# THE RESTLESS DARK

SOMETHING WICKED THIS WAY COMES
DISCOVER MORE BOOKS BY ERICA WATERS

# PRAISE FOR *THE RIVER HAS TEETH*

"Potent, atmospheric, and wholly satisfying."
**—*Kirkus Reviews* (starred review)**

"A backwoods murder ballad of a book that draws from the old
songs and legends that underpin so many areas of rural America.
[*The River Has Teeth*] is well worth a listen."
**—NPR**

"The perfect story for anyone who is tired of feeling
helpless. This book has teeth, too."
**—Hannah Whitten, *New York Times* bestselling
author of *For the Wolf***

"Waters weaves a spell on the page, seeped with dark
and murky magic, both beautiful and terrifying, just
as her girls are beautiful and terrifying."
**—Emma Berquist, author of *Missing, Presumed Dead***

"Fierce and flawless."
**—Kat Ellis, author of *Harrow Lake***

"From its eerie opening pages to its gripping finale,
it kept me enthralled."
**—Kate Alice Marshall, author of *Rules for Vanishing***

"The lush, haunting story gave me the most
gorgeous nightmares I've ever had."
**—Kylie Schachte, author of *You're Next***

"A hypnotic, suspenseful read."
**—Wendy Heard, author of *She's Too Pretty to Burn***

# PRAISE FOR *GHOST WOOD SONG*

"A gorgeous, creepy gem of a book."
**—Claire Legrand, *New York Times* bestselling author
of *Furyborn* and *Sawkill Girls***

"*Ghost Wood Song* sings a high and lonesome love
song to family, to place, to music, and to love itself.
It will make your heart dance."
**—Jeff Zentner, Morris Award–winning author of
*The Serpent King* and *Goodbye Days***

"These haunted pages are full to bursting with intricate family
dynamics, a nuanced queer romance, and a crescendo of an
ending readers won't see coming."
**—Rosiee Thor, author of *Tarnished Are the Stars***

"Strikes the perfect balance of atmospheric chills, dark familial secrets,
and a yearning for the warm comforts of home. I could hear the
cicadas' call and feel the smothering humidity, even as I shivered!"
**—Erin A. Craig, *New York Times* bestselling author of
*House of Salt and Sorrows***

"A dusky, haunting daydream that hits all the right notes."
**—Dahlia Adler, author of *Under the Lights* and editor
of *His Hideous Heart***

"A gorgeously written debut filled with ghosts, a queer love
triangle, a murder mystery, and a healthy dose of bluegrass."
**—Amanda Lovelace, author of *The Princess Saves
Herself in this One***

"Haunting and alluring."
**—*Kirkus Reviews***

# THE
# RESTLESS
# DARK

## ERICA WATERS

HARPER TEEN

*An Imprint of HarperCollinsPublishers*

HarperTeen is an imprint of HarperCollins Publishers.

Library of Congress Control Number: 2022930302
ISBN 978-0-06-311590-3

Typography by Corina Lupp

22 23 24 25 26   PC/LSCH   10 9 8 7 6  5 4 3 2 1

First Edition

*To John and Ashton, my brightest lights in a dark year*

# THE RESTLESS DARK

# KILLER QUEST: THE SEARCH FOR THE CLOUDKISS KILLER'S BONES

Hosted by the *Human Beasties* Podcast
*Six days of true crime gory glory*

## EVENT SCHEDULE

### DAY 1

7:00 a.m.–12:00 p.m. Registration*
7:00 a.m.–12:00 p.m. Canteen Open
12:00 p.m.–2:00 p.m. Welcome Lunch*
2:00 p.m. *Human Beasties* Live Show
6:00–8:00 p.m. Dinner
8:00 p.m. Happy Hour with Sandra and Kevin

### DAYS 2–5

6:00–9:00 a.m. Canteen Open
8:00–9:00 a.m. Forensics & Crime Scene
Instructions (Day 2 only)*
6:00–8:00 p.m. Dinner
8:00 p.m. True Crime Campfire Activities

### DAY 6

6:00–9:00 a.m. Canteen Open
12:00–2:00 p.m. Celebratory Killer Quest Luncheon
and Awards
2:00–5:00 p.m. Checkout*/Last chance to purchase
*Human Beasties* and Killer Quest merch
*mandatory*

# ONE

## LUCY

### DAY 1

**This is where** he jumped. Where he edged out past the wooden barrier, onto the lichen-covered rocks. Where he gripped the trunk of a twisted pine and gazed into the depths below.

I remember his face was ghostly white against the fog, his dark eyes wide. He looked between the police and the yawning canyon, and chose the canyon.

He leapt into the mist.

I spent half an hour with the Cloudkiss Killer, but the thing I think about most is the moment of his death.

The space against the sky where he was until he wasn't.

I stare at it now, the lone white pine clinging to the side of the cliff. The green-brown mountains in the distance, barely visible through the fog.

He must be dead because no one could survive that fall. Not even a monster like Joseph Kincaid. But the police never found his body. They searched the canyon for days and days, and all they found was a shoe.

I glance around now to make sure no one is watching, and then I hop the barrier and edge out as far as I can. I go the last few feet on my hands and knees, gripping the rock. I slide on my belly until I can stare straight down to the bottom of the canyon. But there's nothing to see except fog—thick as smoke, gray and heavy as a funeral dress.

Maybe Kincaid's still down there.

Maybe the fog swallowed him whole.

Maybe he is the fog now. The thought sends a shiver down my spine.

"L'appel du vide," someone murmurs from behind me.

I startle, coming at least an inch off the ground, which moves me closer to the edge of the cliff, so that half my body dangles into space. Panic surges through me, and I clutch hard at the rock, hard enough that my fingernails skitter on the stone and one of them splinters. All the breath has left my body, and I'm frozen, not breathing, not moving, staring down into the canyon, sure that it is eager to swallow me up too.

"Sorry," the person says. It's a girl's voice. "I didn't mean to scare you. Are you all right?" She does sound sorry, her voice soft with contrition.

My breath releases in a cloud of vapor that reminds me it's cold, it's autumn, and I am lying on bare stone 1,800 feet in the air. "Yeah, I'm fine," I say roughly. I climb backward, away from the edge, until my body meets the post of the wooden railing. As I press my back against it, I realize I'm trembling.

"I'm Carolina," the girl says. It's a name that ought to sound like molasses, but in her voice it's only melodic. I tip back my head and look up at her, where she sits on top of the barrier a few feet away.

I don't think I've ever met someone while looking up at them from the ground before. Black leggings and old brown hiking boots, the heavy kind. A burgundy raincoat over a lavender sweater. Long red-brown hair under a white beanie. Peaches-and-cream skin, a round, dramatically pretty face. A pair of dark brown eyes, staring out at the canyon, a dreamy lost look in them.

"Lucy," I finally say.

Carolina's eyes flick down to me. "Your name tag says 'Geraldine.'"

I touch the plastic name tag hanging from my neck. It was waiting for me at registration, along with the rest of my false identity. Geraldine is my grandmother's name. I paid for the contest with her credit card and used all her information to register since I'm underage. She never looks at her credit card bills, so she probably won't even notice before I can pay her back. If I'm lucky, my parents will never find out I came here either. They think I'm visiting my cousin at Sewanee.

"I go by my middle name . . . for obvious reasons," I say.

Carolina smiles, but I can't read the expression behind it. "I don't know. I like Geraldine. It sounds vintage."

"Are you here for the *Human Beasties* contest too?" I ask. The park is closed to regular visitors for the week, so she must be another contestant. But she's not wearing a name tag and isn't at all what I imagined a true crime nut would look like. She holds a lead pencil and a sketchbook, open to a drawing I can't quite make out from my place on the ground.

She sees me looking at the sketchbook and closes it quickly. "Just sketching the landscape," she explains. "And, yeah, I'm here for Killer Quest. You know, I've never been camping before. Have you?"

Not in two years. Not since the Cloudkiss Killer found me. Not since I watched him leap off this cliff. I've barely even been on a hike.

"Yeah, my family went camping all the time," I say, trying to sound casual. "What did you say to me earlier? It sounded French." I took one semester of French, but I was awful at it. I couldn't get my stubborn Tennessee accent to swallow all those unpronounced letters.

"L'appel du vide," Carolina says. "It means 'the call of the void.' It's that urge you get to leap off high places for no reason. Haven't you ever had it?"

"No," I say.

"Hmm," Carolina says before lapsing back into silence. I feel like I gave her the wrong answer and she thinks less of me for it, as silly as that sounds.

Not that it matters what one of these true crime buffs thinks of me. Even if she is painfully beautiful. I'm only here to find Joseph Kincaid's bones and get rid of the hold he has on me. To lay what happened to me two years ago to rest and go back to who I was before.

That way, I won't have to think about him while I lace my shoes, while I drive to school, while I walk alone down a hallway. That way, I can get on with my life.

Cloudkiss Canyon is oppressive and terrifying, and the thought of a whole week here with a bunch of true crime fans is deeply unnerving, but the thought of living with Kincaid in my head for the rest of my life is way scarier.

"Did you come by yourself?" Carolina asks.

I nod.

"Me too. Where are you from?"

I pretend to be checking my jacket pocket for something while I take a moment to think. Has she already figured out who I am? Or are these just innocent questions? The media never released my name and age, but of course those details leaked out, the way they always do. People love a survival story. A few reporters even managed to snap my photo. I was never remarkable-looking to begin with, and now that I've cut off most of my hair and grown several inches, there's no reason for anyone to recognize me. At least that's what I'm telling myself. But that doesn't mean I have to say I'm from Nashville.

"I'm from the Outer Banks in North Carolina," I finally say, remembering our last family vacation. Ocean and wild horses. "You?"

"Honey Valley, just a few towns over from Racksen," she says.

Racksen is the nearest town to here. It's a dismal place full of convenience stores and auto repair shops. "What's Honey Valley like?" I ask, conjuring green fields humming with bees.

Carolina shrugs. "There's nothing interesting about it. God and guns like every other little Georgia town." But she doesn't sound like a Georgia girl—her accent's as neutral as a newscaster's. I'd think she were lying if it weren't for the bitterness in her voice.

"Did you join the contest group chat? There are people from all over," Carolina says, as if eager to change the subject. "One guy's even flying in from Alaska. Can you believe that? I wonder who all we'll meet. Should be a lot of interesting people."

I don't reply. Meeting new people isn't really my thing. Plus, I did look into the group chat, and it was exactly what I expected. A bunch of people with safe, boring lives getting vicarious thrills from true crime. There were fifty spots, but only forty-seven have been taken. Apparently, most true crime enthusiasts prefer their gore from the safety of their cars while they commute home to the suburbs. Few are willing to take a trip to north Georgia, to climb through rough terrain, to camp outdoors in all weather, to touch a corpse. The ones who are willing to come are the die-hard Beastie Babes, as fans of the *Human Beasties* podcast like to call themselves. I'm pretty sure I'll hate every single one of them.

My silence must make Carolina uneasy because she glances over her shoulder. "Looks like more people are arriving. I'm going to go check them out. See you later, Geraldine. Oh, and watch out for the fog—there's no telling what might come out of it." I think she's joking, but she doesn't smile. She throws her legs over the barrier, sliding clumsily to the ground.

"Bye," I say weakly, unsettled by her words. I go back to staring at the canyon, where over and over again I imagine Joseph Kincaid's ghost-white face looking back at me, his eyes wide and dark behind his wire-rimmed glasses. The moment he leapt and disappeared.

What does a serial killer think about as he plummets to the earth?

Did he think of me, the girl he broke, the girl he ruined, without ever touching my skin?

I shake my head. I can't sit around like this, thinking of Kincaid, or I'll never make it through the week. I get up off the ground and brush the dirt from my hiking pants, stretch the cold stiffness from my limbs.

I turn my back resolutely to the canyon and wander into the woods instead, along a trail lined with pine needles. Once the trees close around me, blocking out the sky, I realize how alone I am. This is exactly the thing I've avoided for the last two years. I always surround myself with people—my family, my softball team, my classmates—even though a part of me longs to be alone.

Well, for the first time in two years, I am. Alone in the place that made me afraid to ever be alone again. My pulse ratchets back up, and I feel once more like I'm hanging halfway into the canyon, annihilation only a hairbreadth away.

The trees lean toward me, and the fog rises up around me, alive in a way that doesn't feel quite right. There should be birds flitting and chirping in the trees—tufted titmice and cardinals and blue jays—but there's only the steady sound of the wind blowing through the branches. I'm alone in the fog of Cloudkiss Canyon.

A branch snaps behind me, and I spin, my heart in my throat.

There's no one there. I let out a painful breath.

"Lucy," a man says, somewhere to my right, his form hidden in the fog. I recognize that voice. But it can't be him. He's dead. Is it someone else—someone playing a trick on me?

"Who's there?" I call, squeezing my fists so tight it feels like my fingers will break. I peer into the gloom, though I can't make out so much as a silhouette. But I can feel some-one there, just beyond my sight, waiting and watching. Chill bumps erupt across my arms.

My heart is lodged in my throat, blocking my voice, my air. The trees lean in closer, a wooden cage.

A heavy breeze blows through the trees, and the fog thins, revealing empty woods. No one's here. I'm alone. It wasn't a prank. It wasn't anything at all.

*It wasn't real.*

I lean against a towering longleaf pine and close my eyes, try to steady my breathing.

"I'm safe," I gasp to the trees, to the fog, to my own heart still pulsing painfully in my throat. "That wasn't real." Kincaid is dead. He's been dead a long time. It was only because of what Carolina said, about watching out for the fog. Only because I was alone and frightened and already thinking of Kincaid. My imagination got away from me.

I run through the grounding techniques the counselor from church taught me: feel the sticky sap against my palm, the tree's rough bark, the firm ground beneath my feet, the cool air on my face. I open my eyes and stare again at the place the man's voice came from, to assure myself no one is there.

He never was there. A hallucination, I remind myself. A product of my anxious mind.

As my heart rate slows, I listen to the beat of blood in my veins, a steady rhythm that says *I'm alive, I'm alive, I'm alive.*

I'm alive and Kincaid isn't.

And now I'm going to find his bones and prove it.

# TWO

## LUCY

**By the time** I regain the use of my legs and head back toward the campsite, most of the Killer Quest contestants have arrived. Many have already begun to pitch their tents—and badly. I survey the crowd, unsurprised by what I see. Mostly white people, a mix of genders, nearly all of them sporting expensive outdoorsy clothes and gear. They laugh and joke, exchange conspiracy theories about various unsolved murders, lay out their newly acquired camping gear, confer over large maps.

Someone bumps into me from behind, and then several people, as if I'm not only small but also invisible. I startle but quickly realize there's no threat. It's a group of five or six women, all with various hues of blond hair and artificially tanned skin. One of them has a pageant-style banner across her torso that says *BRIDE* in pink cursive letters. They are all cackling at some joke, their heads thrown back. It's a bachelorette party, I realize. This is how a bride-to-be chose to party with her friends before getting married. By searching for the corpse of a serial murderer.

I have a sudden urge to grab them by the backs of their puffy North Face coats. To scream at them. To demand to know what the hell is wrong with them. But I don't. Of course I don't. Instead, I go back to my tent and sit in the mouth of it, shivering and watching these strangers become ever more strange.

I see Carolina several times. She seems to move easily between various groups, laughing and joking, making new friends. I bet all these people know what she means about the call of the void. Isn't that all this contest is for them: the lure of an unknowable darkness? What else is a serial killer but that?

By lunchtime, all the fog has dissipated, leaving the canyon clear all the way to the bottom. The oppressive feeling of the morning has disappeared with the mist, clearing my head as well. The canyon is just a canyon now, its sinister gaze gone. It's more like I remember it from two years ago, just a beautiful place to hike. A beautiful place that's free of Joseph Kincaid. He's only in my head now, and the only paths he can haunt are the ones I allow him on.

The contestants are growing rowdy, excited by the coming festivities. But Killer Quest won't officially begin until the *Human Beasties* podcast's hosts, Kevin Wright and Sandra Delaney, arrive. So for now we eat our welcome lunch in the lodge and everyone half listens to the instructions of a disgruntled-looking forest ranger about the campground and hiking trails.

After the ranger finishes, I notice Carolina at a table with the bachelorette party, laughing so loudly I can hear it all the way across the room. The sight of her enjoying herself makes me feel strangely lonely. I put my head down and eat fast, doing my best to ignore the three forensics-obsessed geeks at my table who are deep into a conversation about blood spatter.

By two o'clock, an event staff member with a clipboard and a *Human Beasties* sweatshirt has assembled us in a small out-door amphitheater that's really just logs circling a small stone stage, a place for nature guides to give their talks. All the seats are taken, and some people lounge in the grass. I notice Carolina has ditched the bachelorettes and is wedged between two guys who look like college students—their name tags say Brandon and Noah. She's flirting outrageously with Brandon, an athletic-looking guy with curly blond hair and a huge grin on his face.

Finally, the long-awaited hosts stroll onstage. You wouldn't think two people who are famous for their voices would be immediately recognizable, but Kevin and Sandra stand out dramatically. A collective cheer goes up once they're spotted, the crowd leaning toward the pair like metal filaments strain-ing to reach a powerful magnet.

Kevin looks like he was birthed in an NPR station—pasty white skin, carefully coifed red hair, a terrible pencil mustache, and clothes that look thrifted but probably cost more than my Subaru. Sandra is as pale as milk, raven-haired, red-lipped, and dressed head to toe in black, including her 1970s-style cat-eye glasses. She looks like a Goth librarian.

"Hey, everybody! Welcome to Killer Quest!" Sandra yells. "I'm Sandra Delaney, and this is Kevin Wright. We are the hosts of *Human Beasties*." The two do pageant waves, and Kevin throws kisses into the crowd. "We are so excited to be here at Cloudkiss Canyon with all of you die-hard Beasties, just a stone's throw away from where the notorious Cloudkiss Killer's ghastly career came to its strange and mysterious end."

The crowd cheers, as if she's mentioned their favorite football team defeating its rival.

Kevin smiles a perfectly white and even smile. "We decided the best way to start this week off is with a review of the facts of the case." He presses a finger to his phone's screen, and the podcast's theme song plays, eerie yet vaguely reminiscent of electronic dance music. Everyone cheers again.

When the music ends, Sandra starts speaking. "In the months leading up to Killer Quest, Kevin and I have done a ton of research into the history of Cloudkiss Canyon, our home for the next six days. Some of you may have already heard whispers about the place, perhaps been warned off at gas stations and diners along the way. To outsiders, Cloudkiss Canyon is a beautiful place to hike and camp, three thousand acres of woodland and wildlife, with waterfalls and hidden pools, sandstone caves and stellar views from the cliffs. It truly is a place that's 'cloud-kissed,' where land and sky seem nearer, and where people come to feel closer to something bigger than themselves.

"But the tourism website doesn't tell you about Cloudkiss's dark history. See, locals know a different Cloudkiss. For nearly as long as Europeans have lived in the area, it has been a dumping ground. Racksen locals and those from neighboring towns came to its edge to dispose of unwanted and shameful things. Into its mists they tossed ill-gotten goods, murder weapons, bodies, and anything else they couldn't carry into the light.

"We also learned that Cloudkiss used to be a place people came to rid themselves of unwanted memories, emotions, and desires. For example, a few elderly locals told us that a popular break-up ritual for girls in their day was to write their ex-boyfriend's name on a piece of paper, set it on fire, and drop it into the canyon. For them, Cloudkiss Canyon has long been a place of discarding and forgetting. Just toss the thing you wish to be rid of into its depths, and the canyon will do the rest."

Sandra's voice takes on a deeper, slower quality. "But all crimes have a cost. That's why past generations of locals knew to drop their unwanted things and leave, not to linger too long at the edge of the canyon, not to get caught up in the spell of the place. They believed it would pull you in along with your misdeeds and make you face the truth of yourself in the dark."

Kevin butts in. "Of course, when the canyon became part of the national forest, dumping was outlawed. Dump something here now, and you'll get a hefty fine for littering."

"True," Sandra says. "But some locals still sneak to the edge of the canyon in the dead of night to drop the things they wish to hide or forget into the canyon's foggy maw. Some of them do it for convenience. Others do it out of superstition, believing in the canyon's power. Drop your sins, they say, your mistakes, your regrets. Leave them to the foggy chasm of the canyon, and go on your way."

Sandra cocks her head to one side, a small, strange smile on her face. "Is that what Joseph Kincaid was doing, when he came here to hunt and dispose of his victims? Did he choose the canyon because he hoped it was a place to hide his sins?"

Kevin tents his fingers beneath his chin. "Or did he, like the locals say, stand too close to the edge of the canyon?" he asks, his voice thoughtful. "Did he get pulled into the fog?"

Chill bumps spread along my arms, up the back of my neck. A shiver runs though me. I remember my strange thought as I gazed down into the canyon—that maybe Kincaid is the fog now, his sick essence dispersed through the canyon, all around us in the mists.

But that's stupid, and I'm not going to let these assholes make me feel any worse about being here than I already do. Sandra and Kevin are attempting to heighten the already-macabre nature of this event, trying to add drama where there's no need for it. Hunting for a serial killer's bones is already dramatic enough.

"You may have noticed the heavy fog this morning when you arrived," Kevin says. "Turns out, that's not unusual. The canyon is foggy most days of the year, and it's become a sort of boogeyman in these parts. Whether the locals we talked to described the canyon as cursed, haunted, or evil, they all agreed on one thing: it's the fog you've got to watch out for. A malevolent spirit, perhaps? The ghosts of the dead? No one could tell us exactly what it was. But they all agreed, it was the fog that would get you into trouble."

Sandra laughs. "Don't tell me you're falling for local superstition, Kev. Remember, this is *Human Beasties*, not *Lore*."

Kevin laughs too. "I'm just reporting what the people said."

"Uh-huh," Sandra says skeptically. She focuses on the crowd again. "Well, how about we turn to the facts of the case? Let's give our attention to the man of the hour, the notorious Cloudkiss Killer!"

She lets everyone cheer again, clapping along with them. "Kevin?" she says brightly, prompting him to step forward.

"As a respected veterinarian and a loving husband, Joseph Kincaid was the last guy in the world you'd expect to murder and mutilate five people," Kevin says, the words familiar as the intro to the *Human Beasties* episode I've already listened to a dozen times. Episode 133. The one about Joseph Kincaid. Serial murderer and suicide. The man who gave himself to the fog.

I know the words of the episode by heart now. I know every note of the dramatic music interludes, every rueful laugh of the dark-humored hosts. I know Joseph Kincaid's family history, his early signs of trouble. I know the names of all his victims. I know what he left behind.

Sandra and Kevin follow the well-worn trails of the story, their voices soft but clear. As they go into great detail about each of Kincaid's victims, how he tracked and abducted them, how he killed them, how he ritualistically displayed their remains, a hush falls over the previously unruly crowd. This is the part of the podcast you can't laugh at. It's the brutal, gory, hideous part that makes mothers clutch their children close, that makes women double-check the locks on their doors and windows. It's the part of the podcast fans think about when they go running on the greenway alone, when they walk down a city block at two in the morning. This is the closest they get to seeing this podcast as something more than entertainment.

Even the male contestants don't get to feel their usual invincibility because they know Kincaid killed both men and women, young and old, whoever he could catch in a vulnerable moment.

I study each face in the crowd, many of them open-mouthed, though they must already know the whole sordid story, if they are serious enough fans to show up for this contest. But Sandra and Kevin weave the details like a campfire tale, and even I find myself getting caught up in the story, lulled like a child.

First, there was the thirty-year-old solo hiker who'd sprained his ankle. Then a lonely middle-aged woman sitting by the creek, striking up conversations with anyone who passed by. Third, an elderly man with dementia who'd gotten separated from his family. The next two were mysteries—both young women, seemingly healthy and sound of mind. Maybe he charmed them. Maybe they asked him for directions. Maybe he pulled a Ted Bundy and asked them for help. We'll never know.

It's when Sandra and Kevin get to my part of the story that my defenses come back up. I clench my jaw, braced to hear my deepest trauma rendered as a fascinating tale, with several inaccuracies and exaggerations thrown in for dramatic effect. Sandra and Kevin simply call me Lucy W., but my name is less relevant than the role I play in this tale: the Cloudkiss Killer's youngest victim, his botched finale, the canvas he never got to paint.

Kevin Wright actually says that, in exactly those words: "Lucy was Joseph Kincaid's youngest victim, his botched finale, the canvas he never got to paint."

Sandra groans. "Gross, Kevin. Do better."

Then banter, banter, banter.

Finally, Sandra says, "I hope Lucy's doing well. I hope she's thriving."

Fuck you, I think. Fuck you and the fucked-up podcast you rode to fame on.

This is about the point at which an ad for a meal-kit subscription box would be playing if this were a recorded podcast episode, but instead Kevin rubs his hands together and smiles boyishly, as if we're all about to get a wonderful treat.

"Finally, the reason we're all here today. *Human Beasties* is hosting this incredible contest to find the missing remains of Joseph Kincaid, the Cloudkiss Killer. As you know, after he leapt into the canyon, the police couldn't find his body anywhere. It's as if it disappeared, like everything else locals have tossed into the fog. The police were content to chalk it up to a mystery and move on. But not us. No way. Because we're. Gonna. Find. It." He punctuates each word with a pump of his small, bony fist. Everyone leaps to their feet to clap, whoops spreading across the crowd.

I stand too. Anxiety and expectation build in my chest and send a sour, bitter taste up my throat.

"Six days, forty-seven contestants. One haunted-ass canyon. As you already know, whoever finds the Cloudkiss Killer's bones wins a twenty-thousand-dollar reward and claims eternal true crime bragging rights."

Everyone cheers again. The woman next to me, who is wearing a *Friday the 13th* hoodie and skull-shaped earrings, lets out an earsplitting scream of excitement.

A guy in front of us turns around to look at her, an annoyed expression on his face. In the same moment, a scent hits me so hard the noise of the crowd fades and my ears fill with a dull buzzing sound. Spicy cloves, a hint of smoke.

Immediately, all my muscles seize up, and my body is frozen and trembling. I'm no longer surrounded by dozens of other people, but alone with a single man near the bottom of the waterfall trail, the roar of the water in my ears.

The wooden stairs beneath my boots are slick with mist and algae. Skinny trees loom like twisted witch's fingers in the fog. Seven a.m. and there's no one here but us.

Enormous rocks jut out of the side of the mountain, forming crags and crevices, endless hiding places. The mist curls strangely beneath one huge overhang, creating wraiths. The fog is alive, and it watches.

Joseph Kincaid smiles at me from beneath a navy-blue beanie, his eyes inviting behind his glasses, harmless and friendly. He wears a faded brown bomber jacket. A sweet, smoky smell comes off him, mixing with the scent of damp earth and pines. Nothing about him says danger, says to run. He looks like a young high school teacher, one of those almost-handsome ones the straight girls all get crushes on. He's solid and reassuring in the fog that made me lose my way.

So why do I feel so afraid?

He takes a step toward me and lifts his hand, and before I know it, I've thrown an arm out wild and connected with a sharp cheekbone. "Don't touch me!" I hear myself snarl.

Kincaid falls back, and I close the distance between us, one fist balled up tight, ready to strike again. The moves I learned in my self-defense class come naturally, without my having to think about them. This time, I won't run. I can fight. I *want* to fight. As I move to elbow him in the face, his blue eyes widen in shock, and his mouth opens as he raises his hands to fend me off.

Kincaid doesn't have blue eyes, I realize, just as someone yanks me from behind. "Come on, let's get you out of here," she says. It's a woman's voice, or a girl's, and I feel her softness at my back, feel the grip of her hands on my shoulders. My chest heaves, and the world returns to me—so startlingly clear that my body sags in the girl's arms.

"What's going on back there? Is everything all right?" Kevin asks, trying to see through the crowd of bodies.

"Some girl punched a guy," I hear someone tell him.

Sobs well up in me, but I can't let them out here, where everyone is staring at me, watching me, whispering about me.

"Come on," the voice in my ear says, and I let her lead me away. Away from the smell of cloves and smoke, away from the man who's angrily clutching his cheek, the man who's not Joseph Kincaid at all, just some other guy in a blue beanie, some other guy with a smoothly shaven face. I think it's that college boy Carolina was with earlier—Noah.

I follow meekly, my face burning, my heart still hammering in my chest. A soft hand pulls me into a tent, down to my knees, and I'm crawling into a dimness that smells like hibiscus and honey. I can breathe again, I can move, I can see.

A girl sits across from me. She wears a denim jacket with faded black jeans and scuffed combat boots. Her hair is cut short, chin-length and boyish. Her lips are painted dark plum. I'm embarrassed to find myself staring. It isn't because she's beautiful exactly, at least not in the way that girl Carolina is. Her face is just compelling somehow, slightly asymmetrical, as if all her features on the right side shifted a fraction of a centimeter. She has dark, heavy eyebrows and a slightly-too-big nose. Her eyes are really, actually gray, not just blue masquerading as something rarer. I wonder how I missed seeing her earlier when everyone was setting their tents up.

She leans toward me over the light of an electric camping lantern, and her lips slide into a crooked smile, showing a small gap between her top incisor and canine. "You really whaled on that guy," she says.

I pass a shaking hand over my face. The adrenaline has almost completely left my body, regret taking its place. I thought I was hurting Kincaid, but it was only some random guy, an innocent bystander. "I'm sorry," I say. "I don't know what happened."

She laughs. "Oh, don't be sorry. The guy was cosplaying Kincaid. Thinks he's at Serial Killer Con."

I look up at her in surprise. "Cosplaying?" I try to recall how he looked, but I'm not sure how much of it was real. Was he wearing a bomber jacket, or was that in my head?

"Same clothes, same glasses, same hat," she says, counting each one off on her fingers.

I nod slowly. "I think—I think he was even wearing the same cologne as Kincaid. Is that possible?"

The girl grimaces. "He could have been. Kincaid's wife let a reporter take pictures of their house, even in the bathroom. I think there was a picture of all his toiletries."

"But it could have been a coincidence," I say. "He— I shouldn't have—"

She waves my words away. "Look, don't feel bad about it. He deserved a wallop, and you gave him one. You've got a killer right hook, by the way—no pun intended."

I flex the fingers on my right hand, which are sore and tender, the knuckles already starting to bruise. I should have used the heel of my hand, like I learned in class. But it all happened so fast. A rush of fear and rage and . . . release?

"It did feel good to hit him," I admit.

She grins. "Oh, you and me are going to be great friends."

I laugh. "Anyway, thank you for getting me out of there," I say. "My name's—" I pause, wondering whether I ought to be going by Geraldine after all, especially after a display like that. But when I meet the girl's eyes, my real name slips out. "I'm Lucy Wilson," I say.

I expect her eyes to widen, or for her to gasp. She literally just heard my sad story rendered by Sandra and Kevin after all.

Instead, she smiles and sticks out a slightly bony hand. "I'm Maggie Rey. Don't tell anyone, but I'm not a Beastie Babe either."

"You're not?"

She shakes her head. "I'm a sophomore at Duke, and I'm studying these weirdos for a psychology paper. The dark underbelly of true crime fandom. Deep dive and all that. I'm going to publish this paper and get into any grad school I want. Or at least that's the plan."

My head is still spinning from everything that's happened, and I just stare at her. Maggie laughs and runs a hand through her hair. "Sorry, that sounded cocky, didn't it? I'm just— Well, it's nice to have someone to talk to. I've been camping out here for a week already, getting the lay of the land, and it's— Well, all this fog and everything, you sort of lose track of reality, you know? And I don't think any of these people are going to help me find it again."

"But I might?" I ask, surprised to feel a smile tugging at the corner of my mouth. "Did you not just see me punch that guy in the face?"

Maggie laughs. "Well, I guess we can be lost out here together. How's that sound?" She squeezes my forearm with warm, soft fingers.

"Good," I say honestly, relief welling up inside me.

I thought I could handle being alone out here, but clearly, I can't. Not if I'm hallucinating Kincaid and punching people.

And now I don't have to be alone. Besides, after meeting Maggie, I don't want to.

Maggie and I stay in her tent until the live show disperses. I expect someone to come get me and tell me I have to leave the contest, but no one appears. When I voice my relief to Maggie, she laughs. "You think they'd throw you out for that? Why do you think they made us sign waivers before we came? They expect a wild week—in fact, I'd say they're banking on it."

"Why?" I ask.

"Well, *Human Beasties* isn't really branding itself as one of the morally upright true crime podcasts, are they?"

"What do you mean?"

Maggie rummages in a backpack and pulls out an aluminum water bottle. She offers it to me, but I shake my head. "They aren't donating money to organizations for victims of sexual assault or crusading for racial reform in the criminal justice system. Sandra might try to rein Kevin in when he gets too creepy, but the show is running on good old-fashioned sensationalism. None of the other popular podcasts would have hosted a contest like this."

I shrug. "They all seem the same to me."

Maggie shakes her head. "Maybe deep down at heart they're all the same, but they style themselves differently. Some of the hosts of these podcasts genuinely believe they're doing good, valuable, meaningful work that makes the world a better place."

"Do you think they are?" I ask.

She takes a sip of water, considering. "A few. But *Human Beasties* definitely isn't one of them, and they really aren't pretending to be."

"So you think they're hoping for some real-life true crime to happen this week?" God, what have I gotten myself into?

Maggie seems to sense my worry. "I mean, they don't want anyone murdered or anything, but I think they'd love it if something newsworthy happened, something they could spin into a good publicity opportunity. That's why they're *really* hosting this contest, I think."

"They don't actually expect anyone to find the bones?" I ask, surprised.

Maggie leans toward me. "To tell you the truth, I think they're hoping we'll find more than one set."

"More of Kincaid's victims?" My stomach turns.

Maggie winces. "Hey, I'm sorry. I shouldn't be saying all this to you. I'm such an ass."

"It's okay," I say. "I asked for your opinion."

"No, it's not okay. These are just my own silly theories. Like I said, I've been out here in this creepy canyon for too long. I'm imagining all sorts of scenarios. That's always been a problem for me, but out here . . . I'm turning into a conspiracy theorist or something." Maggie laughs, relieving the tense atmosphere.

I smile. "I like that you told me what you really think and that you didn't shy away from talking about it. I'm sick of everyone handling me with kid gloves, as if I'll disintegrate."

"Really?" Maggie asks.

When I nod, her shoulders slump in relief. "I'm glad, because to tell you the truth, I'm not so good with the whole, uh, kid-gloves thing."

"I'd noticed that," I say with a laugh, and Maggie joins in.

"You ready to get out there and see what sort of trouble all the Beastie Babes are getting up to?" Maggie asks with a grin. "Maybe get up to a little of our own?"

"Mess around and find some bones?" I ask around a smile.

"We've got a few hours before dinner," she says. "Let's go."

When Maggie unzips the tent, late-afternoon sunlight falls across her face, golden and leaf-patterned from the scarlet oak overhead. She looks like a merry wood elf stepping out into an enchanted forest, and for a moment I forget to be afraid of Cloudkiss Canyon.

I forget to be afraid at all.

# THREE

## CAROLINA

**Flames dance in** the campfire, voices rise and fall. Shrill, hysterical laughter starts up in the middle of a circle of contestants and then spreads, contagious, through the campsite. The night feels wild and alive, full of possibility. There's a freedom here you don't find back home. It's like everyone has left their normal lives and come here to be unrestrained, another version of themselves.

I edge closer to the circle of people where the laugh came from. Sandra is at its center, her head thrown back, the white column of her throat lit by flames. She looks like a woman from a John William Waterhouse painting—one of his pale goddesses, fierce, wild, insatiable. And the contestants are her worshippers, their faces lit with reflected radiance. They hang on her every word, follow her every movement.

I can't help but be drawn in too, my blood suffused with the thrill of her, of this place, of this contest. It feels like coming home somehow, like finding a family whose names I don't know, who I'll probably never speak to again, but who are like me. People drawn to the dark, the twisted, the dangerous.

I accidentally brush against a big, bearded guy who smiles at me and shuffles over to make room for me in the circle. Sandra notices me and gives a little wave before continuing what she was saying to the others.

As I settle into the conversation, I take a look around. I've already met everyone in the circle except for a peculiar-looking girl with short brown hair and dark lipstick. The lanyard around her neck says her name is Maggie. I realize she's the one who pulled Lucy off Noah and ushered her back to the campsite earlier. I saw them sitting alone at dinner, deep in conversation, though it looked like Maggie did most of the talking. I would love to know why Lucy hit Noah, what was going through her head. Of everyone here, she's the biggest question mark. First, I found her dangling off the edge of a cliff, and then she's punching people at random. I can't help but want to figure her out. There's this intense, wiry energy radiating off her—a story waiting to be told. This morning, I lied and said I was sketching the landscape, but really I was sketching her.

"So, Carolina," Sandra says with a glance at my name tag, "we've been debating nature versus nurture in the creation of serial killers. What makes them do what they do."

"And what has everyone decided?" I ask, pleased that Sandra is taking pains to include me.

Sandra huffs out a laugh. "We're very divided on the subject. I say it's definitely their parents' fault. Over and over again we learn that serial killers experienced childhood trauma, almost always at the hands of their parents. If that hadn't happened, they might have grown up to be good, healthy, normal adults."

Maggie lets out a disbelieving laugh. "Lots of people's parents abused them or traumatized them somehow, and they grew up perfectly well-adjusted. They didn't go out and kill people and mutilate people like Kincaid did. There has to be much, much more to it," she says.

"It's the fog," a guy says in a Halloweeny voice, wiggling his fingers in a spooky dance. Everyone laughs.

But then someone else jumps in to challenge Maggie. The conversation spins on and on, everyone recounting what they know about various serial killers' pasts, how they were portrayed in biopics, what pop psychologists say on the matter. I could debate this stuff all night long, and finally, I've got the right sort of people to talk about it with, who won't side-eye me or call me morbid. I laugh along with them, for once feeling like I belong.

But then Maggie cocks her head, studying me. "What do you think, Carolina? Are some people just born evil? Is it in their DNA?" She can't possibly know anything about me, yet the questions feel strangely pointed.

All eyes turn to me, and I struggle to maintain my composure, to look as cool and unruffled as Maggie does. I know how my father would answer: with Bible verses about original sin and generational curses. But I don't want to think about him—about his fanaticism, his cruelty. His blood beating in my veins. I came here to get away from all that, to find new answers.

I force a mischievous smile onto my face. "The human heart is darkness and chaos," I say airily. "Even the most buttoned-up, law-abiding citizen has badness inside him."

The bearded guy to my left leers at me. "And do you?"

"Of course," I say lightly, edging away from him. I don't like the eager look in his eyes.

"But she's not a serial killer," Sandra says.

"That we know of," Maggie says, and everyone laughs. I laugh too, though it sounds nervous and weak. But at least the spotlight is off me, and I breathe a sigh of relief.

This is all theoretical to them, but for me it's personal. Because, no matter how hard I try to make light of it, there *is* badness inside me. More than my fair share of it. And it's already cost one person his life.

I try to get out of my own head, to focus on the people around me, but the conversation gets further and further away from me. The night loses its luster. Sandra doesn't look like a Waterhouse painting anymore, her makeup caked into her frown lines, her lipstick uneven. I slip out of the circle and head toward the nearly empty drink table and make myself a hot cocoa.

"Sweet Carolina!" someone yells, their singsong voice pulling me from my thoughts. It's my new favorite college boy, Brandon, sitting with his roommate, Noah, by the fire. I didn't even realize I'd wandered back over. I force a smile and join them on the seat. Sandra and her circle of contestants have dispersed, spreading out across the campsite. Only a few people remain by the fire.

"The song is 'Sweet Caroline,'" Noah points out pedantically before he takes a sip of his beer. Sandra and Kevin couldn't officially provide booze for happy hour, but plenty of the Beastie Babes were happy to oblige. Coolers of beer dot the campsite, and bottles of spirits pass from hand to hand.

"You're the one who got decked by a little girl," Brandon says to Noah, and cracks up for the fifteenth time today.

And for the fifteenth time, Noah doesn't laugh with him. He's got a bruise on his cheek, running just under his eye. A muscle in his jaw ticks. I've been hanging out with them on and off all day, and Noah's mood has only gotten more and more sour. Dinner didn't cheer him up and neither did the happy hour. He's edging into brooding territory. Which I know from experience means only bad things to come.

Even when one of the event staff members tried to find out what happened between him and Lucy, Noah clammed right up, said not to worry about it. He said it was a misunderstanding, and the guy seemed eager to let it drop. He didn't even go looking for Lucy. Then Kevin and Sandra just made some statement at happy hour saying that anyone engaging in behavior that posed a risk to others would be asked to leave and that we should all remember the waivers we signed.

In other words, we're responsible for anything we do and anything done to us. We're all grown-ups here, after all, or at least we're supposed to be. I've been telling everyone I'm a freshman at UNC Chapel Hill, which is almost true. I will be next year, so long as my financial aid package works out.

So I'm excited for the chance to hang out with college students. Noah and Brandon go to UT in Chattanooga. Both freshmen. That's the end of what they have in common. Brandon is sexy and athletic and fun, while Noah is forgettable—brown hair, average everything, and a shit personality to complete the package. The only thing about him that stands out is that he's dressed like Kincaid was in the most famous picture of him, a snapshot taken here at Cloudkiss. Noah's outfit choices can't possibly be a coincidence. I'm not really sure what to make of it. Why dress like a serial killer? That's a level of true crime fandom I didn't even know existed.

"You really don't know why she attacked you?" I ask Noah, itching to solve the mystery of tiny Lucy going feral with her fists.

"Because she's a crazy bitch," Noah spits, staring sullenly at the fire.

Brandon smacks Noah on the arm. "Don't call women bitches. It's disrespectful. Anyway, I told you the sort of people who would show up to something like this would be un-hinged," he says. "No offense," he adds, looking in my direction with what I can only describe as a sweet smile, all dimples and sparkling blue eyes.

"Might I remind you that *you* are also here, searching for the Cloudkiss Killer's remains?" I ask him. "So doesn't that make you unhinged too?"

"Nuh-uh," Brandon says. "I don't like true crime. I'm only here for the moola. Tuition money. Don't get me wrong though—I'm absolutely delighted to have your unhinged company, Carolina." He winks at me. "And I'm so glad not to have to be alone with this asshole all week," he adds, smacking Noah's arm again.

Noah does seem like a prick. But Brandon has no idea who I am, what I've done, what I might do again.

I study Brandon's unruly curls, his unblemished skin. He looks like he's never had a single hard thing happen to him in his whole life. Is it possible that he could walk away from me unscathed, as untouched as he is now? I wish I could believe it.

Brandon catches me staring and smirks. "This girl's already got a crush on me," he says.

Noah huffs in disgust and stomps away from the campfire, and we both crack up. Brandon edges a little closer to me on the log.

"So what's your deal, Carolina?" he asks. "Why are you really here?"

"Because I love true crime, duh," I say, laughing. That at least is true—I love podcasts like *Human Beasties*, serial killer documentaries on Netflix, pretty much anything I can get my hands on. Their subject matter is so much more fucked up than anything I've had to deal with, even in my family. Even with my dad. It's comforting.

Or at least it used to be. Until I started scrutinizing every episode looking for traces of myself in the killers. Until it felt like I had more in common with Kincaid than with his victims.

Brandon is shaking his head, clearly unsatisfied with my answer. "Nuh-uh. I don't buy it. There's got to be more to it than liking murder podcasts," he says.

He's right, but I can't tell him I came here because I want to spend time with people who are into this stuff and find out if they're all as damaged as I am. Or that I'm here because I want to prove to myself I'm not like Kincaid—not made of the same evil materials.

I don't actually, truly believe the local legend of the canyon, that it possesses some supernatural force to show humans their own evil, but maybe that is why I'm here, metaphorically speaking: to look into my heart of hearts and face myself in the dark. And if I thought the fog could actually tell me the truth about who I am . . . maybe I would dive right in.

But there's nothing I can say to Brandon to make him understand why I'm so drawn to this place, these people. So I fall back on my oldest, most cherished persona—the girl who's up for anything. "Maybe it just sounded fun, did you ever think of that?" I say, my mouth sliding into an enormous grin.

Brandon's smile echoes my own as he leans toward me. He wants to kiss me—his pupils are dilated, lashes fluttering as he eyes my lips. But he's too polite to make such a rash move. And he's only had about half a beer, so he's as sober as I am. "Aren't you afraid of the ghosts?" he asks flirtatiously. "Aren't you afraid they'll slip into your tent at night?"

"Might not be ghosts," I say, quirking my eyebrows at him. "Might be the fog that drives you mad, like the locals believe. I've heard all sorts of stories over the years. The checkout lady at my town's grocery store said she saw Mothman here. And this girl from my school said a werewolf chased her through the wildflower meadow."

Brandon laughs.

I lower my voice to a conspiratorial whisper. "But the scariest stories are the ones where they couldn't see the monster, only feel it. My ex-boyfriend's uncle camped here overnight once on a dare, and he said he felt someone's hot breath on his cheek while he slept beneath the stars. He was too afraid to open his eyes."

Brandon shivers, half in earnest, half in jest. But then his eyes light up. "Ex-boyfriend, you said? Does that mean—"

I close my eyes at the rush of pain in my chest, the dread that settles cold in my belly. I shouldn't have mentioned Michael. I don't want to talk about Michael. Before I can think too hard about it, I lean toward Brandon and kiss him, stopping his question mid-sentence. He's so startled he laughs, I pull back and laugh too. I touch my lips, as though surprised at my own daring. But I knew exactly what I was doing.

"All right, then," Brandon says with a chuckle, leaning in for another kiss. He puts one hand at the back of my head, the other on my knee. He's a good kisser, all soft lips and just the right amount of tongue. I melt into the kiss, let it take me over.

Michael was a good kisser too. It was the one thing that always worked between us, that we never ever fought about. The thing that almost made up for all the bad parts of our relationship. Almost.

I haven't kissed anyone since him.

Suddenly I'm hungry, desperate to feel like that again. I slide into Brandon's lap, and he wraps a strong arm around me, pulling me closer. We kiss for I don't know how long—long enough that Brandon starts pulling away, giving me that look that asks if we're going to take it any further, if we should head toward his tent.

And I want to. I want to because it seems so simple and so easy, no thinking, only bodies and breath. But I make myself pull away from him. I'm dizzy with desire, my heart pounding, the rest of me aching. My thoughts spin so fast, and Brandon just stares at me, his pupils blown wide. I know he feels the same way I do, his brain fogged with wanting.

"Carolina?" he breathes. "We can stop if you want to. That's all right."

I don't want to, not at all. But I have to, for both our sakes.

I close my eyes, and my father's face swims there, a warning frown etched into his eyebrows, his jaw hard, but his eyes lit with a fierce radiance. "You got a curse inside you, baby, just like I did," he says. "God is visiting the sins of the father to the fourth generation, just like he said in the Bible. It's up to you to get free."

Dad has spent years telling me I've got the curse of his blood inside me, an evil that will take me over if I don't root it out. For a long time, I refused to believe him.

Until Michael died.

And now I'm not so sure. Maybe he's right. Dad's a third-generation felon. He spent the first eight years of my life in prison for manslaughter. He's also the reason my mother will always walk with a limp. But he got hold of some jailhouse religion and a King James Bible and now he says he's free.

Now he says the curse is only in my blood and, if I don't get right with Jesus, it will claim me like it did his grandfather and his mother, like it tried to claim him. Then I'll be an instrument of evil.

That's all my dad can see when he looks at me. A generational curse. Sometimes I think I can feel the curse inside me, rushing through my veins with every pump of my heart.

"Carolina?" Brandon whispers, his eyes searching mine. He doesn't see evil in me, only a nice, fun girl he'd like to get naked.

Defiance makes up my mind. "Let's go to my tent," I say. "No Noah."

Brandon smirks. I climb off him and lead him away from the fire by the hand, one giant fuck-you to my father. We pass through a stand of trees, where it's nearly pitch black. The air feels dense and moist, like we're walking through a fog.

Suddenly, my tent feels impossibly far away. I pull Brandon against a tree and kiss him again. "Oh my God," he says against my mouth. He presses the solid length of his body against me, and I'm pinioned between him and the tree, and it's the best I've felt in months. It's the first time I haven't felt like I was on a tightrope over an abyss.

He was holding back before, but now he kisses me hard, unzips my coat and runs his hands over the front of my sweater and across the bare skin underneath. I must make some little unconscious sound because Brandon chuckles. "You're a wild one, aren't you?"

"Shut up before you ruin it," I rasp, and he laughs again.

"Yes, ma'am," he says, and presses his lips against my neck.

A man's scream comes from somewhere inside the trees, terrified and helpless. The sound runs through me like an electric shock. I swear I hear it echo back from the canyon.

Brandon grabs my shoulders and pulls his lips from my skin, and he must be staring into the trees, but I can't see his expression. It's far too dark out here. "What was that?" he asks, his voice laced with fear. I can feel his heart beating against my chest.

We wait, listening, but the sound doesn't come again. I start to feel the cold seeping through my jacket as the frenzied heat leaves my body.

"Come on, let's go back to the fire," Brandon says. "That— that sounded bad."

"We are literally here to find a serial killer's bones, surrounded by the freakiest of true crime freaks. It was probably just someone fooling around," I say.

"No," Brandon says. "I don't think so. That—that was, like, some primeval shit. I felt it in my guts."

"You mean in your gut?"

"No, like, literally in my intestines or something. That was very, very real." His breath hitches, but it's not with desire. It's fear. I wonder why I don't feel it too. All I feel is cold. I zip my jacket back up.

Brandon tugs me away from the tree and toward the camp. He turns his phone's flashlight on and doesn't turn it off again until the flames of the campfire come into view.

Several people are sitting around the fire, talking in whispers. When we approach, their heads all snap up like those of antelopes at the water hole, scenting a lion.

"Jesus Christ," a woman with a shaved head says, clutching her girlfriend's hand. "You two scared the shit out of me."

"I guess y'all heard it too?" Brandon asks.

They all nod. "Fucking ghosts," the woman says. "My mom told me not to come here. I should have listened."

"It's not ghosts, Rosa," her freckled, red-haired girlfriend says.

"Maybe it's the local legend," another woman says. "The fog. Maybe it pulled someone in and showed them who they are. And they didn't like what they saw." She wraps her arms around herself, clearly unnerved by the idea. It sounded funny to everyone earlier, but now, late at night, with fog rolling along the ground, it feels more plausible and more frightening.

I squeeze Brandon's hand, grounding myself in the warmth of his skin. Curses aren't real, and canyons aren't sentient.

"You're all so gullible. Paranormal phenomena can always be explained," a boy in a turtleneck says, his voice slightly slurred, probably thanks to the silver flask in his hand. "Perhaps there are noxious gasses here that cause hallucinations."

"If there were gasses, the park wouldn't be open to visitors, dumbass," one of his friends says, snatching away the flask. "You're such a fucking know-it-all." They start arguing in a half-drunk, fond sort of way that makes me smile.

Everyone else is too freaked out to be charmed by the pair.

They huddle together in one area, except for the girl from the canyon's edge this morning, the one who punched Noah in the face. Lucy. She sits at the very end of a log bench, as far from the others as she can get. She's hunched over in her coat, staring at the ground. She glances at me, and I can see she's sitting with everyone grudgingly, probably only because she's too afraid to be alone in her tent in the dark.

I remember telling her to watch out for the fog this morning. I meant it to be a joke, but it didn't quite come out that way. Maybe because she looked so serious and intense, staring into the canyon like she expected something to walk right out of the mists.

I loosen my fingers from Brandon's and go sit beside her, I don't even know why. Maybe because she looks so miserable. "Hey, Geraldine," I say. "How's your hand?"

"Hurts," she admits before looking away into the night, a lock of dirty-blond hair falling into her eyes. Her hair is shaved at the back and short at the sides, with a fall of bangs in the front that she runs her fingers through. It's a surprisingly daring haircut for a person who doesn't seem to want anyone to look at her.

"If it makes you feel any better, the guy you decked is a real asshole," I say. "I've been around him all day, and I can assure you that he deserved to be punched for something, even if you didn't know it."

Lucy doesn't even crack a smile. She just keeps staring stonily at the ground.

God, this girl is wound tight. You'd think she was the one with cursed blood. I'm tempted to offer to find her a beer.

"Where are the glorious hosts of *Human Beasties* when you need them, huh? They'd have no trouble making a man screaming in terror in the woods funny."

Lucy snorts, but there's no humor in it. Only disgust. "Yeah, if they can laugh at murdered girls, they can definitely spin a joke out of this."

"Wait, do you not like *Human Beasties*?" I ask. Why would someone be here if they didn't like the podcast?

Lucy shifts uncomfortably on the bench.

Just then, there's a loud crunch of feet, the sound of someone running fast through the trees. The girl with the shaved head Rosa swears again.

A few people stand up, straining to see into the dark woods. Brandon turns and looks for me, and I feel a moment of warmth, that his first instinct was to protect me.

But then Noah crashes into the circle of light and collapses a few feet away from the fire. He's on his hands and knees, breathing heavily and weeping, tears flowing down his face. His expression is wild and terrified, and with the flames playing over his face, he looks like an actor in a church hell-house production. I half expect to see a horned devil standing over him with a pitchfork.

"What the hell, man?" Brandon says, rushing toward his roommate.

"I wanna go home, I wanna go home, I want to go home," Noah sobs out.

"What happened?" Brandon asks, putting a hand on Noah's shoulder. Noah shudders at his touch and cringes away. "Did someone come after you? Or . . . some*thing*?"

Noah raises a shaky hand and points in my direction. Everyone turns and looks past me, right at Lucy, and I follow their movement. Her eyes go wide and her mouth opens, as if to defend herself. But no sound comes out.

"What are you trying to say, bro?" Brandon asks, his eyes flicking between me and Lucy.

But Noah won't speak again. He lets out a single sob and then slumps down beside the fire, his head between his knees, and starts to shiver.

"She was here by the fire with all of you," I say to the others. "She didn't do anything to him."

But everyone else around the fire steps away from Lucy, so subtly they probably don't even realize they've done it. As if she's dangerous. As if she somehow could have been out in the woods, terrorizing Noah, instead of sitting right here. They've all let the ghost stories get to them.

"That's the girl who attacked him earlier today," a blond woman says in a stage whisper to someone. I think her name is Kiersten. She's here with the big bachelorette party from Texas. "Freaaaak," she adds, singsong, as if Lucy's not right here listening.

"Hey," I say, surprised by the anger that surges up into my chest. "I don't know what happened earlier, but there's no way she did anything to Noah tonight. She's been sitting here the whole time."

"You just got here. You don't know anything," Kiersten says. "God, they should have made everyone get a background check before coming here. What a total psycho."

"What a vapid bitch," I shoot back.

"Excuse me?" Kiersten says, standing up and putting a hand on one hip.

Before I can reply, a rush of images assaults me, so intense and so real, they make me lightheaded. *I rush her and throw a fist into her smug, fake-tanned face. I put my hands around her neck and choke her until her face turns maroon. I push her into a tree and bash her head against it. I—*

"Look, I didn't chase him," Lucy says, disbelief in her voice, only loud enough for me to hear. "I would never try to mess with someone like that." Her voice shakes the violent images from my mind, but they still leave me trembling. What the hell was that?

"Of course you wouldn't," I say, my voice hard, my eyes still on Kiersten.

*But I would.*

The thought hits me like a thunderbolt, more startling than Noah's scream. More forceful than the collective paranoid gaze of a dozen Beastie Babes.

I haven't been anywhere near Noah, yet I can't help but wonder if somehow I'm to blame. If some evil inside me slipped out and chased him, frightened and weeping, through the woods. It's a foolish thought, but it terrifies me anyway. To think that I might be capable of making someone scream like that in the dark . . . and worse, that a part of me—a horrible, monstrous part of me—might want to.

All the anger goes out of me, and I wrap my arms around myself, suddenly cold and weak. For the first time tonight, I feel afraid.

Maybe this creepy canyon has already told me everything about myself I need to know.

That I am my father's daughter. The fourth generation. Violence waiting to be unleashed.

# FOUR

## CAROLINA

### DAY 2

**My alarm goes** off at six in the morning, and I wake up stiff and shivering, halfway out of my sleeping bag. Wind blows against my face, stirring my hair, and I realize my tent is open, the canvas flapping like broken bird wings. No wonder I'm freezing. When I lean forward to zip it back up, I see there's blood on my hand, caked in my fingernails.

My stomach drops.

I dreamed—

Trembling, I raise both of my hands and study every inch of my skin.

It was only a dream, wasn't it?

I blink and breathe, blink and breathe. I try to remember what I dreamed about. All I remember is blood. But I must have been dreaming of Michael's death again, like I have a hundred times before. It was Michael's blood. Dream blood.

But this is real blood on my hand, dark red, metallic-smelling, caked into my cuticles and under the nail beds. My mind flits to Kiersten last night, how angry I was. The violent attack that played like a movie in my head. Hitting her, choking her. How I wanted to—

I run a shaking hand over my eyes. When I try to pull my hair over my shoulders, I realize a few strands of it are stuck to my face and neck. I pull them gingerly, wincing as they come loose. I touch my neck and wince again as my fingers find a stinging line of skin. There is blood caked there too. It's a scratch, a deep one.

I laugh, relieved. I only scratched myself in my sleep. That's what it must have been. But nausea still roils in my gut. It doesn't explain why my tent was open.

"Evil always finds its way out, no matter how hard you try to keep it at bay," Dad said to me, more than a few times, when I argued with him about the curse. "I'd try so hard to be good, to keep my temper, to be the man I thought I should be. But that monster always found its moment to burst from my skin. It was always lying in wait—I could feel it. It's gone now, but I can see it in you, can practically hear it humming under your skin. Sooner or later, you're going to let it out."

I close my eyes for a moment, willing my father's words away, and then I crawl out of my tent and into the cold morning, which is filled with a dense fog. The fire went out sometime in the night, and the campsite is still.

I kneel in the dirt until I'm sure I'm not going to puke. Until I'm sure, in my heart and head and stomach, that the blood on my skin is only my own.

I scratched myself in my sleep. That's all. And this tent is secondhand and not in great shape, so it might have come undone in the wind.

There's no such thing as generational curses, no evil carried in our DNA. That's just Pentecostal bullshit, a way to reject responsibility and guilt. We are the choices we make, the actions we commit. We decide for ourselves whether we are good or bad. This is real life, not a fucking Greek tragedy.

I will not let my father's beliefs be my own. I won't let his behavior be my own.

I won't let him remake me in his own bloody, violent image. No matter what I might have done to Michael, I will not do it again.

Never again.

After I get cleaned up, I walk uncertainly through the campsite, still unable to shake my unease. The morning is dim, the sky a cloudy, opaque gray, birds just starting to make a racket in the trees. I don't want to be alone with my thoughts, with myself. But no one is awake yet. People stayed up late last night drinking after the scare from Noah, so I'm not surprised to find my fellow contestants still snoring in their tents.

When Brandon finally got Noah to talk last night, Noah said he thought he saw something weird in the woods. He refused to elaborate, except to say he must have been mistaken. He shot a few surreptitious looks at Lucy, but he didn't point at her again or try to blame her. When Brandon asked if Noah wanted to call the police, he shook his head, said he was fine now. But his fear was a living thing, contagious, infecting all the rest of them.

Not me though. The only person here I'm afraid of is myself.

I'm not sure what to do, where to go. I need to kill a few hours before the forensics lecture, but I'm not too eager to set off into the canyon with no sense of direction or wilderness know-how. Finally, I decide to find Brandon. He said I could hang out with him and Noah today.

But when I reach their tent—a big gray-and-blue one underneath some pine trees, I find Brandon standing outside it, looking around nervously.

"Good morning," I call, and he flinches. "What is it?"

"Noah's missing."

"He probably went to the canteen or showers or something."

Brandon shakes his head, rubs a hand down his face. "Nah, I looked for him. I looked for him everywhere. He's gone. Like, he just vanished."

"Maybe he decided to get an early start without you?" I venture, but misgiving roils in my stomach and the scratch on my neck stings. I pull my hair forward to hide it.

Brandon shakes his head again. "I don't care what he told the rest of y'all, but he was so freaked out last night. Even after he fell asleep, he was, like, whimpering in his sleep. One time he woke me up screaming. There's no way he'd go back out there on his own."

"Maybe he went home?"

"His car is still in the lot, and he left his wallet and phone in the tent. So I know he didn't leave," Brandon says.

"Shit. What do you want to do? Should we track down one of the event staff? Call the police?"

"I don't know," Brandon says quietly, looking away into the fog. "That seems extreme."

"Did he ever tell you more about what he thought he saw out there?" I ask, my eyes straying to the shadowy woods. Brandon only shakes his head.

"Do you want me to help you look for him?" My voice sounds natural and easy, but my insides are stretched taut as a fresh canvas.

Brandon nods. "He's gotta be around here somewhere. Maybe he got lost? Maybe he's hurt?"

"He could totally be lost in the fog," I say, relief welling up with the words. Of course I didn't do anything to Noah. Why would I? He's no one to me.

"What if he fell?" I ask after we walk a few minutes. I think of how Lucy gazed down into the canyon yesterday, how I startled her, how she lurched forward into empty air. What if Noah found himself on the canyon's rim, listening to the call of the void? You don't survive a fall from that height. And yet so many of us can't seem to stay away from the edge.

"He could have been sleepwalking or something," I say, my imagination running wild. I can see it so clearly: Noah roaming in the fog, stumbling over the barrier, pitching down into the dark.

Brandon shrugs. "He's never sleepwalked before. If we don't find him soon though, I'm going to get the park staff involved. Noah's not exactly the rough-it-in-the-wilds type."

"Yeah, makes sense. Let's check the main overlook first."

"Where the Cloudkiss Killer jumped?" Brandon asks, an expression I can't quite read on his face.

"It's just an idea," I say, pulling him toward the popular park vista. The touch of his warm skin against mine is soothing. It makes all my thoughts of curses and evil disappear. "Noah definitely has Kincaid on the brain, so maybe he'd go there."

Brandon's mouth thins into a disapproving line. "Noah is way too into that guy. He learned everything he could about him. Sometimes I think it isn't just curiosity, you know? Like, sometimes it seems like Noah admires him."

"What's to admire?" I ask as innocently as I can, as if I'm not obsessed with Kincaid too, as if I haven't learned every detail of his life and every act he committed on his years-long murder spree.

Brandon sighs, eyes on the pine needles under our feet. "Noah said Kincaid was smart and careful, cerebral. He wasn't a butcher. He was an—an artist."

I wrinkle my nose. "You think Noah wants to be like him?"

"If I thought that, I wouldn't be rooming with the guy."

"He is kind of a creep though," I admit.

Brandon shrugs. "But he's clean and quiet and way better than a lot of my friends' roommates. No dirty underwear on the floor. No parties."

"You hear yourself, right?"

"Noah's not a serial killer. He's just a weird guy. Totally harmless." Brandon laughs, and the sound is wrong somehow, like someone laughing at a funeral. A sense of dread fills my stomach, though this time it doesn't have anything to do with my fears about myself. It's something else, something bigger than me.

"Shhh," I say. We're nearing the overlook, and my palms are sweating, even though it's forty degrees out. Fog covers the whole area, dense and drifting like clouds. Wrongness builds around me, a feeling of being watched from all sides.

To my surprise, Brandon takes my hand, as if he feels it too. "This place ain't right," he whispers.

"No, it really isn't," I agree. "Noah?" I call quietly.

There's no answer, but Brandon and I both move toward the edge of the canyon, inexorably drawn. By intuition? Or something else?

We have to drop each other's hand to climb over the barrier. And then we stand together, shoulder to shoulder, gazing into the fog.

We might as well be standing inside a cloud. I'm reminded powerfully of the painting on the cover of my English textbook, Caspar David Friedrich's *Wanderer Above the Sea of Fog*, in which a man stands confidently on a jutting bit of rock over a valley of mists, walking stick in hand, shoulders thrown back. An explorer, a conqueror, even though he's insignificant in the vast landscape.

I've always loved that painting, though standing here above the fogs of Cloudkiss, I don't feel anything like the man in the painting. I feel as vulnerable as a still-pink newborn. Lost and small and afraid.

I pull Brandon down to the ground, and we crawl, on our hands and knees, feeling carefully. "Noah?" I call again. I should feel foolish, but I don't. I don't think Brandon does either.

"Stop," Brandon says urgently. "I hit the edge." I go still, closing my fingers over a jutting bit of rock. I peer down into the canyon, but the fog is too thick to see anything. I realize I'm on my belly looking down into the canyon just like Lucy was yesterday. Exactly as I drew her. A strange sort of déjà vu washes over me.

"I think this is what purgatory must be like," Brandon says, his voice distant. "A kind of nothingness in between heaven and hell."

There's no such thing as purgatory in my father's religion. Either you're saved or you're not, holy or evil, a child of God or a servant of the devil. You walk the streets of heaven or you burn.

"This isn't nothingness though," I say. "Don't you feel it?"

"Feel what?" Brandon asks, though I suspect he knows exactly what I mean.

Just then a breeze blows against my face, cold as ice and carrying the damp smell of growing, decaying life—moss and mushrooms and mist. The fog seems to dance in response, moving its sinuous way up and away, giving me the first clear view. Trees and rocks, green and brown, below us. And there, a flash of blue. Noah's hat?

"Look," I say, pointing.

"I see it," Brandon says grimly.

The wind blows again, and the fog lifts, and I expect to see Noah. I expect it so completely that my brain fills in all the details before the fog finishes clearing: his body in a clump of bushes thirty feet down the canyon wall, his limbs splayed at unnatural angles. His face bleeding. His neck broken.

But there's nothing there. No Noah. Just rocks and trees and fog.

Brandon laughs, hardly more than a relieved exhalation of breath. "Jesus, this place really gets to you."

"Yeah," I agree, pulling him back toward the barrier. "I don't know what I was thinking. Let's try one of the trails. He's probably just out for a walk. I bet that wasn't even his hat." We climb over the railing and walk in silence for a few minutes, both lost in our own thoughts.

"I really thought he was going to be dead down there," Brandon says as we start down the waterfall hiking trail, which soon turns into a steep, twisting staircase, surrounded by rhododendron. He shakes his head and laughs again, more loudly this time, as if to show the fog he's not afraid. "I felt so sure."

We descend the slick steps carefully, holding on to the mossy banister. But Brandon almost trips on something, and a glass bottle goes rolling down a few steps. He leans down and picks it up. "Cabernet sauvignon," he says. "Looks expensive. Somebody was having a real good time last night." He studies the blandly artful label.

But my eyes are locked on something else. There's a body lying at the bottom of the staircase. Arms and legs spread out awkwardly. Bloody face turned up toward us. Long blond hair fanned out around her face.

"Brandon," I say, my body frozen. "Look."

The joke he was about to make dies on his lips. He drops the bottle, and it lands on the wooden step with a heavy thunk and rolls down, all the way to the bottom, to land at the woman's feet.

"Who is that?" he asks quietly.

I close my eyes as horrible recognition dawns. "Kiersten. She's here with that bachelorette party." She's wearing the same clothes she had on last night—purple yoga pants, a black North Face coat.

Images flit through my head, lightning fast: *Kiersten turns in the dark, her eyes wide with fear. My hands reach out to shove her. She reaches out, scratches my neck. She tumbles down the stairs, landing at the bottom with a sickening crunch.*

"Is she dead?" Brandon asks, his voice hoarse.

"I don't know," I say, my vocal cords strangled. The idea that she could be alive breaks through my paralysis. "I'll go see."

The scratch on my neck throbs as I go down the last few steps. More bloody, confused images fragment and flash behind my eyes.

All the forensic trivia I've picked up from *Human Beasties* rushes through my mind. This is my chance to get my fingerprints on her skin in front of a witness. To get my DNA under her nails.

Kiersten's eyes are closed as if she's sleeping, a puddle of blood her only pillow. I put my shaking fingers to her neck. To my shock, her skin is still a little warm. I feel her pulse, weak and low, at the same moment I see her chest rise.

"She's alive!" I yell back to Brandon. "Call 911."

I stare down into Kiersten's face, pale beneath its artificial tan. I should try to stop her head from bleeding. I should cover her with my coat.

*No*, whispers a voice I recognize as my own: *You should smother her with it.*

# FIVE

## LUCY

**After the woman** is found, the gray morning becomes a blur of red and blue lights. Police, EMTs, and rangers, questions asked and answered. I manage to stay calm through it all though dread lodges in my stomach like a stone. But as the EMTs painstakingly carry Kiersten up on a stretcher, my heart starts to race and my breath comes short. Flashes of another day, another ambulance, other officers and barely restrained journalists crowd in.

Everyone says it's lucky Kiersten wasn't on a more remote trail. Lucky there were stairs and not a rocky, muddy path.

But all I can think about is the last time I walked that trail and who I walked it with. How I heard him in the woods yesterday morning. How he disappeared.

What if it wasn't a hallucination? What if he— What if it's starting again?

I make it to the shelter of an oak tree before my legs go weak and I have to drop into a crouch. Cold sweat runs down my face, and my chest tightens like a clenched fist. I feel death at my back, breathing down my neck, relentless and inescapable. I squeeze my eyes shut, trying to fend off the panic attack.

"Hey," Maggie says, appearing at my side, on her knees in the dirt. She puts a hand on my shoulder. "Are you all right?" When I look up at her, her eyes widen slightly. "Shit, you're not all right."

All I can manage is a head shake. My breath is gone. My words are gone.

I stare ahead, watching as Kiersten is loaded into an ambulance. Her friends follow behind the stretcher, crying and hugging one another.

"You're triggered right now, but you're okay, you're safe. Nothing bad is going to happen to you," Maggie says. "Remember, Kincaid is dead. He's gone." It's the first time she's ever alluded to my history with this place, to what happened to me.

I lock my eyes onto Maggie's face, focusing on the reality of her: the solid grasp of her hand on my shoulder, her concerned gray eyes, the contraction of her brow. "That's right, just look at me," she says, smiling. I manage to gasp in a painful breath, and Maggie's honey scent comes with it.

I gaze at her, taking in every detail. Her hair is pushed behind her ear on the right side, and she has three small studs in the cartilage of her ear, each one a tiny silver star. There's a small silver hoop in her earlobe. My eyes travel down to her neck, which has a scatter of dark freckles like a constellation.

My breathing eases, and the tension in my body releases, leaving my muscles sore and tired. I cough a few times and then slump onto my rear in the pine needles.

"Better?" Maggie asks.

I nod, looking past her to the ambulance. The doors close, and all the bachelorettes walk away from the parking lot, back toward the gathered crowd, whispering angrily to each other. They pass by me and Maggie without noticing us. "We ought to sue their asses," one of them hisses.

Maggie snorts, so she must have heard it too. But her eyes are still on me. Now that the adrenaline has left my body, I'm embarrassed, like I always am after a panic attack. I drop my face into my hands. "Sorry," I say.

Maggie clears her throat. "You know, I had something awful happen to me too, something that I think might stick with me forever. I understand how hard some experiences can be to get over."

"Really?" I can't keep the surprise from my voice. Maggie is so self-assured and confident, not at all like someone who's been through something bad—not at all like me.

She nods, bites her lip, as if deciding how much to reveal. "It's partly why I switched my major to psychology. It used to be music composition. I wanted to understand how someone could do to me what this person did." She laughs. "And look at me now, here at Killer Quest."

"What happened?" I ask, then quickly add, "Of course, you don't have to tell me if you don't want to." People always want to hear a tragic story, and they try to find subtle ways to manipulate it out of you. I never want to do that to someone.

Maggie's eyes are trained on the trees in the distance. "I got mugged my first semester in college. I was out late with friends and walked home alone. This guy pulled a gun on me and demanded my money and jewelry. I gave him my phone and my wallet. But I wouldn't take off this necklace." She pulls a silver locket from beneath her shirt and shows it to me. It's old-fashioned, a tarnished heart with a small garnet embedded in it.

"It was my grandma's," she says. "The guy reached out to yank it off me, and I fought him. He got so mad, like, I watched his face transform with rage." She shakes her head. "He hit me in the head with the gun, right here." Maggie points to an inch-long scar along her hairline.

"Oh my God," I say. "I'm so sorry."

Maggie smiles from the corner of her mouth. "Luckily, a group of guys came by right then and the mugger ran off. But it took me a long time before I could feel safe again."

"I still don't feel safe," I say, drawing my knees up to my chest. "And Kincaid never even laid a hand on me."

"But you know he would have, if the police hadn't come," Maggie says. "And that knowledge is enough to make you afraid."

"Yes," I breathe out, relieved she understands. "It was just luck that my body didn't end up mutilated and displayed on some rock like an offering to the gods."

Maggie's eyes light up for a moment, as if with a flash of insight, but then it's gone again. Before I can ask about it, she's talking. "Do you want to tell me what happened that day? You can if you want to." Her voice is gentle.

I close my eyes. I haven't told this story in a long time, not since the early days of police interviews and meetings with a child psychologist. But it's festering inside me, and I realize I do want to tell her. I want to let it out.

"It was foggy," I say, and Maggie nods. "It was early morning, and I wanted to hike by myself. I used to do that all the time. It made my parents nervous, but I liked the feeling of being completely alone in the woods. Only, I had stepped off the trail for a minute. I wanted to look at a clump of mushrooms I hadn't seen before. I had my loupe with me, for magnifying the small details," I explain, pulling the silver loupe on its chain from beneath my sweater to show her the thick lens. "We were in the middle of a unit on fungi in my junior naturalist class," I add with a small smile. "I was taking pictures of them, trying to see the undersides to help me identify them. When I looked up again, the fog had just . . . descended.

"I thought I could find my way back. I tried. But I got more and more lost. And normally I wouldn't have been scared because I knew what to do if you get lost in the woods. But something about this place . . . it frightened me. I started to get really nervous.

"So when a man appeared, a nice man who seemed really kind and safe and offered to help me get back, I went with him."

A tear runs down my cheek. "I was so stupid."

Maggie wipes the tear away with her thumb. "You were fifteen, Lucy. You were afraid."

"I knew that people had been killed here, but it had been a few years since it happened. Back then they were trying to keep the grisly details out of the news. And he didn't look like a killer. He had a really nice smile." A surge of anger wipes away the last of my panic. "I know better now."

"What happened after he found you?" Maggie asks.

I take a breath. "We walked. He seemed to know exactly where he was going, like he could see through the fog. He asked me questions about myself."

"Like what?" She cocks her head.

"Like, what I wanted to be when I grew up. What my hobbies were. My favorite subjects in school."

"Wow," Maggie says. "Most killers want to depersonalize their victims, not get to know them."

I shrug. "Maybe he wanted to keep me calm. Anyway, it worked. Plus, he really did take me back up the way he said he would. We made it to the stairs at the start of the waterfall trail. It was even foggier there, but you couldn't lose your way in it because you just had to follow the handrail up.

"I went ahead of him, not thinking anything of it. But I started to feel scared then. I'm not even sure why. I wasn't lost anymore. But maybe I sensed it the way animals do. I turned, and there was a hypodermic needle in his hand."

"Jesus," Maggie breathes.

"Later, the police found his kill site several yards off the trail, under this rocky overhang close to where we were when he pulled out the needle. They said there was plastic sheeting, surgical instruments. It's where I would have ended up." My throat goes tight, making my last words a rasp.

"But you didn't," Maggie says, putting her hand on my knee.

I take a shuddering breath. "He lunged for me, but he slipped on the steps. It was all the head start I needed. I ran as fast as I could. He chased after me, calling my name, saying he wasn't going to hurt me. I still remember the thud of his boots, the panic in his voice.

"I guess you know the rest from the podcast," I say. "One of the rangers had recognized his car. She'd called the police the second she saw it, and they were standing near the overlook when I came up. They heard me screaming and pulled out their guns.

"Kincaid saw them. He looked at me, and there was regret in his eyes."

"You think he felt sorry for what he was going to do to you?"

I shake my head. "No, he felt sorry for what he'd never get the chance to do."

"And he jumped?"

"He ran straight for the edge and vaulted over the railing. He looked back at us and then down into the canyon, making up his mind. And then he jumped. I don't think the police thought he would really do it; they didn't even try to shoot him. He was there and then he was gone."

"And you were still here. You lived," Maggie says.

I shrug. "If you can call it living." I reach down and select a brown oak leaf, twirling it between my fingers. The underside of it is studded with hard little galls.

"Thank you for telling me your story," Maggie says. "Did it help—to get it out?"

"No," I say honestly. "I thought it might, but talking never helps."

"We all process trauma differently," Maggie says. "We all find our own ways to heal."

"Like finding a serial killer's bones?" I say with a broken laugh, tossing down my oak leaf.

"Exactly. And I think you're going to find them." She holds my gaze, her own unwavering, sure. "You're going to find them, and you're going to get your life back."

"You can't promise that," I say. "It's like finding a needle in a haystack."

"Maybe not, but I promise I'll do anything I can to help you find them." Maggie touches my hand. "Anything to help you walk away from this place with your mind more at peace."

"Thanks," I say, managing a small smile for her. "I'm really, really glad you're here."

"Me too," Maggie says. "Now let's go find that fucker's bones."

But first we have a mandatory event to attend.

Despite what happened to Kiersten, *Human Beasties* decided not to cancel the contest yet, and so at 10:00, the event staff herds us all into the lodge, two hours late for the scheduled talk from a forensics expert who has come to instruct us in how to avoid contaminating any evidence we may find. Don't touch the body, she says, or anything that might be related to Kincaid. Leave it where it is, take a picture, record your coordinates, and call the ranger's office or the police station. The woman is clearly horrified the contest is happening at all and looks like she's trying not to have a stroke over the prospect of one us contaminating a crime scene or, worse, taking home a part of Kincaid as a macabre souvenir.

I assume this bunch would normally be thrilled to have access to a forensics expert. But they're all too distracted. Whispers and glances run like electricity among the contestants, and more than a few eyes land on Carolina since she called Kiersten a vapid bitch last night. Dozens of true crime fans in the creepiest canyon in the US? It's hard to imagine anything except a violent scene in the dead of night.

Even I can picture it clearly because I've imagined Kincaid coming after me in the same way a hundred times. I can see the shadow at Kiersten's back, the muffled footsteps in the fog. Her staccato breaths misting the air, panic and desperation squeezing the oxygen from her lungs. A hypodermic needle sending cold sedatives into her bloodstream. The knife raised, the cold white fingers reaching for her arm. The horrible, inevitable moment she looks into her killer's eyes and knows she doesn't have a chance.

But it's clear the police have formed a different picture: a young woman drinking, wandering alone in the park. She slips and tumbles down the stairs. She hits her head and lies there until someone finds her. The police and rangers didn't even seem surprised, as if such an accident was inevitable. They were only surprised that she's alive—that she's so battered and still breathing. That someone found her in time.

After a long, distracted hour, the forensics talk finally wraps up. While we clap for her, the speaker eyes us warily, as if wondering which of us is going to be first to compromise a crime scene.

Then one of the harried-looking event staff stands up to announce in a voice of forced cheer that we're all asked to stay close to camp until further notice, but they aren't able to answer any other questions. The moment he sits down, the room breaks into frenzied conversation, the sound like swarming yellow jackets. As we all file out of the lodge, the other contestants pass around theories about Kiersten's accident like this is their favorite TV show and they're trying to unravel this season's big mystery. I hear someone mention Noah's name. Apparently, he was unaccounted for this morning, around the same time Kiersten was found.

The bachelorettes put their heads together, just outside the door, trying to figure out their next move. "I think we should all stay and finish the contest. It's what our sweet, sweet Kiersten would want us to do," the bride says through her pretty tears.

I roll my eyes. Kiersten's friends might have all cried and wailed and yelled about lawsuits, but not a single one of them got into the ambulance with her. None of them packed their things or started their cars. Kiersten left Cloudkiss Canyon all alone, lost in the foggy landscape of unconsciousness.

I grab a YA sci-fi novel from my tent and prop myself under a nearby tree to read, but I spend most of the morning peering over the pages at the other contestants. Only the two who found Kiersten seem to sincerely feel anything for her. The college boy, Brandon, seems genuinely moved. After the talk in the lodge, he sits all morning by the fire, a blanket over his shoulders, a stunned look on his face. Noah comes out of his tent a handful of times to check on Brandon, his dark hair tousled and his eyes red from lack of sleep. It turns out he was missing this morning because he'd locked himself in his car to sleep. Whatever happened to him last night must have really left its mark.

He catches sight of me beneath the tree and stares at me for a long moment, his gaze a strange mixture of anger and desire. It sends a chill across my skin. But after that, he studiously avoids looking at me. I can't tell whether he's embarrassed for pointing at me last night, afraid of me, or something worse.

Carolina sits next to Brandon, staring into the cold black remains of the campfire. But there's a foot of space between them, so different from their behavior yesterday. All of Carolina's flirtatious smiles are gone, and I suspect that whatever little romance they started up yesterday is over. Finding a bloodied body must have that effect.

The rest of us wait, restless and tense, to learn our fate. Maggie watches everyone carefully, surreptitiously taking notes on a reporter's notepad, a small groove between her eyebrows. She walks calmly between groups, occasionally joining in their conversations but mostly listening, gathering up their theories, analyzing their responses, cataloging their thoughts and hopes and fears. I can tell that Maggie likes to observe people, to try to figure out how they tick.

And I like to watch her. I'm a little mesmerized by the way she moves practically unseen in the crowd. How do they all not stop what they're doing to stare at her, to watch her every movement? She might as well be a breath of wind stirring the leaves of a tree for all the notice most of them take of her. But I can't pull my eyes off her. Every now and then, she looks my way and smiles, a solid and reassuring expression. Or she raises her eyebrows at me, cocking her head at some particularly foolish person. Watching Maggie is the only thing that keeps my mind from Kincaid, from remembering how close I came to getting hurt just like Kiersten. She's the only thing keeping my panic at bay.

Finally, the *Human Beasties* hosts, Sandra and Kevin, call an emergency meeting in the early afternoon, after all the police are gone. The atmosphere among the contestants is strikingly different from the day before, the excitement transmuted into a simmering titillation. Everyone is watchful, a little jumpy, but expectant in the same way as a line of cars waiting their turn to rubberneck at an interstate accident.

"Thank you all for your patience today," Sandra says, her voice somber. "It has been a terrible shock, and not at all how we imagined Killer Quest to go."

Maggie cuts her eyes at me and purses her lips, shaking her head at the same time. I almost laugh.

"I know you must all have a lot of questions, and I'm going to answer as many of them as I can," Sandra says. "Today's events were deeply upsetting and have given us a great deal to think about. Let's take a moment of silence for Kiersten, to send up prayers or good vibes or whatever you want to send up."

Everyone bows their heads, but many people shuffle uneasily or maybe impatiently, I can't tell. The seconds seem to stretch out like toffee, the silence feeling louder and louder with every cough, every leaf crunched underfoot.

"Thank you," Sandra says, lifting her head. Her eyes look slightly misty. "The first thing I want you to know is that Killer Quest will continue, despite this terrible accident. And I want to assure you that it *was* an accident. As true crime buffs, we expect to see the worst in the world at times, but the police are certain that there was no foul play. Kiersten was drinking and tripped and fell on the slippery stairs.

"Nonetheless, we understand that some of you may want to go home." Sandra looks at the contestants with concern, as if they're normal, instead of the kind of freaks who spend a week in a canyon searching for a serial killer's bones. As if they have such tender hearts that a little bloody fall is going to send them packing.

Fat chance of that. Even Kiersten's coterie of dewy-eyed friends isn't budging.

Sandra smiles. "Kevin and I hope you will choose to stay. We've got an amazing week ahead of us. *Human Beasties* trivia, campfire stories—all kinds of stuff. And, of course, the awards ceremony for the winners of Killer Quest."

The crowd murmurs, their solemnity already giving way to stirring excitement.

"But," says Sandra, holding up one carefully manicured hand, "there's one change to the contest that you need to know about. The national forest officials have thrown up a bit of red tape for us, but we feel it's a very reasonable request and will make the contest safer for everyone. We really don't want any more accidents, do we?" She pauses dramatically and takes a deep breath. "Contestants will now only be allowed to participate in Killer Quest if they are part of a group of at least three individuals. This is for everyone's safety."

My heart plummets into my stomach. I didn't plan on this.

I'm not the only one who's upset. The crowd groans and begins to buzz with angry whispers. Kevin and Sandra exchange worried glances.

One man's voice rises above the tumult. He's big and bearded and has his arms crossed over his chest. "Excuse me? Some bimbo gets drunk and falls down some stairs and now we're going to be treated like children?" Murmurs of agreement steal over the crowd.

"Will the winners have to split the twenty thousand dollars?" a woman asks, an edge of anger in her voice. A bunch of other people yell support for her question.

Sandra looks apologetic. "I'm afraid so."

"This is bullshit," a man growls. Sandra flinches, as if he's struck her.

Kevin raises his arms to quiet the crowd. When they finally let him speak, his voice is earnest. "We're very sorry about this new rule, but let's not lose track of why we're here. Remember where you are. Remember what's at stake. This week, all of us have a chance to lay the Cloudkiss Killer's hideous legacy to rest."

The crowd shifts uneasily, as if they've been caught out. Caught being the greedy, unfeeling, exploitative people they are. How could I possibly team up with any of them? How could I spend a whole week hiding who I am, what I've been through, while they wax poetic about the fascinating lives of serial killers?

Maybe I should just go home. Maybe this was a mistake.

But then Maggie nudges me with her elbow. "Killer Quest buddies," she whispers. The pressure building in my chest eases. At least there's Maggie.

The crowd now subdued, Sandra and Kevin wind down their speech by giving us instructions to register our new team configurations by dinnertime. Anyone not in a group of three or more will be asked to go home, they say. The contestants disperse into smaller groups, most of them whispering angrily.

"We were pretty much going to team up anyway, right?" Maggie asks. "I mean, we spent all day together yesterday. And I think we get along pretty well, don't you?" She smiles, but I'm surprised to see a shadow of anxiety in her eyes, as if she's afraid I don't like her, that I'll say no.

"Of course," I say, smiling back. I touch her arm. "It was already a done deal." I mean it too. I don't think I've ever felt so immediately comfortable with someone as I do with Maggie. She made me laugh all day yesterday, which was the last thing I expected to do this week. And she helped me through this morning's panic.

Relief washes over her features. "We've just got to find one more partner, then." We turn as one and look out over the crowd. A few people eye us and look away quickly, and I realize none of them are going to want to be on my team. Not after I punched Noah in front of everyone, not after he pointed at me when he ran screaming from the woods. The Beastie Babes are a jumpy and paranoid bunch. And I've pretty much already made my reputation as a weirdo.

I glance at Maggie and realize she's staring at me, a thoughtful look in her gray eyes. She's thinking the same thing I am. "Look, you don't have to be on my team," I say. "I'll understand if you want to join someone else. Maybe that couple I saw you talking to at breakfast?"

"Rosa and Bridget? They're cool, but not a chance, Luce. You're stuck with me," she says, breaking into a radiant smile. She pushes a piece of hair behind my ear, making my stomach flutter. And for the first time in a very long time, I realize, it isn't a flutter of fear.

It's desire. And desire feels a lot like hope.

# SIX

## CAROLINA

**I sit in** the entrance of my tent, watching the Killer Quest contestants mill around, talking and negotiating, forming alliances. That's what I should be doing too. But I'm caught up in a spiral of thoughts that won't let me go.

Whether my eyes are open or closed, whether I want to or not, all I can see is Kiersten's unconscious form, alone at the bottom of the stairs, covered over in mist. The way her limbs were sprawled, her head lolling. The congealing pool of blood beneath her head, soaked into her hair. Her slightly open mouth, the vague emptiness of her face.

A normal person would have felt pity for her, sympathy, maybe even empathy. A normal person would have been moved by her vulnerability, the precariousness of the faint pulse beating at her neck. But I didn't feel any of that. I couldn't feel any of it.

My own pulse was beating far too hard and too fast for those feelings. The scratches on my own skin stung, the scrubbed-clean beds of my fingernails throbbed. I looked at Kiersten and saw the gaping mouth of my tent, felt the night-cold air on my face, heard the way my steps must have sounded in the darkness behind her.

Dismay filled me at the sight of her bleeding body, followed quickly by shame. Because I was more afraid for myself than for her, because the idea of her waking up to blame me seemed worse than letting her die.

Of course, I didn't let her die. Brandon ripped his hoodie off, and I wrapped it around her head. I covered her body with my coat. We called 911, and we stayed with her until help came.

I kept wondering if I'd done it though, and if I had, was it because of the curse or because of the fog? Was it because of my blood or because the stories everyone else laughed off as hillbilly superstition were true? Or both? My thoughts tumbled over one another, contradictory and impossible.

All I know for sure is that the whole time I knelt over Kiersten's body, watching her chest rise and fall, I thought about Michael. I thought about his blood on my hands.

The police said I didn't kill him. That it was a freak accident. And the doctors said I don't fully remember what happened because of shock and trauma. Apparently, forgetting is the self's way of protecting a person from something too painful to process. They say that one day I might get to a point where I remember nearly everything.

Only I'm not so sure I want to. Who knows what I did in those unaccounted-for hours, minutes, and seconds?

And now it's happened again.

This afternoon, I stood at the back of the crowd listening to Sandra Delaney's radio voice turn the events of the morning into a neat and packaged story, just like it turns the heinous acts of serial killers into a tale good people can bear, a tidy forty-five-minute episode to make order from the chaos. But I couldn't believe a word she said.

Brandon stood beside me, but he was a thousand miles away, as inaccessible as the stars. His previously carefree features were scrunched and furrowed, worry in every line of his face. Whatever Sandra and Kevin might say, whatever the police and the EMTs might say, Brandon doesn't buy the story of Kiersten's drunken fall any more than I do. This morning spooked him deeply, and I think I spooked him too though I'm not sure how. Did he see something in my face? Sense something in the way I crouched over Kiersten's body?

Whatever it was, it cut him off from me. I could read it in his posture: arms wrapped around himself, shoulders slightly hunched, head down. A self-protective stance if ever I've seen one. I knew our plans to hunt for Kincaid together were over. So when Kevin and Sandra dismissed us, I didn't even bother to ask him if we were done. Why bother, when I already knew? I just walked away. And he didn't follow me. He didn't call me back.

I'm on my own again.

That's all right. I can be on my own. I'm always on my own, aren't I? And I always manage. But with Brandon gone, I have to find a new team. Otherwise, I'm out of this contest before it's even properly begun.

And then what? Back to Honey Valley and sleeping on my friend Sheena's couch? Back to pretending I'm just a smart girl dealt a bad hand, who's trying to make a better life? Back to pretending, without ever facing the truth about myself?

No. I won't leave here without being sure of myself, without leaving Dad's curse far, far behind me.

I stand up fast, as if that's enough to banish my hateful thoughts. I take a deep breath and leave my tent behind. I walk around the camping area, scoping everyone out. When I spot Rosa and Bridget, I make a beeline for them. Rosa's eyes widen slightly as I approach.

"Hey, you two," I say, making my voice as friendly as possible.

"Hey," Bridget says curtly. Rosa only nods.

"So you look like you maybe need another team member?" I ask brightly.

They glance at each other, wordlessly communicating in the way couples do. "Actually, I think we're gonna ask that guy Denny over there," Rosa says, pointing at a tall, skinny dude in a slouchy beanie and colorful knit sweater.

"Oh, well . . . okay," I say, my smile faltering.

"Look, it's nothing personal," Bridget says. "It's just Denny was in the Peace Corps, so he's got experience, you know?"

I shrug. "Sure, of course." I know they're lying. Denny's only experience is in smoking a lot of pot and making patchouli-scented soap, but I don't blame them for choosing him over me. They saw how I was last night—losing my temper for no reason, unreasonably angry, swearing at Kiersten. That's already someone you don't want on your team. And then I just happen to be the one who finds her unconscious and bleeding? A little too convenient.

But I'm desperate, so I have to try again. "You know, we're allowed to have more than three in a group," I say, my face burning with embarrassment.

"I'm sure you'll find someone," Bridget says, looking at her phone. "Don't worry."

"Anyway, we'd better go, but good luck," Rosa says, then pulls Bridget away. They call out to Denny, who yawns and rubs his eyes as he watches them approach.

"I hope you enjoy having a human sloth for a partner," I mumble, already scanning the area for another option.

But the few contestants who aren't already grouped up seem to avoid meeting my eyes. A middle-aged couple literally turns and walks away when I look in their direction. Like I'm a leper. Can they smell it on me—the evil?

Or is it only in my head? My own guilt and fears written on their faces?

I want to believe that. I came here at least partly for them, to meet other true crime fans. But now I see my mistake. They aren't like me. While I was busy comparing myself to the killers on *Human Beasties*, the other contestants were learning how to recognize people like me.

There's only one group that might take me in. Lucy and her friend—Maggie, I think her name was. After all, Lucy's a pariah too. Noah might not have explained why he pointed at her last night, but he has called her a "crazy, psycho bitch" to anyone who would listen. Hell, maybe he's been badmouthing me too. It would make sense, given the instant dislike he took to me once I started flirting with Brandon.

I open my sketchbook to the page with the drawing of Lucy, belly down at the edge of the canyon. I only managed to get a few lines on the page before I stupidly spoke up and frightened her. But I filled the rest in later: the wiry tension in her limbs, the tightness at her mouth. I've looked at it a dozen times since I drew it, unable to forget the way she hung over the canyon, the fierce longing on her face. It reminded me of myself.

But it's more than that. Something about her draws me in, intrigues me. She's a girl whose story I want to know. But she's so closed off, I honestly don't know how Maggie got her to team up at all. Or if they'll take me on as their third. But it seems like my best bet. Maybe my only bet.

"Have you seen that short blond girl who punched a guy yesterday?" I ask Addison, one of the women from the bachelorette group. Yesterday, she talked my ear off about how her grandmother once met Ted Bundy, but now she only eyes me with distrust and wordlessly points at a picnic table partially hidden in a stand of trees. I can just make out Lucy and Maggie eating a late lunch.

As I approach, I'm surprised to see Lucy is laughing so hard her shoulders shake. Her expression is so, so changed from the one on the page I was just looking at, as if she's a completely different person. Maggie has a hand on her arm, leaning toward her, whispering something mischievous, judging by the look on Maggie's face. It's an interesting face too, the kind you take a second look at when you pass it in the street.

Lucy said she was here alone, but they look like old friends—or maybe something more? I hesitate, unsure how to approach them. I'm not sure my ego can handle getting shot down again.

Maggie looks up and catches sight of me, and a warm, liquid smile spreads over her face, drawing me nearer. "Hey," she says, motioning me over. "I'm Maggie Rey. You know Lucy?"

When Lucy turns and spots me, the laugh in her eyes dies. "Hey," she says brusquely.

"Hey," I say. Then to Maggie, "I'm Carolina Cassels."

"You two had better be friends," she says. "Everyone's been looking at you like you're the spooky sisters."

Lucy rolls her eyes. "Bunch of paranoid, crime-obsessed idiots."

"So it's not in my head?" I ask. "They really are scared of me? Jesus." I had hoped maybe I was reading into things.

"'It is much safer to be feared than loved,'" Maggie says, breaking into another grin.

"Wow, quoting Machiavelli," I say, mustering up a smile for her. It's nice that she's trying to make me feel better. "But 'one should wish to be both,'" I add, remembering the English essay I wrote on the subject.

Maggie raises her eyebrows in approval and pats the seat next to her. "Come sit. I'll share my lunch." She slides a plastic container of dried apricots and almonds toward me.

I sit next to her and gather all my hair over one shoulder, smoothing it down. Lucy's eyes follow the movement, and it's the same way the boys in Honey Valley look at my hair. I feel heat rise to my cheeks.

Unsure what to say or do, I distract myself by popping an apricot into my mouth. Lucy watches me chew it. "Why'd you yell at Kiersten last night?" she asks. "It was kind of an overreaction, wasn't it?"

"You're the one who punched a guy in the face," I point out.

Maggie snorts and pushes Lucy's shoulder playfully from across the table, drawing a smile from the girl's thinly pressed lips. Her face transforms when she smiles, her hazel eyes brightening, the sharp planes of her face softening. I'm already memorizing the expression, thinking of how I'd render it in pastels.

"So you need a team, right?" Maggie asks me, getting down to business.

I nod, pulling my eyes from Lucy's face before things can get weird. "Got an opening?"

Maggie quirks her eyebrows and smiles mysteriously. "Maybe."

"What? Do I have to audition? Quote more Machiavelli? Maybe some Shakespeare?"

Maggie laughs. "You just have to answer one question for us."

"O-kay," I say, suddenly nervous. Maggie is staring at me like she can read my soul.

"Why do you want to find the bones?" she asks. It's the same question Brandon asked me, but it feels different coming from her. Like a test. Especially with Lucy looking on.

I open my mouth and then close it again. I try to think of a lie. Lying has always come easy to me, easy as breathing. It was a survival tool in my house because Dad didn't only come home from prison with talk of curses. He also came bearing restrictions I was forever lying my way out of, like dress codes and curfews and mandatory Bible study. But now my mind is blank except for one, completely unspeakable thing: the truth.

Lucy cocks her head at me.

"First, tell me why you two want to find them," I say, hedging. There's no way I'm telling these girls my worst fears about myself. I fiddle with a leaf on the tabletop, twirling its stem between my fingers.

Maggie shakes her head, her chin-length brown hair swaying around her face. Lucy only stares. Those two have the power here, and they know it.

I huff, frustrated that I can't think of a single lie. I look back toward the people who are starting to disperse, walking off in groups toward the registration tent. None of them are going to want me. If I tell Maggie and Lucy the truth, they won't want me either.

"I don't even want the money. Seriously, y'all can split it between you," I say, feigning casualness. That's not at all true—that money would help me pay for college, not to mention my current living expenses, and I need every penny. But I'm desperate to avoid Maggie's question.

Lucy looks surprised but still doesn't say anything.

I turn back to Maggie's unwavering gaze. I bite my lip. She raises her thick, dark brows, her gray eyes piercing. I glance to Lucy again, whose patience is beginning to wane. She's almost ready to write me off, to turn me away. And I sense that she's not a girl who gives second chances.

There's nothing to do but tell the truth. My heart pounds so hard I can hear it. "I guess . . . I guess that people like Kincaid make me feel better about myself. Like, compared to most people maybe I'm not so great, but compared to serial killers, I'm all right," I say, all in a rush, my eyes on the table-top. It's not the whole truth, only a small part of it, but even this admission is shameful. I look up to see their reactions.

Lucy glances nervously at Maggie. "What's that got to do with the bones?" she asks me.

I shrug. "Not sure. But I think finding them will help me somehow." I think again of the legend of the canyon, of the possibility I might find the true version of myself here in its shadows and mists. I barely suppress a shiver.

"The human heart is darkness and chaos," Maggie says, quoting what I said to her last night. She rests her chin in her hand. "Well, I'm satisfied. Are you, Lucy?"

Lucy clearly is not satisfied. In fact, she's eyeing me like I've got three heads, but she shrugs in resignation. Maybe I earned points by sticking up for her last night, even if that's the thing that has the rest of the camp ostracizing me.

"What about you two?" I ask again, feeling defensive. "I told you mine."

Maggie pushes herself up from the table and hops lightly over the bench. "I never said we'd reciprocate." She winks at me and saunters off toward the registration tent, impossibly cool in her faded black jeans and combat boots, her hands in the pockets of her denim jacket. She turns and looks back at us over her shoulder, that cocky smile on her face again. "You two coming? Gotta register our team."

I should be annoyed they made me spill my guts without sharing anything themselves, but I'm not. If anything, I'm intrigued. What stories are they hiding? What impulses brought them here?

Lucy and I both get up and follow Maggie through the trees.

Once we've registered, we head back to the picnic table. Lucy is quiet and avoids looking at me entirely, but she shoots surreptitious little glances at Maggie. So she *was* looking at my hair the way I thought. Only, it's Maggie she has a crush on. I feel a little twinge that almost seems like jealousy. I ignore it.

Maggie does most of the talking for us, detailing the parts of the park she's already explored on her own and theorizing where we would be most likely to find Kincaid's body. I envy her confidence, the way she takes charge so easily. It's the self-assurance of someone who comes from money. That I'm certain of. She's got wealth written all over her—expensive schools and Ivy League ambitions, private tutors, piano lessons. This is a girl the world has made way for, and so she walks into every new place expecting to thrive.

Lucy pulls out a park map and lays it out flat on the table. "Where do you think we should start?" she asks Maggie.

Maggie is quiet for a long moment. "Well," she finally says, "what might happen to a dead body left out in the open here?"

"Wouldn't it just . . . rot?" I ask. I've always paid more attention to the crimes on true crime podcasts, not so much what happens to the victims afterward.

Lucy looks up. "What about vultures, coyotes, insects? Ravens, foxes, bears? Do you seriously think a body could lie untouched in a wild place?" She stares at me, apparently stunned by my ignorance.

My cheeks flame. "I told you yesterday that I've never even been hiking before. I don't know anything about this shit," I say, instantly defensive. I hate to feel incompetent, less than. I've spent a lot of effort over the last few years to hide where I'm from, to seem smarter, more confident, more worldly than I am. To be someone like Maggie. But I can't fake my way through this.

"Hey, we've all got our strengths and weaknesses," Maggie says. "That's why we're working together, right?"

"Sorry," Lucy says. "I didn't mean to be rude." She shifts uncomfortably.

"It's okay." I clear my throat and lift my chin. I'm determined not to be cowed by either of them. "If he jumped right off the main overlook and fell straight down, I don't see why the police couldn't find his body. That wouldn't be a very big area, would it?"

"No, it wouldn't," Lucy agrees. "They should have found him." Something like fear flashes in her eyes.

"Well, he couldn't have survived that fall," I say. "Even if he didn't die right away, he would have broken enough bones to make walking impossible."

"Could an animal have dragged him off before the police could get to him?" Maggie asks Lucy, who is apparently our resident wildlife expert.

Lucy shrugs, still preoccupied. "It's possible, I guess. A large mammal could have dragged him to its den or at least to a sheltered place to eat in peace. Maybe a bear. Or a pack of animals, like coyotes or even feral dogs."

I shiver at the thought of a pack of animals dragging Kincaid through the canyon, ripping the skin from his muscles, the muscles from his bones, gnawing at his marrow. Anyone else would say it's what he deserved, retribution for the lives he took, the pain he caused. But I—

"How do you know all this stuff?" I ask Lucy, pushing away the thoughts.

She looks down at the map. "I used to be in this junior naturalist program, where we learned about local plants and animals and everything." Her mouth thins into a hard line, and I realize I've somehow stumbled into some painful territory for her.

I hurry to change the subject. "So we should search the caves?" I ask, making my voice brisk and formal.

Lucy lets out a breath, clearly relieved I'm not asking more questions about her. "Caves, sure, or even large holes under tree roots, hollowed-out trees . . . anywhere animals could dig a big enough space for themselves."

"I like that idea," says Maggie. "If the body was left out in the open, someone would have found it by now. It must be hidden. Don't you think so, Lucy?"

Lucy chews her lip. "Yeah, that makes sense to me. It would probably be somewhere out of the way at the very least."

"That doesn't really narrow it down much," I say, staring at the map and wishing I had any idea how to read it. The skinny trail lines spread over enormous green spaces like stitches in human skin. I think errantly of my grandmother, who had throat cancer, of the fresh blue stitches in her swollen throat. The medicine I spread over the red wound with hands too small for the task. But Dad was in prison and Mom hated her mother-in-law, so it was left to me. I tended her as best I could, never flinching from her wound, even though to a child it seemed as grotesque as it was terrifying.

Is that why the thought of finding Kincaid's bones has no fear for me? What are old, yellowing bones compared to cancerous flesh, inflammation and pus, the stink of a dying woman?

I look away from the map and watch Lucy instead, the way her forehead furrows as she studies the features of the park. She's so serious. I wonder if she's always been that way or if something happened to make her like that.

Of course something happened. Of course. She is wary, watchful, and about as misanthropic as it's possible to be. You don't end up like that from a safe and normal life. She came here with secrets and wounds, same as me. Maybe that's why I feel drawn to her.

But she's not trying to hide any of it, not like I am. Some of the people here might look at her and see a strange, quiet, shy girl. But I see the disdain in her eyes, the flashes of revulsion. She isn't diffident or afraid of us. She's repulsed by us, by this place, by the task before us. And yet she won't leave. There's steel in her gaze, determination in the line of her jaw. She won't go home without the Cloudkiss Killer's bones.

Maggie leans over and whispers something in Lucy's ear, and Lucy takes a deep breath and nods, her expression almost stern. She sits up straighter and squares her shoulders, never taking her eyes off the map.

"Carolina?" Maggie says, and I pull my eyes from Lucy's studious, glaring face. Maggie raises an eyebrow at me, and I realize she caught me staring.

"Yeah?" I say, trying to make my voice sound innocent, unconcerned.

"I asked how you feel about the waterfall trail."

"What? Why?" I ask, my heart stuttering. The same old horrible reel plays through my mind. *Kiersten turns in the darkness at the sound of a step, her face pale and shocked, her mouth opening to cry out. Her feet scramble for purchase on the slick treads of the stairs, and she falls backward, smashing her head as she drops.* It feels so real, so visceral that nausea surges in my gut. I clench my teeth to hide it.

"Well, I wondered if you'd mind if we start in that area since it's close. We've only got a few hours before it gets dark, so we don't want to go too far. But if it would be too upsetting for you after what happened with Kiersten . . ." She cocks her head at me, her voice trailing off. Her strange gray eyes seem to look right through me, inside me, straight into my thoughts. "It must have been awful to find her like that." A soft, sympathetic smile edges her lips.

"No. I mean, yeah, it was terrible," I say, rubbing my eyes. "But the waterfall trail would be fine. It's fine. Whatever you guys want. Lucy?" I ask, desperate to have Maggie's attention off me.

"Hmm?" Lucy asks, her eyes still on the map. She's oblivious to the tense exchange going on between Maggie and me. But she must have heard part of it because she taps the broken white line on the map that indicates the water-fall trail. "Yes, I think we may as well start our search at the bottom of the waterfall trail. We'll have to go off marked paths though, and in this fog, it may be a little risky." Her eyebrows draw together in an emotion I can't read.

"Oh," Maggie says, "I think we can handle it. We're together after all. Safety troupe of three." She holds up three fingers in a Boy Scout salute and gives Lucy a reassuring smile. Lucy's shoulders loosen.

"Tomorrow I think we should try the gulch trail and search for places in the rock face where there might be dens. There are a lot of rocky overhangs. It will be strenuous though," Lucy adds, her eyes landing on me. I feel my cheeks heat up again.

I've never been athletic. I'm not willowy thin like Maggie or compact like Lucy. I'm soft all over, from my baby fat face to my heavy thighs. But I've never been ashamed of it, and I won't be now. I sit up straighter. "I can handle it."

Lucy nods. "Okay, great. You told me you don't have any hiking experience, so I thought it might be tough for you. That's all."

"Oh," I say, realizing she wasn't making a dig about my weight. I give her a quick smile. "Well, I'm a fast learner."

"She's clearly brilliant," Maggie says to Lucy, throwing an arm around me. "I think we snagged exactly the right teammate."

Lucy eyes us, biting her lip. If I didn't know better, I'd say she feels threatened. As if Maggie might like me instead of her—which is the last impression I want to give her.

"Let's go, then," I say, pushing up from the table and out of Maggie's reach. "Onward, brave soldiers, and into the fog."

# SEVEN

## LUCY

**My heart beats** hard and fast as we descend the stairs at the top of the waterfall trail, dropping down and down and down into the mists. It's like reliving my abduction in reverse. I can see Kincaid racing after me up these stairs, both of us desperate. I pass the overhanging rock where Kincaid pulled out his syringe. Where I ran. If I walked a few yards off trail, I'd find his kill site. I clench my jaw and continue on, ignoring the pools of darkness where a person might crouch in shadow, waiting.

"Are you sure you can handle this?" Maggie whispers. "You look really pale. We can start somewhere else."

"I'm fine," I assure her. Earlier, when she whispered in my ear, asking if I wanted to try the waterfall trail today, I didn't really let myself think through what it would be like to return here, to walk this path. I just knew it was unavoidable, that we'd have to come this way eventually. I figured I ought to get it over with. So I said yes. Maggie told me it was brave to face it head-on. In the moment, I felt brave.

But now I feel afraid. My hands are clammy, my stomach leaden.

The air grows cooler and moister, and the fog thickens, making our footsteps on the wooden stairs muffled. Carolina is quiet and preoccupied, and I wonder if she's thinking of Kiersten, or maybe just of the end of her fling with Brandon. A part of me wishes she would act more like the chatty girl I met yesterday, brimming with excitement and questions.

Because right now our silence feels like a weight, rather than an absence, lying heavy in the air around us. Maggie must sense it too because she starts asking Carolina about herself. "So, Carolina, I think I heard you tell someone you are a freshman at Chapel Hill? What are you studying?"

Carolina's eyes light up. "I want to study art history, maybe minor in French. But I've considered an English major too."

"So you're undecided?"

Carolina shrugs and then laughs. "I guess I may as well come clean. I'm still in high school."

"You are?" I ask, shocked. I hadn't even considered that someone else here might be as young as I am. I try to picture her at a high school—eating in the cafeteria, going to pep rallies, raising her hand in class. She'd probably hang out with the artsy kids at my school.

"Yeah, but I'm eighteen. I did the early action application for Chapel Hill, so I should hear back soon." Her voice is defensive, as if we're going to tell her she doesn't have a chance of fulfilling her dreams.

"I visited Chapel Hill with my parents," I say. "But I haven't applied anywhere yet." My parents want me to go to

Vanderbilt so I'll be close to home, but they took me around to a few other southern colleges. I doubt my grades are good enough for Vandy anyway. Before Kincaid, I knew what I wanted: to go to the school with the best environmental program I could get into, to become an ecologist. To work in the field, restoring habitats and protecting endangered species. But that's all over now. How can I work alone in the wilderness when I can't even walk down a greenway alone? Kincaid didn't just take my peace of mind; he took my whole future.

Now I'm stalled out, frozen with indecision. I can't even decide where to apply, and application deadlines are looming.

"You got to visit Chapel Hill? What was it like there?" Carolina's voice is so excited, but then she pauses. "Wait, so you're still in high school too?"

"Shh," Maggie says, raising her hand. "Do you hear that?"

Carolina and I both stop and listen. Angry voices come from somewhere below. Two women, arguing. Then another voice, softer and calmer, as if trying to reason with the other two.

"I know you slept with him, you slutty bitch!" rings out. And then sounds of scuffling. The women below are fighting.

"Come on," Maggie says. "I bet you ten bucks that's our bachelorette party down there." She sounds delighted.

Sure enough, when we reach the bottom of the stairs, two of the blond, orange-tanned women are flying at each other, scratching and screaming and pulling each other's hair. One of them was wearing the pink bridal sash yesterday. She's the one screaming at the other, calling her a dirty whore.

"That's Addison that Bridezilla is yelling at," Carolina whispers. "She told me they were sorority sisters."

Their friends keep trying to step in and break up the fight, but the women are like wolves, jaws locked on the jugular. There's something unnerving and unnatural about it. It would be easy to laugh at these privileged women having a trashy brawl, but there's no humor inside me. When I glance at Carolina, I see she's not laughing either. Her mouth is pursed, as if she's trying to think of a way to break up the fight.

That's the one thing I feel like I know about Carolina so far—she's not afraid to step in. She seems to care about other people, even if they don't care about her.

Maggie must realize that too because she takes Carolina's arm. "Come on, let's leave them to it. We've got bones to find," she says.

Carolina pulls away from Maggie, moving closer to the bachelorettes. "What if they get hurt?" she says.

Maggie shrugs. "It's none of our business. They're all, like, thirty years old. They can handle themselves."

"I guess so," Carolina concedes, following us reluctantly, still looking back at the fighting women.

"They'll be okay," I assure her, and she gives me a surprised smile. I must have been ruder to her earlier than I realized. I should try to be nice, give her more of a chance.

The bachelorette party doesn't even notice us pass by, and we continue on down by the base of the waterfall, where the water pounds against rocks and flows into the creek that cuts through the length of the canyon. As I gaze up at the top of the waterfall, I imagine Kincaid standing there. He leaps, plummeting from the top, and smashes onto the rocks below, lost to the surge of the water. I flinch and then blink several times, trying to will the horrible image away.

Maggie and Carolina are still talking about the bachelorettes. "Those two were best friends yesterday," Carolina says. "They braided each other's hair, for God's sake. What happened to them?"

A shiver runs through me, that strange sense of wrongness seeming to follow me, even once we're out of earshot of the fighting women. But Maggie laughs. "That's straight girls for you."

Carolina snorts, and some of the tension breaks. I feel a smile tug the corners of my mouth. Carolina's eyes land on me, and she studies me a moment too long. "So y'all are both . . ." She trails off, as if losing her courage.

"Queer?" I say. "Yeah."

"I mean, I'm not super into labels," Maggie says, "but I do lean sapphic." She winks at me.

"Cool," Carolina says, blushing deeply. "I, um . . . cool." She doesn't say anything else. Maggie shoots me an amused look, but I don't return it. Someone being unsure about their sexual orientation isn't anything to laugh at, and Carolina is clearly still figuring things out.

I look back at the waterfall, and a memory stirs. "There's a ledge behind there," I say, pointing. "You can squeeze between the water and the rock, and there's a big space worn away."

"How can you tell?" Carolina asks, clearly eager for the subject change.

I open my mouth to tell her about exploring it with my sister, but then I remember I'm pretending to have never been here before. "Just a guess," I say. "It's a common feature for waterfalls."

"Let's try it," Maggie says, bounding toward the falls. We follow her, picking our way over rocks and tree roots to reach the base of the waterfall. Without a word, Maggie clambers up onto a rock at the edge and then disappears behind the curtain of water.

"Whoa," Carolina says. I can barely hear her over the rush of water. She follows Maggie in more carefully. But I stand and wait for them to return, not eager to go into a dark, confined place.

"Nothing," Maggie calls when she appears again, climbing down easily. I love the way she moves, always certain and fluid, like a dancer, though it's hard to picture her in a leotard. She moves past me, her eyes on something in the air. I'm about to follow her when I hear Carolina cry out.

She's slipped off the rocks, and one boot is in the water. She cries out again, whether from pain or the shock of the cold water, I can't tell. I rush forward to help her.

"Here, give me your hand," I say, reaching out. She's got one knee and both hands against the rock, and her arms are trembling. There are tears in her eyes.

"You're okay," I say, waiting. She gives me a tremulous smile and puts her hand in mine. It's cold and a little damp from the boulder, but soft and pretty against my rougher, calloused one. I pull her forward, and she gets her footing back and jumps down beside me, grimacing at the impact.

"Thanks," she says. "I've never had great balance." She wipes the tears from her eyes.

"Did you hurt your knee?" I ask. "Can you walk all right?"

"I think I'm okay." Carolina takes a few tentative steps. "I just banged my knee and pulled something in my leg, I think," she says. "Give me a few minutes and I'll be fine."

"Sure," I say, looking behind me for Maggie, but she's gone, disappeared again, this time into the fog.

"Maggie?" I call, but there's no answer. I turn back to Carolina, who is pressing the top of her thigh and wincing. "I can show you some stretches if you want, to work that pain out of your, uh, groin."

Carolina blushes yet again, and I laugh. "There should really be a better word for that area of the body," I say. Carolina laughs too, her cheeks a vibrant pink against the rest of her creamy skin.

"I shouldn't have skipped all those PE classes," she says.

"What did you do instead?"

Carolina laughs. "You'll think I'm a nerd. I went to the library and read."

An image of her hiding out at a back table in the library, maybe a pair of glasses perched on her nose, enters my mind. I can't help but smile. "Yeah, that's pretty nerdy. Did you at least read something fun?"

"Do you think Dostoevsky and Proust are fun?"

I grimace. "Definitely not. I'm more of a sci-fi and fantasy girl myself."

"Aliens and dragons?" Carolina smirks. "Do you go to Comic-Con and cosplay your favorite characters? Wield an elven sword?"

I laugh and push her arm. "You're such a lit-fic snob."

"Nuh-uh," Carolina protests. "I read Lord of the Rings and liked it."

"Oh my God, those books are, like, eighty years old," I laugh. "I bet you listen to, like, The Smiths and play vinyl records too. You are *such* a snob."

Carolina gives me a very dignified look. "I like some horror books. That's not snobby. I even read a Stephen King novel last year."

I shake my head. "You're hopeless! I'm giving you a list of books published within the last five years, and you better promise to read them."

"Okay," Carolina says. "I will read anything you tell me to." Flushed and smiling, she looks out of place here among the dead leaves and rocks and mist. But then her face turns serious. "You don't really think I'm a snob, do you?"

I pause, studying her. "No, but would it bother you if I did?"

She bites her lip. "My ex used to call me that. He was, like, a sports guy, you know? Sports and hunting and stuff. He didn't get my bookishness. But he'd try sometimes. Like, once he bought me one of those romance novels with the buff, shirtless guy on the cover, which was kind of sweet, you know? But right away he could tell I didn't like the gift, even if he didn't under-stand why. Novels all seemed like the same thing to him. When I tried to explain the difference between, like, supermarket novels and what I usually read, he got embarrassed and said I was stuck up." She shrugs. "Maybe I am, I don't know. I guess I could have tried harder to pretend."

"Well, I guess there's a reason he's your ex, right?" I say. "You shouldn't have to pretend for people who love you."

Carolina nods, then clears her throat and looks away, her eyes a little shiny. "It kind of feels like we've been dropped into one of Stephen King's books, doesn't it?" She nods at the ever-growing fog. "Or a horror movie or something." As if on cue, a crow caws in the distance.

I look around again and shiver, the easy mood from our banter already gone. Maggie is still nowhere to be seen. I think about the legends of the fog, which are just undefined and ambiguous enough to be frightening, whether you believe in them or not.

"Maggie? Where'd you go?" I yell. "You're freaking me out."

A canine's howl comes from somewhere up above. I startle, but then laughter follows it.

"I'm up here," Maggie calls back. "Follow my voice." She wolf-howls again and again until we find her up on a ledge of rock peering into a cave. She clings to the side of the cliff like a bat, and when I call up to her, she turns, excitement on her face. "You won't believe what I found."

The crevice she's looking into is too small for a body, surely, but chill bumps break out all over my skin.

"Catch," she says, tossing down a small, lightweight object.

I grab it out of the air. It's a sewn patch ripped from brown leather, faded and unraveling but unmistakable. WWII aviator wings.

It's exactly like the patch that was on the front breast of Kincaid's jacket. When he saw me looking at it that day in the fog, he'd said the jacket belonged to his grandfather, a war hero.

I drop the patch like it's on fire.

I feel like *I'm* on fire, my hands suddenly hot and tingling.

"Holy shit," Carolina says, bending down to retrieve the patch. "Is it his?"

"Aren't we supposed to leave stuff where we find it?" I ask through the lump in my throat. "That's what the forensics expert said."

"But we don't even know if it's his. Seems like a lot of fuss over a bit of thread," Carolina says.

Maggie leaps down from the cliff. "Besides, rules were made to be broken," she says, then throws back her head and howls again.

# EIGHT

## LUCY

**I'm not aware** of much for the next few hours. We hike off trail, peer around boulders, use sticks to poke at the ground in areas with thick foliage. But I don't really see any of it, my entire being fixed on the aviator patch in Carolina's pocket. We don't find anything else.

When our stomachs start growling, Maggie suggests we head back for dinner. The fog is thick as we ascend the rocky trail, and we have to keep our eyes on our feet to make sure we don't blunder away from the path and get lost. The fog seems to rise with us, following us once we reach the stairs, twisting around us when we pause to catch our breath at each turn.

On a bench at the top of the third set of stairs we come across a middle-aged man. He sits with his feet drawn up, his head buried on his knees. His back shakes as he weeps. He's wearing a flat cap, his curly hair poking out of it in a bushy, mist-covered tangle. He doesn't notice us approach.

I don't want to just walk by him, but I don't want to bother him either. I glance at Maggie and Carolina to see if they feel the same. Carolina steps forward. "Levi?" she asks. "Is that you? Are you all right? Are you hurt?"

The man startles at the sound of her voice. He hastily wipes the tears and snot off his face with a handkerchief. "I'm fine, I'm fine," he says, waving us away, without even looking to see who we are. "A bad memory is all. Please . . . continue."

Carolina hesitates but does as he asks, waving us forward. I resist the urge to pat his shoulder as we pass by. It feels wrong to leave a man weeping alone in the fog like that, but what else can we do?

"Who was that?" Maggie whispers to Carolina once we're far enough away.

Carolina shrugs. "He's a contestant. I talked to him the first night. He's a math professor. He was really nice. He works on unsolved crimes as a hobby, especially missing persons cases. He said he focuses on the cases that don't get much media attention, mostly victims from minority communities. He said he's actually managed to crack a few cases."

"Wow," I say. "That's actually really cool."

"See," Carolina says, "not all true crime fans are total monsters."

"I guess not. So at least two of you are all right."

Carolina laughs.

"So do you think he has a personal history that made him get into it, like a loved one he lost who was never found, something like that?" I ask. "Maybe being here is bringing up bad memories."

"Or maybe the fog is getting to him," Maggie says. At first, I think she's joking, but she doesn't laugh or smile or even raise her eyebrows theatrically.

"You believe in the legend?" Carolina asks, her voice cautious. "You think it's why people are acting so weird?"

Maggie shrugs. "A legend doesn't have to be true for it to have power."

"What do you mean?" I ask.

"Well, if people believe in something, it can be true for them. We create a lot more of our own reality than we realize."

"One thing I've learned from landscape painting," Carolina says, "is that we think we make the landscape, but the landscape makes us too. It shapes us in ways we aren't even aware of."

"Exactly," Maggie says. "A place can exert a powerful force on the human mind."

"And this place is really creepy," I admit, "even without Kincaid's influence. All the fog, the isolation." I pause. "Do you think that's what the legend boils down to? Why all the locals believe in it? Because they live next to it, in its shadow?"

"Mmm," Maggie says. "I think there's more to it than that. The power of a shared belief plus a foreboding landscape, those both go a long way. But isn't it compelling, the idea of being forced to confront yourself, to find out who you really are, what you're really capable of? Of seeing the drama that plays out in your mind made real and concrete, where you can get at it in the physical realm?"

"Maggie, you can't possibly believe in this stuff," I insist.

She shrugs. "It's just interesting, that's all."

"It is interesting," Carolina agrees, her voice tentative.

I don't reply, and we lapse into silence after that. There are plenty of reasons the legend can't be true—obviously, because it's superstitious nonsense but also because human beings are much more than the worst impulses they possess. I need to believe that or I could never trust another person again.

Besides, what happens in our minds isn't necessarily real, isn't who we truly are. Thoughts are synapses firing, brain chemicals at work. Who we are is what we *do*.

Kincaid wasn't a monster because he had terrible desires. He was a monster because he did terrible things. That's all I need to know about him.

When we finally walk into the campsite, the mood is strange and tense, filled with sullen silences and occasional explosions of temper. I'm sure Maggie and Carolina are still thinking about the legend and the fog, wondering if that's what's making everyone act like the worst versions of themselves. But I don't have time or headspace for ideas like that. Even the weeping math professor barely intrudes on my thoughts. All I can think of is that dirty, weather-worn insignia patch in Carolina's pocket. What does it mean that Maggie found it caught halfway up the rock face, clearly torn from a jacket? Was it caught by the wind, torn away by a curious crow? It feels more like a message from Kincaid, a sign that he is here and watching. I shrug the thought away as we get our food.

Carolina, Maggie, and I huddle at the end of a long table, shoveling down the evening's fare of tacos, trying to ignore the simmering pot of ill will that surrounds us. I thought that given a little time, people would forget Kiersten's accident and the silly incident with Noah and move on to other things. But if anything, the other contestants' distrust of Carolina and me has intensified.

They seem less sure about Maggie. The bachelorette party watches her with the same suspicious glares they're giving Carolina and me. But I noticed that Rosa and Bridget waved to Maggie and called some friendly greetings from across the room when we came in.

"I'm going to refill my drink. Want anything?" Maggie asks.

I hand her my empty glass. "More sweet tea?"

Maggie wrinkles her nose at me. "Southerners," she says with a disbelieving head shake before walking off.

"Where is Maggie from? I know she goes to Duke, but that's all I really know about her," Carolina says.

"Oh, she's from . . ." I start to say, but then I realize I don't know. "Up north somewhere?"

"Her accent's vaguely New England–ish, I guess," Carolina says. "She—" But then her eyes widen. I follow her gaze across the room to the drinks table, where Maggie is deep in conversation with Noah, of all people.

My stomach lurches. "What the hell?" I whisper.

"Well, would you look at that," Carolina says. "That's the most animated I've seen Noah yet." It's true—he's talking fast, gesturing with his hands, his eyes lit up. Even from across the room, I can see that he's enjoying talking to Maggie. And, even weirder, Maggie seems to be enjoying the conversation too. She smiles at him and mirrors his body language, leaning toward him like he's saying something fascinating. But why? She said he was a creep. Why's she talking to him? Why's she being nice to him?

Carolina and I watch them, both of us riveted. I try to ignore the anger bubbling up inside me. Maybe she has a good reason for talking to him. It's not fair for me to feel like she's betrayed me somehow.

But then Maggie touches Noah's arm and lets her fingers linger against his skin. My own skin prickles in response, and my jaw goes tight. I hate seeing her touch him. I hate the thought of his repulsive body anywhere near her. I silently will her to push him away, show him the disgust he deserves. But she keeps smiling and laughing.

When Maggie finally breaks off from the conversation and heads back to our table, she notices our attention. She does a mock full-body shiver when she reaches us, nearly spilling both my sweet tea and her soda. "Eugh," she says. "What a head case."

"Why were you talking to him?" I ask, not quite able to keep the edge out of my voice.

Maggie laughs. "I'm here to write a paper about his ilk, remember? Noah's the epitome of this fucked-up sub-culture."

"Hey," Carolina says, her voice sharp. "You're talking about me too, you know. I'm a true crime fan."

Maggie waves her objection away. "Please, you've barely got your foot in the door. Noah is the real deal. He's obsessed with Kincaid, just like I thought. I'm going to try to stay on his good side and feature him heavily in my paper."

"I thought you were only observing, not interviewing people," I say. My voice comes out high and tight.

"Well, I'm not doing any official interviews," Maggie says. "But some people are too withdrawn to just observe. You have to coax them out. Get them to share what they like to keep hidden."

"And how are you going to do that?" I ask.

Maggie waggles her eyebrows.

"Ugh, you're flirting with him, aren't you?" Carolina says, grimacing.

Maggie laughs. But I don't think it's funny. A guy who cosplays a serial killer isn't someone to mess around with. And how could she when she knows how he makes me feel? She's supposed to be on my side.

But I can't say any of that. It's too clingy, too needy. So I focus on the obvious. "You should be careful with him, Maggie. You don't know what he's capable of."

"That's what I'm going to find out," Maggie says. "Plus, it's fun to pull his string and watch him go."

I'm still pissed. I can't help it. I don't like Maggie talking to Noah, let alone flirting with him. I know it's for her paper, but still. It feels wrong and . . . gross. Suddenly, I'm desperate to put some space between us.

I push away my plate and stand up from the table with enough force to make my chair squeal on the hardwood floor. "I'm going to use the bathroom," I tell them.

"Shit, is she mad at me?" I hear Maggie ask Carolina, but I ignore it.

I make my way through the crowded dining room, careful to keep my eyes straight ahead. A foot juts out suddenly into the aisle, and I trip, stumble forward a few feet, but don't fall. I turn and glare at the table. It's a bunch of pimply-faced basement-dwelling sort of guys in their early twenties. "Sorry," one of them says. "Long legs."

I ignore the low, pleased laughter at my back, grit my teeth at the rush of anger in my chest, and make it out the door and into the narrow hallway. I have to push past a hulking bearded dude who's talking on his cell phone, taking up most of the hallway. When our eyes meet, he glances away, uninterested, but then he does a double take. After I pass him, I feel his gaze on my back.

The bathroom is mercifully empty, and I luxuriate in the silence and solitude while I pee, my head cradled in my hands. I feel shaky and strung out and . . . exposed, like a deer in the open, no shelter in sight. I wish I could hide out in this bathroom stall until the week is over.

I'm not sure I realized how exhausting this contest was going to be. How much it would require of me. How complicated it would all get. Just pulling up the zipper of my pants makes me tired. I think longingly of home, of my bed, the terrariums on my dresser, the framed national parks posters on my walls. Everything that is safe and warm and—

And stifling. And false.

I shake my head. That safety is an illusion. It can be snatched away in a moment.

Any safety I get will be earned, here in this canyon, by finding Kincaid's bones.

I breathe out my fear and open the stall door. I stare at myself in the mirror, assessing. Dark half-moons beneath my hazel eyes. Sadness in the curve of my lips. Even my hair looks tired, hanging limp against my head. The girl in the mirror looks far too much like the one described in the *Human Beasties* podcast: a girl whose innocence was stolen, whose safety was obliterated. I look down into the chipped sink while I wash my hands so I don't have to see her anymore.

I go back into the hallway and nearly jump out of my skin. The bearded man from before is right outside the bathroom door, leaning casually against the wall, staring at his phone. I go to move past him, but his hand darts out and grabs my forearm. "You're Lucy Wilson." He holds up his phone for me to see.

*Shit.*

My fifteen-year-old self smiles back at me from a school picture. Her hair is long, clipped back with a pin shaped like a daisy, and her smile is big and happy and carefree. It's the photo that ended up on all the true crime fan websites. The one my parents paid lawyers to have taken down over and over again until the image proliferated, a virus no one could contain.

"This is you, isn't it?" he says, looking between me and the image on the phone's screen.

"It's not," I say. "My name is Geraldine." I snatch my arm from his fingers and start walking.

"It is," he says, following me, crowding me against the wall. "You have the same scar under your eye. That's what gave you away." He points at the small scar shaped like a Nike check under my right eye, where my uncle's chow chow bit me when I was five. "Lucy Wilson." He laughs. "I can't believe it."

"You're blocking my way," I manage to say before my throat closes up with fear. The man is overpowering, towering over me like a mountain. He seems to fill the entire dark hallway. I try again to push past him, but this time his meaty hand pushes me against the wall and holds me there. He does it casually, so smoothly it almost seems like a friendly gesture. But my heart rate explodes in my ears, and my breath lodges in my chest.

"Lucy Wilson," he says again. "The last and youngest victim. The canvas Kincaid never got to paint." The man grins, a sick pleasure in every line of his smile. "I'm surprised you're brave enough to leave your house," he says, his eyes glittering. "Now that you know what the world is like. Let alone to come back here."

I close my eyes, the ground suddenly lurching beneath my feet, as if I'm on a ship at sea. My ears ring, and blackness looms at the corners of my vision.

"You know what he would have done to you, right? If the police hadn't come?" The man leans forward and whispers in my ear, his whiskers tickling my skin as nausea rises up my throat. I try not to listen, try not to hear, as he croons Kincaid's atrocities in my ear like a lover's sweet nothings.

And instead of fighting, I go limp. I let the tears stream down my cheeks. My body resigns itself to weakness.

"And then," the man says, "once he had finished—"

But his words are cut short and the pressure of his hand leaves my shoulder. I open my eyes to find him being pulled off me, and roughly. "Hey!" he yells. I expect to see another guy defending me, but it's Carolina. Carolina, her lovely features gone hard with rage. "The fuck is wrong with you?" she yells, pushing him as hard as she can. He stumbles back, whether from surprise or the force of her shove, I can't tell. She balls her hands into fists, like she wants to deck him. Or maybe to keep herself from strangling him, I don't know which.

His jaw tightens with anger, and I'm afraid he's going to come at her with those meaty hands of his. But a man and woman appear at the end of the hallway, apparently drawn by the commotion, and he must think better of it. "Crazy bitch," he hisses before he laughs loudly and shakes his head, clearly for the couple's benefit. Then he turns away, sauntering off down the hall. He turns after a few feet and snaps a picture of me with his phone. Carolina lunges forward, fingers already outstretched, but I grab her hand. "Please," I say. "Let him go. Let it go."

I hear him make some excuse to the couple. The woman shrugs and turns away, but the man watches us for a moment, concern in his eyes, before his wife snatches his sleeve and he follows her out.

"What the hell happened, Lucy?" Carolina asks, not letting go of my hand. She's breathing hard, and I can feel her trembling.

I hang my head. "He figured out who I am." Which means pretty soon everyone else is going to know too.

"Who are you?" she asks. I meet her eyes. She really has no idea.

"Lucy Wilson," I say, but her face remains blank. So much for her Beastie Babes cred.

"I was—I'm the last person Kincaid tried to . . ."

Understanding widens her eyes. "Oh. Oh Jesus Christ, Lucy." Anger flits across her features again, and she looks back over her shoulder like she's thinking of following the guy and beating the shit out of him. But then she turns to me. "I'm sorry that happened to you." She says it simply, without pity or intrigue. No one ever acts like that when they find out. Even in my receding panic, I can tell that whatever Carolina is, she's not like most of the other people here.

"Come on. Let's get out of here," she says, pulling me by the hand down the hallway. I let her lead me, exhausted in every fiber of my being. We break out of the lodge and into the smoky darkness of the camp. Maggie is leaning against an oak tree, from which she parts like a shadow when she notices us.

"Everything okay?" she asks, glancing at my and Carolina's still-joined hands, our troubled expressions.

"Yeah," I say, pulling my hand from Carolina's and sticking it into the pocket of my sweater. My fingertips tingle. "Just this guy was harassing me. Carolina took care of it." I glance at her, torn between gratitude that she rescued me and embarrassment that I needed to be rescued. I realize that I didn't even once consider fighting him myself. I froze, and I hate that. I hate the weakness inside me. But it wasn't like in my self-defense classes or even like my run-in with Noah. Maybe the shock of being recognized is what paralyzed me. Or just the sheer size of him.

"It was that oaf, Rufus," Carolina tells Maggie. "You remember him from the first night when we were all talking to Sandra? Big bear of a guy, looks like a fucking Viking in a polo shirt?"

Maggie nods. "Did he . . . ?" She trails off but touches my arm as though to make sure I'm all in one piece. "Are you all right?"

"He so much as looks at you again and he's going to find himself missing his eyes," Carolina growls.

Maggie looks between us, her expression hard to read. Maybe she feels bad she wasn't there to help.

"There's more," I say. "He figured out who I am. He took my picture."

Maggie's eyebrows raise, and her mouth opens. I prepare myself for the sight of pity in her eyes. But instead, she throws an arm over my shoulders and ruffles my hair. "Well, goodbye, anonymity. I guess things are about to get very interesting, aren't they?"

"Yep," I say through a long breath. Everyone's going to know who I am. And once the hosts of the contest find out . . . they might even send me home. They might—

Maggie lets out a little cackle, distracting me before my thoughts can spiral. "Maybe we should thank Rufus by luring a racoon into his tent," she says. "Or put some beetles in his trail mix. Whatcha think?" She smiles mischievously, and I can't help but laugh, despite my building anxiety. Maggie takes nothing seriously, and right now I'm glad of it.

But Carolina doesn't join in our laughter. Her eyes are on the darkness, watchful and waiting. I think if Rufus came back, she truly would scratch out his eyes.

And maybe I'm glad of that too.

# NINE

## LUCY

**I want to** keep laughing. But as the evening wears on and the stares of the other campers become more and more pointed, their whispers rising like a murmuration of starlings whenever I'm near, I begin to feel the cold wind of my exposure. Rufus took no time at all to spread my true identity around camp. The other contestants study me, their expressions full of curiosity, suspicion, and sometimes pity. When it looks like a group of them are about to approach me, I retreat to my tent, Maggie and Carolina on my heels.

None of us says it, but we all know what might happen now. Kevin and Sandra are bound to find out eventually. Maybe not tonight, but soon. And then they're going to send me home.

We hang out for half an hour in my tent, making half-hearted plans for tomorrow's search in the light of the electric lantern, the mood heavy and awkward. "Let's go to the campfire story competition," Carolina finally says. "It will take your mind off things."

"But everyone knows who I am now."

"So what?" Maggie says. "Don't give them the satisfaction of seeing you hide. They're the ones with something to be ashamed of, not you."

"Why should they be ashamed?" Carolina asks.

Maggie cocks an eyebrow. "Because Lucy represents everything that's wrong with the media they love, how exploitative it is, how it makes entertainment out of the worst thing that could ever happen to a person."

Carolina seems to shrink a little, as if realizing she should be ashamed too. "I guess," she says, though her expression is thoughtful and conflicted.

Maggie turns to me. "Come with us, sit and listen to some stories, let them see you. That you're real and alive and more than a story they heard on a podcast."

"She's right," Carolina says, brightening. "You shouldn't hide out in here all night. Plus, it might be fun. We are in desperate need of fun." She bites her lip and raises her eyebrows hopefully. The expression is such a contrast to her earlier rage. I can't keep up with this girl.

"Okay," I say, relenting, "but if anyone gets weird, I'm going to bed."

"Deal," Carolina and Maggie say in unison. Carolina grabs one of my hands, and Maggie grabs the other, and we walk together back to the campfire.

I don't really want to listen to all these ghouls tell scary stories, but I definitely can't go back to my tent and lie alone in the dark thinking about Kincaid, so I decide I'll stick it out for as long as I can. I sandwich myself between Maggie and

Carolina, ignoring the way people stare at me. When an older couple tries to approach me for a chat, Maggie jumps up and steers them away, jabbering loudly about wanting to know where they bought their fetching Beastie Babes sweatshirts.

Carolina and I crack up as soon as their backs are turned, and Maggie shoots us a wink over her shoulder.

Thankfully, once Sandra and Kevin arrive, all eyes turn to them. I try to sink into the shadows between Carolina and Maggie, praying people will forget I'm here. After a showy introduction, Sandra opens up the floor for spooky stories, which contestants are all too happy to supply. Each one is as gruesome and macabre as I expected. But none of their stories can touch what's inside my head, or begin to match the fear that already lives inside me. Their tales of ghosts, ax murderers, and monsters are more like bedtime stories for my younger, more innocent self.

I half expect Maggie to offer up a story, but instead Carolina raises her hand. To my surprise, she pulls a folded packet of papers out of her jacket. "Is it all right if I read it?" she asks. "It's one I wrote myself."

"Of course," Kevin says, and leans forward, elbows on his knees, as if eager to hear what such a beautiful girl might have to say. He doesn't even glance at me. A few of the bachelorettes murmur to each other and laugh unkindly, but Carolina ignores them, unfolding the papers and holding them so that their pages catch the light from the fire.

"There once was a girl who sang to the dead," Carolina reads. "Every evening, at twilight, she walked out to the cemetery at the end of her street, carrying a song in her heart." Her voice is low but strong, polished as old silver. I realize right away that this won't be a tawdry, gore-speckled tale like the others have told. It's a ghost story.

Carolina smiles to herself, a sad, yearning sort of smile that goes straight to my heart. "The girl was an orphan, and everyone she loved lay in the cemetery. They had all died together, tragically, and the girl was the only survivor. So every evening she walked alone among their gravestones, caressing the moss and lichen that adorned their names. Others might have scraped the stones clean, but the girl encouraged the little plants to grow. She liked to see green there, signs that life can grow from rot and ruin."

Carolina reads on, and I feel as though her words have caught me up in a spell. I can see the girl and the cemetery, the blue of twilight, the creeping moss and lichen. Carolina renders it all so perfectly, so lovingly, with an artist's eye for detail. I feel like I'm inside the orphan girl's body, singing to the dead. Far from Cloudkiss Canyon and this horrible contest, these horrible people. An ache starts up inside me.

"Her neighbors in the town thought the girl was so kind and so gentle, to sing to her lost relatives as they slept, to ease their passage into the dark. But what they didn't know was that the girl was truly singing to wake the dead, to draw them from their wormy graves and into the moonlight with her."

Every hair on my arms raises, a chill sweeping through me. I'm not sure I want to hear the rest, but I'm riveted to my seat, entranced by Carolina's voice. I can't look away from her firelit face, bent over the creased pages of her story.

"She wished to wake them, not because she was afraid to be alone, or even because she missed those who'd gone on. It was because she needed to ask them a question that they alone could answer. She needed to understand how she'd lost them all so suddenly, and if she could have done anything to prevent their deaths.

"And so every night for weeks and weeks she came to them and sang. She called to them, giving their souls no rest. She knew it was selfish, but there was a dark space in her heart, one that could only be filled with the answers of the dead. After two months of this, the dead finally began to stir, to wake.

"The girl was frightened, alone in the cemetery, with night coming on fast and the spirits of her dead family all around her. But she was brave and determined, and so she continued to sing. The first relative to appear to her was her mother. The girl asked her mother a question in her ear, but the mother would not answer. She hid her face and wept. The girl wept too, shame filling her heart."

Carolina's story continues with each of the relatives appearing to the girl one by one, each refusing to answer her question. With each denial, the shame in her heart grows. Carolina's voice turns husky, as if there are tears lodged in her throat. I feel them in mine too, as well as a deep dread. I find myself hoping none of the relatives will answer the girl's question.

"Finally, the last ghost appeared to the girl. It was her little brother, a child of no more than four. After she whispered her question to him, he stared at her with enormous, frightened eyes. Then he cupped his hands around her ear and gave her the answer she sought.

"The ghosts disappeared, and the girl's voice went silent. She lay down on the ground, surrounded by her family, and closed her eyes. She lay very still, so still that the moss and lichen spread over her, so long that wildflowers grew up through the strands of her hair. She lay there until her body turned to rot and ruin, and the girl was no more."

My hand is over my mouth, as if to keep my breaths from making noise. Everyone else must feel the same because the campsite is still, the crackle of the fire and the sad melody of Carolina's voice the only sounds.

"The townspeople didn't wish to leave the girl's body like that. They wanted to bury her with her kin, but they were too afraid to draw near. Whenever someone stepped into the section of cemetery where the girl's family was buried, her voice echoed in their ears, and their hearts grew full with a grief and shame so great they dropped to their knees. They had to be carried away before they too lay down to die.

"So the townspeople built a wrought-iron fence around that section of the cemetery. They left the girl to the elements, let the grass grow up around her, the leaves of trees fall to cover her. Her family's graves were swallowed up too, and a small sort of meadow grew there, filled with wildflowers that drew buzzing bees and butterflies.

"As generations passed, the town forgot the girl and her family, and people would pause beside the fence to admire the flowers and listen to the drone of bees. It was curious, they thought, but the sound seemed to hold a girl's voice inside, a mournful song that made their knees go weak, that made their heart leave them.

"Every now and then, the girl's song was too much for someone, and he would open the gate and walk into the meadow, and lie in the grass to sleep until he too was covered over and forgotten." Carolina pauses for a long moment.

"But the girl wasn't aware of any of this. She and her family slept on through the years, their bodies feeding the earth. Only the sad echo of the orphan girl's shame remained behind." With that, Carolina refolds the pages of her story and smiles, ducking her head. The endings of the other stories prompted clapping and swearing and laughter, but now there's only silence. Everyone sits still, as if entranced.

Carolina looks up and meets my eyes, and I want to say something. I want to tell her that the story is beautiful and sad and moving. But the words won't come.

Finally, Kevin rouses himself. "That was . . . really lovely. Thank you." He starts up a polite round of applause.

"It reminded me of a folk song, like a murder ballad," Sandra adds. Carolina smiles, pleased by the compliment.

"So the girl killed her family, right?" Rosa asks. "That's fucked up. Scary shit."

Carolina shrugs.

"Okay, I've got one about a murderous lady too," a guy across from us says. He launches into a sordid tale about a vengeful stripper, which feels like my cue to get the hell out of here. I push up from the bench.

"Your story was really good," I tell Carolina. "Seriously. But I'm wiped out, so I'm going to go to bed."

"Do you want me to come with you?" Maggie asks absently, her attention still half on the storyteller.

"Nah, you guys have fun," I say.

"I'll walk with you!" Carolina says, hopping up quickly, surprising me and apparently Maggie too, who snaps her head to look at us.

"Good night, then," Maggie says, clearly thrown off balance, her eyes searching our faces. I think she might be jealous.

"Night," I say, a little guiltily.

Carolina and I walk shoulder to shoulder away from the bright orange light and buzz of the campfire and into the foggy field of tents.

"I couldn't tell whether people liked my story or not," she says.

"I think they did, but this is a weird crowd. Anyway, I liked it. I kind of can't believe you wrote it," I say. "It was like if Shirley Jackson wrote fairy tales."

Carolina's face breaks into a giddy expression. "I was sort of channeling *We Have Always Lived in the Castle*, if I'm honest."

"Oh, I love that book. I think it's way better than *The Haunting of Hill House*."

"Me too," Carolina agrees. "Shirley Jackson is gothic perfection."

"And she's been dead for, like, sixty years, so that tracks for you," I say with a laugh.

Carolina snorts. "Fine, yes, I'm predictable." After a beat, she adds, "So you really liked my story?"

"I thought it was beautiful and sad."

"No critiques?" She bites her lip.

I smile. "Well, lichen isn't technically a plant. Just plantlike."

"What?" She laughs, surprised.

"The lichen on the tombstones. In the story, you call it a small plant. But it's actually its own sort of organism."

"Are you serious?" Carolina asks. At first I think she's annoyed I'm nitpicking, but then I realize she's really interested. So I explain how lichen is a meeting of fungi and algae, an ancient symbiosis of organisms.

"That's so cool. I'm going to have to pay a lot more attention to all the lichen growing here. Maybe I'll draw some tomorrow."

"Oh! Then here," I say, pulling the loupe from around my neck. "Look at it with this. It's what jewelers use to look at, like, diamonds and stuff. You can see all the tiny details. Look at some moss too while you're at it."

"Wow, thank you," Carolina says, playing with the lens for a moment before putting it around her own neck. "I'll make sure to give it back to you soon."

"Okay. Well, here's my tent," I say. It looks lonely and forlorn in the fog.

"Are you going to be all right on your own?" Carolina asks. "I can—I mean, I'd be happy to—to stay with you." She sounds more uncertain than I've ever heard her.

"Thanks, but I'm fine. It will be fine," I say, steeling myself for the long night. A long night of listening for noises outside my tent, of startling awake at every scrabbling animal, every calling owl. Of feeling fear in every cell of my body, constant expectation of danger. It's how I feel all the time, but it's magnified here, less a nervous wariness than a bone-deep, exhausted terror.

Maybe if I let Carolina stay with me, it would be more bearable. But that's not what I came here for. I came to here to face what happened to me, to lay Kincaid's last victim to rest and walk out of here someone new. I can't do that if I can't even spend a night alone in my tent.

"Okay, but I'm right over there if you need me," Carolina says, pointing away into the darkness. "Maybe tomorrow you and Maggie and I should put our tents closer together," she adds. "No reason for us to all be so spread out, I guess." She steps closer to me in the dark.

"Sure," I say, stepping away. "Night, Carolina."

She watches as I crawl into my tent and turn on my lantern, which illuminates the small green space.

"Night," she says, the word so soft it sounds like a caress. She pauses for a moment, a dark silhouette at the mouth of my tent, before she walks away into the fog.

Once she's gone, I brush my teeth with water from my bottle and then zip the tent closed, set my battery alarm clock for 6:00 a.m., and huddle into my sleeping bag in the clothes I'm wearing, not even bothering to remove my boots and coat. I should have showered first, but I'm exhausted.

Even so, I can't sleep for a long time. I lie awake thinking of the orphan girl in Carolina's story, of how she lay down to die. I feel like that's what I've been doing for the last two years. Letting the moss and lichen grow over me, giving myself to the dead.

Maybe it's a mistake to sing to the dead, to call them up and demand an answer. Maybe it will only make things worse. But like the girl in Carolina's story, I need the truth. There's a dark hole in my heart that only one answer can fill.

And there's only one person—one body—that can give it to me.

I dream of Kincaid, like always. Only this time we're not in Cloudkiss Canyon. We're in my church, in the cheerful wing of Sunday-school classrooms and offices. I stand alone in the small, windowless room that holds the photocopier and shelves of art supplies. I'm making copies of coloring sheets for vacation Bible school when I catch a shadow from the corner of my eye.

I turn, expecting the Sunday-school teacher. A scream lodges in my throat, and my body goes cold and numb and frozen. The coloring sheets fall from my hands, dispersing into mist.

Kincaid leans casually in the doorway, blocking my only exit. He looks exactly the same, in his navy-blue beanie and brown bomber jacket with the shearling lining. Only the aviator patch has been ripped away, leaving a hole where his heart should be.

His eyes are an empty void.

He says my name, and the room vanishes around me, dissipating into gray fog. Someone screams. But it isn't me. Not this time.

I wake with a jolt and a gasp, the smell of smoke in my nose.

"Fire! Oh my God, fire!" a woman screams. Then the sounds of running feet all through the camp. The lingering horror of my dream morphs into a full-body panic.

I try to leap up, but I'm securely zipped into my sleeping bag, a caterpillar in its cocoon. I yank and yank at the zipper, but it's stuck in the fabric of the bag, locking me inside. What if the fire is spreading? What if it's coming for me?

I start thrashing like a fish on land, desperately trying to work myself out of the bag.

"Shit, my tent!" a woman's voice yells. Maggie, I think.

I get halfway out of the bag and unzip my tent, falling forward from the opening onto the hard-packed ground, fully prepared to army crawl my way to safety. But there aren't any flames, only smoke and the stink of synthetic fibers burning.

"Maggie?" I call into the darkness, my voice a terrified croak.

"Over here. Someone set my fucking tent on fire!" she yells. "Creepy fucking assholes!"

Voices murmur, and someone laughs.

"Go fuck yourself!" Maggie yells at them. "You useless voyeurs!" More laughter follows her words.

By the time I crawl completely from my sleeping bag and make my way over to her, her angry, profanity-laced rant has gone silent. The people who had gathered to see the spectacle have started to disperse, going back to their own tents, shaking their heads. I weave through them and find Maggie standing over the smoking ruins of her tent, her fingers clutched in her hair. All her cool steadiness is gone. She's rattled.

A tall, muscular woman wearing a *Human Beasties* sweatshirt jogs toward us, her hair in disarray, as if she just woke up. I recognize her as one of the event staff. "Are you all right? What happened?" she asks. "Did anyone get hurt?"

Maggie waves her away. "No one is hurt. It's fine. It's over now."

"Are you sure?" the woman asks, blinking sleepily at the charred remains of the tent. "Maybe I should . . ." Her words trail off. She has no idea what to do, and all she really wants is to go back to bed.

Maggie shakes her head. "It was an accident. I just remembered I left a candle burning. God, that was so stupid. I—I'm really sorry. I shouldn't have . . ."

She seems too overwhelmed to go on, so I step in. "She can stay with me tonight. There's not really anything else we can do now, is there?"

The woman nods, clearly relieved. "Sure, that's fine. But let's do a full report first thing tomorrow, all right?"

Maggie nods but doesn't reply. The woman takes one last look at us before trudging away to bed.

I put a tentative hand on Maggie's lower back. "You all right?" I ask. "Was it really a candle? I thought I heard you say someone set it on fire."

Maggie lets out a strained, incredulous laugh. "They did. I was on my way here from the campfire when I saw the flames. Fucking hell."

"I think it looked worse than it was," Carolina says. "It went out easily with water and dirt." I didn't even realize Carolina was standing there. Her hair is disheveled, dirt or soot on her face.

"She put the fire out," Maggie says, nodding to Carolina.

I'm struggling to catch up. "But you told that woman it was a candle. Why'd you lie?"

Maggie shrugs. "What's the point? We won't be able to figure out who did it anyway."

"Why would someone do this?" I ask.

Carolina glances around, making sure we're alone. "Maybe it was a message," she says.

"A burning bush?" I ask distractedly, thinking of the sign of God in the Book of Exodus. That's what was on the coloring sheets in my dreams.

Carolina snorts. "No, more like a Beastie Babe telling us to watch our backs."

"No way would someone—" I start to say, but I don't bother finishing the sentence. Of course they would. Look how people have been acting all day. Tripping me in the cafeteria, cornering me in the hallway. People are turning vicious.

Suddenly I feel the chill of the autumn air, not just on my skin but in my marrow. I shiver, and Maggie puts her arm around me, draws me into her side.

"But why did they burn *your* tent?" I ask Maggie. "Why not mine or Carolina's?"

"I don't know," she says. "Maybe they mixed mine up with yours. People probably saw you in mine."

"Shit, I'm so sorry, Maggie. This is all my fault. Maybe I— Maybe this has all gone too far. Maybe I should go home," I say. "Everyone knows who I am. I'm probably going to get kicked out anyway."

"What? No fucking way," Maggie says, turning me around to face her. "You can't go home. If you go home, they win."

"If I don't go home, one of us might get hurt," I counter. "I would never forgive myself if something happened to you because of me." The world seems to spin around me like a haunted amusement park ride. "God, it was so stupid of me to come here. What was I thinking? That no one would recognize me? That I would actually be able to find Kincaid's bones?"

Maggie tries to interrupt, but I keep talking. "How many more signs do I need that this was a mistake? First Noah, then that guy who recognized me, now this." And Kincaid's voice in the woods, I think, but I keep that to myself.

Maggie stares into my eyes, her pupils glinting. "Lucy, if you go home now, you'll leave worse than you were when you got here. You'll be more Kincaid's victim than ever. You'll go home feeling weak and breakable and ashamed. Isn't that right?"

It's like she's reading my thoughts. That's almost exactly what I've been thinking about myself.

I shrug, but she only tightens her hold on my arms, her fingers digging into the fabric of my coat. She gives me one quick, gentle shake. "But you're so much more than that monster's victim. So much more than entertainment for podcasts. I've only known you for two days and already I can see what you could be."

"What could I be?" I ask, my lips trembling, tears looming.

"Powerful," she says, conviction in every syllable of her voice. "Unafraid. A goddamned force to be reckoned with."

I want to believe her. I want so badly to believe her.

I have to believe her because I can't live this way anymore. Like a shell of a person. Seeing Kincaid everywhere I go. Dreaming of him.

The tears I tried to hold back are falling now, coursing hot and then cold on my cheeks. Maggie wipes them away with her warm fingertips. Her hands cup my face. She pauses, eyes glistening as they search mine. "Will you stay?" she asks. "We're so close—I can feel it. We're going to find him. Promise me . . . promise me you'll stay and be a part of it."

I hesitate, afraid to agree to stay, afraid to leave. Maggie's gaze never wavers.

If I go home, Kincaid will keep invading every aspect of my life until there's nothing he hasn't tainted. He will follow me into every single place I'm supposed to be safe until there's nowhere left to hide.

"Yes," I finally whisper. "Yes, I'll stay."

Maggie's face breaks into a fierce, triumphant smile. Then she does the last thing in the world I expect her to do: she leans forward and presses her lips to mine.

At first, I'm so startled I don't move, but then I realize what's happening and I kiss her back. Nothing about this moment is ideal for a first kiss—the chemical-laden smoke in the air, the tears coursing down my cheeks, the fear lodged in my throat. But Maggie has her hands cupped around my face and her lips are warm, and she wants me. Despite everything, my body responds to her, and my fingers are suddenly clutched in her hair and my mouth is moving against hers. There is heat between us, and want and need.

For a moment, I forget where we are, who I am—aware of nothing except every point on my body where Maggie's skin is touching mine.

# TEN

## CAROLINA

**I don't fully** grasp what I'm seeing until Maggie pulls her face from Lucy's and laughs. They stare into each other's eyes, and I realize they've forgotten I'm here. I may as well be a ghost for all the notice they take of me.

I take a step back, and then another. With a last look at them, I turn away, my insides writhing painfully, an ache starting up somewhere around my sternum. I don't know why I'm surprised. I knew Lucy liked Maggie, that Maggie liked Lucy. And now they've kissed. And now they will go back to Lucy's tent, and Maggie will sleep next to Lucy. Or *not sleep* next to Lucy.

I kick at a stray rock as I walk, sending up a spray of dirt. I clench my fists so hard my nails dig into my palms, a stinging pain. But why am I so upset? I've known Lucy for all of two days. Plus, if Lucy and Maggie are together, that will only make it easier for me to ignore these feelings. If I care about Lucy at all, the best thing I can do is keep my distance. Not get too close. Not risk getting near enough to hurt her. The way I might have hurt Michael. And maybe Kiersten too.

Because since I got here it feels like whatever good there is in me is withering in the shadow of the bad. The way I felt seeing that guy corner Lucy in the hallway. I wanted to kill him. Rage ran through me like electricity. I saw it all play out in my head: *my fingernails in his eye sockets, him on his knees, begging. How I punched him over and over and over again, until his face was a bloody mess.*

If Lucy hadn't asked me to let it go, I would have attacked him. I would have found a way to hurt him. Badly. Some part of me would still like to go find his tent and burn it to the ground, the way someone burned Maggie's.

Lucy has already faced one killer, escaping by the skin of her teeth. And clearly though he left no physical scars on her body, he left serious damage behind. She is guarded, wary, skittish, cynical, and—though she tries hard to hide it—terribly afraid. Maggie is the only person who seems to bring out a different side of her, maybe the side of her left undamaged by Kincaid. I wish it were me.

Because this secret part of myself—the word I've never said aloud—this part I've always denied, ignored, pushed down and pushed down, that I've refused to believe in, that I've never admitted fully, even to myself—now it feels unavoidable. Lucy has made it real, has put a face and a body and heart to it.

But why now? Why Lucy?

Just another thing I can't want, can't have.

God, it feels like something inside me is going to explode. It feels like my chest is going to burst open. It feels like—like—

Like what Dad said the curse in him always felt like. A thing he tried to suppress and couldn't, a thing that rose up inside him to devour anyone who got near.

I'm a time bomb, just walking around, waiting to explode and destroy anyone within range. Except I already have exploded, haven't I? And Michael was the one who died for it. Just because I can't remember it doesn't make it untrue. If anything, it makes it even more true.

The fog and smoke surround me as I walk, making me feel cut off from humankind, a thing apart. Like a monster stalking a wasteland. Cursed.

Michael's dead, staring eyes flash through my mind, sending a wave of nausea through me. And suddenly I can't breathe, like the very air is being sucked from my lungs. I stagger to my tent and throw myself inside, zipping it up. I curl into a ball and rock myself, back and forth, back and forth, as if I can soothe the beast inside me. As if I can keep it from coming out again.

I try to make my mind go blank, but my thoughts are inescapable, coming in torrents to drown me. Lucy and Maggie. Kiersten. Michael.

The night he died. The night everything changed for me.

I gasp in a fractured breath, and the thoughts come with it, filling my lungs. I am bad and I am broken, and I will never be anything else.

I killed him. I am a killer.

Whatever the police report might say, it's wrong. I've gone over it and over it, their version of the story. But it never quite adds up.

They say we were riding an ATV on his family's property at twilight, the same path Michael had ridden on hundreds of times before. As we approached the back of his house, Michael lost control of the four-wheeler, and we careened toward the cliff. There was a galvanized metal wire strung between two trees. And Michael ran into it going very fast, fast enough that the wire sliced deeply into his throat, severing his windpipe. The wire caught him, and he fell, taking me down with him, while the ATV continued on without us, crashing over the side of the mountain.

I walked away with only a sprained wrist. Michael never got up from the ground. When the paramedics arrived, I was clutching him, covered in his blood, while he stared blank-eyed at the stars.

But I don't remember any of that.

I only remember the taste of his blood on my tongue, the feel of it on my skin. That's it. Anything else that happened, that I felt, that I saw—it's gone. Vanished into the dark recesses of my mind.

Well, except for one small, very important detail: I'm the one who hung the wire.

It was the start of a wire-and-glass installation for the experiential arts unit in my junior art class—not my favorite medium, but I was doing my best. I was going to hang stained-glass panels from the wire and photograph the effect for my portfolio. Michael didn't know the wire was there, but I did. I'd put it up only a few hours before the accident.

I'm terrible at math, but I keep trying to calculate the odds of the ATV going off the cliff at exactly that point, at exactly that four-foot stretch of wire. I haven't found the exact number yet, but I know it's tiny.

People say I'm lucky. That if it weren't for that wire, the ATV wouldn't have been able to stop and we both would have died. We both would have plummeted into the abyss. I'm not sure that would be so bad. Maybe the abyss is where I belong.

If I could just remember. If I could know for sure what happened, what I did . . . But no matter how hard I try, I can't call up those moments, that handful of seconds that it took to send the ATV careening toward a four-foot stretch of galvanized wire.

Or even the minutes, or hours, before.

I remember hanging the wire. I remember staring down at the slash it left in Michael's neck, the blood that spread over my hands. Blood that left a taste in my mouth like old pennies.

But everything in between those moments is gone.

The hours after are gone too. The next thing I remember is waking up on my friend Sheena's couch just before dinner-time the following day, my wrist bandaged. As soon as I woke, I knew Michael was dead. But I didn't know why.

Even now, all these months later, my mind refuses to show me what I need to see, refuses to remember. I've tried sketching and painting and writing it. I've tried talking it out with my doctors. But maybe I just don't want to remember.

Maybe remembering would be like the answer the orphan girl gets in my ghost story. More shame than I can bear. Maybe remembering would seal my fate. Yet still I try—was I angry that day? Was I sad? Frustrated?

I might have felt any of those things. After all, Michael wasn't easy to be with. He was controlling and possessive, even petty.

Not at first, of course. We were only fifteen when we started dating. Back then, he was fun and funny, charming, protective. He was a shelter. A refuge from my dad and all his rules, all his lectures. All his little meannesses.

But then gradually Michael had meannesses of his own. Demands. Meltdowns. Words hurled like punches.

And it was always my fault. Always something I'd said, or the way I laughed at another guy's joke, or forgetting to check my texts. I read too much, cared too much about school, got too absorbed in my art. I didn't pay enough attention to him. There was always something to apologize for.

By the end, I was always on eggshells, waiting for the next blowup.

Maybe that blowup came, but I was its lit fuse, not Michael.

I try to imagine how it might have happened. How I might have done it. Maybe I grabbed the handlebars at the last moment, jerking us off the trail. Did I duck before we hit the wire? Did I leap off?

None of that sounds right. None of it sounds familiar.

But does it really matter how I did it? Maybe my very presence was enough, drawing death to me with the force of fate. The end result is the same: Michael is dead, and it must be my fault. It has to be my fault.

And if anything happens to Lucy, it will be my fault too.

*Lucy dead, her eyes open and staring. My hands wet with her blood.*

I whimper, curling myself even more tightly into a ball. I try to will the horrible image away, but it only grows more vivid, more real. I squeeze my eyes closed, so hard stars burst behind my eyelids.

But maybe with Maggie by her side, Lucy will be safe from me. I can just be their teammate, someone to pass the next few days with while we hunt for Kincaid's bones. And then I'll go my own way and they'll go theirs, and whatever track I'm on will guide me toward whatever the hell I'm becoming.

So what if that thought makes my heart ache. So what if it leaves me cold.

I reach into my pocket and pull out the aviator patch that Maggie found. A little piece of Kincaid. This man that I've spent months thinking about. This monster who makes me feel a little more whole inside.

Is this who I am? I clench the worn fibers of the patch against my chest, but then I feel something hard there, under my shirt.

It's Lucy's loupe. I drop Kincaid's patch and hold the cold metal of the lens in my fist instead. I clench it tight, letting it warm against my skin.

I hold it as I lie awake, trying as hard as I can not to picture Lucy and Maggie in their tent, trying as hard as I can not to dream. Instead of open, staring eyes and spreading blood, I try to I think of lichen and moss on tombstones, life growing out of death.

Maybe it's not too late for me. Maybe I too can become something different, something else. Something better than I am.

# ELEVEN

## LUCY

**Someone wolf-whistles from** across the campsite, breaking the spell of our kiss. Maggie pulls away, studying me almost shyly. "Was that all right? I should have asked first."

I touch my lips, unsure how to respond. After the heat of Maggie's mouth and skin, the air feels cold, clotted with the scent of burning nylon. Everything happened so fast.

"Come on," she says, taking my hand and leading me to my own tent. I start to follow her, but then I remember Carolina and look over my shoulder for her. But there is only fog and darkness, the last vestiges of smoke making their way up into the atmosphere. Was Carolina here at all? My mind feels muddled, confused. I want to get back to the warmth of Maggie's touch, the honey taste of her lips.

"Are you all right?" Maggie asks once we're zipped up inside my tent. "I didn't mean to kiss you. It sort of— Well, suddenly I was kissing you." She smiles apologetically and smooths my hair across my forehead. Here, in the green warmth of the tent, with the rest of the world on the outside, I can finally appreciate what just happened.

Maggie kissed me.

I want her to kiss me again. I unzip and peel off my coat, and Maggie shrugs out of her jacket, her eyes on mine.

I can't seem to find my voice. So I do the only thing I can: I lean forward and press my lips to hers. She smiles against my mouth and kisses me back, soft at first, but then hard, eager. And it's everything I wanted.

I run my fingers up the back of her neck and into her hair, which flows like silk against my skin. I press close to her, my pulse thrumming. In this moment, I feel like what Maggie says I am. Powerful. Unafraid.

I lean her back against my sleeping bag and kiss her harder, sliding my thigh between her legs. She whispers something I can't quite hear, running her hands up my back, beneath my shirt. I kiss her neck, my hands everywhere, desperate to touch every part of her. She pulls my sweater and the shirt underneath it over my head, and I shiver in the cool air. Maggie looks at me like I am a wild, rare thing, her expression rapt and awed.

I lean back down and kiss her, long and deep, until we're both gasping. My fingers fumble for the button on her jeans. I've never moved this fast with a girl before, but everything seems to be happening on its own, a wave of feeling that is carrying me with it. I want to make her gasp and tremble, turn to liquid beneath my touch.

I get her jeans undone, but then her hand closes over mine. "Lucy, are you all right?"

"Of course I am," I say. "You don't want to—"

"Lucy, you're crying," she says. "Stop for a minute."

"I'm not crying," I say, but then I feel the tears on my cheeks, running down my chin. Embarrassed, I pull away from her, wiping my face. Without her skin on mine, the world feels cold. I feel cold.

"I wanted to," I say. "I don't know why I'm crying." And I don't. I'm as surprised by the tears as Maggie is.

"It's all right. Things have been really stressful." She hands me my sweater, and I put it on. The wool feels dry and scratchy and smells of smoke. "Maybe we should get some sleep. I'll go back to my . . ."

"Your tent burned down," I say unnecessarily. "You'll have to sleep here. Or go bunk with Carolina."

"Right. Come here, then," Maggie says, unzipping the sleeping bag. "We'll keep each other warm."

I lie down in the circle of her arms, my back against her stomach, my head beneath her chin. She holds me close, and I lie still, wondering what the hell happened. How I messed things up so fast. Why did I start crying? Is it stress, like Maggie said? The aftereffects of Rufus cornering me, my worries about Sandra and Kevin finding out who I am? That must be it. It's probably like how when you're trying not to cry and someone hugs you and suddenly you're sobbing. Kissing Maggie must have let out all the emotion I've been holding in.

God, what horrible timing. My face burns with humiliation. I honestly don't know why Maggie even likes me at all. How could she, when I don't even like myself—this weak, fearful person I've become.

But I'm going to earn her interest, her affection. I'm going to make sure she looks at me again the way she did tonight. Tomorrow I'm going to be a better, braver version of myself. A person worthy of someone like Maggie. A person who doesn't cry while trying to have sex, for God's sake. Tomorrow I'll make everything right.

But when I wake, Maggie is gone. The tent is cold, and my memories of last night seem slightly unreal. Did someone really set Maggie's tent on fire? Did she and I really make out and nearly do more than that? Did we spend the night sleeping back-to-back, her steady breathing lulling me to sleep?

I roll over and sit up, peering around the dim tent for some sign that she was here, that I didn't dream it all. I turn the lantern on, flooding the space with cool, unromantic light. I touch my hand to the soft fabric of her side of the sleeping bag, hoping some of her warmth will still be there. The material is cool to the touch.

Hurriedly, I change my clothes and throw my boots on. I run my fingers through my hair to tidy it. I open the tent flap, ready to run out into the early morning to find her, but she's already here, just a few feet away, coming back to me.

"Maggie!" I say, a little breathlessly, "I was coming to look for you."

"Hey, Luce," she says, but her face is serious, preoccupied. There's no sign of the wild, impulsive girl who kissed me last night. Maybe I really did ruin things by crying.

"What's the matter?" I ask, my voice shaky.

"Just saw Sandra and Kevin," she says, crouching in front of the tent. "They want to talk to you."

"Oh." My stomach drops sickeningly. I knew this moment was coming, but it still feels terrible. "They know?"

Maggie nods. "I think so. It was bound to happen. All the contestants—there was no way they'd all keep their mouths shut."

"They're going to send me home," I say. "I'm underage, and I registered with my grandma's information. They'll kick me out of the contest."

"Maybe not," Maggie says, but there isn't much optimism in her voice. Hell, maybe she changed her mind and wants me to go too.

"Shit." I slump to the floor of the tent, my head in my hands. "We've barely even gotten started. I haven't even had a chance to do what I came here for."

"What's wrong?" someone asks. When I look up, Carolina is standing over us, her expression concerned.

"Sandra and Kevin know Lucy is here."

"What did they say?"

"Nothing yet," Maggie says. "They asked me to bring her to them in the lodge. We're worried they'll make her leave."

"Do you want to go?" Carolina asks me. She kneels down next to Maggie.

"No," I say, certain now. And not just because of Maggie and what's happening between us. I want to stay for myself. So I can find Kincaid's bones and finish what I started. "I can't go," I add, and even I hear the desperation in my voice, the clawing, begging sound of it.

Carolina is quiet for a long moment, considering me. "Then better not let them find you," she finally says, flashing an unexpectedly mischievous smile.

"What do you mean?"

"They can't kick you out if they don't know where you are," she says, smiling that wicked smile again. "Let's hit the trails and find some nasty old bones."

Maggie laughs, clearly impressed. "It'll give you another day at least."

"Won't they come after me?" I ask, unsure, though my heart lifts knowing Maggie wants me to stay.

"Have you seen the shoes Sandra wears?" Carolina says. "She's not hiking in Cloudkiss Canyon."

"They could send a ranger or one of the event staff," I point out.

"Nah," Maggie says. "They won't want to let anyone know you're here before they get a chance to talk to you."

"I guess so."

"It'll be like playing hooky from school," Carolina says, waggling her eyebrows. "Or like . . . sneaking into a movie."

Maggie looks at my uncertain expression and laughs. "She's definitely never done either of those things."

Carolina beams. "Well, I've got plenty of practice."

"Me too," Maggie says. "We'll be your tour guides to getting up to no good."

I can't help but laugh, despite my worry. "I guess let's get outta here, then."

# TWELVE

## CAROLINA

### DAY 3

**Without any more** discussion, we trek down the waterfall trail and then onto the gulch trail, a steady path down into the heart of the canyon. But soon we veer far off the path, clambering among rocks and crags and caves, searching for another sign of Kincaid. It's sunny and there's hardly any fog for once, which makes our way easier. It also makes the canyon feel lighter, less oppressive. My thoughts don't feel so weighted with guilt and dread.

We pass a few contestants at the start of the trail, but once we get down past the waterfalls, we don't see anyone else, so we've got the place all to ourselves. The chaos of last night's fire seems far, far away.

"Did you make a report about your tent?" I ask Maggie.

"Yeah. I stuck with my candle story, which earned me a nice lecture from the ranger on duty. He did a great Smokey Bear impersonation."

"Are you sure you shouldn't have told the truth?" Lucy asks.

Maggie looks between us. "If I say it was arson, then the police get involved. It becomes a whole giant thing, and I have to spend my time on that instead of this." She says it so matter-of-factly it almost sounds reasonable.

"But there is still a flame-happy arsonist walking around camp," I point out.

Maggie shrugs. "It was probably just some drunk asshole. Besides, I don't want to draw more attention to us. We really don't need the drama, you know?"

She's not wrong. We've attracted more than enough attention already. But we'll probably have even more drama to deal with once we return to camp tonight, now that Sandra and Kevin know Lucy is here.

Was it foolish of me to suggest we run from them? It would be better for Lucy if she went home, I know it would. But I could hear in her voice how badly she needs this search for Kincaid's bones. And they are sure to make her go home tonight or tomorrow, so what's one more day? One stolen day?

Lucy and Maggie exchange a few more words about the fire, but then Lucy decides to let it go. She must know it's in her best interest.

I expected Lucy and Maggie to be flirtatious and giddy with a new hookup, but instead they're quiet and a little shy with each other. They keep shooting one another questioning glances when the other isn't looking.

So the kiss must have been all that happened between them. Maybe they just got caught up in the moment. Or maybe that's only my wishful thinking. At any rate, Lucy's back to her usual sharp-eyed, quiet self, as wary and watchful as ever.

She's probably too busy worrying about her identity being revealed, about Sandra and Kevin kicking her out of the contest. Or maybe hiking here, near the waterfall trail, so close to the place her life nearly ended, overwhelms even her infatuation with Maggie.

I swat my jealous feelings away and focus on pushing myself up yet another rock face to peer into a cavity in the mountainside. "Are we really going to do this for three more days?" I groan once I climb back down. My legs are jelly, and my arms are trembling with effort. Blisters are forming on my heels from the unfamiliar boots I borrowed off my friend Sheena's mom. She had handed them to me with a smile, all too glad to get me off her couch for a week.

Lucy moves through this canyon like a damn mountain goat, tireless and sure. And Maggie isn't even wearing proper footwear yet hasn't complained once.

"This glorious contest is not for the weak of heart," Maggie says in a nearly perfect imitation of Kevin Wright, posh British accent and all. "It's a test of grit and mettle, fortitude and faith. If you can survive these six days, you can survive anything."

"The only grits he's testing have cheese in them," Lucy grumbles, and Maggie and I both crack up laughing. Lucy looks up, surprised, apparently unaware she made a joke. "He and Sandra aren't even joining the search," she says defensively, but the tiniest smile plays around her lips. "They're too lazy to even come looking for me."

"Do English people know what grits are?" I wonder aloud, and this time Lucy laughs with us. Her laugh is tentative, but it lights up her whole face. I try to think of something to make her laugh again.

"Do you think he's really even British?" I ask. "Or is it a fake accent for the show? I mean, Sandra's from, like, Iowa. How did they even meet?"

"The accent is real," Maggie says, stopping to brush some dirt off her black jeans, "but the degrees are not."

"What?" Lucy and I demand.

"He doesn't actually have degrees in criminology and psychology. He's an absolute fraud," Maggie says knowledgably.

"How do you know that?" I ask. "He sounds like he knows what he's talking about."

"He lies in bed at night and worries he'll be found out," Maggie says dreamily. "He worries there'll be a big scandal and all his fame and money will go away."

"You're full of shit," I say, laughing, and Maggie shrugs. Lucy watches us, torn between laughter and outrage at the thought that Kevin made up his impressive CV.

"That's the trouble with being an imposter," Maggie says, cutting her eyes at me. "You're never quite secure, no matter how many successes you rack up."

Her words crawl down my throat, cutting off my laugh. Is this her sly way of letting me know that she's onto me? That she knows what I'm hiding? All the ways I'm pretending? Or is she really still talking about Kevin Wright?

Maggie shoots me a lighthearted grin, and I realize she was just kidding. Of course she doesn't mean me. How could she possibly know anything about me? I'm being paranoid.

"What about Sandra?" Lucy asks, hefting herself up over a pile of fallen rocks and onto what looks like a deer track. Maggie and I follow her. "Do you think she's the real deal?"

"Hmmmm. With a pseudonym like Sandra D., she must be trying a little too hard to prove her innocence," Maggie muses.

I snort-laugh, even though it's not a very good joke, relieved to realize Maggie's theories are just her way of showing off for Lucy. She wants to seem like a worldly and wise college student among us naive high schoolers. "Was that a *Grease* reference? What decade are you from?"

"*Grease* is a classic, thank you very much," Maggie retorts. She pretends to smooth back her hair with an invisible comb, greaser style. Total show-off.

"Sandra's not exactly wearing poodle skirts," Lucy points out. "She—" Lucy stops talking, staring straight ahead at something above us.

"What is it?" I ask, following her gaze.

"Bones," she whispers.

I make out the play of sunlight on something bleached white on a ledge a few feet above us. Could it really be over already? We've hardly gotten started.

We climb a little higher until we're looking down on what is definitely a skeleton, or at least part of one. Rib cage and leg bones. What looks like a pelvis. A series of long lines, shadows beneath.

"Is—is it him?" Lucy asks, her skin suddenly as white as the bones. I'm worried she's going to get dizzy and fall, but her fingers are digging into the rock and her feet look sure.

"Maggie?" I ask.

Maggie climbs higher, until she's on the rock with the skeleton. She kneels down and picks up what must be a skull.

"Don't touch it!" I exclaim. "Forensic protocol!" But Maggie raises the skull higher, and I realize my mistake. It's too big to be human, the jaw too long. She holds it in her hands and gazes down at it thoughtfully, like Hamlet contemplating Yorick's skull. Its empty eye sockets gaze back up at her. My fingers itch for a pencil, to capture the unlikely scene.

"Is it him?" Lucy asks again, her voice hoarse, emotion restricting her vocal cords. She's too upset to see anything except Kincaid there. I want to reach for her, to comfort her. But the image from last night flashes through my mind again—*my hands red with Lucy's blood*. I keep my fingers clenched on the rock.

"What is it?" I ask, craning to see.

Maggie turns the skull toward us so we can see its face. I stare into the darkness of its eyes, the absence of its life, and something inside me goes still and quiet.

Lucy suddenly slides down the rock several feet, scrabbling all the way. When her feet hit solid ground again, she turns and retches. I watch her, strangely undisturbed by her distress, quiet inside like rich people say they feel when they do yoga or meditate. I tried to do both with YouTube videos after Michael died, but they only made me feel trapped and restless. But there's quiet in these bones for me. Something almost like peace. I wish I had time to draw them so I could take them with me, carry them inside me.

But I make myself turn to Lucy, make myself care. "I think it's a bear's, Lucy," I tell her.

"She knows that," Maggie says quietly. "She knows. Just give her some space."

I reach out for the skull, and Maggie puts it into my hands. It's less smooth than I expected, and less heavy. The feel of it in my hands settles me somehow, the same way Brandon's body pressed against mine did that first night here.

Bones cannot pretend, cannot hide from themselves. They can't overthink or be afraid. They just *are*.

"It's strange that we found these, isn't it?" I ask Maggie.

She's eyeing Lucy intensely now, watching as Lucy wipes her mouth and puts her head between her knees. Eyeing her like she's weighing her on silver scales, considering how to adjust the balance. The psychiatrist I saw at the hospital looked at me like that.

"Do you feel surprised?" Maggie asks me, without taking her eyes from Lucy.

"No," I say. I ought to—how often do you come across a bear's skeleton, let alone while searching for a serial killer's bones? Yet somehow these bones feel inevitable, as if they were waiting here for me. Like a lesson I needed to learn.

"Valley of dry bones," I whisper, thinking of one of my father's favorite Bible passages. It's how he described his own salvation. A valley of bones brought back to life. As a kid, I thought it was a beautiful idea, like something from a fairy tale. I thought it meant that Dad would be so different from how my mom described him to me in my earliest years, that the cruel, tempestuous man would be knitted together anew, with kindness and gentleness.

In a way, I was right. He was different. But different does not mean better. "'And behold, there were very many in the open valley; and, lo, they were very dry,'" I murmur, hearing the words in my father's gravelly voice, lifted in fervent prayer.

"What?" Maggie asks, finally looking away from Lucy.

"It's scripture. From the Book of Ezekiel."

"'Son of man, can these bones live?'" Maggie quotes, snapping me out of my trancelike state.

I meet her intelligent gray eyes. "'O Sovereign Lord, you alone know.'"

We both look down at the bear's head and its scattered, dusty bones. A thrill runs up my spine, a sense of expectation, as if the bones are going to rattle in the earth, knitting themselves together again, like the bones of the dead army in the valley in Ezekiel.

But of course the valley of dry bones is just a story, merely words on a page, despite my father's belief in its power. The bear's bones lie where the creature fell, white and dead and peaceful, at rest.

Dad always said I should be afraid of death because I'll finally have to face judgment for my sins. But he was wrong. These bones tell me there's nothing in death to fear. It's only the living who need to be afraid.

Maggie's eyes settle on mine again, and it's like she can sense the way the world is reshaping around me. But she only smiles, a little sadly, and jerks her head. "Come on, let's get Lucy back to camp."

I take one last look at the bear and then climb down after her, thinking suddenly of Michael, of Michael's bones beneath the earth, still hidden beneath his embalmed flesh, swathed in the white satin lining of his coffin, beneath a granite head-stone that says he was beloved.

If I had the power to speak to his bones, to command them to live, would I? Would I give him life again?

No, I realize. He's better off where he is, and so am I. Let the dead stay dead.

Lucy is withdrawn on the way back to camp, absorbed in her thoughts. She walks several paces ahead of us, as if unable to stand the thought that we might talk to her. Instinctively, Maggie and I both leave her alone. We hike in silence for a long time.

The closer we get to camp, the more I lose that sense of quiet the bones gave me. Thoughts crowd in, my father's voice, as well as my own, telling me I am bad, wrong, danger-ous. I wish I'd brought one of the bear's bones with me, to hold and draw strength from, a talisman against all my fears, my shame, my regrets. I fiddle with the loupe Lucy loaned me instead, opening and closing the lens cover.

"So how come you know your Bible so well?" I ask Maggie, desperate to distract myself.

"Probably the same reason you do."

"I doubt it," I say, the weight of bitter thoughts in my voice.

She flits her eyes over me as we walk. "Your parents are religious fundamentalists who forced it on you from a young age. And you submitted to it until you got sick of it and decided to rebel. The tighter they tried to hold on to you, the wilder you got."

Her words stop me in my tracks. Anger surges through me. I grab her arm and turn her to face me in the path. "What the fuck, Maggie. Did you look me up or something? You know about my dad?" I think of his mean-looking mug shot online, the list of his crimes. Public and shameful and on the internet forever, whether Jesus cleansed him from his sins or not.

"What?" Maggie asks, startled. "Of course not."

"Oh, you're just that good at reading people? You can see all my fears and shames? Like you knew Kevin Wright lies awake at night worried the world will find out he's a fraud?"

She laughs. "That was a joke. I don't know anything about Kevin Wright. He just seems like a phony."

"You're good at reading people. I can tell that," I say. "You think you've got the number of everybody here? Well, you don't have mine," I spit. Panic wraps around me, the shock of being found out, of being laid bare.

"I *am* good at reading people," Maggie admits. She holds her palms out, conciliatory. "It's a fun party trick. But I only can tell about you because I have the same kind of story."

"Really? You expect me to believe that?" I don't see a trace of myself in this girl.

"Come on, let's keep walking before Lucy leaves us in the dust," she says. I hesitate and then continue on with her.

"Well?" I ask, the word barbed and brutal.

Maggie sighs. "Look, my parents didn't want a kid. They liked their money and their parties and all the drinking and drugs that went with them, and they were always fobbing me off on my grandparents. After a while, my grandparents insisted I come live with them. In some ways, I was glad. They were actually home and paid attention to me and seemed to care that I existed."

"Wow, grandparents who love and dote on you. Sounds terrible," I say, still seething.

"It wasn't, not at first. It was nice." Maggie smiles, as if recalling a good memory, but then her face clouds over. "It was nice until I made a mistake. Until I disappointed them. I was in eighth grade and I snuck out one night and went to a high school party. When my grandparents found out, they totally freaked. They thought I was going to turn into my mother and grow up to be selfish and an alcoholic and all that. And they saw me as their second chance—you know, to have a good daughter. And now they had these horrible visions of me wrecking my life."

"What did they do?"

"They sent me to a Catholic boarding school."

"Are you serious? Because you went to a party?"

Maggie nods. "And it wasn't one of the nice, progressive Catholic schools. It was really, really strict. They taught you to be ashamed of yourself and your body, your desires. They weren't allowed to use corporal punishment, but they really didn't even need it because they were so good at making us all feel like absolute deviants."

"Wow," I say, softening. "I'm sorry. That's horrible."

Maggie shrugs. "So I'm saying, I get it. I see you."

"You see me?" I say with the barest trace of a smile.

"I mean, not all of you. Just this part. Because I've got it too," Maggie says.

"Okay," I say. "I'm sorry I jumped down your throat."

"So I guessed correctly about your parents, then?" she asks, annoyingly proud of herself.

I nod. "Do you ever wonder . . . ?" I meet Maggie's strange gray eyes. "Do you ever wonder if maybe . . . ?"

"If they were right and we really are as bad as they say?" Maggie grins. "If we are, so is everybody else, including them. Maybe we're just more honest about it."

This isn't what I expected from Maggie. I didn't expect her to have crappy parents or any problems at all really. She glides through the world like nothing can hurt her, like she carries no shame on her back. How does she do that? Maybe if I watch her hard enough, I'll figure it out. Then I can do it too. Throw off my baggage and be free.

We spend the rest of the walk back to camp comparing our religious horror stories, laughing over Catholic school dress codes and lectures about the evils of masturbation. I try to explain altar calls and speaking in tongues, and Maggie's eyes widen in disbelief. We keep it light—we don't share how much it all hurt us, warped us, kept us in the dark. We laugh at it, and I wonder if that's Maggie's secret. The reason she doesn't seem to take anything seriously.

Maybe if you laugh at the dark, it can't you hurt you so much. It can't get inside you and drag you down to hell.

# THIRTEEN

## LUCY

**It wasn't him.** The bones didn't belong to Joseph Kincaid. But for a moment, I'd been so sure. I'd recognized Kincaid in the shape of the skull, the long femurs. It was Kincaid— Kincaid dead, Kincaid vanquished. But then I blinked and the skull was the wrong shape. Teeth too big. Ribcage all wrong. It was an animal's skeleton, a black bear's.

I only got a moment of peace before the world came crashing in again.

I want that moment back.

The return hike to our campsite feels endless, which is fine by me. I'm not ready to be among all the Beastie Babes again. Not ready to face Sandra and Kevin. Not ready to be sent home. I wish we'd brought the tents with us and found a new place to camp—we could hide out in the canyon until the contest is over. Live on Kind Bars and trail mix until we find the bones.

Then again, I'm not sure I'd like to be out in the canyon at night. Maybe it's just from the shock of the bear skeleton, or maybe because of the aviator patch we found yesterday, but the Cloudkiss Killer feels close, as if he's just underfoot. Maggie and Carolina seem to sense it too, each of them lost in her own thoughts as we near the rim of the canyon.

We make it back to camp just as night is beginning to fall, the sky clear for once, dark blue with a few scattered stars. The only fog is close to the ground, rolling up from the canyon. Dinner isn't for another half hour, so we decide to head back to our tents to rest and change.

The campfire is already lit for the night, music plays from someone's tent, and people mill around, exchanging stories from the day, passing around a flask. They all seem normal—no fights or sullen silences like yesterday.

The campsite has the air of a festival, everyone weary but rowdy, still hoping something exciting's going to happen. They're here for Kincaid's bones, but they're here for something else too—community, kinship, connection. They don't want to be out in the canyon on their own. They want to be here, where the warmth and the light and the life is.

It surprises me. Their humanity. Their ordinariness. For the first time, I wonder if maybe I've been wrong about them all. I was wrong about Carolina. What if I've been wrong about Sandra and Kevin too? Maybe if I talk to them, they'll understand and let me stay in the contest.

But when we go to pass by the fire, Maggie points at a small cluster of guys there, and all my good feelings toward these people evaporate. "Look at Noah," she says unnecessarily. He's all I can see.

He is dressed in the same outfit Joseph Kincaid had on when he abducted me, when he leapt from the edge of the canyon. Navy-blue beanie, wire glasses, brown leather bomber jacket, complete with the shearling lining and aviator patch. But it's the knife in his hand that gets my attention, that turns my breathing shallow.

He raises it cinematically over the chest of another guy, who holds his arms up in mock fear. Noah brings down the knife, and even though I know it's a joke, even though I know it's not real, my blood runs cold, the nausea from earlier burning my throat.

The guy pretends to take the thrusts of the knife before falling dramatically to the ground, using his hands to panto-mime the rush of blood from his chest. Once more I hear those hateful, whispered words in the hallway outside the bathroom. *You know what he would have done to you, right?*

I clench my fists.

Noah straddles the guy and pretends to finger his knife thoughtfully, gazing down at his mock victim as if deciding on his first cut. The other dudes around the fire shift nervously, clearly aware the joke has gone too far. But they wait to see what will happen, titillation clearly vying for their good sense.

Carolina starts forward with a snarl, but I push past her, driven toward Noah as if carried on a wave. All the guys look up as I barrel toward them. Noah scrambles hastily off his victim. "It was just a joke," he says. The other guy sits up, and his eyes widen when he recognizes me.

They all recognize me. They all know who I am.

My vocal cords feel strangled, the words I want to say trapped inside my throat.

"We're only kidding around," Noah says. "I swear." He drops the knife on the ground. My eyes follow it, watching the way the flames of the campfire dance across the metal of the blade. It's a hunting knife, the sort you use for gutting animals. I think about using it on him, and I don't hate the idea.

Carolina steps forward, but Maggie puts a restraining hand on her wrist. "Let her handle this herself," I hear Maggie whisper.

Handle it myself. How do you handle something like this? All I feel is disgust, revulsion. And rage. A part of me wants to pick up that knife, is practically begging me to. Noah must see me looking at it because he takes a step backward, toward the fire.

His movement releases a laugh from my throat. "Are you really afraid of me? Am I really the reason you went screaming through the woods? From a teenage girl hardly more than five feet tall?" My words drip with disdain.

Noah takes another step backward. "Look, I don't want any trouble. We were just goofing around."

"You think murder is funny? You think a man ending the life of another human being is a laugh? You're disgusting. You're sick."

"I'm not the one attacking people," Noah mutters.

"You're dressed like the man who planned to murder and dismember me," I say, thrusting my finger at his jacket. "To arrange what was left into some mockery of art. In that order, if I was lucky."

Noah's eyes light up at my words, and his mouth curls cruelly. "It's not my fault you're too damaged to take a joke."

My ears fill with an electric hum, and my vision goes white at the edges. But this isn't like before, when I hit him. Now I'm fully in the present, fully in control of myself.

When I shove him, it's intentional, a choice I make. I push him just hard enough to make him stumble back toward the fire. Just hard enough to make him step into the flames.

It takes a few seconds before Noah realizes he's on fire. Then he looks down and yelps as the flames lick up his leg. He leaps out of the fire, but it's too late. Flames run up one of his pant legs, eagerly consuming the denim.

Time seems to stop as the flames glow and bite. I stare, transfixed, as Noah screams, either in pain or in terror. Either one is fine by me. Because I did it, I made it happen. Satisfaction spreads through me, releasing all the coiled-up anxiety in my muscles, the knots of fear in my stomach.

"Oh my God—Lucy!" Carolina yells, her voice a panicked rasp.

The sound of my name shatters the peace of the moment, and the world comes horribly into focus. The acrid smell of burning fibers. Noah's terrified screams. Growing, hungry flames.

I bolt into action, knocking Noah to the ground and forcing him to roll in the dirt. I yank my half-full water bottle from its pocket in my backpack and douse what's left of the flames. Smoke and steam rise from his quivering body. His jeans must have been fire resistant because they're in better shape than I expected, only burned away in a few patches and not melded to his skin.

"Let me see how bad it is," I say, reaching for him. "I have a first aid kit." But Noah recoils from me, raising his hands in a way that's nearly identical to the pantomime he and the other guy put on before my arrival.

Now I'm not the victim. I'm the one with the knife. I find I like this role much better, maybe a little too much.

The other guys finally break into movement, surrounding Noah. "We've got it, psycho," one of them says, shoving me away. "You've done enough."

"Come on," Maggie says, pulling me by the arm. "He'll be fine. Let's go."

I turn and catch sight of Carolina's face in the red of the flames. She looks stunned.

But Maggie's eyes glitter with something I'd almost call triumph.

The three of us leave behind the smell of charred denim as Maggie guides us toward the picnic table in the trees. I sit on the tabletop, feeling disconnected, disbelieving. I pushed a guy into the fire. I watched him burn.

Carolina puts her hand on my knee. "It was an accident, Lucy. You didn't mean to do it."

Maggie laughs. "No, it wasn't. Lucy knew exactly what she was doing."

"But she helped him. She saved him," Carolina says earnestly. "He'll be fine."

"Not that he deserved her help," Maggie says with a roll of her eyes. "What a fucking creep. I'd have let him burn."

"You would not," Carolina says. "And neither could Lucy."

"Jesus, why are you so intent on making Lucy into an angel?" Maggie demands. "Let her be angry. Let her fucking rage. You're not the only one with a temper, you know."

I listen to them argue about me, neither of them bothering to ask me how I feel. How it felt to push him into the fire. How it felt to watch him burn. Whether I meant to do it. Whether or not I liked it.

I did like it. It made me feel strong, in control. Powerful. What does that say about me?

"Lucy, are you all right?" Carolina finally asks.

"I don't know," I whisper. I lift my head and meet their eyes—Carolina's are concerned, but Maggie's are bright and eager. She looks the way she did last night when she kissed me.

"You took back your power," Maggie says. "What Kincaid stole from you, you took it right back. This is exactly why I told you to stay. Not to run away."

"So I could become a monster too?" I ask around a weak laugh. I'm not sure whether or not I mean it.

"You're not a monster," Carolina says quickly.

"No, you're a fucking queen," Maggie says. She emphasizes her words by pointing a knife at me on each syllable. It's Noah's hunting knife, I realize. She must have stolen it from the campfire in the confusion. "You're on your way to becoming untouchable. A few more days and you'll be pissing on Kincaid's bones." Her face breaks into an enormous, feral grin.

I grin right back, my self-doubt unable to stand against the fierce radiance of Maggie Rey's smile.

"Lucy?" a soft voice asks. It's a woman. She stands a few yards away, a man by her side. They are silhouettes against the deep of twilight. "Are you Lucy Wilson?" The woman takes a few tentative steps forward. "Lucy?" she asks again, her voice strangely hushed, a note of strain in it.

"Yes," I manage to say, my heart sinking into my gut. Now they'll surely make me go home, now that I've attacked Noah twice. Now that I've made sure everyone in this competition sees me as a threat. I look down at the ground, at my dusty hiking boots.

Sandra and Kevin move closer, their shoes crunching on the pine needles. For a moment, everyone is silent, unsure how to begin.

"It's an honor to meet you, Lucy," Sandra says.

My head snaps up. "Oh, I . . ."

"We've often talked about you and wondered how you were faring," Kevin says.

I search their faces, trying to read them in the dim light beneath the trees.

Sandra smiles. "Maybe we could go inside and talk? We could eat dinner together," she offers. "We'll have it brought to my cabin."

"Are you going to make me go home?" I ask.

Sandra and Kevin exchange a glance I can't read. "We'll . . . have to talk about that," Sandra says. "Let's go get some food, all right?"

"All right. Can my teammates come?" The thought of being alone with Sandra and Kevin is too much.

"Well—" Kevin starts to say.

"Of course we're coming," Maggie interrupts, putting an arm around my shoulder. She stares Kevin and Sandra down with smile that's simultaneously affable and threatening.

"All right," Sandra agrees. She pulls out her cell phone and types quickly. "I'm going to have my assistant, Priya, bring us some food. Any dietary restrictions?" We all shake our heads.

Sandra finishes texting and puts her phone away. She gives us a tight smile. "Let's go."

Sandra's rental cabin is rustic but cozy, with a fire burning in the stone fireplace. I find I don't want to look at the dancing flames. The smell of the burning wood makes me feel a little sick.

Once we're all squeezed into a small, square table in the kitchen, plates of chicken Parmesan in front of us, a sense of unreality descends. I'm sitting in a cabin at Cloudkiss Canyon with two true crime podcast hosts who have turned the most painful experience of my life into entertainment. And I have to beg them to let me stay here, in this nightmare canyon, to find my would-be killer's bones.

It's so messed up it's almost funny.

We push our food around in silence for a few minutes, every-one clearly unsure how to begin. Finally, Sandra puts her fork down. "Lucy, help me understand. Why would you come here, lie about who you are, participate in this contest?" Her expression is carefully schooled into an expression I can only described as *concerned adult*. "It must all be very painful for you."

I swallow a bite of chicken, which goes down my throat like sand. I take a sip of water. "It is," I agree. "Very painful." I meet her eyes, and the pity there makes me bold. "Almost as painful as hearing my abduction story on a crass, exploitative podcast like yours."

Maggie lets out a low, admiring whistle.

Sandra and Kevin exchange a worried glance. "If that's how you feel, why on earth are you here?" Kevin asks.

"Because I want to make sure he's dead."

"And you had to come here to see it for yourself?" Sandra asks, her voice gentle.

"I had to come here and find him for myself," I say, lifting my chin.

"I can understand that," Sandra says. "You want closure."

I give a sharp nod.

"But, Lucy, you're underage. Do your parents even know where you are?"

"They aren't worried. I have a cover story," I say. "And I've been texting them every day."

Sandra and Kevin glance at each other again. "It's a legal liability, your being here," Kevin says. "Anything could happen to you, and we would be held responsible."

When I don't say anything, Sandra leans across the table. "Clearly, things have already happened. Other contestants say you've had aggressive run-ins with a man named Noah?"

I nod. "The first time was a mistake. I don't really know what happened. But tonight, he was pretending to be Kincaid, acting like a killer."

Sandra frowns. "You have to understand, Lucy, that Kincaid means different things to people here than he does to you."

"I pushed Noah, but I didn't mean for him to get hurt," I say. I close my eyes for a moment, clenching my jaw so I don't say what I really think. *But he deserved it.* "Is he all right?" I ask instead. I need to at least pretend that I care.

"Noah is fine. No real harm done," Sandra says. "But what if it had gone differently? What if you had gotten hurt? You're too young to be here, Lucy. It's clearly unhealthy for you."

"So you want me to leave?"

"I think it would be best," she says.

I stare down at my nearly untouched plate, trying to find the words I need to convince them. To make them understand.

"What if she gives you an interview?" Maggie says.

"What?" Carolina and I both say at the same time.

Maggie keeps her eyes trained on Sandra and Kevin. "An exclusive interview for *Human Beasties*, about Kincaid and her abduction, his death, everything?"

"Maggie!" Carolina whispers sharply. "You can't be serious."

"I'm dead serious," Maggie says, not even bothering to look at Carolina. "If she agrees to give you an interview, you let her finish out the week." She stares down Kevin and Sandra, her eyebrows raised.

To my shock, they hesitate. They exchange furtive glances, and I can see the gears turning behind their eyes. Their fake concern for my well-being gives way so quickly it's laughable.

"Is that something you'd want to do, Lucy?" Sandra asks carefully. "Tell your story?"

My face heats. I look at Maggie. She shrugs. "I was just trying to win you a chance to stay," she says. "But it's up to you."

"There *are* things you've gotten wrong," I say, and my voice sounds strange in my ears. "About what he was like. About how things went down that morning."

Kevin leans across the table. "Like what, Lucy?" He's practically salivating.

"Isn't this all illegal?" Carolina butts in. "Remember how you said it's a legal liability? You know Lucy is here at this contest, that she's underage. And you want to barter her safety for an interview? Her parents could sue you."

"No one's getting sued," I say, throwing the meanest look at Carolina I can muster before turning back to Kevin and Sandra. "You can pretend you didn't know I was here. I won't tell anyone. As far as you know, I'm Geraldine Franks. Besides, my parents really aren't the suing kind."

But Carolina's words already found their mark, the threat of a lawsuit practically hanging in the air above our table. Kevin and Sandra lean away from us and confer in low voices.

"Damn it, Carolina," Maggie whispers. "We had them."

Carolina ignores her. "Lucy, your story is your own. You don't owe it to anybody. You sure as hell shouldn't have to pay your way here with it."

"Maybe telling her story would be good for her. Did you ever think of that?" Maggie asks. "Keeping things bottled up inside doesn't do anyone any good." She gives Carolina a meaningful look that's lost on me.

"Maggie's right," I say, and the truth of the words settles in my chest. My family has wanted me to put the past in the past, to move on with my life. But I've been mired in the memory of that half hour with Joseph Kincaid for two years now. Maybe trying to forget isn't the answer. Maybe speaking the truth into the air is what it takes to move on.

And if I find the bones, that will be the last step. I'll cut myself free of this cursed place and never look back again.

"I want to tell my story," I say, so loudly that Sandra and Kevin startle. "I want to tell the world what happened." I meet their eyes, my gaze steady. I feel stronger than I have in a long, long time. Because I confronted Noah? Because I told Sandra and Kevin what I really think about their podcast?

"Okay," Sandra says. She's pretending to relent—ever so reluctantly—to my wishes, but there's a glint of greed in her eyes. She knows this is risky, that it could backfire, but she can't resist it. All her condescension and pity are gone. Her expression is all business—straight brows, lifted chin, lips pressed thin. "Let's draw up terms."

I sit up straighter in my chair and fold my hands on the table. Right now, I'm not a teenager and she's not an adult. We are equals, with our own agendas, our own goals, willing to take the risks to get what we want.

"Here's what I'm willing to do," I say. When I speak, everyone listens.

# FOURTEEN

## CAROLINA

**The second Lucy** has finished hammering out the details of her deal with the devil—well, with Sandra and Kevin— she pushes to her feet and strides from the cabin. I jump up and follow her, pursuing her across the open grass toward the tents, where mist rises from the ground. I don't even know what I'm going to say when I catch her. I feel bad for interfering and getting in her way, but I'm afraid for her too. That scene at the campfire with Noah was terrifying. *She* was terrifying. I don't want her to become what I am. It will destroy her.

"Lucy!" I yell. When she doesn't respond, I try again. "Lucy!"

She spins around. "What?" she spits. "What, Carolina? Are you disappointed you didn't manage to ruin things for me in there?"

"Of course not," I say, stung.

"Then have you come to tell me what a mistake I'm making? That it's stupid and shortsighted to give up my story in exchange for staying here? Because if that's what it is, believe me, I've already considered all that."

"That's not it at all," I say. "I—I think you're brave to tell your story. There's a lot of power in taking control of a narrative."

"Oh, I'm brave, am I?" she says, furious—at Sandra and Kevin? At this place, at God, at the world? Maybe all of them. But right now, the full force of her rage is pointed squarely at me. Even in the dark, I catch the flash of her eyes, the intensity of her stare.

It ought to repel me, but instead it draws me near. I step closer to her. "Yes, I think you're very, very brave. You wouldn't be here if you weren't."

Lucy laughs. "That's funny because all you do is act like I'm weak. Like I need to be rescued from everyone, as well as from myself. You argued with Maggie over me tonight like I'm a child."

"I don't think you're weak," I say. "I could never think that. It's just that Maggie—"

"What do you want, Carolina?" she interrupts. "I'm tired. It's been a long day, and I want to go to bed."

I want to tell her that Maggie has more influence over her than Lucy realizes, that Maggie's suggestions for how Lucy can feel powerful aren't the only option. Being violent won't give Lucy what she wants. I know that for sure. All it's done is make me afraid of myself.

But would saying all that confirm Lucy's suspicions, that I see her as a child, someone who doesn't know what's best for herself, whose well-being I feel compelled to argue over? Of course that's not how I feel about her at all.

I think of the drawings of her in my sketchbook, the ones that have multiplied from one to five to nine, though I hardly remember drawing them. If she could see them, could see herself through my eyes . . .

Maybe then she'd see something of me too. Some part of my heart that she wouldn't despise. Maybe she could draw that good out of me, make it stronger than all the bad.

I start to reach into my bag for my sketchbook when Lucy turns away. "Lucy," I say.

She turns back around. "I want to know what you did, Carolina."

"Excuse me?"

"I want to know why serial killers make you feel better about yourself. I want to know what you did that brought you here. Because there has to be something. If there's power in a narrative, then tell me yours." She lifts her chin, a challenge in every line of her body.

I feel myself go cold. If I told her, she'd hate me. She'd never be able to see anything in me but evil.

Maybe I should follow her example: take the risk, tell my story. Maybe I should be as strong as I know she is. I should tell the truth and accept the consequences. But I don't know if I can.

"I hurt someone," I say quietly.

"Did you mean to?"

"I don't know," I say. That's as honest an answer as I can give.

"Did they deserve it?"

"Does anyone deserve violence?"

"Yes," she says, her eyes blazing. "Sometimes they do."

That resolute, righteous look in her eyes tells me I can't possibly tell her the truth, tell her what I am. I'm not nearly as brave as she is.

"Did Noah deserve it?" I ask, looking away from her.

"Are we back on this?" Her voice is hard.

"You could have hurt him badly, Lucy," I hear myself say, even though I know it's the wrong thing to say, the last thing in the world she wants to hear right now. "And you don't know what it's like, to cause that kind of harm. You don't know what it does to you. How it changes you."

"Noah's fine," she says around a sigh, "Sandra said he didn't even need to go the hospital. He's not even limping."

"What about next time?" I ask. "What if next time you hurt him bad enough he does need the hospital? Or what if he hurts you?"

"There won't be a next time," Lucy says. "I'm going to find Kincaid's bones, and I'm going to go home and never think of this place or these people again. That's all that matters."

"Lucy," I say, hating the pleading tone in my voice. But it feels suddenly imperative to make her understand. "Listen, what's happening with you and Noah, it isn't normal. There's something else at play here, something dangerous. Don't you feel it? It's like something is bringing you two together, like it wants one of you to hurt the other."

"What, like the spooky canyon fog?" Lucy asks, laughing.

I hesitate. Maybe I do believe the legends. Maybe I do think it's this place getting into her head, my head—hell, every person here is acting weird. But I can't say it outright. "Haven't you noticed since you've been here, how everything feels heightened?" I ask instead. "Like whatever it is inside you that keeps the bad stuff in check, that it's . . . not working like usual?"

Lucy raises her eyebrows. "Do you hear yourself?"

"Okay, forget that stuff." I wave my previous words away. "Just know . . . just know that I care about you," I say, my voice tentative. The words are so inadequate, so bland. "I don't want you to—"

"You don't even know me," Lucy counters. "You're only worrying about me so you don't have to worry about yourself. So you don't have to deal with your own problems. It's pathetic."

The words are a blow, and I take a step back. Regret flashes in Lucy's eyes, but only for a moment.

"Why Maggie?" I ask abruptly. "Why do you trust her, and not me? Is it because I'm a true crime fan and she isn't?"

Lucy's expression hardens. "What you really mean is, why do I like her instead of you, isn't that it?"

I blush all the way to the roots of my hair, but at least she can't see that in the dark. "That's not— I mean, I'm not . . ." But I can't find the words to defend myself.

"Just back off, Carolina," Lucy says. "I don't need your mothering. I've got a mother of my own back home."

"Fine," I spit. "Forget it." Anger pulses inside me, thrumming through my veins. I turn away before it makes me say something I'll regret. I walk away fast, and I force myself not to look back.

I've done too much of that already.

I consider hanging out in my tent, where I can worry and fume in solitude. But that feels too pathetic, even for me. So instead, I go to trivia night at the campfire, just so I don't have to be alone with my thoughts. Most of the other contestants are still shunning me, but Levi and his fellow middle-aged buddies make space for me on their bench. The first round of trivia is underway, and the three men have their heads together, deep in disagreement about the name of John Wayne Gacy's clown persona.

"No, I'm sure it starts with a *P* and ends with a vowel," Levi says. "Ponyo?"

I snicker to myself. The three men turn to me. "What?" one of them says.

"Ponyo is a mermaid from an animated film. Gacy went by Pogo the Clown."

They all laugh, except for Levi, who shudders. "God, I hate clowns," he says. He looks drawn and wan, and I remember how we found him crying by himself in the canyon. I wonder if the bad memories are still getting to him.

"Well, she's on our team tonight," says one of Levi's friends, a balding man who shakes my hand and tells me his name is Geoffrey and that he's an accountant. The other man, an IT guy named Darius, says I look about his daughter's age. I tell them I'm an art history major at UNC Chapel Hill, and they all shake their heads and mutter about how I ought to study something with more career certainty.

I laugh, and then I wonder if this is what most people's dads are like. Nice, nerdy, practical men who lecture them about their money-making potential. I bet Lucy's dad is like these guys. I bet he makes corny jokes and reads *The Economist*. Then again, I suppose most people's dads don't enter competitions to hunt for serial killers' bones, so these might not be representative of the usual middle-class dads of America. Still, it makes me sad that Lucy would think these men were sickos.

My dad would think they were too, even though I'm sure *they've* never been to jail for manslaughter. The one time Dad caught me listening to a true crime podcast, he confiscated my phone and made me read the Bible at the kitchen table every night for a week. He said I shouldn't fill my head with sordid stories that would only lead me further away from God. I wonder what he'd think of my being here now, if he'd see it as evidence of how lost I am. Maybe he wouldn't be wrong.

I'm so caught up in these thoughts that I miss the next question. "Oh, that's definitely Gary Ridgway," Geoffrey says.

"Nope, Samuel Little," Darius says. "He confessed to more than ninety killings."

Geoffrey whistles in awed surprise.

I tune them out for a moment, watching the other groups of contestants. I'm surprised to see Brandon here, sitting with three older women who are definitely flirting with him, enough to make him look deeply uncomfortable. Noah and Rufus are nowhere in sight.

I almost get up to go check on Lucy before I remember she wants me to leave her alone, to stop mothering her. Fine. That's fine. I can think about other things. Like the way Rosa and Bridget are glaring at one another, clearly pissed off. They're not even bothering to try to answer the trivia questions, leaving it to their third member, Denny, who keeps shooting guilty little glances at them. What the hell happened there?

A lot of the people here look strange, I realize. Angry with one another, strung out and exhausted, or despondent. Brandon is chewing his nails, becoming more nervous by the minute. Addison is telling a long-winded story in a very loud voice, clearly seeking the attention of anyone who will give it to her. No one here actually seems to be having much fun.

I turn back to my little group. Levi's hands are trembling, I realize. He's trying to hide it, but he's obviously having a hard time. Geoffrey has three empty beer bottles at his feet, even though the night has just begun. Darius is eyeing the fourth beer like he wants to say something but is too afraid.

Maybe everyone's tired from hiking all day. Maybe the stress of the competition is getting to some people. But I can't help but notice the fog creeping ever closer to the campfire, rising among the distant tree tops, blotting out the stars.

And no matter how hard I try to keep them here, my thoughts creep too, hungry and wanting, through the fire and through the trees, blundering through the fog, seeking Lucy in the dark.

# FIFTEEN

## LUCY

**I stare at** the words on the pages of the sci-fi novel I've been trying to read. They are stark—black text on white page, stamped unmistakably clear. Yet they seem to disappear the moment I read them. Instead, the words I spoke to Carolina hover in my mind, sharp and cruel, cutting me a little each time I turn them over. I don't know why I got so angry at her. Why I was so harsh. It's not like me, not really.

I want to apologize but not now. I'd probably just say something even worse. Tonight I need to stay here in the silence of the tent with my book I can't read, my thoughts I can't escape. But I only get a few minutes to myself before Maggie is outside the tent asking to come in. It's not like I can say no since her own tent burned down—because of me.

"What's wrong?" she asks when she sees my face. "Is it Carolina? I heard you two fighting." She bites her lip. "Do you want to talk about it?"

I shake my head. I don't know what to say. I'm not even sure what I feel.

I had a moment of clarity after I made my decision, after I told Sandra and Kevin I'd record with them on the last day of Killer Quest. I felt sure it was the right thing to do, that I was taking control. But then Carolina came along to muddle it all. To make me doubt myself. It ought to have been a win—I get to stay and finish out the contest—but I don't feel at all like celebrating.

"You're doing the right thing," Maggie says. "I'm sure of it." She kisses my cheek. "You seem like you need some alone time, so I'm going to go see what the Beastie Babes are up to at the campfire. See if I can score some sweet, sweet anecdotes for my paper. Maybe I'll throw out a comment about the sexualization of serial killers and watch them tie themselves into knots trying to rationalize it." She laughs.

I muster up a smile for her, but I feel too overwhelmed to try to talk. After she leaves, I lie in my sleeping bag and let the events of the day—God, what a long day—roll through my mind. Fleeing the campsite like a fugitive, finding the bear skeleton, confronting Noah, negotiating with Sandra and Kevin over my right to be here. And then fighting with Carolina too. I'm exhausted by all of it.

Hours later, Maggie returns, and I pretend to be asleep. Before long, she's out cold, breathing deeply beside me in her own sleeping bag, or someone else's she borrowed or stole, I guess. Yet all I can do is lie in the dark, haunted by bleached bones and burning flesh, yet more fodder for my nightmares.

Carolina was right about one thing: that Noah and I keep getting drawn together. I just don't understand why.

Attacking him that first day, then his weird terror later that night, his shaking finger pointing at me. And now this. I pushed him into the fire. I watched him burn. In the moment, it felt good. But now the memory makes me feel sick. What if the fire had spread? What if he ended up in the hospital? Or what if he'd pulled me into the flames with him?

If I didn't know any better, I'd say this has been orchestrated. Like Kincaid has come back to haunt me in another form.

But I refuse to believe that some supernatural force is making me act differently. I refuse to believe that anything is controlling me, pushing me into choices I wouldn't otherwise make. That's bullshit. Isn't the contest itself enough of a trigger? Could there be anything more stressful than hunting for my would-be killer's bones in the place he tried to kill me, surrounded by true crime freaks who are fascinated by him? Of course I feel afraid and angry. Of course I want to punish someone.

If I were home in my bed I would toss and turn, maybe turn on the light and read. But I don't want to wake Maggie, so I lie still, waiting for daylight, waiting for some glimmer of understanding. Finally, when the birds begin to wake and sing in the trees, I check my watch. It's just after five. Five in the morning, the camp still asleep in fog and darkness.

But I can't stay here any longer, can't lie here stinking of smoke and haunted by Kincaid, by Noah, by myself. As quietly as I can in the still-dark tent, I climb out of my sleeping bag and gather my things. Maggie murmurs in her sleep and turns over, but she doesn't wake. I crawl out into the cold, damp morning.

I know the way to the showers well enough to leave my flashlight in my pack. I walk softly down the worn path, toward where they are hidden behind a clump of trees. The sky is beginning to lighten from deepest black to smoke gray, a bare handful of hazy stars peeking out. Tufted titmice chirp and flit in the branches of the pines, joined by an occasional cardinal. A barred owl hoots somewhere in the distance—*who cooks for you, who cooks for you all?* But except for the birds, Cloudkiss Canyon sleeps soundly in its chilly blankets of fog, silent and still.

So why do I feel eyes on my back?

I turn, again and again, the hairs on my neck prickling. It must be anxiety, sleeplessness, paranoia. Because there's never anyone there. Just me and the birds and the slate-gray sky, its distant, faded stars. I wonder, not for the first time in the last two years, if anyone is up there watching. If anyone is up there caring what goes on down here.

Before Cloudkiss, before Kincaid, I would have said yes. My family went to church every Sunday, and I grew up in Sunday-school classrooms, church bazaars, summer Bible camps. God was a given, a benign background to the rest of my life. When I came out to my parents, they assured me that God loved me exactly as I am. So did my church. I didn't have the horrible experiences there I've heard about from others, of tearful parents, threats of conversion camps, or even the fake, silent judgment some of my friends endure. The church said God loved me as I was, and they meant it.

And when I escaped Kincaid, that same church said that God loved me, that God had saved me. And I wanted to believe them. They'd never let me down before. But I couldn't help wondering about all those other people God didn't save, the ones who got stabbed and cut and desecrated. Didn't God love them? Why did only I escape?

And so now I'm not so sure about God, about whether They exist, and if They do, whether They are watching. Or whether we're all on our own down here. I still go to church with my parents. I still sing the hymns and hug the old ladies. I still close my eyes and pray. But church, while still safe, still benign, seems a little emptier, a little more like praying to cold and distant stars that do not know my name.

I hope I'm wrong, but as I walk through the fogs of Cloudkiss Canyon, I do not feel the love of God, the protection of the Holy Spirit. I feel only a malevolent regard from someone—or some*thing*. A cold and unyielding ill will that makes me clutch my jacket closer.

Finally, I reach the showers, which sit empty and silent in the fog. They are merely stalls arranged around two corners of the building. The barest nod to privacy.

Getting naked here doesn't sound at all appealing, but better that than the stink of Noah's burning jeans in my hair. I strip quickly, shivering so hard my teeth clack together. I turn on the water and hope desperately for it to turn from freezing to lukewarm at the very least. The cold flows and flows around my feet, and I'm afraid I will die of hypothermia before it starts to warm. But at last it runs hot, piping hot, and I know it's going to leave my skin as red as a lobster, but I don't care. I duck my head under and lather shampoo in, scrubbing hard, my nails scraping my scalp. As I do, I start to cry, I don't even know why. Maybe because I'm alone, maybe because the water can hide it. Better here than while I'm kissing Maggie.

I scrub my body just as hard with the soap, still weeping as if I need to purge last night even from my tear ducts. If anything is out there, I don't care. I can't hear it; I can't see it. I just want to get clean.

Finally, when my skin is nearly blistered from the heat and the force of my scrubbing, I turn off the water and dry myself. I hurry into clean clothes, and even though I'm already shivering again, I decide to leave my coat off. Let it air out. I don't want its smoke stench on my body. At least I brought a spare hat to cover my damp hair. Why couldn't this stupid contest have been in the summer? I'd take the mosquitoes and ticks and poison ivy over the cold any day.

I check to make sure I have all my things before I head back toward camp. I start down the path, still fidgeting with my backpack. When I finally look up, I'm surprised to see it's nearly as dark outside as it was before my shower. The slate-gray sky is the same, only now the stars are gone. And so are the birds. Thick white fog rolls along the ground, and wispy, nearly translucent tendrils of it grab at the empty air like ghostly hands. The entire world is mist and vapor, all the paths and landmarks gone.

"Fuck," I whisper softly. I could go back to the showers, wait there until the fog dissipates. I turn back, but the building I left has vanished. A wall of white fog has taken its place. It's like I'm inside a snow globe, only instead of fluffy white snow and cheerful scenery, there is impenetrable mist and dread.

I stand motionless on the path, trying to think. Fog is only dangerous if you try to move around in it, if you blunder into a pit or off a cliff or get lost in the woods. Or if you trust a serial killer to lead you out of it. But if I stay on this path, if I don't move, the fog will eventually lift. And then I can get back to camp, back to Maggie. I wonder if she is still sleeping. Or if she's up and worried about me. Not that Maggie worries. I know some people would call her careless, thoughtless, and maybe she kind of is. But no one's perfect, and Maggie takes everything with a lightness that I envy. Even before Kincaid, I wasn't like that.

Carolina will worry though, I realize, wincing at the memory of how coldly I spoke to her, how I took out all my anger on her. It's like she's decided she's my personal protector or something. Maybe I should be grateful for it, but her concern feels like a suffocating blanket, reminding me that I'm someone others think needs protection. That I'm weak, vulnerable. Maggie doesn't treat me like that. Maggie doesn't *see* me like that.

So I'll be the person Maggie sees, I decide, squaring my shoulders as I peer into the ever-deepening fog.

Leaves rustle somewhere behind me, off to one side. I close my eyes. It was probably a squirrel. I wait, every nerve of my body straining to hear. The sound comes again, only this time it's longer, more drawn out, like someone dragging their feet through dead leaves. My heart rate accelerates, and my breathing goes shallow.

A wind kicks up, making the treetops moan. The fog above me dances, sinister and strange. A cold breeze hits the back of my neck, making me shiver. Footsteps come toward me from the direction of the showers, the unmistakable sound of heavy boots.

"Who's there?" I call. Despite the cold, despite my wet hair and lack of a coat, I begin to sweat. I squeeze the puffy coat in one fist, waiting. But the footsteps come on, only now I can't tell where they are coming from, the fog making them seem to come from nowhere and everywhere at once. Dizziness makes me sway on my feet, and my vision fills with pinpricks of light.

The wind comes again, and this time it brings more than the smell of moss and mist, earth and pine. Spicy cologne drifts into my nose. I turn, and that's when I see him. Kincaid, emerging from the thickest fog, his face pale, his eyes nearly black with pupil.

And I know I can't be what Maggie sees. I can't reclaim what she says I'm meant to reclaim. I can only shake and scream and wish more than anything to be home, in my bed, with my mother in the next room.

But that's impossible. My only option is to run.

I bolt forward, blindly, heedlessly, into the gray. My backpack slaps my back with every step, the only sensation that makes me feel real in an empty expanse of nothing, with Kincaid's footsteps still coming steadily behind me. At first, I can feel the hard-packed earth of the path beneath my boots, but then I lose it, blundering into leaves. I veer back to the right, but it's gone. Instead, I run into a tree, crashing painfully into it with my shoulder.

I cry out as I fall onto a prickly bed of pine needles, but I roll back to my feet and push away from the tree, my hands outstretched. After a few steps, I don't encounter more trees, so I start running again.

Still, impossibly, Kincaid's footsteps hound me. How can he see me in all this fog? Why isn't he lost and running into things like I am?

Because, I realize, he's dead.

Joseph Kincaid is dead.

It's his ghost that pursues me.

Terror seizes me and I scream again; I can't help it. I should be quiet, but I can't keep my panic inside anymore. Maybe someone will hear me, maybe someone will come.

But no one does. I run and run and run, and no one comes. I'm alone in the fog with the ghost of the Cloudkiss Killer. What's the point of finding his bones if even death can't stop him?

I careen once more into a tree, only this time when I fall, the ground doesn't stop my progress. I crash down through rocks and leaves, brambles and vines, scrambling desperately for something to cling to—before I'm tumbled off the edge of the world, swallowed by fog, never to be seen again. I can feel it, the yawning emptiness of the canyon below, waiting hungrily for my bones.

My fingers scrabble for purchase, nails breaking, thorns stabbing into my palms. But I just keep falling, down and down, a rock cracking into my rib, tearing a gash through my sweater. A branch scratches across my face, and I shriek. This time the fog doesn't swallow my voice. I hear my own scream echo back to me, magnified and terrible.

Finally, I thud painfully into a tree jutting out of rock, my stomach slamming into it so hard the breath is knocked from my body. I lie stunned for several long moments, my whole being focused on trying to rake oxygen back into my lungs. My chest burns for lack of air.

Once I'm breathing normally again, my body floods with pain. I'll be lucky if I didn't crack a rib, if I don't have internal bleeding. I stare down into the canyon, into the fog that's thick as stew. I was one tree away from tumbling into it. I'm not convinced I would ever have hit the bottom. I think the fog might have swallowed me whole and left nothing behind.

I need to get back to camp. I need to get to Maggie and Carolina. But what if he's still up there, waiting for me? I peer up the cliffside. I didn't fall nearly as far as it seemed, only a few yards really. But the fog looks thinner above. The sun is finally starting to rise, sending a yellow band across the gray sky.

With agonizing effort, I climb to my hands and knees. My head spins, and I have to grip tightly to some saplings and close my eyes to stop the vertigo. I go the whole way up like that, a few feet at a time, my arms shaking with effort. Finally, I heave myself back over the edge.

Exhausted to my very marrow, I lie on my back in the cold dirt and breathe painful, jagged breaths for a long time. Finally, I push myself to my feet and stagger toward camp, which turns out to be much nearer than I'd imagined. Everyone is awake, milling around, talking in hushed voices. People stare at me as I pass, their eyes huge. No one approaches or asks if I need help, though I know they can see I'm bleeding.

And then Maggie appears. "Shit, Lucy, what happened?" she asks, hurrying toward me, her hair still mussed from sleeping. "We all heard someone screaming. Was that you? We did a head count, and it's just you and Carolina and Noah missing. Was Carolina with you?"

I shake my head. "I—"

"Oh my God, Luce, you're a mess." She surveys me from my snotty, tearstained face to my torn and bloodied clothes. "What the hell happened?"

To my dismay, I burst into a fresh round of tears.

"Come on," Maggie says, tucking an arm around my waist and guiding me back to our tent. "Let's get you cleaned up."

I crawl gratefully into the tent and ease down on top of my sleeping bag, my backpack still on my back. At least I didn't lose it, like I lost my coat. I shiver, and Maggie grabs her sleeping bag and unzips it before throwing it over me. Then she scoots in behind me and lays down, pressing her body against my back and wrapping her arms gingerly around me. Even though she's gentle, I wince at the pain in my side. But her nearness feels too good to ask her to let go.

"Tell me what happened," Maggie whispers. "Who hurt you?"

But I have no words. All I can do is shiver and weep. Kincaid is out there, and I guess haunting my memories isn't enough for him—now he's trying to kill me. Again.

# SIXTEEN

## CAROLINA

### DAY 4

**I come to** suddenly, jolting into horrible awareness. It's cold and foggy, light just beginning to break through the trees. My breath plumes the air in agitated puffs, and my heart races. I'm standing in the woods, fully dressed, wide awake.

I don't know how I got here. When I got here. Or why.

My mind spins through possibilities, each one more terrible than the last. Why am I out here? What did I do? *Oh God, what did I do? And who did I do it to?*

I spin around, my frantic movements stirring the dry leaves underfoot, but there are no clues to orient me. There's no one else here. Only me and the trees and the fog. I strain my mind, trying to recall something, anything to explain my presence here.

I remember having dinner at Sandra's cabin. I remember fighting with Lucy. I remember going back to my tent alone, feeling like shit because Lucy can't seem to stop thinking the worst of me. I was angry and embarrassed and—

Panic shoots through me. *Lucy.* I had been so angry at her. What if I did something to her? What if I hurt her?

The now-familiar image hits me like a freight train: *Lucy's open, staring eyes. Blood on my hands.*

I stand still, listening hard, my breath lodged in my throat. I can barely make out the low hum of conversation from the camp. People waking up, having coffee, making plans for the day. I follow the sound of their voices, my heart beating a staccato rhythm in my ears. When I break out of the gloom of the woods, I'm standing near the edge of the canyon, where light pierces in shafts through the fog, highlighting the red-and-brown trees in the distance.

All is still and peaceful. No one is out looking for me.

I didn't do anything. I didn't hurt anyone.

I let out my breath in a relieved whoosh, feeling the shaky panic slowly leave my body. Not quite ready to face the others, I walk along the rim of the canyon, watching the light change. My heartbeat slows gradually, becomes a dull metronome again. With a clear head, I take stock of myself: there is no blood on my hands, no dirt or grime on my clothes. I am damp with dew and my feet hurt, as if I walked a long way in these horrible boots. I must have been sleepwalking.

That's all. Just sleepwalking.

So why can't I shake off this dread that's settled over me like mist?

I start toward camp, but after only a few yards, my boot slips on something and I nearly fall. It's a woman's green parka, worn and a little shabby. L.L.Bean but vintage. It's Lucy's. She said it was a hand-me-down from her mom. Lucy loves this jacket.

A cold wave of panic rushes through me, sending ice to my fingers and toes. A flash of memory—blood and screaming.

Half frozen, I turn slowly, searching the area for Lucy or some clue of where she's gone. But there's only the parka, cold and damp and still reeking of last night's fire. Horror sinks its claws into my chest.

I was angry at her last night, hurt. I must have done something to her. I must have hurt her. Is her body lying somewhere, like Kiersten's was? Is she bleeding? Is she dead?

Tears prick my eyes as I stride toward camp, but I try, desperately now, to think of other excuses. She went out for a walk and got hot and took off her coat. She dropped it by accident and didn't notice.

I want to believe it, but I can feel the monster inside me— the evil, dark, churning thing. What did it do to her?

I walk faster, rushing through camp. People stare at me as I pass them, their gazes suspicious. Addison narrows her eyes at me, and Levi looks as if he means to call out to me. But I don't stop, don't even acknowledge them. I need to know the truth, no matter how horrible. I go straight to Lucy's tent, which is zipped up. Low voices come from inside. I hear Maggie speaking, and then a short, jagged-sounding answer from Lucy.

The sound of her voice nearly drives me to my knees.

She's alive. At least she's alive. She's safe. She's with Maggie.

I consider leaving the jacket and going back to my tent, but I need to make sure Lucy is all right. I need to find out if I did anything to her. My heart pounds, my hands are clammy, and a metallic taste spreads across my tongue. I clear my throat, trying to steady myself.

"Lucy?" I call, hovering at the mouth of the tent. "It's Carolina. Are you— Can I come in?"

The tent flap unzips and Maggie's face appears. "Where have you been?" she asks, her voice uncharacteristically strained. "Something happened to Lucy."

Cold panic grips me again. "Is she all right?"

Maggie studies me, her brow furrowed. "Come in. Maybe you can get her to say what happened."

I want to. I want to go in and see her, make sure she's okay. But what if I go inside the tent and Lucy takes one look at me and screams? I hesitate, biting my lip, while Maggie stares at me.

Nothing for it but to find out. I crawl inside the now-cramped tent, leaving the flap open to let in the light—and so I can get out of here fast if I need to. "Lucy, I found your jacket," I tell her gently.

She's lying on her side, shivering, her face a mess of tears. But when she sees the parka, she sits up and reaches out for it. She gathers it to her chest and hugs it close, despite its stench. "Thank you," she says. She stares at me, her bottom lip and chin trembling.

"Are you ready to tell us what happened?" Maggie asks her gently.

Lucy closes her eyes and sighs. Her shoulders slump. "I went to take a shower, and on my way back, someone was following me."

My breath catches in my chest.

"It was foggy and I ran. I was so scared. I fell and rolled down the cliffside. I almost—" She gasps, as if reliving a memory. "I could have died."

"Who was it? Did you see who chased you?" I ask, my voice shaking.

Lucy looks up and meets my eyes again, and fear fills me. She's going to say it was me. She's going to demand to know what I was doing.

But Lucy shakes her head. "You won't believe me."

"Why not?"

"Because the person who chased me is dead."

Maggie and I exchanged a bewildered glance.

"It was Kincaid," Lucy clarifies. "I saw him."

"Joseph Kincaid, the Cloudkiss Killer?" I ask stupidly, barely able to think through a rush of relief. She didn't say it was me.

Maggie rolls her eyes at me before turning back to Lucy. "Luce, you were scared. You imagined it."

"No," Lucy says, her voice sure. "I know what I saw. And it wasn't the only time. I saw him on the first day of the contest too, right after I met you, Carolina. I thought it was just anxiety, but . . ." She shakes her head. "It was him."

"You think you're being haunted?" I ask.

Maggie scoffs. "There's no such things as ghosts."

I'm not sure whether I believe it's a possibility or not. My grandmother called out to my dead grandfather all the time when she was sick, staring across the room and gesturing at an empty wall. Was he there, or did she simply need him to be?

"Well, then maybe he's not dead. He's not dead, and that's why the police never found his body," Lucy says, her voice going up half an octave.

"Lucy, that's ridiculous," Maggie says. "You can't possibly think—"

"What other explanation is there?" Lucy demands, anger edging her words.

Me. I'm the other explanation. She thought it was Kincaid, but it must have been me. I was jealous of Lucy and Maggie's kiss, of their nights in the tent together. I was pissed at Lucy for refusing to listen to me, for practically throwing her feelings for Maggie in my face.

I must have acted on that jealousy and anger. Chased Lucy, terrified her—

"Noah," Maggie says, interrupting my rising panic.

"What?" Lucy and I say at the same time.

"What if it was Noah?" Maggie asks. "He looks so much like Kincaid, especially with the clothes he keeps wearing. He could have been following you."

Lucy pauses, considering. "I guess it's possible. It was really foggy. But he looked exactly like Kincaid, every single detail."

"Maybe you saw Noah and your brain filled in the rest of the details because you were so scared. You saw what you were most afraid of," Maggie says. She turns to me. "Don't you think so, Carolina?"

"Yeah, that could happen," I say. And I mean it—it's the most logical-sounding explanation. If I hadn't just come to in the woods near Lucy's discarded coat, I'd think Maggie was right.

"Seriously, Noah makes way more sense than ghosts," Maggie says. "He wasn't in camp this morning. It could easily have been him. Actually, it could have been him the first time you thought you saw Kincaid too."

"But I'd just gotten here. No one knew who I was yet," Lucy says.

Maggie's eyes widen, as if she's realized something. "I bet he knew who you were all along, since the first day. Maybe this whole time he's been orchestrating run-ins with you. He's been trying to frighten and provoke you. The cologne, the glasses, the clothes . . . that absurd stunt when he ran out of the woods screaming and pointed at you. It's too much to be a coincidence."

"But he was so rattled when Lucy confronted him at the fire last night," I point out, though I'm not sure why I'm defending him. "I don't think he'd seek out more of it."

"But the clothes, the whole cosplay act," Lucy ventures. "It's not normal."

"Yeah," I say, "but maybe he's been doing all that stuff for reasons that have nothing to do with you, Lucy. I mean, Brandon told me that Noah is a fan of Kincaid's, that he admires him. Thinks of him as an artist. That's why he's imitating him, not to scare you."

Maggie raises her eyebrows. "If Noah is a Kincaid fanboy, if he wants to be like his serial killer hero, wouldn't it make sense for him to come after Lucy?"

Lucy's face is drawn in concentration now, her eyes flicking back and forth like she's sorting through memories. "What if—maybe this is paranoid, but what if the real reason he came here was for me, not to hunt for Kincaid?" She looks up at us, dismay written plainly on her face.

"But how would he know you were going to be here?" Maggie asks. "You registered with your grandma's name and everything."

Lucy shakes her head. "How do these assholes know anything about me? Information leaks all the time. My full name, my picture—we couldn't keep them off all the fan message boards. Someone who works for *Human Beasties* could have made the connection and shared it on Reddit or something. Or one of the other contestants did some online sleuthing. Who knows?"

"Shit," Maggie says. "You're right. He definitely could have known you'd be here."

"Aren't we jumping to conclusions?" I ask.

"Some conclusions are so obvious you can skip the steps in between," Maggie shoots back. "Whether he knew Lucy would be here or not, he would have recognized her straightaway. Noah has means and motive and plenty of opportunity out here in the wilderness."

"To do what?" Lucy asks, her arms around her knees.

Maggie bites her lip, her eyebrows furrowed. She doesn't want to say the words, so I say them for her. "To finish Kincaid's last project."

"To kill me?" Lucy asks, her voice hardly more than a tear-filled croak.

Maggie nods, her face grave.

Lucy's head drops to her knees. She's clearly exhausted and overwhelmed. This is the moment to act, to convince her to go home. Where she'll be safe.

I put as much conviction into my voice as I can. "Lucy, Noah has been messing with you. Maybe he even wants to hurt you. That means it's not safe for you here. I know you don't want to hear this, but you should go home. Right now. Get in your car and drive away as quick as you can, and don't ever look back."

Lucy finally raises her head, and her eyes meet mine. She looks haggard, dark circles under her eyes, her skin pale. She looks like a girl who's about to break. And I want to pull her close and hold her and tell her things will be all right, but that's the last thing she needs from me. "Go home, Lucy," I say instead. "Forget about this contest. Go to therapy like everyone else, make friends, get a girlfriend, go to college, and make a life for yourself. Because there's no life for you here."

Maggie looks between Lucy and me, incredulous.

"You're right," Lucy says, and all the tension drains out of my body. "You're right. I should have listened to you last night. You tried to tell me things between Noah and me didn't make sense. It was stupid for me to come here to begin with, and it's even stupider for me to stay. All I've gotten for my trouble is being stared at and whispered about and chased through the woods. I'll go home." She lays her cheek against her knees and lets silent tears stream down her face. That girl who negotiated with Sandra and Kevin last night, who yelled at me, is gone.

Maggie shakes her head, glaring at me. "Bullshit," she says.

"Excuse me?" I say.

"You heard me. That's bullshit. Everything you both said is fucking ridiculous. Go home? Lucy, you think you'll be safe if you go home? You think Noah or some other asshole won't just come after you there? You think you'll ever get free of Kincaid? You think he'll ever stop haunting you? If you run away now, you leave nothing behind except your spine."

"Hey, watch it," I growl, my hands balling into fists. "You have no idea what she's been through."

Maggie laughs. "Of course I do. Everyone here knows what Lucy has been through. And they look at her and they see Kincaid's victim. They see a little doe running through the woods, its white tail flashing, its eyes rolling with terror. They see someone weak and broken." Maggie turns back to Lucy and levels a ferocious stare at her. "That's why Noah is fucking with you, Lucy. That's why that dick Rufus cornered you by the bathrooms. That's why everyone whispers about you but can't quite meet your eyes."

Lucy's quiet tears grow into a gasping sob, her body shaking. I want so badly to reach out and hold her. To protect her.

But Maggie is a driving wind, relentless. "And you think you're the only person Noah will ever target? You think even if he leaves you alone, all the other girls like you will be safe? You have a chance to stop him before he really begins."

"Yes, by reporting him to the police," I butt in.

Maggie laughs. "Haven't you paid attention to the podcasts? Haven't you listened to enough stories like this? Lucy has no proof that Noah did anything to her. If anything, it's the opposite. She hit him. She pushed him into a fire. The police can't do anything about Noah. Maybe after he kills someone, but not now anyway."

Lucy slowly raises her head again. "And it's my job to stop him from killing someone? Is that what you're saying?"

"No," Maggie says, her eyes shining. "It's your *right*. It's your chance to break free of the things you came here to break free of. It's your chance to prove to yourself that you're more than Kincaid's last victim. That you're more than a broken girl. It's your chance to throw off your fear, tap into your power, and be the person you want to be. This isn't an obstacle to your freedom, Lucy." Maggie's voice trembles with passion. "It's how you get free."

Lucy's gaze is trained on Maggie, on her burning eyes and her hard-set jaw, and Lucy's eyes start to burn too. Her chin stops trembling, and her lips form a thin line. It's like Maggie's sureness passes from her and into Lucy, who raises her head high, looking nothing like the battered, terrified girl of a few minutes ago.

"Noah might be the next Kincaid. But you can stop him before he ever takes a life. *We* can stop him. Together," Maggie says, her voice softening on the last word. Her eyes go soft too, like she's just proposed marriage and not some absurd catch-a-killer scheme.

"Yes," Lucy says. "That's what I want. You're right." She wipes her eyes and turns to me. "Will you help too, Carolina?"

My heart sinks. But I can't possibly say no. Because what if I'm wrong and Noah really is after Lucy? Maybe my nighttime wanderings are nothing but that. Maybe Noah's the one who attacked Kiersten, not me. And if I leave, if I go home and leave Lucy here and something happens to her . . . I couldn't bear it.

Lucy is waiting for me to answer, her lips slightly parted. And I don't want to leave her, I realize. Maybe that makes me worse than I possibly imagined, but I don't want to go home and leave her here. I want to guard her with my body and my heart, and protect her from every possible harm.

"Of course I'll help," I say. Lucy smiles, tremulous and grateful, and the horror of the morning fades a little. I want to believe this theory about Noah. I need to believe it.

I need to believe that it's just this place that's getting to me. This place and my father's stories. I can't possibly be what he says I am. Not when I care so much. Not when I want so badly to be good.

So I stay. We talk for an hour, going over every single thing we've seen Noah do or heard him say since the first day. It's surprisingly easy to make a case against him, and soon I've nearly forgotten my fears about myself, the cold panic I felt in the woods, the fear of what I might have done. Noah's guilt seems more and more plausible, and I cling to it like a drowning man to a bit of driftwood.

But then Lucy shifts, drawing her parka across her lap. "How did you find my jacket anyway?" she asks.

The driftwood splinters beneath my fingers. I feel myself begin to sink beneath the waves. I pull out Lucy's loupe, which I still haven't returned, and squeeze the cold metal tight in my fist, as if holding it can make me see the world more clearly.

"Just luck, I guess," I say, not meeting her eyes.

Whatever Noah might be, that doesn't change what I am. What I might have done. What I might still do.

I need to be more careful than ever before.

Because there's a monster inside me, and it's clamoring for release.

# SEVENTEEN

## LUCY

**Carolina tries to** convince me to go back to sleep for an hour or two, but I can't. I'm wide-awake, the world sharp and clear in a way it hasn't been in years. Noah has been psychologically torturing me—following me around, trying to make me think Kincaid is still alive. Why? To make it all the sweeter when he finally kills me?

The thought runs through me like a jolt of electricity. Noah wants to kill me. He wants to do what Kincaid couldn't. And he nearly completed the job this morning, whether he meant to or not. It was a near thing.

Pain lances through my side every time I move, reminding me just how close I came to death. I put my hand against my ribs and close my eyes. I have to let the pain keep me awake, keep me sharp, keep me from giving into the fear.

When we finish discussing Noah, Carolina looks at me like she's seeing my injuries for the first time, taking in all the cuts and bruises. She wants to drive me to the hospital, but when I refuse, she insists on examining me herself. It's like our fight yesterday never happened, like the hard words I spoke to her never touched air. She has forgotten or forgiven me, which either way makes her a kinder person than I'll ever be. But I let the fight go too because there are bigger things to worry about now.

Instead, we head to the bathrooms in the lodge, where people are visiting the canteen and eating their overpriced breakfast bars. Carolina makes sure no one is in either of the stalls before she locks the door. "Show us," she says grimly.

"She's fine," Maggie argues.

I'm not. I have a long, shallow scratch across my cheek. Three broken and bleeding fingernails, dirt-filled scrapes and gouges all over my hands. That's only the damage other people can see.

But Carolina's not going to let us get on with our day until I show her. I pull off my shirt and my pants, and stand in the dim light of the bathroom in only my sports bra and underwear. Stripping in front of other people doesn't bother me after so many years of playing sports. Bodies are just bodies.

Carolina gasps at what she sees. "Oh, Lucy," she says, tears in her voice. Her eyes travel from my shoulders to my shins, and I can feel each bruise under her gaze. "May I . . . ?" she asks, her Georgia accent breaking through. I nod, and her fingers touch my cheek, and then my shoulder. Her touch is warm against my cold skin, soft and endlessly gentle. But when her fingers graze my side, where I smashed into the tree that saved my life, I flinch and suck in a breath.

"Lucy, won't you please go to the hospital?" she asks again. "It would probably only take a few hours."

"It's only bruised," I say. "I've taken first aid classes. There's no serious swelling, and it doesn't hurt to breathe. I was lucky."

"Lucky," Carolina scoffs.

I look over my shoulder to Maggie for help. She's leaning against the locked door, watching us impassively. "If Lucy says she's fine, she's fine," Maggie tells Carolina.

Carolina clenches her jaw. "Don't you care that—"

"Of course I care," Maggie interrupts. "But Lucy's capable of deciding what's best for herself. You can stop babying her."

Carolina huffs. She starts to clean the wounds on my hands, and I let her. Her movements are sure but gentle, wiping away the dirt and blood.

"Great ass, by the way," Maggie says with her crooked grin. She quirks her eyebrows at me.

I laugh and immediately have to clutch my side.

Maggie winces in sympathy. "We'll load you up on Tylenol and ibuprofen and you'll be right as rain," she says. "I'm sure we could even snag some pain pills off one of the bachelorettes. You can put your clothes back on now—unless the doctor objects." She lifts an eyebrow in Carolina's direction.

"I guess I'm outvoted," Carolina says sadly, throwing away the bloody paper towels.

"I'm fine," I tell her again. "I swear, if I thought I needed the hospital, I would go." Is this really the same girl who said serial killers make her feel better about herself? Who's torturing herself over some person she hurt? She's a mother hen, clucking at her chicks.

But not Maggie. She's still practically vibrating with the excitement of our plan. Not that we really have one yet. Just to get Noah before he can get me.

"Let's go eat breakfast and figure out what's next," Maggie says. I start pulling my clothes back on, slowly and carefully. I manage my flannel shirt, but Carolina has to help me pull on my fleece. She zips it up slowly, and when her eyes meet mine, I find it hard to look away from her. Her eyes are warm and worried, glancing across my wounds like she feels every one herself.

We head into the canteen, and I buy pain meds and a granola bar, along with a protein shake, which is all I have the appetite for. I keep my head down, ignoring the curious glances of the other contestants. There are a few genuinely concerned looks thrown my way, but I ignore them too. I pray to God that Noah doesn't walk in. I'm not ready to see him yet. Not ready to face him.

Carolina waits for me to pay, and then we carry our breakfast to our usual picnic table. It's freezing outside, but the cold is more comfortable than being watched by everyone indoors.

Maggie's already sitting on the top of the picnic table, grimacing her way through a cup of bitter tar-colored coffee. She's still wearing black jeans and a denim jacket, but she at least added a black wool scarf as a nod to the bone-chilling cold. She fiddles with it constantly as if it itches, drawing my attention to her hands. Her fingers are slender and delicately boned, but strong, like a pianist's. Her nails are neat but clipped short and unpainted. She said once that she changed her major from music composition. I wonder if she plays the piano. She hardly ever talks about herself in any really personal way, always preferring to spin stories and theories about everyone else. I'll have to remember to ask her about it.

Some other time. When we're not plotting the downfall of a copycat killer.

"Okay, so here's what I'm thinking," Maggie says, hopping off the table and onto the bench, while motioning for us to take the other side. She does all this without spilling her coffee, an excited gleam in her eye. "Today's all about gathering information. Let's really get to know our Noah, see where he goes and what he does, who he looks at and who looks back, that sort of thing."

"What's our endgame here?" Carolina asks. "What are we hoping to do?"

But Maggie shakes her head. "No, we're not there yet. Today's all about recon. We need to do our homework. Find out what's possible. Work up our imaginations." She grins. "And let's give Lucy a taste of turning the tables. Last night he hunted you. Today you hunt him."

I feel a smile pull my lips. I like that idea. Let him be the prey for once. I can't believe I ever felt guilty for hitting him or for pushing him into the fire. He *did* deserve it, even if I didn't know it yet.

"You don't think he'll notice three girls following him all over camp?" Carolina points out.

"So let's give you another mission," Maggie says. "Why don't you cozy up to his roommate again? Ben or whatever. Blondie boy."

"Brandon. What for?"

"To find out how Noah has been acting here. Where he's been disappearing to and how he accounts for it. That sort of thing."

"What makes you think Brandon will tell me anything?" Carolina asks. "He's barely looked at me since the morning we found Kiersten."

Maggie smirks. "I'm sure you'll think of something. Just remind him what he liked so much about you on the first day."

Carolina's face colors, and Maggie lifts her hands, conciliatory. "Hey, I'm not slut-shaming. No Puritan ethics here."

"Fuck you, Maggie. I'm not going to throw myself at him to get information," Carolina says. She glowers at Maggie, her arms crossed over her chest.

I interrupt before Maggie can come up with a clever retort that will only piss Carolina off more. "I think what Maggie means is that you're really good with people. I know some of the contestants are suspicious of you, but you were so nice to everyone on the first day and everyone clearly liked you. You can get back on Brandon's good side easily—just be yourself. Be friendly and, you know, caring . . . like you've been to me."

I think of her soft fingers on my skin in the bathroom this morning, and heat rises up my neck. If Maggie hadn't kissed me first, would something more have happened between Carolina and me? Maybe. But I can't focus on that right now.

"Sure, all right," Carolina says. "For *you*."

Maggie clears her throat, impatient, maybe a little jealous too. Her eyes look smoky. "Anyway—"

"Wait," Carolina interrupts. "Let me tell you what I already know about Noah."

Maggie huffs but leans against the table and spreads her feet out on the ground, as if settling in. "Tell us, then," she says.

"Well, the morning that Brandon and I found Kiersten, we were actually out looking for Noah. It was super early, and he was just gone. Brandon said Noah had been really freaked out by whatever had happened the night before, when he came running out of the woods, remember? And he pointed at you, Lucy?"

As if I could forget that moment. His frightened face, everyone staring at me.

"But he wouldn't say anything more about what he saw in the woods. So he and Brandon went to bed, and Noah kept calling out in his sleep. He was clearly terrified.

"So obviously Brandon was worried when he woke up the next morning and Noah was missing. I mean, it turns out he was sleeping in his car, but that's why we went looking for him. But instead, we found Kiersten."

"But maybe Noah wasn't really sleeping in his car? That was just a weak cover?" I prompt. "And really he was out prowling. Maybe he went after Kiersten and that's why she fell?"

Carolina shrugs. "Maybe. Sleeping alone in a car isn't exactly an alibi. But why go after Kiersten if it's you he wants?"

"Maybe he has a type," I say, a shiver running down my spine. "Blond girls."

"Maybe," Maggie says, her brow scrunched up. "But that wasn't Kincaid's type, was it? He was an opportunistic killer. Anyone vulnerable would do. Men, women, any age."

"Maybe Noah's just not a very good fanboy," Carolina says.

"Okay, I have a theory," Maggie says. "About what Noah's long game might be. See, he could have tried to stay anonymous. Make sure no one would notice him. But he did something more proactive, to reverse the tables and make himself into a victim. First, he triggered Lucy with the cologne, and then he made people suspicious of her by pretending to be afraid of her that night by the fire. He knew he could push it even further by hurting Kiersten, hoping people would blame Lucy. It didn't entirely work, but he planted the seeds." She turns to me. "And then you pushed him into the fire. You gave him exactly what he wanted. What are people whispering about you?"

"That I'm a psycho," I murmur.

"Exactly. And Noah looks like someone you've targeted, not the other way around."

"Jesus," I say. She's right—I can see each step of Noah's plan laid out, all leading toward a trap for me.

But Carolina clearly isn't entirely convinced. "I don't know," she says. "It seems kind of convoluted to me."

Maggie shrugs. "Killers often see themselves as victims. Victims of childhood abuse, victims of man-hating women, victims of a world that couldn't recognize their greatness. Whatever. Noah's just taking it a step further."

"Okaaaaay," Carolina says, "but none of this makes sense or sounds right to me. He—"

"God, Carolina," I interrupt, impatient with her again. "You have to stop fighting me every step of the way. What did we talk about last night? About you not treating me like a child who can't think for herself or make her own decisions?"

Carolina's face turns crimson, and she opens her mouth only to close it again.

Maggie looks kind of pleased by my outburst, but then she shakes her head. "That's really not fair, Luce. It's always good to have a devil's advocate in the group. If Carolina isn't convinced, maybe there's a flaw in our thinking."

I close my eyes, biting back my frustration. "Look, Carolina, I'm sorry. I get why you're hesitant, but I saw him. I mean, I thought it was Kincaid, but that makes no sense, so it had to have been Noah. There's no other logical explanation. We could be wrong about everything else, but it has to have been Noah stalking me. Isn't that enough of a reason to look into him?"

Carolina nods slowly, and I can see we're starting to wear her down. She's starting to consider that Maggie and I might be right.

"I guess I know men like that," Carolina says. "Who blame the women they abuse, the children, always believing it's someone else's fault." She bites her lip, growing thoughtful, and I wonder what men she knows like that and why she knows them. She believes she hurt someone; that's why she's here. But what if the truth is that she's the one who has been hurt? And she's only been led to believe it's her fault?

But Maggie's already back to business. "Exactly," she says. "All right, then. Today we watch Noah, and Carolina talks to Brandon. Simple. If we're wrong, we'll ditch the whole plan and forget about Noah. But I really don't think we're wrong."

Maggie says she saw Noah go into the lodge while we were at the picnic table, so the three of us stand at the side of the building, pretending to confer over a map of the park. But really we're waiting. Finally, Brandon and Noah exit the lodge with the big, burly guy who cornered me outside the bathrooms. Rufus. A sour taste fills my mouth at the sight of him, and I remember the feel of his large hands on my arms, the tickle of his beard as he whispered in my ear. I glance at Carolina and see her jaw go hard when she notices him.

"Is he with them?" I ask Maggie. What if he's their required third member and I have to contend with both Noah and that guy? Anxiety writhes in my gut.

"It looks that way," Maggie says, pursing her lips. "Maybe Noah even told him to mess with you. But don't worry about him. Let's stay focused on Noah. He's the real threat."

She's right, so I force myself to ignore Rufus, keep my eyes on Noah. He really is completely unharmed by his encounter with the fire. I must have put it out in time before it could do any real damage. He ambles along beside Rufus, deep in conversation.

We let the guys get far enough ahead that they won't notice us following them. They've all got packs on and are clearly ready to set out for the day. I can't imagine how Carolina is going to manage to break Brandon off from the other two, though he does look like he'd rather be anywhere but with them, trailing several paces behind, earbuds in his ears.

We follow them for hours. After a long hike, they veer off from the waterfall trail and onto the gulch trail. They don't slow, so they're clearly heading much farther down than we've made it so far.

"Looks like their plan is the same as ours," I whisper. "To try the caves."

Carolina nods. "We can keep following them." She's been staring at the map as she walks, tracing the route with her finger. "This is a strenuous hike though, Lucy. Are you sure you're up for it?"

I sigh. "Yes, I'm fine. I might be injured, but I'll still fare better than you will."

"Play nice, Lucy," Maggie teases, giving me a quick pinch on the arm and winking at me. But Carolina ignores my barb and tucks the map back into the inside pocket of her jacket.

To my surprise, Maggie laces her fingers in mine, sending a thrill of electricity up my arm. I didn't think she was really the hand-holding type. I risk a glance at her and am surprised again: She looks happy, like really, truly happy.

A slow, goofy smile spreads over my face at the thought. I am making Maggie Rey happy. For a few minutes, I forget that we're stalking my would-be killer and whatever the hell that other guy is. I am just a girl holding a beautiful girl's hand in the woods. But then Maggie lets go to take a sip from her water bottle, and cold, moist air takes the place of her skin. Reality comes rushing back.

No, I am a traumatized girl stalking dangerous men in the woods.

But that's the thing. At least *I* am the one stalking them. Maggie was right. It does feel good to turn the tables.

After another hour of hiking, my side is screaming for rest, but I trudge on, down and down into the canyon, knowing that the climb back up will be even worse. We've been paralleling the creek for most of the way, the soothing sound of the water covering our voices and footsteps. A few times we lose sight of the guys around a bend, and my heart plummets into my stomach. But then they come into sight again, still making their slow and steady way down into the bowels of the canyon.

A sign says there's a picnic area in a quarter of a mile, and I remember it from my last trip here. A single picnic table under a tree beside a turquoise pool of water. It's a beautiful spot. They are sure to pause there for a rest.

"Stop," I hiss to Maggie and Lucy. "Stop."

"Hmm?" Maggie says, coming out of a reverie.

"Are you in pain?" Carolina asks.

I am, but that's irrelevant. "They're going to stop up here, and if we keep following them, they'll see us."

Maggie rubs her hands together in mock-diabolical glee. "Then our moment has arrived. Let's sneak up and spy on them."

"I don't know," Carolina says. "Is it—"

Maggie interrupts her. "What do you think we're doing out here? This is our chance. Otherwise, all we've done is go for a nice autumnal hike."

"She's right," I say, giving Carolina an apologetic look. I feel bad that I'm always snapping at her and taking Maggie's side, but this is what we agreed to. "Let's take our chance while we've got it."

"How? Where will we hide?" Carolina demands. "Most of the trees are bare. There isn't much cover. They'll hear us if they don't see us."

I point to the left, where huge boulders cluster and climb above the pool. "There's a little trail behind them we can take and then climb up. We should be able to watch them and probably hear what they're talking about."

I climbed those same boulders with my little sister two years ago. We lay flat in the bramble and listened to our parents' voices float across the water. They were making plans for the next day, of which trail we should hike, which nature talks we should go to. Whether it was worth paying for the ranger-led hot-chocolate hike when we could run to the grocery store in town and buy a whole box of cocoa for two bucks.

We never did any of that. Joseph Kincaid put a swift end to our vacation the next morning.

But I won't be chased from this place again.

"Come on," I say, leading the way. The trail offshoot is just as I remember it, narrow as a deer track, curving around a patch of elms. You'd miss it if you didn't know it was there. Maggie and Carolina follow me without comment, and it's strange to be in the lead, strange to be the one with a plan. But it feels good too.

When we reach the boulders, I hear Carolina sigh behind me. I'm not sure whether she's sighing because she'll have to climb the rocks or because I will. Probably the latter. I feel a flash of annoyance at her mothering, but I let it go. Honestly, I'm nervous about this climb too, worried I might worsen the injuries I've already got. But if my little sister, who was only nine at the time, could manage it, surely I can handle it. Besides, we don't have to go all the way to the top. We just need to get close enough to listen.

I survey the gray boulders, which are slick with moss and algae, and covered in lichen, like barnacles on the hull of a ship. Ferns grow out of the gaps, their leaves still verdant green, even in this autumn landscape. I think errantly of Carolina's story, the little signs of life growing on tombstones. If we weren't spying on a couple of sickos, I'd tell Carolina to pull out the loupe I loaned her and finally take a good look at the lichen.

Instead, I choose a point of attack: a waist-high, nearly flat rock. I put my hands on its surface, ready to push myself up, but the barest pressure makes my bruised ribs scream.

"We'll boost you up," Maggie says, realizing my trouble. She makes a cradle for my foot, and when I step into it, she lifts me up while Carolina pushes from behind. I scramble onto the rock on my knees, gritting my teeth against the pain, and Maggie follows me up. Carolina comes more slowly, but I keep moving. The next few boulders are easier, and I'm soon high enough. I stop going up and crawl forward to reach the side that hugs the water.

And there they are: Brandon, Noah, and Evil Bearded Dude, aka Rufus. They throw off their packs and collapse onto the picnic table. They are silent for a few moments, intent on drinking water and cramming protein bars into their mouths.

"Guys, are you sure about this route?" Brandon says, staring away down the trail. "I mean, this is a long, long way from where our dude fell off the cliff." He pulls his curly hair up into a bun, tying it off with an elastic from his wrist.

Rufus wipes his mouth with a meaty paw. "If his body was closer, they'd have found it already. I'm telling you, if we're gonna find him, we're gonna find him out here. If he's here at all."

"What's that supposed to mean?" Brandon says. "Earlier, you told me a coyote probably dragged his nasty carcass away."

Rufus shrugs his hulking shoulders. "Some of us aren't sure he died. We think he faked it. More than a few people on the message boards have said they spotted him out here, hiding out in the caves."

A tremor runs from the base of my skull and down my spine, settling with a cold weight in my stomach.

"What message boards?" Brandon asks, suspicious. He glances at Noah, who stares off into the distance.

"Where your boy Noah and I met," Rufus says, smacking Noah heartily on the arm, hard enough that Noah nearly pitches off the bench. "On the *Human Beasties* board. We dissect every episode, bring in new theories, that kind of thing."

"I told you," Maggie hisses. "They already knew each other."

I close my eyes, nauseated. I can only imagine what they've said about me on those boards—threads and threads of morbid speculation. Is that where Rufus found my picture, the one he showed me in the hallway?

"Man, what if we find him alive?" Rufus says, his voice laced with excitement.

"If he's alive, we don't get any money," Brandon points out.

"I don't need money. I'm an investment banker," Rufus says with a guffaw before turning to Noah. "What'd you bring this guy for anyway?" Rufus asks. "He's a wet blanket."

"Just because I'm not obsessed with a guy who killed people and cut them up and displayed their bodies like fucking museum pieces, I'm a wet blanket?" Brandon says, incredulous.

"Don't you have any darkness in your heart?" Rufus asks, leaning toward Brandon, his face lit with the kind of fervor you see on those TV preachers. He's a believer, like Noah. "Haven't you ever wanted to do something bloody and terrible, and only stopped because you don't want to go to prison?"

"No!" Brandon exclaims, pushing back from the table in disgust.

"See?" Rufus says. "Wet. Blanket." He laughs, the sound booming out. There's something unnerving about him—the combination of jollity and violence, like a satanic Santa.

But Noah is unnerving too, sitting there quiet as a cat. What schemes is he dreaming up? What desecrations is he planning?

Brandon seems to be wondering the same thing. He stares down at his roommate, biting his nails and waiting. For what? For him to be disgusted by Rufus too?

"Noah, I don't like this," Brandon says, rubbing the back of his neck.

Noah finally looks up. "Rufus is joking. And how are you creeped out by this? Look at the people who came to this contest. There's a bachelorette party, for God's sake. They could have gone to Nashville and hit the honky-tonks, but they're here. What does that tell you about true crime? It's harmless. How many times do I have to explain that to you? I don't judge you for listening to rap music about shooting people. Why are you judging me for this?"

"Are you seriously comparing—" Brandon starts to say, but he's too angry to finish the sentence. "You know what? Fuck you. I'm going back to camp."

He throws his backpack on and thuds away from the picnic table, his boots scattering leaves. "I should have stayed with Carolina," he yells over his shoulder.

"What a pussy," Rufus says. "That man bun tells you everything you need to know about him."

Noah laughs.

"Carolina," Maggie whispers. "Go. This is your chance. Follow Brandon back to camp and talk to him. He's pissed off at Noah, so it's the perfect time."

Carolina gives me one appraising look before climbing down. She must bang a knee or an elbow because she swears in a full Georgia drawl. I turn and see her slip down onto the next rock, flailing to free her one thigh that's stuck on the ledge.

The sight of her struggling down the rocks erases the last of my anger at her. I shoot her an encouraging smile as she finds her footing, and she gives me a cheesy thumbs-up before she disappears. As much as I've felt suffocated by her concern, I'm surprised to find her absence makes me feel . . . untethered. But I turn my attention back to the guys, hoping they'll speak more freely now that Brandon's civilizing presence is gone.

"You didn't actually believe any of that shit you just said, did you?" Rufus asks, leaning over the table. "About the bachelorettes?"

Noah avoids making eye contact with Rufus. "Of course not. But I've got to live with Brandon when we get back to campus. The last thing I need is him reporting me to the Title IX office or something."

Rufus guffaws and slaps Noah's arm again. This time Noah laughs too.

"I'm glad we teamed up. It was going to be boring as hell doing this whole week by myself," Rufus admits.

I glance at Maggie. So Noah and Rufus hadn't planned on working together. They teamed up for convenience. We were wrong about that. What else might we be wrong about?

"And I'm glad I didn't get stuck with that bitch Carolina," Noah says.

"Who was that anyway?" Rufus asks around a yawn.

"This slutty girl Brandon hooked up with on the first day. The one who's with Lucy Wilson now."

"Thunder Thighs?" Rufus asks. "She's hot, but that girl is crazy. The way she looked at me when she saw me talking to little Lucy. Wild. I'd like to take a run at her though."

Noah shrugs. "Not my type."

"I know. I've seen your twisted taste on Reddit. You like 'em young and scared and bleeding." Rufus laughs and smacks the table. "All right, let's get back to it." He climbs to his feet and throws his backpack on.

"Do you want to follow them?" Maggie asks, but I shake my head. I've heard enough.

Noah likes his women young and scared and bleeding. That's all I need to know. That's enough to convince me that even if we've gotten some of the details wrong, the heart of our plan is sound: Noah needs to be exposed for what he is. And I'm the one who needs to do it. I *want* to be the one to do it.

The cold pool of fear in my stomach hardens into ice and splinters into diamond-sharp shards.

Let him come for me.

He might find me young and scared and bleeding, but he won't find me unprepared.

# EIGHTEEN

## CAROLINA

**I scrabble down** the giant rocks, trying not to swear as my leggings catch on every uneven surface. After I tear a hole in the fabric at the back of my knee, I decide I'd better take my time climbing down. It's fine if Brandon gets ahead of me. I probably shouldn't approach him until we get to camp anyway so he doesn't get weirded out that I'm following him.

Finally back on solid ground, I start walking as quickly as I can manage on my tired, achy feet. It was bitchy of Lucy to say she'd handle this hike in her battered condition better than I would, but she wasn't wrong. I've never worked out or played sports apart from PE class. I put all my efforts into my academic subjects because it seemed the best possible means of escape. Get smart, get a degree, and get the hell away from where I came from.

And after college, I'll get even farther away. Move to London or Paris or Rome, live in cafés and museums. Surround myself with beautiful things, beautiful words, beautiful people. And those people will never know where I came from. My accent's already nearly gone. I'll scrub off the dirt of my family just the same. I'll be reborn—maybe I'll even change my name.

But can I scrub off the inside—this monster that's grown so big inside me it wakes me from my bed in the dead of night and sends me walking through the woods after a girl who picked someone else? A monster that wakens at the slightest reason, claws out, ready to devour? I thought coming here would make what happened with Michael all those months ago make sense. I thought I'd figure out who I am and lay Dad's stories about me to rest.

But I'm more lost than ever, less sure of myself than I ever thought possible.

I stumble over a root and flail in space for a moment before thudding painfully to my knees. "Fuck!" I grunt. When I look up, Brandon is staring at me from a few yards away, shadowed by the trees. I wasn't paying attention. I was so lost in thought, I forgot to watch for him. I forgot I was following him.

Shit.

"Carolina?" he asks, striding toward me.

"Hey," I say weakly from the ground. To my surprise, he offers me a hand up. I groan as he pulls me to my feet.

"You all right?" he asks.

"Yeah, just clumsy." I rub my smarting knees, and Brandon winces sympathetically.

"Why are you out here by yourself?" He looks around, as if searching for Maggie and Lucy.

"Why are you?" I shoot back.

Brandon laughs. "Fair enough."

"I have a headache, so I'm going back to camp," I lie. "My team is looking around the caves today."

Brandon's mouth thins into a line. "Mine too. I hope yours doesn't have the misfortune of running into mine."

"What do you mean?" I ask as innocently as I can. I turn and start walking toward camp, and Brandon follows.

"I honestly don't know what to believe anymore. It's this fucking canyon"—he gestures angrily at the creek and the trees, the ascending path—"it messes with your head, you know?"

"Sure," I say, noncommittal. I'm not about to reveal what's been going on in my head.

"I'm serious," Brandon insists, earnest now. "There's something wrong about this place, Carolina. Haven't you noticed?"

"I mean, it's foggy and a little scary sometimes," I say, hedging. "But I'm not really Nature Girl, so I figured this is what the great outdoors is like."

Brandon shakes his head. "It's not. My family visited a bunch of the national parks when I was growing up. We went to the Smokies, the Appalachians, Yellowstone, even up to Acadia in Maine. No place ever felt like this place."

"Maybe it's just the fog," I offer. "That's what freaks everyone out."

Brandon huffs, frustrated that I don't see his point. "Yeah, and about the fog—it doesn't make any sense for it to be so foggy all the time. The climatic conditions aren't right for it. There's no reason for constant mists, even with the waterfalls and everything. It's abnormal." He shivers.

That shiver reminds me of how Brandon behaved when he heard Noah screaming in the woods the night we were together—how afraid he was, how he said he felt that scream in his guts.

I study him, and I can see the signs of fear and weariness all over him: in the overgrown blond stubble on his face, the lines around his eyes, the way he keeps looking around, hyper-vigilant.

Haunted or not, I understand now how this canyon has gained its reputation. How its landscape and atmosphere work on people. Maggie was right: the canyon's isolation and severity make it into the perfect mirror to show us the darkest parts of our minds, the things we're most afraid of. We are jumping at our own shadows. Right? Because the alternative is . . .

I touch Brandon's arm, wanting to steady both of us. "I think you got spooked early on because of Noah's scream that night, and then we found Kiersten . . . so now the place feels threatening to you."

Brandon shakes his head but all he says is "Yeah, maybe."

"So how is Noah?" I ask as nonchalantly as I can. "Did he ever open up any more about what made him come screaming out of the woods?"

"Nah. He refused to talk about it after that night. The next day, he started acting like nothing had happened, and then things were so bananas with us finding Kiersten and then this guy Rufus joining our team." Brandon clenches his jaw. "I guess I didn't really know what I was signing up for coming here."

"Me neither," I admit. I wasn't prepared to come here and fall for someone. Wasn't prepared to watch her fall for someone else. Wasn't prepared to find myself sleepwalking all over the damn canyon, doing only God knows what. "You thinking about leaving early?"

"I drove here with Noah," Brandon says. "I'm stuck."

"Only a few more days." I offer him a sympathetic half smile.

"Look, Carolina," Brandon says, stopping in the path. He turns to me and looks me in the eye. "I wanted to say I'm sorry. It was a jerk move for me to drop you like I did. I just got weirded out. I don't even know how to explain it."

"You and everybody else," I say wryly. "Don't worry about it."

"That's what I'm saying." Brandon gestures emphatically toward camp. "Why are all these people so suspicious of you? You did, like, nothing. And your friend Lucy, they turned on her before they even all knew who she was. But why? Why would someone burn down your other teammate's tent? Why do they all act like you three are walking around here performing witchcraft and human sacrifices? You're just girls. Three girls, one of whom almost died because of their beloved Cloudkiss Killer. It's sick and it's twisted and it doesn't make any sense."

"Are you on about the canyon's mystical powers again?" I ask, squinting at him.

"Don't say it like that, as if I'm some New Age druid wannabe or something," Brandon says, laughing. "But yeah,

I mean, most of these people were normal when they got here. They were nice. A little weird maybe, a little too obsessed with true crime, but normal. Now . . ." He shakes his head.

"Has Noah done something?" I prod, trying to steer the conversation back to helpful ground.

Brandon bites his lip. "He keeps disappearing. Won't say where he's gone or why. Won't say what he did or who he was with. He's always been quiet, but now he's cagey, kind of secretive. I don't like the way he looks at the women here. I don't like that guy Rufus he's with. I just . . . I've got a bad feeling."

"Do you think he lied about sleeping in his car that night, that he had something to do with Kiersten?" I ask, my throat tight. I hate how much I want him to say yes.

Brandon grips his forehead and squeezes. "Gahhhh. I don't know."

"Do you think I did?" I ask quietly.

Brandon meets my eyes again, searching my face. His cheeks flush. "I'm sorry, but yeah, I did."

*And maybe you were right.*

"But I realize now I was wrong," Brandon says. "I let everybody here get to me. Let this place get to me. I haven't known you very long, but I do think you're a good person. A little intense maybe," he adds, raising his eyebrows and smiling, "but I think you've got a good heart. I've seen how you've been watching out for Lucy. She's lucky to have you on her team."

"Thank you," I say. I want so much to believe him. That my heart is good. That I am capable of goodness.

We hike in silence for a while, both lost in our thoughts and trying to keep breathing up this steep incline. But then I remember I haven't asked him everything I was supposed to. I don't want to deal with Maggie's attitude if I come back without the intel she wanted.

"So can I ask you something else?" I venture. "About Noah?"

Brandon nods, his eyes straight ahead.

"Before you came here, did he ever do anything that makes you think he might have been involved with what happened to Kiersten?"

Brandon exhales loudly. "There was this girl." He takes a minute to gather his thoughts. "Her name was Emily, and he was really into her. She was, like, very girl-next-door. White girl, long blond hair, wore all these, like, pastel dresses with little cardigans. She was pretty and really nice, so she actually talked to him sometimes in class and in the cafeteria. Which is more than he gets from most girls."

"Sure," I say, thinking of how he lit up at Maggie's attention that time at dinner.

"But then she just, like, out of the blue stopped talking to him. Would go in the other direction if she saw him. He clearly did something to scare her. When I asked him about it, he said he asked her out and it got awkward, but it really seemed like more than that."

"Wow." This is a neon red warning sign if I've ever seen one. "Did you ever talk to Emily?" I ask, trying to keep the accusation from my voice.

Brandon shakes his head. "I should have. But I let it go."
He pauses for a long time, as if wrestling with himself.
"Seems like I'm always letting stuff go with Noah. Maybe
I'm a shittier person than I thought." He starts chewing on
his thumbnail.

I could reassure him, but I don't. He should have talked to
Emily, should have looked harder at his roommate. Brandon's
feelings about Noah give me worse vibes than any of Maggie
and Lucy's theories about him. But maybe they're right, and
I couldn't see past my own hang-ups about myself. Maybe
Noah is targeting Lucy. Maybe he is more than a harmlessly
creepy guy. Maybe this is our chance to catch him before he
does something irreversible, something a girl like Emily or
Lucy can't walk away from.

And if Noah really is the one who went after Lucy this
morning, which seems increasingly possible . . . maybe I'm
not a danger to Lucy after all. Maybe I'm not the monster in
this canyon.

# NINETEEN

## LUCY

**We meet up** with Carolina again for a late lunch, and I'm surprised to find her more cooperative than she was before. She listens to everything Maggie and I say, and then shares what she learned from Brandon. When Carolina finishes talking, Maggie shakes her head. "Textbook stuff here, girls."

I think at this point I should be terrified, knowing that I'm sharing a campground with one, maybe two dangerous men. Knowing I'm Noah's target. Knowing what he is. But I feel a giddy expectation running like electricity through my limbs. For once in my life, when I feel afraid, I don't want to run from that fear; I want to let it reshape me, let it fuel me. I want to feel everything I feel and act on it.

"So we have a sense of who he is now," Maggie says thoughtfully. "He's different from Kincaid. Sexually motivated. He's clearly opportunistic and reactionary, emotional. He might worship the Cloudkiss Killer, but he's nothing like him. And that means he's going to be easy to catch," she says, a slow smile spreading across her face.

"What should we do?" I ask, my arms and legs tingling with excitement and nerves. "How do we prove any of this to the police?"

"We could get him on camera, try to get him to admit to why he's here," Carolina offers. She looks nervously around the picnic area, as if someone is eavesdropping in the trees.

Maggie chews her bottom lip. "That's a good idea," she says, "but we need more than that, I think. We need to catch him in the act."

"The act of what?" Carolina asks, her eager tone turning cautious.

"Murder," Maggie says, her eyes alight.

A shiver runs through me, half fear and half pleasure. "You have a plan?"

"I think so," Maggie says, "but it's risky." She waits for us to say something, biting her lip again. "It's a lot to ask of you, Lucy. But I wouldn't suggest it if I didn't think we could pull it off."

"Well, I don't like the sound of that," Carolina says.

I wave my hand to shush her. "Tell us. What do you want to do?"

Maggie leans forward. "We're going to set a trap for Noah, but we need bait." She raises her eyebrows and twists her mouth to one side, and I finally realize what she means.

"I'm the bait," I guess.

"Absolutely not," Carolina says. "It's too dangerous."

Maggie sighs. "Just listen, Carolina. Lucy can decide what she's up for. You know I wouldn't do anything to get her hurt." She turns back to me. "Here's what I'm thinking: at dinner tonight, we'll let Noah see how injured you are. We'll spread the word that we're camping alone in the canyon, make it clear where we're going to be. Maybe talk about how you're going to need to take a lot of breaks alone in the tent because of your injuries . . . or say we plan to split up to search more ground."

"And you think Noah will come to find me? Just like that?"

"I know he will. It fits his profile perfectly. He won't be able to resist the temptation."

"What if he doesn't come alone?" I ask, picturing the fervor in Rufus's face when he talked about violence.

"He'll come alone," Maggie says with certainty. "He wouldn't want to share the moment with anyone."

"And we'll do what?" Carolina asks, her voice shaking. "Secretly film him trying to attack Lucy?"

"Obviously," Maggie says. "And I bet you anything we'll get a confession too. He'll want to brag to Lucy about how he came here for her, how he has been tracking her, setting her up. And we'll record it all. Of course, we'll intervene before he can hurt Lucy."

"What if something goes wrong?" Carolina asks. "What if we don't get to Lucy in time? What if he really hurts her?"

"Then she'll use this," Maggie says, sliding a sheathed hunting knife across the table. It's Noah's.

I take it in my hand, my fingers gripping the worn leather. I pull the blade out, admiring the cold metallic sheen of it. Unbidden, the image of me stabbing it into Noah's chest, over and over and over again, appears. Except his face is Kincaid's.

When I look up, Carolina must see something of my thoughts in my expression because her mouth falls open.

"She's not going to have to use it," Maggie says with a laugh. "We won't let anything happen to her, I promise."

Carolina shakes her head. "It's too dangerous."

"I think it's just dangerous enough," I say, meeting her gaze without flinching. I find I want to meet face-to-face with Noah, to have a chance to redo what happened to me here two years ago. This time, I won't run. This time I'll fight back. This time, the bad guy won't get away. He'll have to pay for what he's done.

"Lucy, this isn't you," Carolina says. "The way you pushed Noah into the fire, the way you watched him burn . . ." Anxiety laces her voice. "I understand that you're angry and scared, but this plan is— Well, what if it leads you somewhere you don't want to go? What if it turns you into someone you don't want to be?"

"I'd rather be anyone than that girl you met at the start of this contest. I'd rather be anyone than the scared, weak shell of a person I was," I say evenly.

"What if you went home?" Carolina continues. "What if you let Maggie and me handle this for you? We could still get Noah," she pleads, though there's no conviction in her voice.

I shake my head. "Carolina, I know you care about me, but that doesn't mean you know what's best for me."

"I want you to be safe," she says earnestly, reaching across the table to take my hand.

"No, you don't." I snatch my fingers away, all my calm dissolving. I don't bother to keep my voice quiet this time. "You want to rescue me so you can feel better about yourself."

"That's not true," Carolina says desperately.

"I'll always be Kincaid's victim to you. You're the same as everyone else here."

"Is that what you think or what *Maggie* wants you to think?" Carolina spits Maggie's name like it's poison.

"Hey, leave me out of this," Maggie says, raising both palms in the air.

I feel a bitter laugh leave my throat. "See, Carolina? According to you, I can't even think for myself!"

"Lucy," Carolina says gently, her eyes suddenly damp, and my insides twist like she's gutting me with the hunting knife.

"Either get on board or butt out," I say. "We're going forward with this plan." And with that, I snatch up Noah's knife and stalk away from the picnic table, leaving Carolina standing there looking lost, her shoulders slumped in defeat.

There. That showed her. I'm not a baby. I'm not weak. I don't need her to save me.

After a few moments, I hear someone following me into the trees. Thankfully, it's Maggie. She throws her arm over my shoulder.

"That's my girl," she says admiringly, planting a kiss on my cheek. Pride surges through me, filling up the dark and gaping chasm that's been inside my chest for the last two years.

I am taking back my life.

# TWENTY

## CAROLINA

**I don't see** Lucy and Maggie for the rest of the day. I can't stop feeling shame flood through me every time I relive Lucy's words. Is that really how she sees me? As someone in her way? And does she really think I see her the same way the other Killer Quest contestants do—that when I look at her, I only see Kincaid's handiwork, a damaged girl?

Lucy's not the only one who escaped someone who tried to damage her irrevocably. How do I make her see how alike we are? How afraid I am that she might become what I am and lose her soul in the process? Because I wouldn't wish my monstrousness on her for anything. And this place—whether it's the fog or Maggie's influence or the atmosphere of the contest—it's having an effect on her that she can't see. It's driving her to the edge, and I'm afraid she's going to leap right off it.

I'm slumped over in the mouth of my tent, going over these thoughts for the thousandth time when Maggie appears, standing over me. "Knock, knock," she says.

I look up. Anger floods my entire body, filling my mouth with a metallic taste. "What do you want, Maggie?"

But Maggie acts like nothing happened earlier, her voice breezy. "You weren't at dinner. I thought you might be hungry." She hands me a hamburger wrapped inside brown napkins. "No fries, I'm afraid."

I was too upset to even think about dinner, but the smell of the food makes my stomach growl. Maggie laughs. "Just take it, please. Consider it a peace offering."

I accept the burger and, after a tentative bite, inhale the whole thing in a matter of minutes. I'm washing it down with water when Maggie finally speaks.

"Look, I'm sorry if you feel like you're being pushed out or something," she says. "Me and Lucy are . . . Maybe we've been a little wrapped up in each other." Maggie laughs nervously, running her fingers through her hair. "But I'm not trying to keep you two from being friends."

"Aren't you?" That's sure as hell what it feels like.

Maggie crouches down next to me. "I swear I'm not. Like, yeah, fine, I've been jealous of you a few times. I mean, look at you. Jesus. But I also know that Lucy needs a friend like you."

"You were jealous of me?" I ask incredulously.

"I mean, don't get bigheaded about it," Maggie says, smiling. "I want you to be her friend and to make sure we don't get too carried away. But I still think your worry for her is misplaced. I'm not pushing her to do anything she isn't up for. I just want to help her get what she came here for. She's got this fire inside her, and I'm trying to . . . let it out."

"I'm worried she's going to get hurt," I say. "Worse than she already has."

Maggie shakes her head. "She's stronger than she looks. She can handle herself. I mean, look at that beating she took from falling down the cliff, and she's still thrashing both our asses on the trail."

"True," I laugh. "She's like a little mountain goat."

Maggie cackles. "Do *not* repeat that to her. She'll totally headbutt you."

"She's hardheaded enough," I say ruefully.

"Exactly. So whether or not you think the plan is a bad idea, Lucy is going to go through with it," Maggie says. "Even I couldn't stop her at this point. She's made up her mind."

"I know," I say.

"And the plan will be a lot safer if you help."

"I guess."

Maggie puts her cool hand on my arm, and I finally look at her. The starlight glints in her strange gray eyes. Her mouth quirks into a contagious smile. "I'm asking for your help here. Groveling and everything."

I laugh, and in this moment, I see exactly what Lucy sees in Maggie. There's a quickness and lightness in her that neither Lucy nor I possess, and it's intoxicating. The thrill of letting go of solid earth and floating out over empty air.

"Plus, I've got booze," Maggie says, pulling a half-full bottle of whiskey from her buttoned-up jean jacket.

"Is that how you've been keeping warm?"

Maggie laughs. "I stole it out of some asshole's tent a few hours ago."

"Score."

"Come have a drink with us," Maggie says, lifting her eyebrows hopefully. "It's twenty-one-year-old Scotch for God's sake. Lucy wants you to come too."

"All right," I say, making my voice sound grudging, but really, I'm grateful. I don't want to sit alone in this tent for one more gloomy minute. I want to see Lucy—even if she isn't excited to see me. I want to be near her.

We walk in silence across the campground, away from the roaring fire, where half the contestants are gathered, laughing and joking and swapping theories about unsolved murders. The air is clear tonight, no fog to lead us astray. There's a nearly full moon and a sky full of stars, and a bottle of stolen whiskey to make us brave.

And when I catch sight of Lucy, her hair and skin dappled silver in the moonlight, I feel something I haven't felt in a very long time.

I feel my age. Only eighteen.

Not a monster, not a demon.

Just a human girl under an enormous, ancient sky.

An hour later, Maggie pours yet another shot of whiskey into my plastic cup. I've lost track of how many times the neck of the bottle has crossed the space between us. At first the whiskey tasted like expensive paint thinner, but now that my tongue is coated all over and I've gotten used to the way it burns going down my throat, I can see why rich old men like to drink it. It tastes like the world has been distilled into amber liquid, the sweetness and the smokiness, the shivery feeling of bodies touching, the sun setting over a briny ocean. The whole world in a glass.

I am nearly dizzy with pleasure. The tent glows softly with beeswax candles, the smell of honey permeating the space, working its way into my hair and my clothes, maybe even my skin. And Maggie is incandescent, laughing and telling jokes, every movement she makes beautiful and arresting. Lucy watches her with quiet, shining eyes, a perpetual half smile. I watch them both and am struck again and again by how lovely they are. They are like light rippling across water. And even though I wish Lucy were staring at me the way she's staring at Maggie, I still feel caught in their light, rocking gently in a small boat at sunrise, feeling as if every atom of me is the same as that light. As if there is no separation between us.

They must feel it too, because when I lie down with my head in Lucy's lap, she strokes my hair and Maggie smiles at me. I think this is what I imagined heaven would be like as a child, all soft light and a sense of rightness, your body floating and intermingling with everything else. No part of you is alone, no part of you lives in darkness.

Only that's not true. There is a part of me I can't show to the light. Even here, in the haze of candlelight and liquor, I can still feel it festering inside me like an ugly black wound.

"Hey, Carolina, you're from around here, right?" Maggie asks.

I nod and smile, trying to find my way back into the light.

"So why don't you have an accent?"

But I am in the water now, tossed in the waves. My mind moves slowly beneath its film of whiskey. "My accent? I trained it away."

"Like with a speech therapist?" Maggie asks, cocking her head at me like a bird.

I laugh, imaging her as a glittering bird, fluffing its wings. "Sorry, no, I did it by myself. Just got rid of it," I say.

"Why?" Lucy asks. "I don't mind my accent."

I turn over in her lap and gaze up at her. "Because one day I'm going to get away from here. I'm going to fly across the world and live somewhere else. And when people ask where I'm from, I'm going to lie."

Lucy frowns at me. "Are you ashamed of the South?"

*I'm ashamed of myself*, I think.

"Why are you ashamed of yourself?" Lucy asks, and I realize I didn't only think it, I said it aloud.

I close my eyes. I've held my secrets for so long, never breathed a word to anyone, except for Maggie, and only because she guessed. But before I can stop myself, the story is tumbling out. About my parents. What Dad was like when he came home from prison. How he told me, again, and again and again, that I'm evil. That I have an unclean spirit, a rebellious, wicked heart. A curse in my blood that will damn me.

"He was right. There's badness inside me," I say, a tear running off the edge of my cheek. With my eyes closed, I can see it, the darkness swirling in me, waiting for a chance to get out.

Lucy gently pulls me up from her lap and turns me to look at her. She cups my face in her hands. "He was wrong," she says, an angry certainty burning like fire in her eyes. "He lied to you. You aren't evil. You aren't demon-possessed. God doesn't hate you."

"How do you know?" I whisper.

Lucy smiles, candlelight turning her fair features angelic. "Because there's so much goodness in you, I almost can't stand it. You've protected me since you got here, whether I wanted you to or not. You've looked out for me and been a friend to me even though you barely know me."

"I do know you," I say.

Lucy's lips twist to one side. "And I know you too. You are not evil. And believe me, I've gotten pretty good at seeing the evil in other people. But everything I see in you is good. And I grew up in church too, you know, if that carries any weight. You are 'fearfully and wonderfully made.'" She smiles again, and I want so badly to kiss her, to cross the distance between us. Most of all though, I want to believe her.

Lucy holds my gaze, the guttering candles making the light waver over her face. But her eyes never waver. They are sure of me.

"Parents are assholes, aren't they?" Maggie says from beside me. I turn, surprised. For a moment, I'd forgotten she was here too. She's lying on her back now, staring up at the ceiling. I turn my head and look at Lucy again, but the spell between us is broken. Her eyes are on Maggie.

"You want to know why I really came here a week early?" Maggie adds. "It wasn't to get the lay of the land. It was because my school was on break and I couldn't stand to be home. Couldn't stand to be where I wasn't wanted, where I wasn't accepted."

Lucy puts her hand on Maggie's shoulder. "Well, you're wanted here." Maggie smiles gratefully and grips Lucy's hand.

"Families really are the fucking worst," I say, lying back down, trying to ignore the way the alcohol sloshes in my stomach.

"Not mine," Lucy says. "They've always been great. Sorry," she adds. "That sounded braggy, didn't it? I'm a little tipsy." She laughs nervously. "I'll be right back. I gotta pee." She gently moves past me and exits the tent.

Maggie and I sigh at the same moment, and then we laugh. "That must be nice, huh?" Maggie says. "You know, she told me that when she came out, her youth group all bought rainbow T-shirts in support."

"Jesus," I say.

"If she'd never met Joseph Kincaid, can you imagine what she'd be like?"

"She'd be happy," I say.

"She'd be boring though," Maggie shoots back. "It's our trauma that makes us interesting."

"Do you really think that? That's kind of a sad worldview."

"Is it? Hmm. You gotta build your sense of self from something, I guess." She turns over onto her stomach and props her head on her hands, her boots in the air behind her. "Whatever you're built from, it's not only about your parents, is it? That's not why you're here."

"No," I admit.

"Tell me," Maggie says. "I'll be your confessor."

"I'm not Catholic."

"Neither am I," Maggie says with a wicked smile, pushing the nearly empty bottle of Scotch toward me. "At least not anymore."

I sit up and take a long swig, feeling the light burst inside me again. I want to confess. I want to cut this tumor out of my side.

"You won't tell Lucy?" I ask.

"Of course not. She has enough of her own burdens to bear."

I nod. I close my eyes. I see Michael dying in my arms, his blood dark against his pale skin. I feel myself holding him, a metallic taste in my mouth.

"I think I killed my boyfriend," I say, eyes still closed. "Michael. I think I killed him."

Maggie stirs beside me, as if she's sitting up. "What do you mean you *think* you killed him? Wouldn't you know?"

"I can't remember exactly how it happened. I only remember what I felt when the light left his eyes."

"What did you feel?"

"Relief," I whisper. "And then shame."

Maggie doesn't say anything. I open my eyes and look at her. She gives me a half smile. "So you killed your boyfriend."

"You don't care?"

"People are what they are," Maggie says. "You killed your boyfriend. I helped my roommate try to burn down her ex's house." She shrugs.

"You did what? Why?"

Maggie laughs. "He was a total dick, and he deserved it."

"Did you get in trouble?"

Maggie rolls her eyes. "No, because I'm not an idiot. And apparently neither are you."

I open my mouth to protest, but Maggie interrupts. "Do you really think we're any different from the rest of these people here? The Killer Quest contestants aren't here because they are fascinated by true crime. They are obsessed with it because they see themselves in the killers—their fears and desires. And that titillates and terrifies them, just like it does you. But as long as they aren't the ones doing the killing, they think they're still good."

"Aren't they?"

"No," Maggie says. "People are what they are."

Before either of us can say anything else, the tent unzips and Lucy climbs back in. "What's the matter?" she asks, looking between us.

"We thought you got lost out there," Maggie says, pulling Lucy down and tickling her. Lucy shrieks and thrashes, and the two of them dissolve into laughter.

Just like that, the moment is over. A second ago, I told Maggie I killed my boyfriend, and now she's cracking jokes. I almost feel like I imagined our exchange. Was she really not surprised or horrified by what I said? Did she really take it in stride, a fact as mundane as my hair color or my college major? Maybe it's more of her bravado, her refusal to take anything seriously.

But which of them is right, I wonder: Am I good, or am I . . . simply what I am?

Either way, I don't want to think about it anymore. I just want to be the girl in a tent under a sky full of stars again.

I find the whiskey bottle and take a long slug. "Last call," I say, handing the bottle to Lucy. She smiles and takes a sip, then passes it to Maggie, who holds the bottle over her head, letting the final precious drops drip onto her tongue. We all cackle like it's the funniest thing in the world.

Hours pass, stories and jokes and innuendoes blooming like flowers. We laugh and feel our blood buzz in our veins. Despite the weirdness with Maggie, despite how much I resent their relationship, despite Noah and what might happen tomorrow, despite everything, I feel . . . happy.

Around two in the morning, we finally blow out the guttering candles and fall asleep in a tangle of limbs and sleeping bags, and for the first time in a long time, I don't feel alone or afraid as I drift into the dark.

# TWENTY-ONE

## LUCY

### DAY 5

**The sun has** barely begun rising when Maggie shakes me awake. "Hey, we should get moving," she says, her voice hushed but excited. Despite my foggy head, a thrill runs through me. Today's the day. We're going to catch Noah, expose him for what he is, and make sure he never hurts another person.

I sit up and my head spins. Maggie runs her fingers through my hair and lays her hand on the back of my neck. "You ready for this?" she asks. "It's not too late to back out."

I blink at her, surprised. "No way. I'm a little hungover, but I'm ready."

Maggie beams at me and plants a kiss on my lips. "Let's hit the showers and the canteen and get on the trail, then. We need to pack everything up to take with us."

"Did you wake Carolina yet?" I ask, rubbing the sleep from my eyes.

"Yeah, and she headed straight into the woods to throw up." Maggie laughs. "She drank most of that bottle last night."

I wince. I have only gotten that drunk once—with my softball team after a game last year—and I have never wished to repeat that sort of hangover experience. "I hope she's okay. Maybe I should go check on her."

"She'll be fine," Maggie says, waving her hand dismissively. "I'm going to go get a shower. See you in a bit."

I close my eyes and drop my throbbing head on my knees as she exits the tent. My body wants to go back to bed, but my mind is already wide awake, churning through everything that might happen today. If things go the way we plan, Noah might end up in jail, or at least on the police's radar. At the very least, we can show everyone who he is. And me—I could be someone I'm proud of—someone who makes a difference in the world instead of hiding from it. The thought propels me into action. I drink some water and gather up my shower supplies and some clean clothes.

Carolina hasn't appeared, so I grab her water bottle and head out into the gray morning to look for her. I find her only a few yards away, crouched halfway behind some rhododendron.

"Carolina," I call out, and she looks out from the twisted branches, her face pale with nausea, her eyes struggling to focus on me as I draw near. "Here's your water."

She takes the bottle and drinks gingerly. "Thanks," she says, her voice hoarse. She manages a weak smile. "Me and whiskey aren't friends anymore. I take back every nice thing I said about it."

Her words are pure Georgia drawl. It must take a lot of control to keep that accent hidden, but that's hard to do when you're hungover and exhausted. I wonder how many other parts of herself she's had to hide—from her religiously abusive parents, from teachers and friends, maybe even from herself. Like the fact that she is most definitely into girls.

"My head isn't too happy with me," I admit. "I'm going to go take a shower before we hit the trail. You wanna come?"

"Yes, please," Carolina says. I can see she's having a hard time getting to her feet, so I help her up. We grab her stuff from her tent on the way and walk slowly toward the showers. Considering what happened to me last time I headed down this path, I'm grateful to have Carolina next to me, even if she is shivering and looks like a zombie.

"Last night was actually fun," I say. "I haven't really had fun in a long time."

"Me neither," Carolina says.

"Was it worth it?" I ask with a laugh.

Carolina groans. "I'll let you know once we start hiking."

I grimace. Carolina isn't a good hiker at the best of times, so today's going to be especially rough for her. Not that I'm in much better shape, with my bruised ribs, my body a canvas of contusions, and now my head pounding. "We'll go slow," I promise.

Just as we round the path and the showers come into sight, Carolina stops dead. Her face drains of color.

"What?" I whisper, looking around frantically. Did she see Noah? Rufus? Kincaid?

But then she runs into the bushes and pukes. Relief floods me. After the paralysis leaves my limbs, I walk over to her. She's on her hands and knees, her legs trembling. I put my hand on her back. "I'm so sorry you're sick. You can stay back today if you want to. I think Maggie and I could manage. . . ."

"Absolutely not," Carolina says. "I'm going."

She dry-heaves, and I pull back her long hair, holding it gently in one fist.

"Sorry. I know I'm disgusting," Carolina says, putting a trembling hand over her mouth. "But I'll feel better soon. I promise." She pushes herself up off the ground just as Maggie comes striding from the direction of the showers.

Maggie waves. She doesn't even look tired, let alone hungover. She's got on a fresh black Henley and a forest-green beanie, her denim jacket in one hand. She radiates her usual intelligence and energy. I wonder if she feels afraid or even nervous about what we're planning to do today. It doesn't seem like it. She grins at us excitedly when she gets close.

"Come on, you two, we're burning daylight," she says. "See you in ten?" She continues on down the path.

Carolina rolls her eyes and then closes them as if the motion hurt. "Yeah, don't want to lose all this daylight," she murmurs, motioning at the rolling gray fog that covers everything.

"She's right though. It's a long hike," I say. "Let's do quick showers and get some breakfast."

Carolina holds out a fistful of hair. "I should wash this, but I really don't have the energy."

"I can braid it for you," I offer. "I braid my little sister's all the time."

Carolina nods and gives me a shy smile. "I would love that."

We stop beside a loblolly pine near the showers, and Carolina turns her back to me, pushing her mass of hair behind her shoulders. I run my fingers through it to get the tangles out. Even unwashed, it's beautiful and soft, the color of cherry wood. She lets her head fall back, an instinctual surrender to the comfort of my hands in her hair.

"French braid or schoolgirl braids?" I ask.

"French. I love all things French."

"Like what?" I ask as I start to separate her hair into sections.

"French pastry. French novels. French movies," she says dreamily. "The French language. French fries." She laughs.

I remember the way she spoke French the first time we met, the sounds so smooth and natural, even though she was describing something terrible. "Remember you asked me that first day we met if I'd ever felt the call of the void?" I ask her. "And I said no?"

"Yeah?" she asks, surprised by the turn of the conversation.

"Today feels like that."

"Like a leap into a chasm?" Carolina asks, turning to look at me, worry furrowing her brow. "I'm sure I've already told you this enough times, but you don't actually have to jump."

I shake my head and turn her back around, resuming my work. "No, it feels like it did when I fell down the cliffside. Like, the prospect of tumbling down the cliff and dying . . . it made me realize how badly I want to live. Really live. Not just exist, not just get through. I want my life back."

"What are you saying?" Her shoulders feel suddenly tense.

"I'm saying that going after Noah isn't jumping. Going on like I've been doing . . . that's what would really kill me. Does that make sense at all?"

Carolina gives me a complicated smile over her shoulder. "I know exactly what you mean."

I smile back, my fingers moving deftly over her hair. I feel almost sad when I reach the end of the braid. "Okay, I'm done. I don't have anything to tie it off with . . . except . . ." I rummage in my backpack. "I have a rubber band. Do you want me to use it? Not very chic."

Carolina laughs. "There is nothing chic about me today."

"Me neither," I say, laughing too. I lean my head against her back for a moment, feeling the vibration of her laughter through her skin. I'm not sure why we're getting along so well. Maybe it was because of last night, bonding over a bottle of whiskey, or maybe because Maggie isn't here. We do always seem to get along better when it's just the two of us.

I'm glad for it. Because being here, in this hollow place, I'd forgotten how nice it feels to care for someone, to do something simple and gentle and human. I want to savor it because it might be the last nice moment I get in this canyon.

Everything here is hard and cold and angry. Necessary, if I want my life back. But still, this moment with Carolina feels like a shelter in the storm. A part of me wishes I didn't have to leave it.

The hike down to the caves is every bit as grueling as I'd imagined it would be in my injured, sleep-deprived state. My head throbs and my ribs scream. We go slow and take a lot of breaks, but it still feels like every step is going to be my last. A few other groups of contestants pass us on their way to other trailheads, including a trio of sisters who must be at least sixty-five. "Look alive, girls!" one of them calls as they storm past us with their tanned, athletic legs and sporty silver hair. I can't help but wonder if I'll get to live long enough to look like that.

Maggie is impatient, barely able to stop herself from sighing every time Carolina throws down her pack or stops for a drink of water. After the third time this happens, I snap at Maggie and tell her to give Carolina a break. Even so, I push myself harder than I want to, maybe harder than I should.

Finally, we descend into the lowest elevation of the canyon, where sandstone caves loom out of the rock like open mouths. The fog is thicker than ever here, a dense and sinister wall of white. I imagine that you could disappear into it and never be heard from again. I don't know where you'd end up—swallowed into nothingness maybe. The thought makes me shiver.

Maggie leads us off the main trail and onto a deer track. After only a few minutes, she stops. "Here."

"Here where?" Carolina demands.

"This cave," Maggie says, pointing out a narrow opening in the rock.

"It's tiny," Carolina protests.

"It opens up inside. I found it last week." She clicks on her flashlight and walks straight into the cave, lowering her head at the threshold.

I go right behind her, but Carolina hesitates.

"What's wrong?" I ask, turning back around.

"I don't think I want to go in there." She looks scared.

"Oh, okay. Well, um, stay here and I'll check it out. I'll get the lantern turned on before you have to come in. Be right back."

Carolina wraps her arms around herself and nods. I turn and follow Maggie into the dark. Maggie was right about the cave. The ceiling slopes upward after a couple of yards, finally opening into a cavern the size of my bedroom back home. The walls are damp, and stalagmites hang down from the ceiling. I bet this is a perfect spot to hunt for salamanders.

Maggie points her flashlight up, probably to check the corners for bats. But the cave is completely empty. It's musty and cold, but it will keep us dry if we have to stay the night. I find my camping lantern and turn it on, filling the cave with light and shadows.

I head back toward the entrance to get Carolina, but when I emerge from the cave, she's gone.

"Carolina?" I call. My voice disappears into the fog. "Where are you?"

I take a few steps out of the cave, peering into the gloom. "Carolina?" I listen for her voice, the sound of her boots, anything, but the world has gone silent. "Are you all right?" I walk forward a few more steps.

The fog moves around me, sinuous as a snake, coiling and taut, as if ready to spring. Chill bumps spread across my arms beneath my flannel shirt and wool sweater, and up the back of my neck. My heart beats loudly in my ears, a drumming I can feel painfully around my bruised ribs. I feel watched, as if with an ill will. With resentment. With malicious intent.

"Carolina," I try to say, but it comes out more like a croak. "Carolina?" I try again, and my voice breaks on the third syllable. I take in a deep breath to call again, and that's when I smell it. Cologne. Cloves and smoke. My breathing goes shallow, as if the scent is closing up my lungs.

*He's here.* He's here, somewhere. Watching me.

I take a step backward, back toward the cave and Maggie. But then I remember Carolina. She's still out here somewhere. What if he got her? What if he—

Someone grabs me from behind, bony fingers closing over my shoulders. I scream and spin around, my hands tightening into fists.

Gray eyes, widened with surprise. Hands half in the air, stunned into stillness.

"Maggie," I breathe.

"Hey, I'm sorry I scared you. I thought you heard me behind you. I said your name."

I sink into a crouch before the vertigo can bring me down. I put my head between my knees and breathe. But I still smell the cologne.

Footsteps come crashing toward me out of the fog, and then Carolina is bending over me, her face pale and her chest heaving. "Are you all right? What happened?" she asks.

I shake my head. "I didn't know where you were."

"Sorry. I had to throw up again," she admits. "I didn't mean to scare you."

"Do y'all smell it—the cologne?" I ask.

Maggie takes a deep breath and shakes her head.

"No, but do you think—could Noah be here already?" Carolina asks.

And I realize my mistake. Noah. I'd forgotten about Noah having the same cologne. All I could think of was Kincaid. What if Noah's already come looking for us?

"No," Maggie says, certain. "He couldn't possibly be here yet. While you were showering, I saw Rufus over at Noah and Brandon's tent, trying to drag them out. They had just made it into the lodge for breakfast when you came back. There's no way they hiked here that fast. Even if they had, we would have seen them on the trail."

"Or heard them," Carolina says. "Rufus is so loud."

"Exactly," Maggie agrees. "Besides, I think it will take Noah a bit to find a chance to break off from the others. I'm sure we have plenty of time."

I nod. It must just be nerves. My mind playing tricks in the fog.

"Come on, let's go make camp," Maggie says, pulling me up gently by the arm. After she goes into the cave, I take Carolina's hand and lead her inside, watching her reaction by the light of the lantern. She eyes the space warily but doesn't look ready to bolt.

"Is it all right?" I ask, and she nods stiffly, setting down her pack. We unload our stuff and lay our sleeping bags on the hard floor. We work quietly, but every sound is magnified in the cave, rustles and coughs and footsteps. Finally, we sit in a circle, facing one another in the quiet, an expectant hush all around us. It feels like the lull in a cicada chorus at the height of summer, when the shrill pulse of their tymbals ceases for the space of a second or two, reminding you what silence sounds like.

Soft light from the lantern illuminates Maggie's and Carolina's faces, throwing the back of the cave into shadow.

Suddenly, Carolina laughs, a weak, croaky rasp.

"What?" Maggie asks eagerly, always ready to join in on a joke.

"When I talked to Brandon, he said it was weird how all the other contestants were acting like the three of us were witches doing human sacrifices or something. If they could see us now, a little coven in a cave." She lets out a hoarse, witchy cackle. Maggie cracks up, and Carolina starts laughing again too.

Their laughter should be cheerful, but instead it's vaguely unsettling. It echoes strangely in the cave, making me shiver. "So how are we going to do this?" I ask, hoping getting down to business will ease my nerves. When we first started planning this trap for Noah, it was so exciting that I didn't really think through all the details. Now that we're here, I'm not exactly sure how it's going to work. Now our plan seems flimsy and far-fetched.

The same thing seems to occur to the other girls. They look around the cave, Carolina somewhat blearily, Maggie with her brow furrowed, biting her bottom lip.

"Here's what I think," Maggie says after a long moment. "Noah knows we're out here. Last night at dinner, I talked really loudly with Rosa and Bridget about how we'd decided to camp in the caves. Noah and Rufus were sitting at the next table, and I know they were listening. I complained about how Lucy was banged up, and said she was going to be pretty much useless. So I think Noah will be expecting you to be here alone in the cave at some point."

I nod, steeling myself against the fear that skitters like a spider's legs up my arms, toward my ears. I rub my neck to ease the sensation.

"So how about this: one of us will keep watch for Noah outside, far enough from the cave that he won't see but that we can follow him in quickly so we're not all trapped. We won't be able to give any warning, I don't think, so the others will have to be prepared. The best we can do is to try to get whatever he does or says on camera. That's pretty much it. And then the three of us will scare him away."

"That's not much of a plan," Carolina says. "Not much of anything. How will he even know what cave we're in?"

Undeterred, Maggie plows ahead. "My phone is fully charged and I took off the password, so I'll leave it here for whoever's closest. Just get the camera rolling as quickly as you can and make sure Noah doesn't see you do it." She puts the phone on a small ledge in the wall. "And if you can manage it, there's a tunnel over here in the corner you can hide in to film him." She goes over to the far left of the cave, feeling with her hands before she disappears into the shadows.

"Where does that tunnel go?" I ask, a lump tightening my throat.

Maggie comes back out and shrugs. "Probably into another cave."

I shiver, imagining tunnels branching all through the rock of the canyon—deep, dark places where ghosts drift like netherworld shades. I glance at Carolina and see my thoughts echoed in her expression.

"You two look completely awful by the way," Maggie says, "so how about I take the first shift outside? Lucy, why don't you keep watch while Carolina gets some sleep, and then you can switch off in maybe an hour or so?" she suggests.

Carolina and I exchange another glance, neither of us entirely convinced by Maggie's plan. But we're too exhausted to argue further. Maggie gives us two thumbs up and stalks out of the cave.

"Maggie's right. You really should get some sleep," I tell Carolina. "If I start falling asleep too, I'll wake you up."

Carolina must feel too lousy to resist the offer because she burrows down into her sleeping bag right next to me without a word. In moments, she's breathing steadily, fast asleep. I exhale an enormous breath, realizing how relieved I am to have a moment to myself. I pick up Maggie's phone and open the camera app to make sure I'm ready to use it. I find the recording setting and fiddle with it, zooming in and out on Carolina's face.

Looking at her through the screen, she acquires a strange distance, as if she's from another time and place. I admire the soft curve of her cheek, her long, dark eyelashes, her carefully sculpted eyebrows. Her lips are full, and there's a little dip beneath the bottom one that makes her look like she's pouting. I smile and reach out a finger, as if to trace them, before I realize how creepy that would be. I settle for the slightly less creepy choice of watching her sleep.

I put Maggie's phone back on the ledge and settle down on the cave floor next to Carolina. I try not to let my eyes travel over to the tunnel in the wall. I try not to think about all the invisible passages in the stone.

The cold from below drifts up into my bones, making my hips and knees ache. Even so, my eyes start to grow heavy, and I jolt again and again into wakefulness. Each time I come to, it gets a little harder to resist the weight of the dark. The cold and the dim emptiness of the cave pull at me, whispering of sleep and forgetfulness.

I know I shouldn't, but I prop my heavy head in my hands and close my stinging eyes. I'm nearly asleep when suddenly all the hairs on my arms and legs rise, as if a cold wind is blowing through the cave. I raise my head and blink into the darkness.

A white face and dark, frightened eyes stare back at me.

I don't even have time to scream before he disappears.

# TWENTY-TWO

## CAROLINA

**I dream of** the fog. It swirls around me, alive and intent, plucking at my clothes, my hair, trying to get inside. There is no sky and no ground, nothing in the world except me and mist, locked in a battle of wills. Finally, I wrest myself from its grip and run, screaming, smack into a wall and utter blackness.

I wake, opening my eyes on a soft light. The electric lantern. For a moment, I think I'm in my tent in the campsite, that it's the middle of the night.

But then I remember—the cave. The cave in the canyon. The cave that is a poorly designed trap for a potential killer. I shift in my sleeping bag and feel something wet against my cheek.

It must be water, maybe condensation dripping from the roof of the cave. But when I touch my cheek, the wetness isn't cool. It's warm. Almost hot.

And when I raise my fingers to the level of my eyes, they are dark. I sit up quickly, so fast my head spins and I think I'll vomit.

Blood.

Blood on my hands, blood on my clothes.

Blood spreading across the floor of the cave.

I take a shuddering breath and turn my head, already knowing what I'll see. The image has been lodged in my head for days.

Lucy lies sprawled across the cave floor on her back. Her eyes are open and staring, a red grin of blood slashed across her neck. Knife wounds gouged into her chest and stomach, at least a dozen.

Blood pours from her body, forming a hot, sticky, metallic pool around her head and shoulders.

Lucy is dead.

A knife is gripped in my hand, blood running down the hilt to coat my hands.

I killed her.

A scream wells up from inside me, terror and rage and horror. I kneel before her spent body and scream until my voice cuts out, until only a hoarse wail leaves my lips.

He was right about me. He was right.

I grip the knife in my hand, knowing what I have to do. I have to kill the demon that lives inside my skin. I have to cut it out of my own chest. My vision goes black with intent. I turn the knife around in my hand, blade against my heart.

But someone knocks it from my hands, shakes me, hard, and screams into my face. "Carolina," they yell. "Carolina, listen to me. Carolina!"

I come to, kneeling on the cave floor, a scream in my mouth. Panic grips me, squeezing my heart until I'm afraid it

will burst. My breath comes in heaves, and I don't know where
I am, who I am.

Lucy's face swims into view, her skin pale, her eyes wide.
"Carolina," she says, gripping my shoulders. "You're safe. It's
all right."

"You're alive," I manage to say. She nods, her forehead
furrowed in concern.

A single, relieved sob leaves my mouth. Tears pour down
my cheeks. Lucy takes me in her arms and holds me, and I cry
against her hair. "You were dead," I say, again and again.

"You were dreaming," she croons, smoothing down my
hair.

"Where's the knife?" I ask, cold terror gripping me again.

"It's right here," Maggie says. She's standing at the entrance
of the cave, breathing hard. She comes forward and tosses the
sheathed weapon onto my sleeping bag. "Sorry, I should have
left it here. I forgot. What the hell's going on in here? Did
something happen? I heard screaming and thought Noah had
somehow gotten here already."

"She had a nightmare," Lucy says.

I stare at Lucy, struck dumb as reality finally descends on
me. She's speaking. She's moving. There is no blood at her
neck, no wounds in her chest. She's alive. I didn't hurt her. I
didn't kill her. Relief washes over me, so profound my knees
give way and I slip down to the cave floor, shivering.

Lucy tucks herself against me and holds me, and I grip
her hands. "It wasn't a nightmare," I say. "I saw it. You were
dead."

Lucy shakes her head, and I feel her cheek move against my mine. Her skin is soft and her hair smells like clementines. "It's not real. I promise you it's not real." She pauses for a long time. "But you aren't the only one . . . hallucinating. I thought I saw Kincaid again. Just for a second, in the corner of the cave. It was terrifying." She squeezes the sleeve of my coat.

I sit up, and Lucy follows, her hand still gripping my arm. Maggie watches us, her expression unreadable.

"Something's wrong out here," I say. "Brandon tried to tell me. . . ."

"Brandon?" Maggie asks.

"He said this place wasn't right, that something is wrong in this canyon. I've tried to ignore it, tried to explain it away, but I think he's right. I think . . . I think the legends are true. This place is evil." Saying it out loud, I realize I mean it. I do believe the legends. There's something here that feels dangerous.

"It's not *evil*," Maggie says. Her voice turns gentle. "You're just freaked out."

"No," I say. "This place is messing with our minds. It's trying to—trying to . . ." I can't find the words.

"Trying to what?" Maggie asks, cocking her head at me, curious.

"I don't know. I don't know," I say, tugging at the end of my braid.

Lucy reaches for my hand again. "Maggie's right. We're just scared and tired." She's trying to seem calm, but I can see the cracks in her armor. She wants a logical explanation for what she saw in the corner of the cave.

"No, it's more than that," I insist. "There's something here."

"Well," Maggie says, running her fingers through her hair, "if you really think this place is what the legends say . . . well, why not lean into the fear, lean into whatever it is you're seeing or feeling? Maybe instead of running from it, you need to look for the truth in it. You look for the possibility. Give yourself over to it, see where it takes you."

I gape at her. She can't be serious. "What the fuck is wrong with you?" I finally say.

"Seriously, Maggie," Lucy says. "Everything isn't a game."

Maggie holds her hands up, conciliatory. "Sorry, I'm sorry, okay?" She sighs. "Look, you're both overwhelmed. It's probably just all the whiskey and lack of sleep. Why don't you go take a walk? You can clear your heads."

"What about Noah? You said I should stay here," Lucy argues.

"If Noah came now, the plan wouldn't even work. You're too out of it. Go clear your heads. Seriously. You're both a mess."

We get shakily to our feet, and I grab my water bottle from the floor. "Maybe she's right," I say. Getting out of this cave does sound good.

Lucy nods. "A short walk, then."

"It's going to be fine, you guys," Maggie says, moving from the cave's entrance to make room for us. "We're going to get what we need from Noah, and no one is going to get hurt. Everything will be fine." She squeezes Lucy's hand and smiles. "Just go get some air. We can do this. I promise."

Lucy and I stumble into the gray light of the canyon, and I'm surprised by the dark circles under her eyes, the heavy way she carries herself. "You didn't get to sleep," I say.

She shakes her head. "I nodded off a few times. But to tell you the truth, I didn't want to fall asleep."

"Did you really see Kincaid?"

"Yeah. And not Noah pretending to be him. The real Kincaid." She shivers.

"And I saw you dead," I say again. Lucy shakes her head and looks away.

Our worst fears. That's what we both saw. The things we're most afraid of. For Lucy, that's the fear that Kincaid might still be alive and after her. For me, it's the fear that I might kill her. And Maggie wants us to lean into that? *Jesus.* If the inside of her head looked anything like mine, she wouldn't act so blasé. I'm glad that Lucy called her out on it. Maybe Lucy isn't quite as deep under Maggie's spell as I thought.

We choose a side trail and walk slowly, in silence, for a few minutes. My mind feels fuzzy, hazed over, just like the canyon that surrounds us. And even though I slept, I still feel exhausted, as if it was more tiring to dream than to be awake. When we reach a huge, mossy tree stump that borders the path, I slump down onto it and put my head in my hands.

"Hey, did you use that yet?" Lucy asks, pointing at the silver loupe that dangles from my neck.

"Oh. No, I guess I haven't had a chance," I say. "Do you want it back?" I start to pull it over my head.

"No, no. You should keep it," Lucy says. "My gift to you. The world in micro. Something to remember me by when we go home."

"Thanks," I say, warming the metal in my hand. I'm glad I get to keep it, this little part of Lucy. "Every time I look at lichen, I'll think of you."

Lucy tries to smile but can't quite manage it. "I wanna go home," she whispers, wrapping her arms tightly around herself.

Me too, I think, but not back to my parents and not back to sleeping on Sheena's couch. I want to go to a home of my own creation. A small place that's mine, with a lock on the door—not to keep the monsters out but to keep them in. A place I can feel safe.

"Please don't tell Maggie I said that," Lucy adds.

I look up. "You don't have to prove anything to her, you know."

Lucy shakes her head. "You don't understand."

"Try me."

"Okay." She pauses, thinking. "I know Maggie can be demanding and kind of over-the-top. But she's giving me my life back," Lucy says, settling next to me on the log. "For so long, all I've been able to do is feel afraid, to feel weak and small and—" She shakes her head. "Ever since Kincaid, everyone wants to protect me, to coddle me. My mom freaks out if I even get home from school late. And everyone watches me all the time, waiting for me to break."

"Because they love you," I say. "I wish I knew what it was like to be loved like that."

"No, you don't," Lucy says, tears shimmering in her eyes. "I promise that you don't." When I don't argue, she goes on. "Maggie is the first person who has ever seen me differently. Who isn't afraid I'll break. Who expects something from me, who believes in me. Maggie believes I can do this, so I believe it too. I don't want to let her down . . . because I don't want to let myself down. Does that make sense?"

I nod. "But for the record, Lucy, I don't think of you as weak and breakable either. I keep telling you that, but you never believe me."

She laughs bitterly. "Carolina, you literally just hallucinated me dead. Of course you see me that way." She stands up from the log and brushes off the seat of her pants.

I want to correct her. I want to tell her the truth—that it's me I'm afraid of—but the words won't leave my mouth. I hang my head.

"Shit, and now I'm hallucinating his cologne again," she says, tears in her voice. She pulls her hair in frustration.

I sniff the air. "No, I smell it too." I shoot to my feet. "It must be Noah." Lucy's eyes widen.

Suddenly, the fog feels like it's closing in on us, pressing against our bodies, cutting off sight and sound. Just like in my dream, or hallucination, or whatever the hell it was. I start to shake.

"Come on, let's go back. What if he's there, and Maggie's all alone?" Lucy says, her voice panicked. She takes off down the path, her boots barely making a sound in the thick fog. It is agony to run—each step feels like it will crack open my skull—but I don't want to lose sight of Lucy for a moment. I jog after her, holding my side.

Oh God, this is just like the dream too. Running blind in the fog. Only instead of a wall of darkness, there are bushes and vines, rocks and fallen limbs, all of them trying to trip my feet. "We're off the path," I say, doubling back.

"Shit," Lucy hisses, turning around.

A girl's scream rends the air, and Lucy is moving again. I follow her and soon feel the even ground of the trail under my feet, then the narrower deer track.

"Here," she finally says as the cave rushes into view. She disappears inside, swallowed up by the canyon.

I throw myself in after her and stumble into a waking nightmare.

# TWENTY-THREE

## LUCY

**I move through** the dark opening of the cave as quickly as the cramped space will allow, fingertips scraping along the cool stone, heart in my throat. What if she's already dead? What if he's already—

"Maggie!" I scream as the dim interior of the cave comes into view. She's slumped on the ground on her knees, gripping her right arm, blood running out between her fingers.

Noah stands over her, his arms hanging at his sides, a knife in his hand.

They both turn to look at me at the same moment, Maggie's eyes wide with fear, and Noah's with surprise.

I've been so afraid all morning, but suddenly my fear vanishes. Without stopping to think, I hurl myself at Noah, slamming into him hard enough that he drops the knife, which skitters across the cave floor behind me. "You son of a bitch!" I scream.

I hit every part of him I can reach, my fists flying and connecting with his chest and arms and stomach. He puts up his hands, trying to push me away. Finally, he grabs my wrists and shakes me. "Stop it!" he screams into my face, his eyes wild.

"Get your hands off her!" Carolina yells, and rushes in from behind me, shoving Noah away from me. He crashes into the wall of the cave. Maggie, Carolina, and I surround him.

Maggie starts talking, her voice high and agitated, so unlike how she normally sounds I know she must be terrified. "He was already in here. He was hiding! He must have come in while you were sleeping and hidden in the tunnel. After you left, I guess he decided to get me out of the way. He came at me with the knife, and . . . and—"

"What the fuck are you talking about?" Noah yells. "You're crazy."

Maggie laughs, the sound hysterical and unnerving. "Oh yeah, all women are crazy. Was Kiersten crazy too?"

"What? What are you . . . ?" Noah shakes his head, turning to Carolina and me instead. "She's deranged," he says, his voice pleading. "I didn't do anything to her. Or to Kiersten."

But as he continues talking, my blood runs cold. *He's* who I saw when I nearly fell asleep earlier. It wasn't Kincaid's ghost. It was Noah. Noah hiding in the dark tunnel, watching us. He must have slipped back into the tunnel when I opened my eyes. A shiver runs through me—fear and disgust and rage.

"We know what you are, Noah, and we know why you're here," I say, surprised by how even my voice is. "We know you worship Kincaid, that you want to be like him. That you came here to finish his work." I cross my arms over my chest to hide the way my hands shake. "Admit it. You're a copycat killer."

Noah's mouth gapes. "I . . . Look, I'm not saying I'm a good guy. But I didn't hurt that girl Kiersten, and I wasn't going to do anything to you. It was just a fantasy."

"A fantasy?" Maggie says. "A fantasy is imagining a hot actress coming into your dorm room at night and begging you for sex. A fantasy is pretending you won the lottery and imagining all the shit you're going to buy. A fantasy is *not* hunting down a girl whose life has already been ruined to make it even worse. A fantasy is not stalking her through the woods and—"

"I didn't stalk her!" Noah retorts. "I—"

"*I* am not a fantasy!" I roar, drowning out his voice, all my calm gone. "I'm a human being!"

When my voice stops echoing, a stunned silence falls in the cave. It's Carolina who finally breaks it. "Noah, why did you point at Lucy that night by the fire, when you came screaming from the woods?" she asks. "That's never made any sense to me."

"What the hell does it matter?" Maggie asks. "He's clearly—"

But Carolina holds up a hand to quiet her. "Let him talk."

Noah clenches his teeth, his jaw a hard line. He shakes his head. "I got confused out there in the fog. I started seeing things."

"Seeing what?" I demand. "Did you see Kincaid?"

"What? Of course not. I saw *you*," he says to me.

"I wasn't anywhere near you," I say.

Noah rubs his face. "I saw your body, laid out the same way Kincaid laid out his victims. The same cuts, the same—" He shakes his head. "I thought I'd done it. I thought . . . and

I got scared and ran, and then when I got to the fire, you were there. I thought you were fucking with me."

"That's ridiculous," I say. "And a lie."

Noah shrugs. "I wasn't thinking straight when I pointed at you. But the more I thought about it, the more I realized you couldn't have done it. It didn't make sense." He pulls off his beanie and runs a hand through his hair, making it stand on end. "Something's out here, something evil."

I flinch. Noah's the third person to say this about the canyon. Carolina believes it, and she said Brandon does too. But it doesn't matter what they believe about this place. It only matters what they do. And Noah has done nothing but try to hurt me.

I force myself to laugh. "The evil thing is *you*. And I'm going to expose you. You're going to go to prison. You're never going to hurt another girl."

"God, how many times do I have to tell you that I didn't do anything?" Noah says, holding out his hands, palms up in supplication.

"You literally followed me out here to kill me," I spit.

Noah glances between the three of us, a desperate look in his eyes. "Why would I—"

Maggie lunges at him, her fist raised. "Tell the truth, you sick fuck."

Noah stumbles away from her until his back is against the cave wall. "You're all insane," he says. "I'm leaving." He tries to push past me.

"You're not going anywhere until you tell the truth," I say, blocking his exit.

"Get out of my way," Noah snarls. "God, I wish Kincaid *had* killed you. He left a crazy bitch behind."

Like a dam bursting, two years' worth of fury explodes inside me. I'm barely aware of what I'm doing, but I pick up the knife at my feet and hurl myself at Noah.

Before I can get the steel into his skin, he throws out an arm and slams his elbow into my chest. Pain bursts along my clavicle like a firecracker. I reel back, losing the knife, before I throw myself at him again with a scream. He grabs me and slams me powerfully to the cave floor, knocking all the breath from my body. He straddles me, pinning me in place, and his hands find my throat.

"You want a killer? I'll give you a fucking killer," he snarls, and his thumbs press into my windpipe, cutting off my air.

I buck under him, trying to get him off, but he's far too heavy. I'm desperate for air, my fingers scrabbling uselessly at his face and neck. Dimly, I hear Carolina and Maggie screaming, but all I can see is Noah's blotchy white face floating above me, contorted with anger. His eyes are dark, pupils blown wide, his features inhuman.

And I realize that this time I'm not going to escape. The police aren't coming to rescue me. This time I really am going to die in Cloudkiss Canyon.

I get one single second to pray they find my body so I don't have to spend my afterlife here too, and then the world goes black.

# TWENTY-FOUR

## CAROLINA

**There's always this** moment in action movies when a bomb has gone off and debris is flying through the air, people running and screaming in terror, explosions spreading like felled dominoes. But for one person, the world goes still and nearly silent, like time has slowed down only for them. They alone get to step outside the chaos and see with clear eyes.

I always found those scenes unconvincing and cliché. But that's what's happening now.

It's like a bomb went off in the cave, sound and panic ricocheting off the walls. Noah is on top of Lucy, choking the life from her body. Maggie is crying and screaming, begging Noah to stop. And I am standing still, frozen like a bad action hero in the eye of the storm.

But then Lucy makes this small, desperate noise, and my body simply reacts, throwing me back into the chaos. I yank at Noah's arms, trying to make him let Lucy go, but he doesn't budge. It's like he's turned to stone, impossibly heavy and strong. I pull his hair, but even that doesn't get a reaction. It's like he's in another world, another reality. But Lucy's face is turning purple in this one.

And the knife is still lying there, right next to them both.

Without thinking, I snatch it up, grip its handle tight, and bring the blade down as hard as I can. The knife goes into Noah's back more easily than I expect—a thud and then a sick, wet slide. Once, twice, three times. He finally lets go of Lucy and reaches for me. With a desperate cry, I slam the knife down into his chest.

Noah's eyes widen, turn lost and scared as a child's, and then he slumps forward, halfway on top of Lucy. She opens her mouth to scream but only manages to cough and rasp. She flails weakly, trying to get up.

I drop the knife, which clatters dully on the cave floor, and help Lucy to roll Noah's body off her. He falls heavily onto his side, blood leaking from his mouth. I fall to my knees beside him, my hands going uselessly, unthinkingly to the wound in his chest.

But his eyes are open and staring. Empty.

He's already dead.

Lucy sits up and leans forward, her hands at her throat, whimpering and gasping for air. I glance over at Maggie and my frantic heart goes cold in my chest.

Maggie's face is red and streaming with tears, but she isn't afraid. She isn't traumatized. She isn't even numb.

Maggie is smiling.

I just killed someone, and Maggie is smiling, her mouth curved into a small, satisfied smirk.

I raise my bloodied, shaking hands, staring in horror as rivulets of red snake down my wrists and disappear into the sleeves of my jacket. My mouth fills with a metallic numbness.

The room sways. Everything is distorted—Noah's body, the walls of the cave, my own hands stretched out before me, bloody like in every nightmare. "No. No no no no no no," I whisper.

"What is it? Are you hurt?" Lucy croaks, coming toward me, hands outstretched.

I back away from her, not wanting her to touch the blood. "I killed him."

"For me," Lucy says. "To protect me. He would have choked me to death." She touches her reddened throat gingerly. "You saved me. And Maggie too."

I look at Maggie again. She's not smiling anymore. Her eyes are grave and serious. Did I imagine her smiling earlier? I must have. Everything feels unreal, wrong, grotesque. A surrealist painting where nothing makes sense, like melting clocks and little girls with hyena heads.

Only here it's wildflowers blooming from the cave's walls, the floors, springing up between my feet. Birds twittering and swooping between long shadows. The sweet, grassy smell of springtime permeates the cave.

And suddenly it's April. Birds making nests, crickets chirping, wildflowers everywhere you look. Michael's driving, I'm sitting behind him on the ATV as we move out of the sun and into the woods, following the worn trail between the trees. Light filters in through the leaves, undulating in golden pools. It's beautiful, but I'm tired of this path, this routine. We drive deeper, until the world is green and shadowy and cool. Michael pulls off the path a little ways and grins at me. I try to smile back. I try to act normal. I get off the ATV and follow him to our usual spot. But I don't want to be here with him. I think of my wire-and-glass project. I wanted to finish it before twilight so I could catch the sunset through the stained-glass panels. Michael could have sat beside me while I worked and kept me company, but I didn't even ask. I knew he wouldn't want to share my attention, not even with inanimate wire and glass.

"Where are you right now?" Michael asks, his hand on my thigh. His fingers creep higher. And I want them to, but also I don't. I am so tired. It's spring and the world is alive, but I feel like I am turning brown and dry as autumn leaves.

"Why are you crying?" His voice isn't tender or soft with concern like it used to be at my tears. It's annoyed.

And suddenly I can't do this anymore. I thought I could wait until graduation. Until I'm leaving town, starting over. I thought I could make a clean, easy break.

But the words are tumbling from my mouth. "I don't want to be with you anymore. I want—I want to break up."

"What? Why?" he asks, reeling back from me like I've said something disgusting.

I hang my head and shake it. "I want to focus on school, on getting into college," I say weakly. Even I know that isn't true. Not the whole truth. I wring my hands.

"No," Michael says. "Forget it. Fuck that."

"This isn't working," I say, my eyes pleading. "We fight all the time. Aren't you tired of it?"

"So is it school or is it me?" he asks. "Pick whatever fight you want to have, Carolina."

"I don't want to fight," I say. "I just want a break."

"A break or to break up? I can give you a break if that's what you want."

"Really?" I ask, looking up quickly, eagerly.

Too eagerly.

His face changes. Rage takes over so fast. "I fucking knew it. I knew one day you'd decide you were too good for me. I knew you'd make up your mind and that would be it. You'd leave and not give a shit about me ever again. You selfish bitch."

"Michael, no. That's not—"

"Come on, let's go," he says, standing up. He pulls me by my arm, hard.

"Ow, stop," I say. Somehow that's all it takes. He explodes. He's screaming at me, pacing back and forth, jabbing his finger at my face. I lean away, against the tree, waiting for it to stop. Waiting for him to run out of words, out of air, out of anger.

Finally, he turns away, bracing himself on another tree. I see his fists clench, his shoulders heave. He's trying to get control of himself. After a few moments, he turns back around. "Come on, let's go," he says. "You should go home." His shoulders are tense, his jaw set, as though he's made up his mind about something.

I study him, trying to figure out what he's thinking. But his face is carefully blank. I think it's okay, that he's okay.

Maybe he's not taking this seriously. He doesn't believe I'll go through with it. "Michael—"

"Just get on and let's go," he says, throwing his leg over the ATV's seat. Hesitantly, I climb on behind him. I wrap my arms around his waist, lean my head against his back. The feel of him is so familiar it's almost comforting, despite everything.

"You're not leaving me," Michael says. "We're meant to be together." His voice is a broken thing, a wounded bird. I close my eyes. He starts the engine.

He drives too fast, barely staying on the path. I cling to his shirt so hard my knuckles ache. "Michael, slow down!" I yell into his ear. My heart races, a hollow feeling spreading through me. "You're going to kill us!"

Instead, he speeds up. "Michael!" I try to reach around him, to gain some control, but it's no good. He slaps my hands away. We break out of the trees and into twilight. It's nearly dark. I didn't realize how much time had passed. How long he was yelling.

We fishtail in the dirt, and I think we're going to crash, but Michael slows down long enough to stabilize the ATV before he guns the engine again, heading off the trail and toward the cliff. "Michael!" I scream.

"You want to be free of me?" he yells over the rushing wind. "Fine, here you go."

I catch a glint of silver just before we hit the wire. I close my eyes, and the world turns upside down. There's a jolting, sickening impact, and a scream—mine, I think.

And then I'm on the ground, dizzy and nauseous. I can't move, can't see. I lie still, panting. After several long minutes, I finally manage to raise my head. There's a body on the ground a few feet away. I crawl toward it on my hands and knees, my head spinning. Every time I put pressure on my left wrist, I nearly scream. But I keep going, dread lodged inside me because I know what we hit. I know what I'm going to see.

The wire still hangs from the trees, dangling and limp, barely visible in the gloaming.

Michael lies on his back, dark spreading out from him. The air is metallic and wet. I crawl through the puddle of his blood and look down at him. His eyes are open, and I think he's dead. He ought to be dead. But his mouth moves slightly, barely more than a tremor. "Michael," I gasp. "Oh, Michael, what did you do?" I cling to his shirt, shake him, beg him to please, please not die. My hands flutter uselessly over the gash in his neck. It's too wide, too deep. There's too much blood.

"I won't leave you," I promise. "We don't have to break up. I was being stupid."

But it's too late. He's already gone. All the life has left his eyes. They are empty, glassy, filled with the night's first stars.

I scream. I scream and I scream and I scream.

But underneath the horror, dull relief spreads through me. It's over.

The next thing I remember is my parents arriving to pick me up. Dad gets out of his truck and slams the door, and Mom creeps like a shadow behind him. They stand over me at the back of the ambulance, where I am draped in a blanket, my clothes still covered in Michael's blood. It's underneath my fingernails and in the creases of my skin. I think it might be on my face because I can taste it.

"Daddy," I say, my voice desperate. But there's no warmth in his eyes.

"I told you you'd be the death of that boy." Dad shakes his head. "I told you and I told you. You wouldn't listen." My mother only peers at me, her eyes blank.

"Sir," says the EMT, an older woman who wrapped my wrist and patiently calmed me down, "your daughter did nothing wrong. It was an accident. The boy drove his four-wheeler into a metal wire that was stretched between two trees. He lost control of the thing, nearly went off the cliff. Your daughter could have died too. It was a near thing."

"You were drinking," my father accuses.

"No, sir, she wasn't," the EMT says, putting her body subtly between Dad's and mine. "It was a freak accident, and maybe a miracle she's alive. She'd be dead at the bottom of that cliff if it weren't for that wire. There'd be two dead kids instead of one."

"A miracle?" Dad says, his eyes lighting up with a fervor I recognize. "No, there was no miracle here today, ma'am. It would be better if she had died."

The words strike me like a punch to the gut.

The EMT glances at me, disbelief in her eyes. She thinks he's mentally ill. She's wrong though. There's nothing wrong with his brain. He's simply a mean, hateful man who got religion. A man who looks at me and sees a reflection of his own shame.

The EMT turns to my mother, thinking that surely my mom's maternal instinct must override my father's disdain. "Ma'am, don't you want to take your daughter home to rest? She's had a terrible shock, and she might need to see the doctor about her wrist. I think it's a minor sprain, but you may want to get an X-ray."

Dead-eyed, cold as a fish, my mother stares at me. "She's no daughter of mine."

"We tried to turn you toward the light," Dad says. "We did everything in our power, but your heart is too rebellious." He shakes his head sadly. "You've chosen the darkness, and I won't let you bring it home with you anymore, to taint us too. Goodbye, Carolina."

With that, my parents turn away, my father tall and straight-backed, my mother limping behind him. Their words seep through my skin and into my bloodstream, spreading through me as surely as the blood that beats through my veins.

Dad's right. It's my fault. I killed him. Because that's what I am. A killer. It's in my DNA. I am bad, all the way through. Everything I touch turns to death.

I gasp back into the present, to my blood-covered hands, to Noah bleeding out on the floor. Another Michael, dead at my hands.

"You did what had to be done," Maggie is saying. "It was horrible, but now Lucy will be safe. And who knows how many other lives you've saved, all the people Noah would have hurt."

"She's right," Lucy says.

"But he's dead," I say, shaking so hard my teeth rattle in my skull. "He's dead, and I killed him." I gesture at Noah's body, but I can't stand to look at it again.

"*We* killed him," Lucy says. "All of us. Not just you." She looks fierce, almost proud.

"I don't think the police are going to see it that way," I say.

"The police are never going to know about it." Maggie strides toward me. She grips my arms, stares into my face. Her gaze is deadly serious. "Never. You understand?"

When I nod, she releases me. "No one knows Noah came out here. We didn't get it on camera, did we?"

Lucy and I both shake our heads. I never even considered trying to film it.

Maggie shrugs. "The canyon already took one serial killer's body. Why not another?"

"What are you saying?" I ask.

"We leave him here," Maggie says. "Let the animals have him."

"Shouldn't we go to the police?" Lucy asks. "Explain what happened? I mean, he attacked us. It was self-defense. We'll tell them what happened, and they'll understand."

Maggie shakes her head. "If we'd gotten him on video confessing, maybe. But otherwise, it looks like we lured him out here and killed him. Especially after all of your confrontations with him, how everyone in camp thinks about you. I don't think it would all go the way you're imagining."

"Shit," Lucy breathes, rubbing her face. "You're right."

Is she right? I can't think straight. I'm so tired. So over-whelmed.

"So we leave him?" I ask. "We go back to camp like nothing happened?"

"Yes," Maggie says coldly. "We dump our bloody clothes somewhere else. We hike back to camp. We go to dinner and then to bed, just like normal. And if anyone asks us about Noah, we tell them we don't know anything."

"Someone will come looking for him. Brandon—he's been keeping a close eye on him," I say.

Maggie shrugs. "Noah got lost in the fog. He wouldn't be the first. And it wouldn't be the first time he disappeared either."

"What other choice do we have?" Lucy asks.

"We could . . ." My words trail off. I have no other ideas. "I don't know, but this feels wrong. To just leave him."

Lucy takes my hands. "You wouldn't have hurt him if you'd had a choice. He was trying to kill me. I'm so sorry that you had to do it. I know it's horrible. But—but he was a bad person. And you're not. You—you deserve to put this behind you. You shouldn't suffer because of him. None of us should." Her eyes are huge and earnest.

"Can we put this behind us? Is that even possible?" I murmur, breaking away from her.

Lucy looks down at Noah's body. "Now that he's dead, I don't think Kincaid will be able to haunt me anymore. I think I'll finally be free." She takes a breath. "I think—I think I already am."

"You feel free?" I ask, some of the weight lifting from my heart. I know what that kind of bloody freedom feels like—I remember it, even if my own was so brief.

Lucy nods. She gives me a small, tremulous smile.

"Okay," I say, too exhausted to do anything except give in. "Let's get cleaned up and go back to camp, then."

In silence, we strip off our clothes and replace them with ones from our bags. Lucy uses gauze from her first aid kit to wrap Maggie's arm. The cut wasn't too deep. Maggie puts her jacket on over it.

Once we've cleaned things up as much as we can, we file out of the cave, taking everything with us—our bloodied clothes and sleeping bags, the camping lantern, the knife. The only thing we leave behind is Noah.

We pause in the fog at the mouth of the cave, and Maggie looks between us. She's been all business for the last half hour, but now her face crumples as if she wants to cry. "Lucy, I'm sorry things went this way. I said no one would get hurt, and I was wrong." She touches Lucy's bruised neck with trembling fingers. "I'm so sorry."

"You couldn't have known," Lucy says. "But it's over now." She squeezes Maggie's hand once and then continues down the path toward camp, leaving the carnage behind her.

Maggie meets my eyes, her expression unreadable. "Well, you said you came to this contest to find out who you are. I guess you did." I flinch, as if she's punched me. But she only shrugs and jogs away to catch up with Lucy.

I stand alone in the fog, swallowing down my shame, trying to make sense of everything that just happened.

I've got my memories back, and now I know the truth. Michael wasn't my fault. I didn't kill him. I didn't make him choose to drive his four-wheeler off a cliff with me on it. I didn't enjoy his death. I only tried to get myself free from another man who wanted to cage and control me. And he tried to kill me for it.

It was Dad's voice in my head all this time, filling in those blank spaces in my memory—his voice saying that I am evil, that I am wrong inside.

I'm not evil. I'm not wrong inside. I was never a murderer.

Until I killed Noah.

A human being. Maybe an innocent one, if there's any such thing.

So what does that mean for me? For who I am? I shake my head, but I can't clear it. Lucy says she found her freedom in Noah's death. And Maggie said I found out who I am, but she's wrong. I don't have a single goddamned clue.

# TWENTY-FIVE

## LUCY

**I walk away** from the cave with certainty beating in my veins.

Noah is dead. Kincaid is dead. There's no one left to hurt me. I'm safe.

There could be others, at some point, someday. The world is filled with monsters. But for now, *my* monsters are gone. Dead. Defeated.

So, despite my pain and exhaustion, despite the horror of the last hours, a sense of freedom stretches out inside me because there's finally room enough inside my chest for something more than fear. Room for dreams and adventures and maybe even love. I'm going to apply to college when I get home. I'm going to plan my future. And Maggie? Is there any possibility for us after we leave here? I want there to be. I think she does too.

But for now, there's a more pressing issue: we need to make ourselves look like we didn't just murder someone. I know I should feel guilty and ashamed as I stuff my bloodied clothes into an abandoned burrow and cover it with rocks. I know I should feel bad for Noah, his family, his friends. But I don't. We didn't plan to kill him today, but he forced us to. And I'm glad he's dead. It was self-defense, and he deserved it.

Shivering in the cold air, we kneel behind some bushes at the edge of the creek to scrub the dried blood from our skin. We stay together, but Carolina keeps her distance, a stunned look on her face. While I finish rinsing Noah's blood out of my hair, out from under my nails, Maggie sits on a fallen log, staring absentmindedly at her open notebook. I've been so caught up in everything else, I had almost forgotten about the academic paper she came here to write. But I don't think she's even reading her notes. Her gaze is far, far away. I can't tell what she's thinking.

I sit next to her, and she looks up at me, brought back to here and now. Maybe it's wrong, but a smile breaks open in my chest and spreads across my face. Maggie's eyes glitter in response. I take her face in my hands and kiss her, long and deep and unafraid. "Thank you," I say.

Carolina might be the one who delivered the killing blow, but it's Maggie who made it possible. Maggie who saw more than Kincaid's last victim when she looked at me. Maggie who made sure I got free.

"You did it all yourself, Luce," Maggie says. Then she smiles, and it's breathtaking. My heart breaks a little because tomorrow we have to get into our cars and drive away from one another. Maggie will go back to college, and I'll go home to my family and to my last year of high school. We might never see each other again.

"You gave me my life back," I say.

Maggie smooths a wayward strand of hair across my forehead. "We had better make it a good one, then."

It's not lost on me that she said *we*.

"What about your paper? Will you still be able to publish it?" I ask, gesturing toward her notebook. "Things got a little . . . off track, didn't they? Plus, no one found Kincaid's body." Kincaid is the reason I came here, but finding his remains seems so unimportant now. Like Noah was his surrogate, and seeing him die released me from Kincaid's power.

"I got everything I need," Maggie says, closing the notebook's cover. She takes my hand in hers, and we lapse into quiet, staring at the creek, listening to the burbling of the water. Cloudkiss Canyon doesn't seem so scary anymore.

Maybe I should be thinking about Noah and what will happen when he's reported missing, or when his body is found, but there's no room in me for second-guesses or recriminations. I'm not looking backward.

Because for the first time since Joseph Kincaid leapt into Cloudkiss Canyon two years ago, I look into my future and see a life I want to live.

I'm going to enjoy my last months of high school. Try to get an internship for the summer, maybe with the parks department. And I'm going to apply for all the best environmental programs. Maybe even one near Maggie. I'm going to start hiking by myself again. As soon as I get back to Nashville, I'm driving out to Beaman Park and disappearing into the woods. Maybe I'll even camp overnight at Bells Bend.

As we head back to camp, these thoughts spin on, giddy and bright, propelling me through the rough terrain and distracting me from my fatigue and even from the pain that creeps across my ribs and up my neck, its fingertips cradling my skull.

Joseph Kincaid has been dead for two years, but now his ghost is banished too.

When we walk into camp, it's late afternoon, the sun going down behind the mountains, though it's hardly noticeable in the heavy pall of fog. A mourning dove coos from the electric pole, solemn and lonesome sounding. It's the last full day of the contest, so camp is mostly deserted, people making what they can of the last bit of daylight to search for Kincaid's bones. Still, I'm nervous that someone will notice something amiss—the bruises peeking out above my sweater, how Maggie moves her injured arm with extra care, or—worst of all—the haunted look in Carolina's eyes. But instead, the few people we encounter are too wrapped up in their own issues to even spare us a glance.

Maybe it's the stress of the contest winding down, the toll of camping for a week in the cold, I don't know. But people are behaving oddly, and this time I know it has nothing to do with me. Everyone we see looks angry or depressed or just . . . fidgety. The woman who always wears the *Friday the 13th* hoodie paces in front of her tent, forward and back, forward and back, as if tranced. She chews at her cuticles, which are bleeding freely. We hurry past a tent where a couple is having extremely loud, deeply disturbing-sounding sex.

Right as we go by, a knife blade rips through the fabric of the tent and a man yells, "Jesus, Bridget!"

Maggie whistles in admiration. "Bridget heard the call of the wild, and she said yes."

"I hope that's not Rosa's Bridget," I say, and Maggie smirks like she knows something.

I glance at Carolina to see what she thinks, but she seems oblivious to our conversation, as well as everything else.

"Hey," I say, nudging her. "Let's get our stuff and go shower, all right?" She nods, her movements listless and her eyes unfocused, as if they're looking back in time, still seeing Noah's body laid out in a pool of his own blood.

Maggie holds my hand as we walk to the showers, and Carolina stumbles along beside us. I finally take her hand too, to try to draw her back to the present. We must make an interesting silhouette—three girls linked together in the fog.

How different this walk is from the last two, when I was thinking about Noah and Kincaid, wondering if God was up there and watching me suffer. Now I feel light and clean, untouchable, even if I'm exhausted and in terrible need of a shower. Carolina looks just as bad now as she did during the height of her hangover this morning, her face gray, purple bags beneath her eyes. Her hand is ice cold in mine.

Hopefully people will only think she's tired. Then again, I don't think anyone's going to notice her. Everyone's clearly too busy with their own personal chaos.

In fact, as we near the showers, I'm not surprised to hear raised, angry voices. Maggie puts her finger to her lips, and we sneak around the side of the building. A middle-aged couple is face-to-face, arguing. I immediately recognize them as the couple that came into the hallway to check what was happening when Carolina rescued me from Rufus. The man is pressed against the wall, the woman bearing down on him, her face contorted with rage. "You humiliated me," she snarls, grabbing his jacket and slamming him hard into the bricks. He cringes and tries to look away from her. But she grabs his face in one iron fist, digging her claws into his skin.

"A deer's rib!" she sneers. "You're a medical professional, for God's sake."

"I'm only a phlebotomist, honey."

"Don't call me 'honey,' you sniveling child!" The woman's eyes are wild, terrifying.

I expect the man to fight back, push her away, but instead he sinks into himself like rotting fruit, his face a mess of tears and snot. "Please, please," he sobs. "I'm sorry. I know I'm a failure. I always let you down. I'm worthless. I'm so sorry, Joyce. I wanted so badly to be the one to find him. I wanted to make you proud."

Joyce slaps him so hard the sound makes me flinch, and he sobs even harder. It's about the saddest thing I've ever seen.

I glance at Carolina to see if she's going to try to intervene like usual, but her eyes are distant, far away. I don't think she even sees what's happening right in front of her. Meanwhile, Maggie is watching the scene play out like it's on TV, her eyes wide and riveted.

"We should do something," I whisper.

"I'm not getting in the middle of a marital spat," Maggie whispers back.

"That's not a spat. She's hurting him. She's, like, sadistic."

"We shouldn't draw attention to ourselves after what just happened."

"Fine, I'll do it myself," I say. "Get ready."

"Hey!" I yell, then quickly pull Maggie and Carolina around the corner and into a shower stall, where the couple can't see us.

"Who's there?" Joyce calls, her voice alarmed. I don't answer. "Excuse me?" she says, now in a more normal tone, ready to pretend it was all a misunderstanding.

I hear her footsteps come around the corner. "There's no one here," she says to herself. "I'm hearing things again. I hate this fucking canyon." She sighs and walks away. "Joe?" she calls. "Joe?" Her husband doesn't answer. "Joe, where the hell did you go?" she yells, then runs away into the woods, presumably to look for him.

"Oh my God," I breathe, leaning my head against Maggie's shoulder. "I hope he's all right."

"He'll be fine," Maggie says, stroking my hair. "He had a head start."

I wonder why she doesn't seem unnerved by what we just witnessed. She called it a marital spat. But as a psychology major, she has to know better. Why did she try to diminish it? Why did she act so unsympathetic? Maybe what happened with Noah affected her more than I thought, more than she was willing to let on. Maybe I expect too much from her. After all, he attacked her too. She almost watched me die.

When I don't answer, Maggie meets my eyes. "He'll be okay, Lucy."

"He won't be okay," Carolina says, her voice hollow. "None of us will be." Without another word, she leaves the stall, and a few seconds later, I hear water running.

"We're going to have to keep an eye on her," Maggie says in a low voice.

I nod. "But we won't be able to do that once she goes home. I hope she can keep it together. Poor Carolina."

Maggie's eyes are thoughtful. She doesn't say anything.

"Maggie?" I ask.

She turns her gaze to me. "Everything will be fine, Luce," she says, stroking my face. "From now on, everything will be fine."

There's a knot of worry trying to form in my stomach, but when Maggie kisses me, I decide to believe her.

We fought too hard for everything to not be fine.

# TWENTY-SIX

## CAROLINA

**The world has** been nothing more than mist and echoes for hours now, but when we walk into the lodge for dinner, the room comes into horrible, severe focus, all right angles and bright light. The hum of conversation is loud, discordant, like poorly played jazz. It feels like every single person looks up from their plates to stare at us. Lucy shrinks down into the scarf she put on to hide the bruises on her neck, and I avoid everyone's gazes, looking at the floor, the walls—anywhere except into their eyes. I shove my hands into my pockets, afraid some traces of blood might linger under my nails or in the creases of my skin. I'm afraid they can hear my crime in the beating of my heart, the breath moving in and out of my lungs. Maggie, though, looks as carefree and natural as if she'd done nothing today except go for a nice hike. As if she feels nothing.

I remember her smile in the cave. Maybe I didn't imagine it.

Or maybe I just don't want to be alone in my guilt, maybe I'm looking for somewhere to put the weight of this horror that's crushing me.

The bachelorettes all lean their heads together to whisper, darting furtive looks at us as we get in line for food. They look like a troupe of mean popular kids in a high school cafeteria, their smiles cruel and cold. I can hear their whispers as I accept my plate of spaghetti and garlic bread, my glass of sweet tea. I find an empty table in the corner and sit facing the wall. But I can feel the other contestants' eyes on me, their gazes pounding my back like an onslaught of waves.

Maggie and Lucy slide into the seats across from me, and they both start to eat. My plate sits untouched. How can they eat when we—I—just killed a man? When I stabbed a knife into him three—or was it four—times? When he bled out on the cave floor and the light left his eyes?

Lucy eats carefully, wincing a little as each small bite goes down her throat. But when she looks up at me, her eyes are shining. It's such a relieved, unburdened look, I want to weep.

Noah's life was the price for that look in her eyes—his life and my innocence. It's a cruel sort of irony, isn't it? I realized I'm not a killer in the same moment I killed someone. I became what I most feared by trying to be good, by trying to take care of her.

I know Lucy thinks Maggie set her free, but it was me. I'm the one who plunged the knife into Noah's chest. I'm the one who saved her. And yet Maggie is the one she kissed when it was all over, the one she'll spend tonight with, the one she will—

"Carolina, you need to eat," Maggie says, making me flinch.

"I'm not hungry." There's an edge of anger in my voice, but either Maggie doesn't notice or chooses to ignore it.

"It doesn't matter if you're hungry. If you don't eat, you look suspicious." She smiles at me like she just said something funny, playing her part for this roomful of spectators.

She's right—I ought to be hungry after a day of hiking. But the food looks disgusting to me, like blood and entrails. I lift my fork and twirl the spaghetti noodles a few times before giving up. Instead, I take a bite of garlic bread, nearly gagging at its oily texture. I manage to swallow down a single painful bite before putting it back on my plate.

"Here, have my pudding," Lucy says, sliding the small white container toward me.

"Thanks," I whisper, and peel it open. Lucy hands me her spoon, and I take a bite. Vanilla sweetness coats my tongue, and I give her a small smile.

"See, you're okay," she says, reaching across the table to squeeze my hand. "And I am too." Her voice still sounds a little raspy. But it could have been much, much worse.

A tray plunks down onto the table next to me, startling all three of us.

"Y'all mind if I sit here?" Brandon asks. "I don't know where Noah is."

"Sure," Maggie says cheerfully. "The more the merrier."

Every muscle in my body tenses, and I keep my eyes trained on my plate. I focus all my energy on keeping my hands from shaking. I killed his roommate. What would Brandon think of me if he knew? Would he still say I'm a good person?

Brandon slides in next to me, his broad shoulder bumping mine. "You all right, Carolina?" he asks.

"Yeah," I say, not meeting his eyes. "Just tired. And I don't like spaghetti."

"Here, I'll trade you for this salad," he says. "I hate salad."

I accept his bowl, and he takes my plate and scrapes it on top of his meal. "Double spaghetti," he says in a funny deep voice, and pretends to strike his chest like King Kong.

The three of us laugh, and I think it sounds normal, ordinary. But there must be a false note somewhere because Brandon looks between Maggie, Lucy, and me with a question in his eyes. I quickly shove a forkful of lettuce into my mouth. It tastes like nothing.

"So how's the search going for your team?" Maggie asks.

Brandon shrugs. "We haven't found anything. To tell you the truth, I'm glad. I think if I found a serial killer's skeleton right now, I would keel over dead. There's only so much a man can take." His eyes flit to Lucy, and he blushes, as if only now remembering who she is. He puts his fingers to his mouth, and I see his nails are bitten down to the quick, the skin red and irritated. He's clearly stressing. About Noah?

"How about you g— Hey, wait, I thought you were camping in the canyon tonight? Isn't that what you said, Maggie?"

Panic constricts my lungs for a moment, but Maggie lies without hesitation, her voice perfectly natural. "Yeah, we were going to, but Carolina got freaked out and wanted to come back."

Brandon smiles at me. "See? I told you about this place, didn't I?" He bumps my shoulder with his again, almost playful. But his eyes are serious, preoccupied.

"Yeah, you did," I manage to say. Is that why things got so out of control? Is there truly something evil here, heightening everything we feel, driving us to the brink of ourselves? I remember how Maggie said we ought to lean into the effects of the fog, see where it takes us. Maybe that's what Noah did. Because the way he snapped, how strong he was . . .

And is that why I killed him? I didn't feel out of control. I felt like myself. And it's not like I wanted to do it, not like I enjoyed it. So what does that mean?

"That headache still bothering you?" Brandon asks, clearly concerned by something he sees in my face or hears in my voice.

"Yeah, I guess so," I say, rubbing my temple, and I'm not even lying. My head does hurt.

Brandon puts his arm around me and gently rubs my shoulder. It's sweet and comforting, and I'm afraid I might burst into tears. I don't deserve any of his kindness.

We eat quietly for a few minutes, listening to contestants talk and laugh all around us. Maggie finally breaks the silence. "Have you heard anything from the other groups? Like, has anyone seen anything, found any signs of Kincaid at all?"

"Nah," Brandon says, then laughs. "That married couple Joyce and Joe, they found a rib bone earlier today and got all excited, but one of the rangers said it was from a deer."

Lucy flinches. She glances between Maggie and me. Joyce and Joe are the couple we saw behind the showers. I was still pretty out of it then, but I remember how he cowered away from her, how enraged she was. I think she mentioned something about a deer.

No one says anything for a while.

"Have you gone to any of the campfire stuff?" Maggie asks, apparently afraid of what might happen if she lets the conversation lag.

"A little, but it's not really . . . I mean, like, I went to trivia night to hang out because Noah and Rufus had disappeared, but I couldn't answer a single question. I looked like an idiot."

Lucy smiles at him. "I don't think that's such a bad thing, considering the subject matter."

"I guess not," Brandon says. "But I've had some interesting conversations with people here. About whether there's anything redemptive in true crime, or if it's only exploitative—that kind of thing. It has opened my eyes a little, I guess."

"How so?" Maggie asks, immediately interested. I'm surprised she doesn't pull her notebook out and jot down his answers for her paper. Maybe that's all we are to her—anecdotes for publication.

"Well, I thought it was creepy to be into serial killers, and I still think it is. But some of the women here told me that for them it's a way of facing the stuff they're most afraid of—like watching a horror movie, you know? Addison told me that hearing these stories on podcasts helps her think through what she might do if she were attacked and makes her be more careful about her surroundings and stuff. I guess that's not so bad, you know?"

Lucy cocks her head. "So they listen to *Human Beasties* because they are afraid of serial killers?"

"Exactly," Brandon says. He shrugs.

Lucy looks around the room, scrunching up her brow. "I'd honestly never thought of that."

Brandon studies her. "Well, you've been on the other side, haven't you? Of hearing your own story used for entertainment?"

Lucy nods and tightens the scarf around her neck.

Pressure builds in my chest, and my ears start to ring. I know I shouldn't do it, know I shouldn't mention Noah's name, but I need to find out if Brandon has any idea where Noah might have gone. If there's any chance we're going to be found out.

"So where did you say Noah was?" I ask.

Lucy widens her eyes at me across the table, and Maggie gives a slight shake of her head. But it's too late—the question is out.

Brandon swallows a big bite of spaghetti and wipes his mouth with the back of his hand. "Dude has been disappearing all week. This morning, we were out on the gulch trail, and he split. Rufus said he saw him talking to a girl, and then he was just gone. I hope—"

"What girl?" I ask.

"I wish I knew," Brandon says. And I can read the rest of his meaning in the grim set of his jaw. He wishes he knew so he could make sure she was okay.

"What time was that?" I ask, an idea niggling at the back of my mind.

"I don't know, maybe ten or eleven? Why?" Brandon looks at me and then at Lucy and Maggie.

"Carolina thinks it's her job to keep tabs on everyone and everything around her," Maggie says. Her voice is light, but her eyes darken to an unnatural, smoky gray. I do a double take, but when I look again, she seems normal.

"Sorry," I say, "too much *Human Beasties*, you know?" I laugh. Brandon laughs too. But my mind is whirring. Lucy and I were out walking in the fog then, leaving Maggie alone in the cave. Noah would have been so close to us, and yet we didn't see him or anyone he was talking to. Unless the girl he was talking to was . . .

I try to recall every detail of our encounter with Noah, every word he said, everything Maggie said too. It's all blurring together. But I do remember how shocked he seemed, as if things were going very differently than planned. The incredulous way he looked at Maggie . . . And how Maggie smiled as he bled out on the ground.

I risk another glance at her now, and she's looking out across the room, absentmindedly fiddling with the left cuff of her denim jacket. I remember the careless way she shrugged it on after Lucy bandaged the cut on her arm. Lucky she wasn't wearing it when Noah attacked her, especially since I've never seen her take it off. The jacket is pristine, blood-free, as unmarred by this morning's events as Maggie seemingly is, though I know it's hiding a four-inch gash on her upper arm.

An image of Maggie drawing the blade across her own skin flashes through my mind.

It's so jarring that I stand up abruptly, upsetting the table so that the dishes rattle. "Sorry, I, uh, have to pee," I say. I ignore Lucy's startled, worried gaze and Maggie's glowering one. I hurry through the room and into the hallway, which is empty. My thoughts come fast and messy, crashing into one another.

I didn't kill Michael. I didn't hurt Kiersten. I know that now, I know it with complete certainty. But I did kill Noah. I did it to protect Lucy, and nothing about it felt good. Nothing about it felt right. Except that it saved Lucy's life, and it freed her up from the fear of Noah coming after her.

But did it really need to happen? Did we need to be out in that cave, setting a trap for him? That wasn't an accident. It was planned, plotted. By all of us? Or by Maggie? It felt like Lucy's idea, but was it?

I slip into a stall and pull out my phone with shaking hands. I type Maggie's name into the Google search bar. I'm not even sure what I'm looking for, but something. Something to tell me the feeling in my gut is wrong. That I'm overreacting, that I'm imagining things. Maybe I want Maggie to be at fault here because I'm threatened by Lucy's feelings for her, because I'm ashamed, because I'm filled with guilt for what I've done.

Maggie has no social media profiles that I can find. I thought she'd at least have a Twitter account where she could mouth off. But there's nothing.

I try adding her university to her name. Still nothing. But then, in desperation, I click the News tab. And there she is, three stories down, highlighted in an article about a fire. She did mention helping her roommate try to burn down a guy's house when we were drinking last night. She bragged about getting away with it.

I open the article, my heart hammering in my throat while I wait for the page to load. An ad pops up instead and refuses to close. "Damn it," I whisper, poking futilely at my screen.

Finally, I get the ad out of the way and skim the article, watching for Maggie's name. Four months ago, a freshman named Rachel Duncan tried to burn down her boyfriend's off-campus house, badly injuring herself in the process. Hospitalized with third-degree burns on her arms, face, and torso, Rachel was unable to give her account to police. But, the article says, her roommate, Maggie Rey, provided insight into the crime. Maggie explained that Rachel's boyfriend, a member of a frat, had dumped her, and Rachel wouldn't accept it. She was obsessed with him, stalking him and sending him threatening messages. There's a direct quote from Maggie: "We were getting coffee when he walked in with his new girlfriend, and I guess Rachel sort of snapped. When he told her to leave him alone, she got all quiet and left the shop. I had no idea she was going to do something so extreme to get back at him. But she had a history of trauma and was always a little fragile, you know? If I'm honest, I really wasn't surprised when I found out what she'd done."

A chill runs through me. Maggie told me she helped her roommate start the fire. Why would she lie and say that if she didn't do it? Clearly, she got away with her part in it, and Rachel got all the blame.

What will Maggie say about me and Lucy when Noah's body is found and it's connected to us? That she had no idea what we were up to? That we were two fragile, damaged girls and she just tried to be our friend?

With a wince, I realize she really could get away with it too. Because Maggie never touched Noah, not that I can remember. In the cave, she yelled and threatened and cried, but I don't think she ever laid a finger on him, not even when he choked Lucy.

My knees go weak, and I sink down onto the toilet lid. My head in my hands, I run through the last week, cataloging it all. How Maggie goaded Lucy on with all those speeches about getting free, how excited she was about our plan to trap Noah, how she forced the idea of the cave even though it didn't really make sense. How we were too tired and hungover from her whiskey to argue.

I'd bet anything that she did the same to Rachel. She probably encouraged Rachel's obsession, helped her spy on the boyfriend, maybe even made the plans for the fire. She wound Rachel up like a toy and watched her go. Just like she did to Lucy. And to me.

Because there's absolutely no reason Noah would have known to go to that particular cave, half-hidden on a deer track. Unless he was led there. Unless it was planned.

But why? What does Maggie get out of it?

I remember her smile, how pleased she looked. Because her plan had worked. Because she'd won the game.

She moved us all around like pawns on a chessboard.

I feel certain now that Maggie was the girl Rufus saw talking to Noah. That she set Noah up too, just like she did us.

She wanted to bring the three of us together in that cave, to see what would happen. I doubt she expected Noah to end up dead. That seems a step too far. Maybe she just thought it would be exciting, a bit of drama to liven up her psychology paper.

Still, now that I'm on this track, I can't get off it. The last five days suddenly feel like a play I've been acting in without realizing I was onstage. How far back does it all go? When did Maggie start weaving this web? Did she burn her own tent down? Tip off Rufus about Lucy's identity? Drug us to make us hallucinate? Is she the reason I've spent all week afraid I might hurt Lucy? Anything seems possible.

I feel delirious, seasick. Maybe nothing that happened this week was even real. Maybe it was all a game that Maggie was playing.

Lucy will be devastated when I tell her.

But I need to tell her now, before Maggie has time to dream up any new schemes.

Quickly, I snap screenshots of the article in case I can't get enough cell signal to open it again. Then I hurry out of the bathroom stall and down the hallway, but the dining room table where I left them is empty. I must have been gone longer than I thought. Panic thrums through me, the only thing able to cut through my haze of exhaustion.

God, if I could sleep. If I could clear my head for an hour, maybe I could figure this out. But I can't. I have to find Lucy.

I head toward the sound of voices and see people crowding around the fire, setting up camping chairs and laying out blankets to sit on. I remember tonight's the last night of Killer Quest, and that everything wraps up tomorrow afternoon. So tonight is the final chance for revelry and storytelling, arguing about cold cases and hooking up. The night's event is Plan the Perfect Murder, and groups are supposed to take turns presenting their murder plan and being grilled by the other contestants. The group with the most solid plan, as decided by Sandra and Kevin, wins a bunch of *Human Beasties* merch. Maggie said we should go tonight at least for a little while so we'll seem less suspicious. The irony alone may kill me.

In the midst of groups of people arguing and gesticulating and laughing, I spot Lucy sitting alone near the fire, staring into the flames, lost in thought. Relief rolls through me, a brief respite from my building anxiety. I rush over and sit beside her. "I need to talk to you. Where's Maggie?"

Lucy startles and looks up at me, flames dancing in her eyes, her skin glowing orange-red. I remember how Maggie said Lucy had a fire inside her, and Maggie just wanted to help let it out.

"I don't know. I think she went to use the bathroom or something. What is it?" Lucy lowers her voice. "Did someone find Noah, or . . . ?"

"No, it's not that. Can we—can we take a walk?" My heart starts to race.

"Let's wait for Maggie."

I bite my lip. "It's about Maggie."

Lucy gets up wordlessly and heads away from the fire and into the trees. I'm reminded powerfully of my first night here, of being in the woods with Brandon when we heard Noah scream. Was that Maggie messing with him, moving him a little closer to what happened today? I don't see how she could have made him hallucinate seeing Lucy's dead and mutilated body. Maybe I'm jumping to conclusions.

Lucy stops suddenly and spins to face me. "So what about Maggie?" She crosses her arms over her chest, already defensive. This is not going to be easy.

I clear my throat, all my urgency fading into nervousness and self-doubt. I'm about to tell Lucy the last thing in the world she wants to hear. And I've got barely any proof. She won't want to listen, but I have to at least try.

"Maggie—Maggie isn't who we thought she was."

Her eyebrows knit together. "What are you talking about?"

"I think she's been . . . manipulating us. Trying to get us to do what she wants. I think she set up what happened today."

"What do you mean?"

"I don't know," I say, running my fingers through my still-damp hair. Everything that felt so clear a few minutes ago feels muddled now. I'm not sure how much of what I suspect is true.

"I think she told Noah to come to the cave, that we'd be there. I think she, like, planned it with him."

Lucy's eyes widen. "Of course she didn't. Noah attacked her. You saw the cut on her arm."

"Yeah, and isn't it weird she wasn't wearing her jacket? It was freezing in that cave."

Lucy scrunches up her face in disbelief. "What? You sound like one of these conspiracy theorists around here." She gestures toward the campfire. I can just make out several voices humming the *Human Beasties* theme song.

She's not wrong. I sound delusional. I should focus on what I saw, not what I suspect. "Look, when I—" I lower my voice to a whisper. "When I stabbed Noah, I looked at Maggie and she was *smiling*. Like she wanted him to die. Or at least like she was glad it happened." I plow on before Lucy can interrupt. "And remember Brandon said Noah was talking to a girl before he disappeared today? There's no one else that could have been but Maggie. I think she led him back to our camp and set him up."

"Carolina," Lucy says, pity in her eyes. "I know today was awful, that what you had to do was awful. Maybe it messed with your head a little. I mean, you were already talking about the canyon being evil and all that. I think you've gotten a little carried away."

"No," I say. "No, actually, for the first time I feel like I know the truth. When I saw Noah's blood, I remembered things that—" I stop. Telling her about Michael, about my fears of being a killer, is the last thing I should do. "I just don't think we can trust her," I say instead.

Lucy shakes her head. "You've always been against Maggie. From day one, you've been contradicting her. You've been trying to keep her away from me. I know you're jealous, but do you really want to take it this far?"

I stare at her, momentarily at a loss for words. Of course I've been jealous of Maggie, but this is so much bigger than that. "Lucy, I'm afraid for you," I say.

"Afraid for me?" Lucy laughs. "There's nothing to be afraid of anymore." She squeezes my wrists, looks into my eyes. "Noah is dead. He can't hurt me."

"But Maggie can," I say.

Lucy lets me go. "What's that supposed to mean?"

"Look. Just look." I pull out my phone and open up the screenshots I took of the article. "Read this."

Lucy scans the text, her brow furrowed.

"She's done this before," I say.

"Done what? What does this fire have to do with anything?"

God, is Lucy really so blind? Can she really not see what Maggie has been doing this whole time? Do I have to spell it out?

"Maggie took a vulnerable girl and played on her fears and insecurities and drove her to act out in a dangerous way. Doesn't that sound familiar?"

Lucy shakes her head. "You have no evidence that Maggie had anything to do with that fire. And when are you going to stop seeing me as vulnerable?"

"We're *all* vulnerable," I spit, suddenly angry, the numbness of the last few hours finally fading. "I am. Every person who's alive is vulnerable in some way. And Maggie is the sort of person who takes advantage of that. She told me she helped

Rachel start the fire. Yet in this article, she lied and said she knew nothing about it."

"Okay," Lucy says, struggling to stay patient. "That's a little weird, I guess, but what exactly do you think she's going to do to me? Set *me* on fire?"

"I don't know," I admit. God, I've bungled this whole thing. I haven't explained everything right.

"Carolina," Lucy says, her voice ragged. "All you've done since we got here is try to rescue me, like I'm some damsel in distress. Maggie saw more than that in me. She wanted more for me. She *made* me more."

"She made us murderers," I say quietly. And I mean it. I didn't kill Noah for Lucy; I did it for Maggie because she set it up and made it happen. The anger kindling in my gut flares up, threatening wildfire.

Lucy clenches her jaw. "I didn't want Noah to die, but I'm glad he's dead. It's like I can breathe again, for the first time in two years. Kincaid has been haunting me all this time, but now he's gone too. I'll never be afraid again. Maggie did that for me." Her eyes flash, and I see a look there that's horribly familiar: it's the same way my father looks when he talks about his salvation, his redemption from sin, his freedom in Jesus. Lucy sees Maggie as her own personal savior.

"And yet *I'm* the one who killed Noah—not Maggie," I snarl.

"Maggie would have handed me the blade and let me do it myself," Lucy hisses, my anger reflected in her eyes. "That's the difference between the two of you."

"Yeah, it is," I say. "Because only one of us actually cares about you."

Lucy laughs, and it's a hard, unkind sound. "Well, do me one last favor, then, Carolina. Stop caring about me."

I gape at her, absorbing the words like a blow. Lucy pushes past me and strides away, back toward the campfire, back toward Maggie and all the plans Maggie's making for her. She didn't believe anything I said.

I stand alone in the darkness, in the ever-present fog. I am hurt, exhausted, ashamed, but for the first time in months, maybe in years, my head is clear and my heart is sure. I am not what my father said I am, what I believed about myself. I'm not a monster. But I think Maggie is.

Lucy can't see it. Maggie is a poison she is determined to drink until it chokes her. But I will knock the cup from her hand. I will save her from that fate, even if I have to swallow the venom myself.

# TWENTY-SEVEN

## LUCY

**As I walk** away from Carolina, I start to shake. How dare she try to take this from me? How dare she try to ruin everything? And for what—some petty jealousy? It's sick.

I know Maggie isn't perfect. I know she can be dramatic and a little insensitive. I know she puts on a big show. But she isn't some evil puppeteer driving us to commit murder. Carolina is clearly cracking under the weight of what we've done—what *she's* done—and is looking for someone else to blame. The canyon, the fog, Maggie. I should have known this would happen with how she was acting at dinner, all those questions she asked Brandon.

I know I probably shouldn't have said some of the things I did, but she's making up lies about Maggie. Trying to turn me against her.

Against the one person who enabled me to get my life back, to get free. The one person who makes me want to dream again.

I won't let Carolina get into my head. I won't let her steal my peace of mind, not when I've only just gotten it back.

When I return to the fire, Maggie is there, chatting with Rosa and Bridget. She shoots me a grin that sends a pang straight to my heart. How could this girl have done anything that Carolina said she did? It's impossible.

I search Rosa's and Bridget's faces for some signs of distress or animosity, but they seem ordinary, happy. If that was Bridget in that tent today, Rosa clearly doesn't know about it . . . unless she was in there too. I really don't want to know. I'm just glad they seem okay and that they seem to have gotten over most of their suspicion of me.

Carolina doesn't come back to the fire. When Maggie asks about her, I lie and say she felt unwell and went to bed early. Maggie shrugs, but she insists that she and I stay at the fire until the small hours of the night, that we stay where people can see us, that we act as normally as we can.

When Sandra and Kevin join all of us at the campfire, Kevin looks around at everyone and shakes his head. "You all look so bummed out. Why? Because no one has found the bones yet?"

People murmur and shrug in response.

Kevin leaps to his feet dramatically. "You know what this means, don't you?" His eyes dance gleefully in the firelight. "If no one finds Kincaid's remains before tomorrow at lunchtime, then Killer Quest lives on to fight another day! We'll have it again next year. Hell, if we need to, we'll make it an annual tradition. Every year we can make it bigger and better. We can bring in new experts and speakers, make it a full-blown convention, my friends. Just imagine the possibilities!"

"Can we get yurts next year, then?" Addison asks. "My back can't take another week sleeping on the ground."

"Anything you want!" Kevin says. "We'll open up a suggestion page on our website."

The contestants around me break into excited conversation. I shake my head. How could they want to come back here, year after year? I thought I was beginning to understand these people, but they are like another species entirely. Kevin and Sandra I get though. I can practically see the dollar signs spinning in Sandra's eyes as she laughs and jokes and answers everyone's questions about Killer Quest 2.0.

Finally, once everyone has settled down, Sandra leads us into our activity for the night: Plan the Perfect Murder. It feels even more ghoulish considering today's events, but I try to keep my expression neutral, try not to give anything away. Just a few more hours and I can go to bed. And tomorrow I can go home.

When it's our group's turn to present our perfect murder, Maggie shares a surprisingly thorough eight-point plan that earns a lot of cheers and gasps. If Carolina heard this, she'd turn it into evidence against Maggie, say it shows how Maggie's mind works, how devious she is. But I don't think so. I think Maggie is just smart, logical, and resourceful. It's an academic exercise for her. I barely listen to the other contestants' questions and objections, my eyes on Maggie as she laughs and argues. I can picture her at college, always raising her hand in class, always having something to say, never afraid or embarrassed.

A team made up of a math professor, an amateur cryptol-
ogist, and an accountant wins the contest. Their murder plan
was so technical I couldn't follow it, but everyone else hung
on every word, mesmerized by each precise detail. I was only
surprised to realize that one of them was Levi, the man we
found weeping in the fog. He still looks pretty depressed to
me, his face drawn and tired, despite his air of intelligence.

The bachelorette group comes in second with a plan so
cool and calculated that everyone's eyes bug out a little. "Oh,
we underestimated them, didn't we?" Maggie whispers to
me, delighted. Maggie and I come in third, which earns us a
lot of stares and two *Human Beasties* branded beer koozies. I
offer mine to Bridget, who immediately drops a can of PBR
into it.

After the awards are given out, the night breaks into a
party—drinking and flirting and jokes and, of course, fighting. Hours pass, and I get so tired I nearly fall off the bench
once. Maggie ventures out into the crowd of people, chatting
with several groups, leaving me on my own. I almost wish
Carolina were here, but not quite, not after what she said
about Maggie.

Finally, even the wildest of the contestants has had enough
of macabre jokes and drunken bickering, and people begin
to head away to bed. The fire burns down to embers, and
someone pours water over them to put them out, plunging
the camp into darkness.

Maggie and I walk hand in hand back to the tent, and I'm
so tired I can barely put one foot in front of the other. I had

hoped we'd make something more of our last night together. But it's enough for me to lie curled against Maggie's back, inhaling her honey and hibiscus scent and listening to her breathe.

I don't fall asleep so much as plummet into darkness.

But sometime in the night I'm awakened by a loud voice, magnified by a megaphone or a speaker or something. I blink blearily into the darkness and reach for Maggie, but she's not there. Instead, she's crouched at the mouth of the tent, staring out.

"What's going on?" I ask, my voice heavy with sleep.

"I'm not sure," she says. "That's a ranger with the megaphone. He said there's been an incident and that we all must report to the lodge for a head count."

I sit up fast, suddenly wide-awake. "They found Noah's body." Fear thrums through me. I realize that we haven't even put together a plan for what to say if we're asked our whereabouts, how we spent our day. I'm not prepared.

"Come on," Maggie says. "It will look bad if we don't show up."

"Carolina," I say, "we need to find her." There's no telling what she might say.

"She's already headed our way," Maggie says wryly. "Your knight in secondhand hiking boots."

I'm too anxious to respond. I roll out of the sleeping bag and pull on my boots. When I'm ready, Maggie gets up, and I follow her out of the tent. Carolina is waiting, arms crossed over her chest, her breath misting the air. She had to ditch her coat because of the blood, and I can see she's shivering beneath a few layers of sweaters.

"Maggie, I need to talk to you about something," she says, her voice tight.

"Talk," Maggie says.

"I need to talk to you alone."

Maggie sighs. "Fine, but can it wait? We're sort of being summoned here."

"No," Carolina says, "it can't wait." She turns to me. "Lucy, can you go ahead and we'll meet you? Save us seats?"

"Carolina, if this about that fire—" I start to say.

Carolina interrupts without even looking at me. Her eyes are trained on Maggie. "Please, Lucy, will you just let me talk to Maggie for a minute? I promise we'll be right behind you. Just tell them we're on our way if they ask."

I don't want to do it. But it will look weird if all three of us show up late for the head count, and Carolina clearly isn't budging. "Fine," I say. "But hurry up." I walk slowly away from them, down the path toward the lodge, looking back over my shoulder for some sign of what they're talking about. Is Carolina accusing Maggie to her face? But they turn away and walk into the shadows so I can't see them anymore, probably for more privacy. God, I hope Carolina isn't about to ruin everything.

I focus on the people around me. The other contestants are half-asleep but clearly alarmed, whispering to one another, already forming theories about what happened. Rufus looms suddenly out of the darkness, and I quicken my steps before I remember: I don't have to obey the small animal impulses of my body, the mouse's scurrying at the hawk's shadow. I don't have to be afraid.

I ignore him and continue on toward the lodge. The atmosphere inside is tense and excited, exactly what you'd expect from a pack of true crime junkies who were pulled from their tents in the middle of the night. I pass by that horrible woman Joyce, and my heart rate explodes when I see Joe isn't with her. But then I spot him wedged between Levi and his teammates across the room. Joyce shoots eye daggers at him, but he ignores her and talks quietly with the other men.

I decide to sit near Rosa and Bridget since they were friendly enough at the fire. It feels dangerous to be alone in this crowd.

"What do y'all think happened?" I ask them, as casually as I can.

"I bet you someone found Kincaid's body," Rosa says.

Bridget shakes her head. "No, because that ranger said it was an incident. I think there must have been another accident, like with Kiersten."

"Or maybe it wasn't an accident," Rosa answers darkly.

"Kiersten or this one?"

Rosa shrugs.

I'm afraid to meet their eyes, so I start scanning the room for Brandon. He wasn't at the Perfect Murder competition, and he's not here now. So he must have been the one to find Noah. Poor guy. That's two bodies he's stumbled upon now. I only hope that doesn't make the police suspect him. But if it came down to that, I'd come forward. I'd admit what happened, only I'd leave Maggie and Carolina out of it. I'd live with the consequences.

But I really hope I don't have to.

Kevin and Sandra walk into the lodge, their faces somber. The crowd goes immediately, shockingly silent.

Sandra raises her hands. "I need everyone to please remain calm," she says, which is strange since everyone is silent and waiting. "There has been an incident, and we'll explain everything soon, but our first order is to make sure that everyone is safe and accounted for. Our assistant, Priya, is going to call out names from the registration sheet, going one team at a time. When you hear your name, raise your hand and say 'here.' Once we're sure everyone is safe and accounted for, we will set your minds at rest."

I look toward the door, but there's no Maggie, no Carolina. My pulse skyrockets. I'm on my own.

Priya steps forward and starts reading names off a tablet and checking them off with a smart pen. It feels, bizarrely, like the first day of school. We all look around at each other as if we're complete strangers, as if we haven't been camping in the same canyon for the last week.

"Carolina Cassels," Priya calls out. For the first time, no one raises their hand or answers. Everyone looks at me.

I open my mouth to offer some excuse, but then suddenly Maggie's coming into the room. "Carolina is too hungover to leave her tent, but she's fine. I just saw her," Maggie lies. Her eyes find mine, and she starts toward me, hands in the pockets of her jacket, head down. She seems agitated, unlike herself.

Priya looks uncertainly at Sandra, who nods for her to go on.

"Maggie Rey," Priya calls.

"That's me," Maggie says with a wave as she sits down.

"Geraldine Franks," Priya says. For a moment, I'm confused to hear my grandmother's name, but then Maggie elbows me in the side.

"Here," I say, one hand going into the air and the other to my throat, automatically adjusting my scarf. I ignore the pointed stares of the rest of the room. They all know who I am. Sandra and Kevin carefully avoid looking at me too, clearly determined to deny all knowledge that I was here, in case the police get too nosy. But I know they'll still claim the interview I promised them.

"Rufus Adams," Priya says, and Rufus grunts and raises his hand.

"I don't know where the rest of my group is," he says. "Brandon went out looking for Noah."

"Yes, we're aware," Sandra says, and whispers sweep across the room. I hear Noah's name from every direction, whispers of "creepy" and "sketchy." So, I guess Noah's behavior hasn't gone unnoticed this week.

My hands shake so badly I have to hide them between my knees. Maggie rubs my back, pushing at a knot in my shoulder. I lean into her warmth, her certainty.

Priya continues down her list, valiantly reading the names over the increasing tumult. Finally, the last person has been accounted for, and the only people missing from the room are Carolina, Noah, and Brandon.

I clench my jaw, hard. There's no mistake, then. They're going to tell us Noah is dead.

Kevin clears his throat. "I'm afraid there's been another . . ." He shakes his head, clearly unsure how to proceed. He glances nervously at Sandra.

She steps forward again, still studiously avoiding looking in my direction. "I'm afraid that another of our contestants has met with an accident. However, unlike with Kiersten, in his case . . ." She bites her lip. "One of our contestants— Brandon Walters—says that he was attacked by an unseen individual tonight while out looking for his missing friend. He was near the edge of the cliff when he was shoved from behind and fell."

Several people gasp.

Sandra nods, as if to acknowledge their shock. "Thankfully, there was a ledge immediately below where he was standing, so he didn't fall very far and only sprained a wrist. But he's very shaken, obviously."

I let out a relieved breath, but my chest immediately tightens again with worry. Who could have attacked Brandon? I'd suspect Noah if he weren't lying dead and cold in a cave. I glance at Maggie, wanting to talk, but her eyes are focused on Sandra, her mouth pursed in concentration.

"When did this happen?" someone asks.

"About an hour ago. Brandon was able to climb back up and immediately reported the incident to the emergency ranger line, who then notified us. The police are on their way."

"So where's his missing friend? Noah, right?" another person asks. "Do we think he's the one who pushed Brandon? Or did someone go after them both?"

Sandra shakes her head. "We don't know. When the police arrive, they will look into everything. In the meantime, you all need to stay here, either in the lodge or in your tents."

The contestants burst into furious conversation. "Why should we stay here when there's a fucking killer on the loose?" someone yells.

"We don't know that," Sandra says. "We don't have enough information to—"

"I'm getting the hell out of here!" the *Friday the 13th* lady yells, her voice high and tremulous. "I've had enough!" She shoots to her feet and runs out of the lodge. A few people follow her.

"We can't force you to stay," Sandra calls after them, "but if you choose to leave the park, the police will have questions for you later." She turns back to the panicked room. "Please keep tabs on one another, and keep your eyes open. We'll give you an update first thing tomorrow morning." She glances at her watch. "Which is in about four hours."

Before Sandra even finishes speaking, the bachelorette group bursts into frantic, feverish conversation. "Clearly, someone here came after Kiersten," the bride says. "It wasn't an accident. What if they want one of us next?" she wails. "Maybe we should leave too!"

I roll my eyes, but I can't ignore the pit forming in my stomach. We're supposed to all be safe now. The killer is dead. Isn't he? Squeezing my eyes tight, I conjure the image of Noah's body, bleeding out onto the cave floor, empty of breath and life. He was dead. He *is* dead.

I turn to Maggie, who is bent forward on the bench, her fingers laced over the back of her head, her face hidden. There's a smear of blood on her thumb. "Maggie?" I ask. "Are you okay? What happened? Where's Carolina?"

When she finally raises her head and looks at me, there are tears in her eyes. "Carolina—she—she lost control and attacked me."

"You mean she yelled at you?"

Maggie shakes her head. "She physically attacked me. I had to fight back." She glances at her hands.

*Fuck.* "Because of what she learned about your room-mate and the fire?" I ask. "She told me about it too, and what she . . . suspected."

Maggie nods. "She had this whole theory about how I'd driven Rachel to burn down Chad's house. And when I told her she was off base, she attacked me. I mean, I knew she had violence in her past, but I had no idea what she really was. If I had—"

My insides go cold. "What do you mean? What violence?"

Maggie looks around, as if only now realizing how many people might overhear. "Not here. Let's go back to our tent," she says, pulling me up from the bench.

I follow her wordlessly, feeling dozens of eyes on my back. Outside, the fog has risen, thick and cold. It feels heavy, oppressive, like it's trapping us here. Maggie and I make our way slowly back toward camp, and I can feel her trembling next to me. Maggie is never cold, so I know it's emotion causing it. Finally, halfway to camp, I stop her with a hand on her arm.

Questions explode out of me, one after another. "What's going on? Where's Carolina? And who do you think attacked Brandon? Please, tell me what's happening. I can't take this anymore."

Maggie faces me in the dark. I can't see her expression, but I can feel the tension rising off her. "I'm so sorry, Lucy, but I was wrong. I was wrong about everything." Her voice breaks on the last word, a near sob. "God, all I've done is let you down."

"What? What do you mean?" I ask, still gripping her arm.

Her voice is anguished when she speaks. "It wasn't Noah who was after you. He was a creep, but he wasn't the one who was chasing you in the fog."

"Who was it? Rufus?" My head buzzes like a yellow jackets' nest. Something horrible is about to come out of Maggie's mouth, I can feel it.

Maggie takes both my hands and squeezes them tight. "You aren't going to want to listen to this, but you need to hear it." She pauses for what feels like ages. "It was Carolina all along."

I'm so startled I laugh. "That's ridiculous. That doesn't make any sense."

"Look at this," Maggie says, pulling a notebook from her jacket and pushing into my hands. It's Carolina's sketchbook.

Maggie opens it to the middle and starts flipping pages. When she turns on her cell phone's flashlight, I see that each page is covered with a drawing of me. "She's obsessed with you."

I peer at the drawings in the light from my cell phone. They're beautiful, detailed. There's one of me on my belly looking down into the canyon, another where I'm smiling, another with my eyebrows drawn together in concentration.

"They're just drawings," I say, handing back the notebook. "She's an artist."

Maggie shakes her head vehemently. "No, they're not just drawings. I'm telling you—she was obsessed with you before she even got here. I've seen this sort of thing before. My room-mate last year, Rachel—she—"

"Carolina told me about her. She showed me an article." I remember how she shoved her phone into my hands, the same way Maggie did with Carolina's sketchbook. The buzzing in my ears grows louder.

Maggie nods. "Rachel was—is—a lot like Carolina actually—this amazing, talented, really passionate person. But sometimes she gets too passionate. To the point of obsessed. She just loses track of reality sometimes. Her boyfriend broke up with her, but she couldn't accept it. She kept showing up at his place, following him, threatening to expose him for crimes he never did. He had to take out a restraining order. It was really scary."

In the silence after Maggie finishes speaking, I hear Carolina's voice in my head: *Maggie took a vulnerable girl and played on her fears and insecurities and drove her to act out in a dangerous way. Doesn't that sound familiar?*

I clear my throat, speaking carefully. "Carolina said that you told her a different version of the story last night."

Maggie puts her face into her hands and groans. "I know, but I was only trying to make Carolina feel better about something she told me. Trying to connect with her. And I do blame myself for what happened with Rachel and Chad. I do feel like I helped her commit arson, even if not directly. It was a mistake, not one I'll make again. I'd hoped I was wrong about Carolina, that she wasn't like Rachel. But it's too clear now to ignore."

"What do you mean?" I feel like I'm on a roller coaster, creeping slowly toward a sheer drop.

"She— Do you remember that first day we put our group together and we asked her why she was here at the contest? What did she say?"

The words spring immediately to mind. "She said that serial killers make her feel better about herself."

"Didn't you ever wonder why? Didn't you wonder what an eighteen-year-old girl could have done to need to compare herself to serial killers?"

"Well, yeah, and I tried to ask her about it once. But she changed the subject."

Maggie raises her eyebrows.

"But she said her dad was abusive, that he called her evil and all that," I argue. "She learned early in life to be ashamed of herself, to think of herself as a bad person. That's religious trauma, not reality."

Maggie shakes her head. "Last night, she told me more. She told me she killed her boyfriend six months ago."

"What?" I reel away from Maggie, stepping out of her reach. "Of course she didn't."

Maggie steps toward me. "His name was Michael, and she killed him. She didn't mean to tell me, but she was drunk."

I shake my head. "I'm sure it was an accident." But I remember what Carolina said last night: *There's a badness inside me.* The buzzing in my head rises into a deafening drone.

"No, she killed him," Maggie says. "On purpose."

"Why didn't you tell me?"

Maggie shakes her head, as if ashamed. "I wanted to tell you, but I promised her I wouldn't. I thought maybe she had her reasons—that maybe he was abusive or something. I didn't realize her boyfriend was only the start of things. I didn't realize she'd gotten a taste for it."

"What does this have to do with anything?" I ask, my head spinning. All the relief and freedom I felt after Noah died are gone now. The old emotions are seeping back in to take their usual place—anxiety, fear, anger. The sense of a warped and horrible world. Joseph Kincaid's wide, frightened eyes as he leapt.

"Now that I know what she is, I see it all so clearly," Maggie says. "I don't know how I missed it. I should have seen."

I shake my head vehemently. "You're wrong. Carolina has been protecting me since we got here. From that girl Kiersten, from Rufus, from Noah. She's tried to get me to leave here and go home a dozen times."

"Because she didn't like you being close to me. She didn't like how I was helping you," Maggie says. "You said it yourself. She wanted you to stay a victim."

I turn away from Maggie. This isn't something I can believe, any more than I could believe Carolina when she told me Maggie set us up. How can they both be so wrong about each other?

"I'm not saying she's acted rationally here," Maggie explains. "That's a misbelief about serial killers, that they are all cold-blooded, coolheaded psychopaths. Carolina feels deeply. In her own twisted way, she cares about you. But she'd rather kill you than see you free of her grasp."

"Serial killers?" I whisper. Those words don't make sense applied to Carolina. I close my eyes, trying to see through the haze in my brain, trying to feel something other than despair and hopelessness, which are swiftly enveloping me like the fog. Every good feeling inside me is being crowded out, replaced by growing dismay. How could Carolina be a killer? How could she do this to me?

"Look," Maggie says, "I'll lay it all out for you, all right?" Her voice takes on an academic quality, like she's reciting a research study. "Kiersten was a bitch to you, so Carolina attacked her. She followed you around scaring the shit out of you, to the point that you were paranoid and thought you were being haunted by Kincaid's ghost. Remember after you fell down the cliff and you came back to camp, and Carolina was the only person missing? And she had your jacket?"

"I mean, I guess—"

"And when she thought Noah was sniffing around you, she decided to go after him too."

"I don't know. . . ."

"She stabbed him three times in the back with a knife, Lucy. That's not self-defense."

"But why would she go after Brandon? She clearly likes him. And he had nothing to do with me."

"Because he suspected her," Maggie says. "He knew Noah went off with some girl, remember? She was worried he thought it was her. She probably has plans for Rufus too."

"But—"

Maggie plows on. "And I saw how he was looking at her during dinner. Carolina is really good at reading people, so she must have noticed it. And she knew I was onto her too, especially after she accidentally revealed what she'd done to her boyfriend to me," Maggie continues. "That's why she went looking for dirt on me. She wanted to discredit me.

"But she knew she didn't find enough. She knew you wouldn't believe her. That's why she confronted me. Tonight, when she sent you ahead without us, she asked if I was going to expose her. That's what she didn't want you to hear."

"What did you say?"

"When I made it clear I was done hiding her secrets, she just . . . lost it." Maggie shakes her head. "She flew at me in a rage."

I don't want to believe any of this, but there's a ring of truth to Maggie's words. My mind churns through the details of the last five days. Carolina flew off the handle at the slightest provocation. She was possessive and controlling. She was antagonistic toward Maggie. Even the way we met was weird: she crept up behind me at the edge of the canyon and was watching me . . . drawing me. That's not normal.

And then there was this afternoon in the cave, when she fell asleep and she woke up screaming, convinced I was dead. She asked where the knife was.

The knife she stabbed into Noah's chest less than an hour later.

While we stand here, the fog rises around us, thick and opaque. My heart rate ticks up a notch, as if my body remembers what happened to me last time in the fog.

"She hallucinated killing me," I say, a horrible certainty blooming in my chest. "When she woke up screaming in the cave, it was because she thought she'd killed me." The truth of Maggie's words is finally sinking in. "She pretended to be my friend, to care about me . . . and all the while she was hunting me, planning my death."

It's like the ground drops out from under me. I stagger and fall forward into Maggie, who catches me and lowers me onto the pine needles. A chasm opens inside me, empty and echoing and cold. The fog that rises up around me feels like it floats through me too, inside me, turning me into a second Cloudkiss Canyon.

"Carolina caused an innocent man's death," Maggie says. "Noah hadn't done anything wrong, not really. But she let us believe he was stalking you. She killed him. But we're all victims here."

Anger surges up the back of my throat, bitter as acid. "I'm not a victim," I spit back.

"What do you want to do?" Maggie asks quietly, her voice hushed in the fog. "Do you want to go tell Sandra and Kevin what we know? Do you want to tell the police?"

I shake my head. I cling to the anger I feel, my only anchor in the yawning emptiness inside me. "No, I want to end this myself," I say. "I'm not going back home afraid."

"Lucy," Maggie says, her voice uncertain.

"Tell me where she is," I say through clenched teeth, tightening my hands into fists. I've been through too much this week to go back to who I was.

I will go home unafraid, or I won't go home at all.

# TWENTY-EIGHT

## CAROLINA

### DAY 6

**I wake up** on the ground in the dark woods, my head throbbing, my entire body an ache. For a moment, I can't remember what happened or how I got here, or even what day it is. The fog closes in, suffocating me.

Images of blood and chaos flash lightning-fast through my mind, and I can't say for sure whether they're real or not. An image of Lucy flashes: *Lucy on the ground, her neck bleeding, her open eyes reflecting the stars.*

But no, that's Michael. Michael is dead. Or was it Lucy?

"Lucy," I croak. I pat the ground around me, searching for I don't know what. My hand closes on a huge, damp rock, and when I finally manage to force open my eyes, I see the rock is covered in what looks like blood.

My blood. Or is it Lucy's blood?

I stagger to my feet, and the world wheels around me. I fall to my knees. My temple throbs, and I when I touch it, my fingers come away bloody.

The fog seems to snake its way inside me, through my eyes and ears and nose, probing and touching and spreading like liquid lead through my veins.

I crouch on the ground, my fingers digging into the moist soil, and I weep. Because Lucy is dead. Because I killed her. I know I did.

Maggie's voice in my head: "People are what they are, Carolina. And you're a killer."

Maggie's gray eyes—

Her eyes. Another flash of memory: Maggie's eyes a swirling gray, like the center of a tornado, the eye of an ocean's whirlpool, a sucking vortex.

I blink. A hallucination? The other images have a shifting, fragmented quality, but this image adheres: Maggie, her eyes gray—storm gray, fog gray, void gray. Fathomless.

Her eyes are a canyon you want to leap into. She throws herself at me, and the force is ten times what it should be, what her lanky body is capable of. She's more than human, or less.

She lifts a rock over my head, and darkness swallows me.

The fog swallows me.

No, there's something in me that resists it. Something that keeps it in check, keeps it at bay.

"Fuck," I whisper to the dirt. "Fuck." I can't keep my thoughts straight, can't tell real from not real. Do I have a concussion? Is this a nervous breakdown?

No. No, I can do this. I search my mind for a true memory, something untouched by the despair of this place.

*Lucy.*

Lucy, washed in pale light from a lantern, squeezing my face between her two warm hands and telling me I am good. That I have helped her.

That was real. The memory and the meaning.

I'm good.

I'm not a monster.

I'm not a killer.

There's no badness inside me, waiting to get out.

I smile, wincing at the pain the small movement of my facial muscles causes.

Maggie did that, I realize. Maggie hurt me. Maggie hurt everyone.

Maggie played us all like pawns on a chessboard—a game of words and stories. She never got her fingers dirty, until now. Because I challenged her.

I take a deep breath and retrace the last hours, clinging to the real memories like a life preserver.

Finally, they begin to adhere, one sticking to the other until a chain of memories leads me out of the fog: The middle of the night, a megaphone. A ranger saying there'd been an incident. I rushed to Lucy. I suspected that Maggie had done something to her, but she was safe. I asked Maggie to stay behind. Lucy went on to the lodge without us. I promised we'd be right behind her. But it didn't work out that way.

"You made it all up," I said to Maggie.

"Made what up?" Maggie shot back.

"Noah. That he was after Lucy, that he was a copycat. You made it all up."

To my shock, she shrugged. She smiled, lazy as a cat. "So what if I did?"

"You made me kill an innocent man!" I whispered furiously.

"I gave you exactly what you wanted. You wanted a chance to find out what you were made of, if your parents were right about you. Well, guess what, Carolina? They were. You're a killer."

I shook my head, ignoring her words. "He didn't deserve to die like that."

"Look, you saw how he behaved in the cave, how he choked Lucy. You heard all the shit he said that day on the trail."

"How did you get him to the cave? That's the part I can't figure out."

Maggie laughed. "I asked him to meet me for a romantic rendezvous. I'd been dropping kinky hints for days, so he thought he was sure to get laid."

"You set him up!"

"So what," Maggie said. "He was a creep. Maybe he wasn't after Lucy in the beginning. Maybe he would never have acted on his fantasies in real life. But he was a bona fide sicko, and he deserved what he got."

"Did your roommate's boyfriend deserve to have his house burned down? Did Rachel deserve to end up burned to pieces and with a criminal record?"

Maggie's eyes glittered, but not with amusement. Finally, I'd managed to rattle her. "You researched me?" she said through gritted teeth. "That's what Lucy meant about the fire?"

"It doesn't take a psychology degree to tap some keywords into Google. Matter of fact, it doesn't take a psychology degree to recognize you for what you are."

"And what's that?" she asked, her eyes intense and strange, smoky like I noticed before in the lodge.

"A monster," I said. "You see people as playthings, as puppets you can move around on a stage for some amusement of your own. You don't care about Lucy; you just get off on gaining power over her, on seeing how far you can push her. You did it to Rachel, and now you did it to Lucy."

"And you," Maggie said.

"You tried anyway."

A slow, pleased smile spread over Maggie's face, but the rage in her eyes didn't waver. "We'll see."

A chill ran through me. I realized I might know only a tenth of everything she'd done. "Did you—did you set your own tent on fire? So you'd have a reason to sleep in Lucy's tent?"

Maggie didn't reply, but her silence was answer enough. Somehow this was the final straw, the thing that sent anger roaring through my chest. "That was the night Lucy and I were getting close, when things might have gone a different way for us. And you saw it and you knew you had to get between us, didn't you?"

Maggie only smirked.

I shook my head. "You're poison, Maggie. I'm going to expose you for what you are, whatever it might cost me." I moved to stalk past her, but Maggie stepped into my path.

"No, you're not," Maggie said. "I'm not letting you fuck up all my work."

"What are you going to do? Hit me? It's clear you don't like to get your hands dirty."

Maggie leaned down and picked up a rock. "Don't like to, but can."

I backed away from her, but she advanced on me, sure and merciless.

Did her eyes really look the way I remember—when she drew back her arm, that rock gripped in her fingers, were her eyes really fog and darkness? I'm not sure. I remember a scuffle and an explosion of pain, and then blackness.

Now I'm bleeding and dizzy and probably have a concussion, but I'm not dead. Why? She could easily have killed me, but she didn't. Does that mean she isn't finished with me? I know she's not going to let Lucy and me go home now. There are too many loose ends, and Maggie's not the type to leave them be.

But it's more than Maggie, isn't it? Now that I know it's there, I can feel the fog's influence. All this time, it's been inside my head, making me hallucinate, drawing out my worst fears, my worst desires. This place is evil, and it wishes us ill. All it wants is for us to destroy one another and then ourselves.

It's the valley of dry bones, a place of death. It calls us in and swallows us whole, leaving nothing to show that we were ever here. Is that what happened to Joseph Kincaid—did he come here, a young man with warped desires, and find a killing ground?

And then Maggie came along with her notebook and her schemes, her desperate need to charm and control, and made us play here, another round of Cloudkiss Killers.

All Lucy wanted was freedom, a life without fear. But maybe it's not too late. Maybe there's still a chance. For both of us.

This time when I climb to my feet, I sway but do not fall. I've got to find Lucy.

I stumble out of my hiding place but keep to the tree line, holding on to the rough bark when I need to. I reach the campground and scan the area, but there's no one in sight. The entire place is dark and apparently deserted. I think errantly of my father's belief in the Rapture, of God's faithful being called up to heaven, snatched like magic from their beds, from airplanes, from jail cells, while the sinners remain behind on earth to face the End Times.

I let out an anguished, stifled laugh. Of course, the sinners would include me. But I'd expect at least a few of my fellow Beastie Babes to stay behind too. Cloudkiss Canyon is the perfect place to endure the final days, after all.

With effort, I refocus my attention. I need to find Lucy.

But there's no one here. I must have been knocked out for less time than I thought and the contestants are all still gathered in the lodge because of whatever incident happened—something I'm sure involved Maggie. Maybe she went after Rufus since he saw Noah talking to her.

Or maybe they've already found Noah.

I sneak as close to the building as I dare and wait in the shadows, trying not to breathe too hard, trying to keep the nausea and dizziness at bay. I'm shivering with cold, and I feel every heartbeat as a throb in my temple, where blood still trickles weakly down my face.

I flinch when the door slams open and a woman comes running out, a few others on her heels, calling her name. She ignores them, sprinting straight toward the parking lot. But after their footsteps die away, it's quiet once more.

Then the door opens again, this time spilling out a crowd of contestants. Each one is illuminated for a moment in the porch lights on either side of the front door before they slip into the foggy darkness. Most of their voices are angry and frightened, and it sounds like some of them are making plans to leave immediately. Others are clearly excited, whooping and roughhousing and jumping around. "Let's get the fire going!" one of them yells. Another shouts something about vodka. They stream toward the campsite, as wild and excited as they were on the first night here.

Finally, Maggie and Lucy come out, Maggie's arm around Lucy's shoulders. It takes all my willpower not to leap from my hiding place and tackle Maggie to the ground. But instead, I wait for them to pass me, and then I follow them into the restless dark.

# TWENTY-NINE

## LUCY

**"How are we** gonna find her?" I ask, peering around the gloomy, wooded area where Maggie said she saw Carolina last.

"I'm not sure," Maggie murmurs, scanning the trees.

"We might have to wait for daylight," I say, "She could be anywhere in the dark."

I hold still, listening. Wind rustles the dry leaves of the oaks and sugar maples, and nocturnal animals move on quiet feet and wings. The stars might be shining above, but they're obscured by clouds and fog. It feels like sunrise is never going to come. The fog swirls around our ankles, alive and vital, like the burbling of a creek.

I kick over a large rock, and my flashlight shows dried blood on its other side.

Maggie must see me looking at it. "I hit her with that," she admits. "I didn't know what else to do."

"I'm just glad you're all right," I say. "God, when I get hold of her . . ." I clench my fists. I can barely think straight, my head a messy collection of competing thoughts and desires. I want to go home—no, I want to beat the shit out of Carolina—no, I want to give up and die because this world is too awful. My skin prickles with anxiety, and the all-too-familiar pit of dread in my stomach seems to grow bigger.

I cling to the anger at Carolina because everything else feels like standing on the edge of a precipice and staring down. At least Carolina is a real, solid problem I can confront.

Maggie suddenly flinches beside me, her face turned away. She takes a step to one side, as if she sees something in the dark.

"What is it?" I ask, hating the fear in my voice.

She turns back to me and touches my arm. "Nothing, I think I just saw an opossum in the bushes. I hate their pointy little teeth." She caresses the back of my hair and neck, then leans down to whisper in my ear. "You know, I think Carolina will find us. She won't be able to stop herself from hunting you, not now."

The words make me feel sick to my stomach. I trusted Carolina. I confided in her. I felt friendship for her, and more than that.

"Let's hike the waterfall trail," Maggie suggests, her voice still hushed.

I look up at her in surprise.

She shrugs. "There's a kind of pattern to things, isn't there? It's where Kincaid found you. It would be irresistible to Carolina."

I nod, even though a well of terror opens up inside me. We head out of the clump of trees where Maggie fought Carolina and walk quickly toward the start of the waterfall trail. I feel like I'm walking back in time. Like I'm fifteen years old and I never left this place. Like there's a monster waiting in the fog for me, like there always will be.

The trees are white in the dark, the path is smooth underfoot, and the mist billows up, dampening my hair. It's all the same. Only this time I'm not lost and I'm not alone. I grip Maggie's hand, hard, letting her warm certainty steady me. Just touching her opens up my chest a little more so that I can breathe.

Still, I feel eyes on my back. I glance behind me, but there's only fog and mist, trees and a slate-gray sky. We continue forward until the path diverges—one trail goes around the rim of the canyon to the top of the falls, and the other winds down toward the creek. I hesitate, but Maggie pulls me gently toward the higher trail. I'm glad. I find I don't want to descend any deeper into the fog.

Halfway to the falls, the hair on the nape of my neck prickles, and I turn, looking for eyes in the dark. I spot someone far behind us, hardly more than a pale blur, half-hidden behind a tree. I turn to face forward again, pretending I didn't notice. "She's back there," I say.

"I know," Maggie says. "It wasn't an opossum I saw. I just didn't want to worry you yet. I thought we ought to draw her away from camp." She's quiet for a moment. "Do you see now? This is what she's been doing the whole time. She's always been sneaking up behind you. Everything you felt, everything you saw—it was all Carolina. She's delusional. She tried to make herself your hero when she was the one threatening you all along." Maggie shakes her head. "It's disgusting. And I'm sorry I didn't see it sooner. I really should have."

"Let's just get to the top," I say. "I don't want to face her in the middle of the trail in all this fog. It will be clearer up there. It's almost daylight."

I clench my jaw and continue on, watching my feet as the trail grows rockier. We hike in silence for several minutes. The fog ought to be lessening the farther we get from the base of the waterfall, but if anything, it's worse. It hugs the ground, forming so densely it's like we're walking through clouds. But above us, it dances, sinuous and watchful.

I shake my head, as if to dislodge the strange thought. The only one watching me is Carolina. Carolina turning herself into another Kincaid, Carolina hurting one person after another. All the while pretending to care about me, to be my friend, to have feelings for me.

Anger simmers inside me, giving me a last surge of energy to make it to the end of the trail. The waterfall pours below us, falling sixty or seventy feet into a green-tinged pool below. I peer over the edge, but the fog is too thick to see the collection of boulders at the bottom, their gray heads rising above the churning water like sea monsters.

Maggie leans against a yellow-leaved tulip poplar. I throw myself to the ground and watch the trail, waiting for Carolina to show her face. I don't want her to see me afraid. I don't want to give her the satisfaction of knowing the pain she's caused me. I want her to see I am not her victim, that after all she's done, I will still walk out of here a different person than the one she met on the first day. The one she frightened with only her voice.

Still, when I hear her footsteps, I scramble up off the ground, my hands balled at my sides, my fingers clenched hard enough to hurt. She staggers out of the fog, and I can see just from her silhouette that she's hurt badly. She deserves it, I remind myself. She's the one who attacked Maggie. And Brandon and probably Kiersten too.

Then her face appears, sweet and heart-shaped, with those big brown eyes, innocent as a doe's. The last person the world would ever imagine as a killer.

Blood runs down the side of her face, which is paler than it ought to be. Her cream-colored sweater is dirty and streaked with red. She looks at me, and I look at her. Maggie stands between us, a little to one side, watching, waiting.

Carolina darts looks between us, her expression uncertain. Finally, as if convinced Maggie isn't going to attack her, she fixes her gaze on me. "Lucy," she says, her voice hoarse and tired. "Why did you come up here?"

"Why did you follow me?"

Carolina looks afraid. "Please, you have to listen to me, Lucy. What I told you about Maggie—it's all true. She's been fucking with us this whole time. She doesn't care about you. She's not capable of caring about anyone."

"You're one to talk," I say. "Maggie told me everything. I know about your boyfriend."

Carolina flinches and takes a step back. Tears form in her eyes. But then she shakes her head and steps toward me again, clenching her jaw as though she's steeling herself. She lifts her head and meets my eyes, her gaze determined. "I thought I was a killer when I came here; that's true. I thought there was something bad in me. For years, my dad has been telling me that I carried a curse inside me, that I would end up just like him. I was terrified that I might hurt you. But I was wrong." Her eyes soften, and she steps toward me again. "I could never, never hurt you, Lucy."

I resist the urge to move away from her. I don't want to show her any fear. "What about your boyfriend? I bet you thought the same about him, that you'd never hurt him. But you killed him."

Carolina shakes her head, then puts her hand to her temple, as if dizzy. "I thought I did," she says, blinking her eyes fast like she's trying to clear her vision. "For a long time, I thought that. I couldn't remember what happened to him—all my memories were just gone. Yet I felt so guilty and so horrible that I knew I must have done it somehow. I thought I was a monster."

"You were right," I spit.

Carolina smiles sadly. "It took coming here to figure out how wrong I was. Because when I stabbed Noah, I remembered everything. I got all my memories back. I know that sounds made up, but I swear it's true. The blood ran down my hands, and it was like—like Proust and his tea and madeleine story in *In Search of Lost Time*, you know? I think it's called sense memory. In my case, a really fucked-up sense memory."

"Spare us," Maggie says dryly.

Carolina ignores her, her eyes locked onto me. "The sight of the blood like that, Noah's body, everything—I—I remembered what happened with Michael, how he really died. I remembered what my dad said to me afterward and how it lodged into my head, taking up all the empty spaces in my memories. And I realized I was wrong about myself. That Michael wasn't my fault. That I wasn't what my dad said I was. That I'm not what I thought I was. You have to believe me." Her last words are laced with desperation and a painful hope. But it must be an act; it has to be just another lie she's telling me.

"You set me up," I say, hardening my voice. "You played with my head."

"No, I didn't," Carolina pleads, taking a step toward me. "That was Maggie. It's like I told you—she's done this before, with her roommate and the fire. She likes playing with people."

"Maggie has does nothing but help me," I say, glancing her way. Maggie remains still, her arms crossed, letting me handle Carolina myself. The way she's let me handle everything myself.

"She charmed you and manipulated you. She got inside your head," Carolina says.

Anger surges through me, making my fingertips tingle. "You think I'm some stupid girl, who gets a crush and falls in line with a killer?"

"No, of course not," Carolina says. "But it's this place. This place"—she gestures to the fog, the trees, all of Cloudkiss Canyon—"it hates us. Don't you feel it? The way it watches us? There's something evil here, and it gets inside our minds and it preys on us. It draws out the worst that's inside us. That must be what it's done to Maggie. She was here a whole week before we got here, remember? If it's messed with us this much, how much damage did it do to her while she was all alone here, with only her thoughts and her memories, feeling unwanted and misunderstood?"

I glance at Maggie again, who snorts and shakes her head. "She's desperate, Lucy. She'll say anything."

Carolina takes a few more steps forward, until I can see the golden ring of her eyes. The world around us has disappeared; we are wreathed in fog, as if removed from time and place.

"Think, Lucy. What do you actually know about Maggie? What has she told you about herself? Do you know what she's afraid of? Do you know what she loves? What has she ever done to earn your trust?"

"Oh, come on—"

"I'm serious," Carolina interrupts. "Tell me what you actually know about Maggie."

"She—" To my shock, Carolina's words have a ring of truth. I barely know anything about Maggie, apart from the name of her university, the subject of the paper she wants to write. That she was mugged once. That she's a musician. That she doesn't like her parents.

Does she have siblings? Hobbies? What's her best friend's name? Where is she from? I can't answer a single question. I don't know anything about her at all.

Maggie is a stranger.

Uncertainty fills me, accompanied by the familiar ache of fear.

"No," I say, pushing it away. "No. I'm not going to let you turn me against the one person who has actually tried to help me. Not when you came here to hurt me, not when you hurt Kiersten and Brandon and—"

"Brandon?" Carolina asks, her brow contracting. "Did something happen to Brandon? Is he all right?" She lunges suddenly toward Maggie. "What did you do to him, you hateful bitch?"

Maggie backs away from Carolina and comes to stand closer to me. "Do you see?" she says. "Look at what she is."

The fog swirls around me, its humid breath moist against my skin. "Bad," I hear myself say, "just like all the others. Kincaid, Noah, Rufus. A monster same as them." I feel so sad, so lost, so empty.

"Some people are just evil," Maggie says. "They're born wrong. The only thing to do is put them down like the rabid dogs they are."

Carolina's eyes widen in fear, and her chin trembles, as if she's trying not to cry. It makes her look like a little girl. Kincaid looked innocent too, but he was a killer. And suddenly I can see what Maggie sees, past the exterior Carolina shows the world: the sharp points of Carolina's teeth, the bloodlust in her eyes. She's a demon, just like her dad said.

"Killing people like her is the only way to make the world safe," Maggie whispers, her breath warm at my neck. "The only way to make *you* safe." Something cool slides against the palm of my hand, and I grip it. It's the knife Carolina used to kill Noah.

Carolina sees it too. "Lucy," she says. "Please, please, Lucy, don't listen to her. Please don't let this place take everything that is good inside you away. Don't let it make you like her. She's hardly even human."

Maggie runs her fingers down the back of my head, her lips close to my ear. "This is the last step, Luce. This is how you get free. Once she's gone, you'll never be afraid again. You'll walk through the world and not a single person will make you hide. No one will ever make you feel weak again. This is all it takes." Her hand squeezes around mine against the knife, and a thrill runs through me.

I nod.

Carolina lets out a sob as I step toward her with the knife raised. But I don't even see Carolina anymore. I only see the worst of humanity before me. The people the *Human Beasties* podcast is devoted to: the demons, the monsters, the beasts. She is Kincaid and Noah. She is Jack the Ripper and Ted Bundy. She is every killer who has prowled this world looking for a victim to feast on.

If I kill her, I will be free.

If I kill her, I will banish Kincaid's ghost for good.

If I kill her, that part of me that Kincaid slaughtered will come back to life.

And I'll be whole again.

# THIRTY

## CAROLINA

**Lucy comes toward** me with the knife. Her hazel eyes are shadowed and vague. She looks more like Maggie than I'd like. Like Maggie when she raised a rock above my head.

"Lucy," I say, as if speaking her name can wake her up. "Lucy, wait."

She doesn't flinch, doesn't stop. But she brushes a fall of hair out of her eyes, and the ordinary humanness of the gesture gives me hope. Lucy isn't lost, not yet. I can bring her back.

But how? If she kills me now, we're both gone, done for. She'd never come back from it, never be Lucy again.

I hold her gaze as she closes the final steps between us. I stare into her eyes, trying to communicate everything I feel: my fear, my hope, but most of all my—love? Can you love someone you've known for less than a week? I don't know, but what I feel for her is pure and burning and sure.

And I think she feels some of it for me too. She picked Maggie because it was easier, I think, because some unconscious part of her knew that it wasn't real. And she turned from me because—because—

My thoughts scatter as Lucy raises the knife in a shaking hand, mere inches from my neck. She presses its tip against the tender skin of my throat, right above the little hollow between my clavicles. I hold my breath, my heart galloping, willing her to come back to me, to change her mind.

The knife trembles in her grip, barely piercing my skin. I feel a warm bead of blood well and roll down into my sweater.

All the warmth in Lucy's eyes vanishes, and I know I have no choice but to fight.

I shove her as hard as I can, so hard she flies backward and sprawls onto the ground, and the knife falls from her hand. She leaps to her feet and runs at me with a scream, barreling straight into my stomach. She's not very big, but her momentum makes me lose my already-precarious balance, and we fall into a heap of limbs.

The zombie-like movements of earlier are gone, and instead she's wild, feral, scratching and punching, yanking my hair. Her eyes are anger and hopelessness and desperation.

I grab her by the front of her jacket and roll her over, slamming her hard into the ground. "Stop it!" I scream. "Stop it!"

She grits her teeth and brings an arm up toward me, and I catch a glint of metal from the corner of my eye just as pain rips into my upper arm. I scream as Lucy yanks the knife from my flesh. The sound seems to startle her, and she pauses, knife in midair, eyes wild and frightened and—clear. Human. Herself.

I knock the knife out of her hand, and it skitters across bare rock toward the waterfall. I straddle her, breathing hard, and ready myself for another attack, but it doesn't come. Lucy lies beneath me, half raised off the ground, gaping at me.

"You can't do it," I tell her. "You can't do it because that's not who you are, Lucy. You're not a killer. And neither am I." I know that with absolutely certainty, for both of us. This isn't who we are. This isn't what we're meant for.

Lucy searches my eyes, afraid and confused. Her mouth opens and then closes again as she searches for words and doesn't find them. I'm relieved to see her eyes are hazel again. Now that I know it's safe, I climb off her, and she sits up, gasping.

"I—I . . ." she stutters. She turns her head, looking around, as if she's not sure how she got here. How she ended up hiking to the top of this waterfall and trying to murder me. She looks at Maggie, but Maggie turns away, her gaze distant. Lucy's eyes land on me again. "The legend about the fog," she whispers. "It's real. It's real, isn't it?" She looks terrified.

I nod, relief stealing through me. Finally, finally she understands.

"It made me believe I was a murderer," I say. "It made you believe everyone wanted to kill you. It took our worst fears and tortured us with them."

Lucy looks at Maggie, realization dawning. "Did you know—did you know what was happening? All that talk of yours about leaning into the fear, letting it drive you . . ." Her eyes slowly fill with accusation.

Maggie comes toward us and gets on her knees, her gaze laser-focused on Lucy. She reaches for Lucy's hands, and to my surprise, Lucy accepts her touch. "Luce, listen. This place isn't trying to torture you."

"But look at us," Lucy says. "I tried to kill Carolina."

"This place isn't evil. It's only a mirror," Maggie says, her voice quivering with passion. "I figured that out after a few days here. It's a mirror and an amplifier. Everything you are, everything you feel, it's magnified, made real and tangible. It's like your psyche turned inside out. It's amazing. I didn't want to tell you outright. I wanted you to figure it out for yourself, wanted to let your story unfold on its own."

"Maggie, we killed someone," Lucy says, snatching her hands away from Maggie's grasp. Tears are streaming down her cheeks now.

Maggie's eyes fill with hurt. "No, we punished someone bad. That's all. Someone who deserved it."

Lucy shakes her head.

"Look how powerful you've become, Lucy. Look how brave you are now. There's nothing you can't do. *That's* what I wanted for you." Maggie's eyes shine with feeling, and I realize that she means it. That's one thing I was wrong about. This wasn't only a game to her, not completely. She really believed she was helping Lucy, at least in the beginning.

"Maggie," Lucy says in a small, broken voice. "Oh, Maggie, no."

"I realized what this place was showing you, leading you toward, and I just helped you lean into it. That's all. I helped you not fight it so hard." Maggie's voice is desperate.

Lucy closes her eyes. "Did you hurt Brandon?"

"For you," Maggie says. "Because he was going to figure it out. I didn't want you to get into trouble."

Lucy glances at me, horror and regret in her eyes. "Why did you want me to kill Carolina? Because she'd figured out what you were doing?"

Maggie's face takes on a cornered, trapped look. "She tried to turn you against me, Luce. She tried to take you from me. Right when things were so good. When *we* were so good. And I realized that with her gone, there wouldn't be anything to worry about. There wouldn't be anything to get between us.

"It's our perfect ending," Maggie says. "I can see it so clearly." There are tears in her voice. "Can't you see how it all fits?" When Lucy doesn't answer, Maggie holds out her hands again. "Don't you love me? Don't you want to be with me?"

Lucy shakes her head. I can see anger building in her eyes, hardening across her jawline. "No," she says, "I don't. I could never love someone who lies and manipulates and hurts people."

"For your own good," Maggie says. "To help you be the best version of yourself. I did all of that because I care about you."

"You did it because you're a monster," Lucy yells. "And you tried to make me one too."

Maggie shakes her head. "Not a monster. Just . . . whole. Complete. Perfect. See, if you let it in, if you let the fog in . . . Lucy, it's amazing. You can't imagine how you'll feel." Maggie laughs. "This place is the best thing that ever happened to me. I finally realized what I really am."

"A killer?" I ask.

Maggie shakes her head, her eyes alight. "I'm an artist. Only instead of shaping clay, I shape people. I write them better stories than they could ever imagine for themselves."

"Is that why you came to this contest? You knew I'd be here? You wanted to write a better story for me?" Lucy asks.

"No," Maggie says. "I came here planning to write my paper, like I told you. But then on the first day of the contest, I recognized you. And I knew I had to meet you, get to know you. That I had to help you."

"You didn't help me," Lucy says. "You only hurt me. Carolina's the only reason I'm even still alive."

Maggie shakes her head, resentment stealing over her features. "Carolina is the one thing that got in your way. That kept you weak. That's why you needed to kill her. It's not too late," she adds.

"You're sick," Lucy says. "You're the one who needs help, not me."

"Let's just go," I say to Lucy. "Let's get out of here." We start to climb to our feet, but Maggie scrambles to block our path.

"No, you can't go," she pleads. "Lucy, please, don't go!"

"Get out of our way, or I'm going to call the police," Lucy says, still beside me on the ground. She reaches into her back pocket for her phone, but Maggie knocks it from her hand. Lucy picks it back up.

"If you tell the police, you'll get in trouble too," Maggie says. "Both of you, but especially Carolina. She's the one who killed Noah. I'll tell the police everything you did," she says to me.

"I don't care," I say. "This is over. Your game is over, Maggie."

Maggie looks at Lucy, her expression beseeching. "Lucy, you don't want to go to jail. You don't want to get in trouble. And you don't have to. We just need to kill Carolina. We can blame it all on her. It's not too late. We can be together."

Lucy shoves her phone back into her pocket and meets Maggie's gaze. "I could never kill Carolina."

Maggie's chest heaves. "We're supposed to be together, Lucy. We're supposed to be a team. We *are* a team, even if you don't see it right now. But you will . . . later on. After she's dead and this is all over." Maggie's gaze flits to me, and my blood runs cold.

"What are you talking about?" Lucy asks, all the anger leached from her voice, replaced by fear.

"You don't want to kill her? That's fine. I understand," Maggie says. "But you don't have to. I'll do it for you! I'll do it for you, and this will all be over." She takes a few steps backward, her eyes still locked on us.

"Lucy," I say, my heart rate accelerating. "We need to get out of here. We need to go, right now!"

But it's already too late.

Maggie lunges for the knife. Before I can move, it's in her hands.

# THIRTY-ONE

## LUCY

**Maggie strides toward** us, her jaw locked, her gaze intent. She grips the hilt of the knife, its blade pointed at Carolina. I realize that she's done pleading with me, done trying to persuade me. She's really going to kill Carolina.

I throw myself in front of Carolina. "Stop this now, Maggie!" I yell. "I am never going to be with you. How could I ever want you after this? We're finished!"

Maggie's eyes register the barest hint of hurt, but then she shakes her head, and all the feeling drains from her expression. The bright sparks of life in her eyes dim and go out, replaced by a scary, smoking gray. "Fine, then I guess I'll kill you too," she says. "And I'll tell them you killed Carolina and then yourself. Lucy Wilson as a murder-suicide? Well, now that will make for an interesting paper." She laughs, the sound both empty and cruel.

I stare at her, stunned into silence. This is the girl I kissed, the girl I shared a tent with, the girl whose warmth I snuggled into only last night as we slept. This is the girl who drew me out of myself with a single smile. The girl who changed my life. Who made safety feel possible again.

Didn't she?

Didn't I love her, this girl with the strange face, the eternal denim jacket, the long and lanky limbs, the girl with her notebook and her raised eyebrows?

Didn't I imagine a life with her, this girl who skims the surface of the world like a dragonfly over water?

All that fades away as she strengthens her grip on the knife and takes another step toward us. Dragonflies might be jewel-bright and lovely, but they are also the world's most efficient predators, nabbing their prey 95 percent of the time. Is that what Maggie was all along—a predator after easy prey?

"Maggie?" I yell, scuttling away from her like a crab and tumbling into Carolina. "You don't want to do this." My whole body shakes. I would run if I could, but there's nowhere to go. "Maggie!"

"Maggie!" Maggie cries back, in a high-pitched voice of mock terror. She grins, but the smile is as cold and hard as rock. She crouches next to me, propping one arm on a knee as she studies me. Carolina fumbles on her knees, trying to put herself between us, which only makes Maggie laugh.

Everything Carolina told me about Maggie was true, but I refused to listen. I refused to see. Instead, I let Maggie turn me against Carolina. I almost *killed* her because Maggie wanted me to. The thought makes me sick.

"You two are pathetic," Maggie says, her voice laced with cruelty. "Weak and stupid and pathetic. You deserve each other."

"I'm not pathetic," I say, though as I hear the way the words tremble, even I don't believe it.

Maggie smiles and reaches a long, bony hand to stroke my face. I flinch when her skin meets mine, my eyes flitting to the knife in her other hand. Her touch is cold and moist, and her fingers smell of damp things—moss and soil and the undersides of rotting logs. "I tried to save you. If you were going to see a monster behind every rock, I thought, at least you could become one too. At least you could take your cynicism to its natural conclusion: that if people are bad, so are you. And that badness would be your armor. It would save you."

"That's not why you did this," I say. "Stop pretending you cared about me at all. You didn't want to save me. You just wanted to entertain yourself."

Maggie shrugs. "Two birds, one stone." But her eyes meet mine, and I think there's something there. A tiny, regretful look, there and gone again, that says maybe she did care, that she was telling me the truth before. Or maybe she just wanted to care. But that's over now.

She taps the knife against her palm, studying me, as if deciding where to stab me.

"And what plans did you have for me all this time?" Carolina asks, apparently determined to draw Maggie's attention away from me. "You needed someone to pin the attacks on, to pin Noah's murder on, didn't you? That's what you were going to do from the beginning." She shakes her head.

"Please, I barely needed to point at you," Maggie says. "You incriminated yourself. Your problem is the same as Lucy's. You two are exactly the same. You let other people define you, let them tell you who you are, let them set your course. So you're both victims, always. You'll never be anything else."

"And you're not *anything* at all," I say sadly. Because I can see now, I can see the emptiness where her humanity used to be. She is a void, a maw, a black hole.

Maggie raises her dark eyebrows. "I am perfectly myself. I made myself, with the fog's help. I saw what this world was and what people were, and I made my choice. I would be more."

"That's what you think," Carolina says, "but it isn't true. You didn't choose this. This place wormed itself inside you and rotted you from the inside out. And now you're just its bitch."

Maggie's face darkens still further, and her gray eyes turn to cumulonimbus clouds: dense, dark, promising destruction. But she's drawing the moment out, relishing it. We're a captive audience, and Maggie can't resist a chance to perform.

"Lucy, on our second day here, you said you were lucky you hadn't ended up as one of Kincaid's offerings to the gods, or a sacrifice . . . something along those lines. And I realized the thing that I hadn't been able to grasp before. Why do you think Kincaid mutilated his victims and arranged them just so?" she asks, running the blade of her knife softly across her palm. "Did you think it was only for his own amusement?" She smiles an evil, menacing smile, with anger around its edges. "Well, it was for his amusement. But it was more than that. It was an offering, like you said. It was a gift to the place that gave him so much."

"What are you talking about?" I say, my voice shaking. Any minute now she's going to turn that knife on me.

"It's true this place will make you face all the darkness in your heart. But only weak, pathetic people like you two are afraid to find out who they really are. Kincaid wasn't afraid. He welcomed it. He loved this place and gave himself over to it."

"Oh, you're a fan of his now?"

Maggie laughs. "Kincaid didn't want to hide his sins from the world. He wasn't ashamed. He wanted to be his true self, and this place allowed him to do that. Just like it did me."

"Where is he now?" I ask. "When I saw him in the woods, it was really him, wasn't it? He's the one who chased me and came after me. Not Noah. It was really Kincaid. He's not dead at all." Panic writhes through me, making my breath come short.

Maggie looks down on me, her eyes mocking. "Of course he's dead. He jumped off a fucking cliff, Lucy. Those were your own pathetic fears chasing you around."

"Then where's his body?" Carolina says. "If the canyon hides people's sins for them, or absorbs them or whatever the hell it's doing, where's his goddamned body?"

Maggie laughs, delighted. "You know, that's the most interesting part. Whose sin was Kincaid that the canyon felt the need to hide it?"

"What?" I ask weakly.

"This really isn't the time for philosophy, Maggie," Carolina says.

"Oh, but you love debates like this, Carolina," Maggie shoots back, grinning. "Is he his parents' sin? Society's? What makes a man like Kincaid? What makes a girl like me?"

"Do you know where his body is or not?" I ask.

Maggie shrugs. "I did rip the aviator patch off his jacket."

A shudder runs down my spine. "His body's actually on that ledge? We were that close to it?"

"I told you we were. Don't you remember?"

"But that ledge wasn't even big enough for a body," I say. Yet I know she isn't lying now. I feel the truth of her words, a chill I can't shake.

"The canyon lets you see what it wants you to see. But now that it's a part of me, I see everything here," she says exultingly. "I see every secret, every sin, every possibility. I tried to let you in, Lucy, but you were too afraid. Too weak."

"She should have been afraid," Carolina says. "Of losing her humanity."

Maggie shakes her head, exasperated. "It isn't about losing your humanity. Don't you get that yet? It's about becoming *fully human*, everything you are. I was eager to face myself, to see what I might be capable of. To let go of anything that would keep me from it."

"And what exactly are you capable of?" Carolina spits.

Maggie smiles that terrifying smile again. She looks toward the east, where the sun will soon rise over the treetops. "I guess it's time to show you." She stands and walks a few paces away from us, and we scramble quickly to our feet. But there's nowhere to run. Fog rises up around us, obscuring the paths of escape. It billows around Maggie, wreathing her, making her appear ghostlike and menacing. She is like a shadow, a phantom, a column of mist. Her eyes are an abyss, a graveyard where bodies are never found.

We have to get away now. Somehow, we have to get away.

Maggie turns, and I see the glint of the knife. I know we'll have to fight our way out. But maybe I can give Carolina a chance. "Go, Carolina!" I yell. "Run!" And then I rush forward and push Maggie's skinny chest with all my strength, making her stumble back several steps.

"Lucy!" Carolina screams, grabbing my arm.

"You chose wrong," Maggie snarls. And then whatever is inside her breaks free of its human cage. She lets out a roar that human vocal cords couldn't make—like tectonic plates crashing, like a million pounds of water rushing over rock, like an eon's worth of sediment compacting in the earth. Fog swirls from her mouth, cold as ice when it touches my skin.

And finally, finally, I see what we face. Carolina tried to tell me, again and again. That something is wrong here, in this place. That this canyon hates us. That it wishes us ill, wishes us dead, wishes us rotting in the earth.

Whatever Maggie was when she came here, whether good or evil or something in between, that girl is long gone. She thinks the canyon gave her freedom, but all it did was take over her mind and her body and make her its home, its hands.

Maggie flies at us, a being of darkness and cold, of mist and rock, impossibly strong, with the worst of humanity at its heart. Carolina takes a single step forward just in time for Maggie to barrel into both of us. My feet go out from under me, and in my mind, I'm tumbling over that cliff again, crashing into rocks and trees, plummeting toward the bottom of the canyon.

I've been plummeting toward the darkness from the moment I returned here, and now the ground itself has risen up to meet me.

I lie stunned for a moment before Carolina grabs me, pulling me to my feet and behind her own body in one clumsy movement. She's still trying to protect me, even now. All along, when I ignored her and chose Maggie instead, when I literally tried to kill her, she has been trying to protect me.

Maggie slashes at Carolina, who manages to dodge her. Carolina strikes out, hitting Maggie's wrist and making her drop the knife. But Maggie doesn't need a knife anyway. She just keeps coming.

I won't let Carolina put her body between Maggie and me again, put her soul between death and me again. I run around her and tackle Maggie from the side, surprising her. She goes down. Before she can throw me off, Carolina leaps into the fray, and we roll across the cold ground in a flailing, punching, writhing, desperate mass of limbs.

Maggie lands a thunderous punch to my chest, and I'm knocked away from them, gasping for breath, my lungs caving in, my already-damaged ribs on fire. Maggie yanks a fistful of Carolina's hair, and Carolina screams and thrashes, scratching at Maggie's face with her nails. Carolina must get her eyes because Maggie lets go and stumbles backward, trying to gain some leverage.

"Look out!" Carolina yells as Maggie steps nearly to the edge of the cliff. Maggie glances behind her, the monster inside her unconcerned by the powerful roar of the waterfall at its back.

There's an opening, but Carolina doesn't take it. She doesn't want to kill again. She hesitates, and that's all the chance Maggie needs. She grabs Carolina by the front of her sweater, and I know she's going to toss her right over the edge.

"Carolina!" I scream, the sound wrenching from my aching throat.

Startled, Maggie glances at me, and I run toward her, faster than she expects. She lets go of Carolina, but she's not quick enough to fight me off. Maggie's mouth opens in a yell as I shove her with all my strength. She stumbles back, one foot halfway off the edge of the earth. She grabs for me even as she falls, and her fingers catch on the edge of my sleeve, pulling me with her.

For a moment, framed against the fog, she's Maggie again, her eyes wide and human—afraid, helpless. Her lips form my name. But it's too late. Carried forward by her weight and my own momentum, we both fall into the abyss of Cloudkiss Canyon.

Hands grab hold of my legs at the last second and bring me to the ground, slamming me painfully against the earth. Maggie's grip is wrenched from my sleeve.

Someone screams, but I don't know who. Maybe it's me.

I hang halfway off the edge, and Maggie disappears into the fog.

And then there's a thud, a sickening crunch, barely audible over the rush of water.

Carolina and I scramble away from the edge, barely stopping ourselves from tipping over into the mist.

We lie panting, our hair and clothes damp from the falls, tremors running through us both. My ears fill with a hollow ringing.

*I pushed her. I killed her.*

Finally, because I have to look, because I have to know, I crawl to the edge of the cliff and peer into the soup of fog, searching the rocky bottom around the waterfall. I don't see her.

Carolina appears next to me. "There," she says, pointing. I let out a strangled gasp. Maggie's body lies smashed against an enormous boulder that juts up at the base of the falls. Her neck is bent at an impossible angle.

"Lucy," someone calls. The voice is disembodied, floating, but I recognize it.

"She's alive!" I scream. "We have to—" I look around desperately, scrabbling on the rocks, searching for a way down to her.

Carolina grabs my arm. "She'd dead, Lucy. Look at her. She's dead. It's just the canyon—it's still messing with your mind."

I stare down at Maggie's broken body, and I know Carolina is right. Maggie is dead. She's dead, and I killed her.

"What have I done? Oh my God, what have I done?" The world reels around me, horror gripping me. "I killed her."

"She tried to kill us," Carolina says, shaking me. "She— It tried to kill us. This fucking place. It's evil. You didn't kill her; this place did."

"She's dead," I say helplessly, and I don't feel triumph or power or freedom. All I feel is loss. Because Maggie was beautiful and strange and wild and some part of me loved her. And now she's dead. Gone forever.

"It's not your fault," Carolina says, reaching up from the ground to hold my hand. "And you saved me. I would be dead instead if you hadn't pushed her. You saved me."

I stare down into the churning water until the fog thickens around Maggie, obscuring her completely. I stay still until the desperate urge to leap after her leaves my body.

And then I fall heavily down beside Carolina. She puts her arms around me.

"Did you hear me, Lucy?" Carolina asks. "You saved me. And not only today. This whole week, who you are—you saved me." She strokes my hair.

"I didn't do anything," I whisper, hopelessness stealing over me. I thought Maggie was rescuing me, but she was manipulating me all this time, playing me like a pawn. Was there any part of her that truly cared for me? Was I anything more than her crowning achievement?

And if nothing this week was real, what do I leave here with? Who am I going home as?

"Lucy," Carolina says, intruding into my thoughts like a gnat that won't stop landing. "It's this place. It's still working on you. It got to Maggie worse than anyone. It got into her and rotted her from the inside. But we're going to make it out."

"Why?" I ask, biting back a sob. "Why Maggie?"

Carolina laces her fingers in mine as we stare down into the fog. She takes a deep breath.

"Because she was alone. She camped here by herself for a whole week before the rest of us arrived. It was just her all alone out here with only her thoughts, her worst impulses."

"I guess so," I say. "But she can't be the first to have done that."

"Yeah, I think it was more than that," Carolina admits. "She didn't have anyone, not here, not anywhere. She was alone because she chose to be alone. People weren't real to her. They—we—were just playthings. She never let anyone in. She never let herself care about anyone. The fog got her so bad because there wasn't anybody she belonged to or anybody who belonged to her."

"I did," I say, but then I shake my head. "No, that isn't true." I turn and look at Carolina, really look at her, for the first time in days. "You cared about me," I say. "You fought for me, over and over again, even when I didn't want you to."

Carolina's eyes are clear and warm and steady. "Even when you were sick to death of my caring."

I laugh, and the sound is a broken, aborted thing. "God, I'm tired," I say, looking away from Carolina and out over the mountains, where the sky is beginning to waken.

"The sun will be up soon," Carolina says, anxiety edging back into her voice. "The contest—it's over today. And no one found Kincaid."

"But we know where he is," I say.

"Won't the canyon hide him again?"

"I don't know." I peer down the fall of water, searching for the place Maggie fell. The fog is clearer now, thin as spider silk, and I can just make out the boulder her body landed on.

"I don't think anyone's ever going to find Kincaid," I say, a chill washing over me.

"Why?" Carolina asks.

I jerk my chin at the waterfall, and Carolina looks over. "Where did she go? Where the fuck did she go?"

Maggie's rock is empty.

"She must have slipped into the water," Carolina says.

"Maybe," I agree, though I know it isn't true. It's the same as what happened to Kincaid. He fell and was gone, swallowed, disappeared. I suspect if we went back to the cave, we wouldn't find Noah either. The canyon has claimed them, hiding the evidence of our crimes, like the legend says. Like Maggie said. We've added to its evil.

"I want to get out of here," I say. "I want to be done with this place."

"Just leave?" Carolina asks, surprised. "Just drive off?"

"While we still can. Before the fog gets us too." I climb to my feet and gaze down into the canyon, which glows gently with dawn light along its ridges, while its belly lies swathed in darkness, in cloud, in mist. Even now, I feel its insidious, persistent pull. The pull of an edge that wants you to jump, the lure of a darkness that wants you to drown, the call of a void that wants you to surrender to nothingness.

Carolina stands beside me so that we're shoulder to shoulder against the fog. "You know, I read once that the call of the void isn't actually a death drive. In fact, it's pretty much the opposite—your brain sending warning signals to your body. It's sort of a paradox. You feel like you're going to jump precisely because you want to live."

"I don't know what I want anymore," I say. "I don't know what to make of who I am, not after this."

Carolina squeezes my hand. "Me neither."

I sigh. "Let's go find him. Let's finish what we started."

# THIRTY-TWO

## LUCY

**We hike back** down with leaden steps, too exhausted even to be afraid anymore. When we reach the base of the waterfall, we look up, searching for the ledge where Maggie found the aviator patch. Slowly, painstakingly, we climb up, using roots and jutting rock for handholds. My ribs scream at me, and Carolina looks like she might pass out and tumble down at any moment, but we grit our teeth and we climb, several feet apart.

"Do you see anything?" I ask.

"No," Carolina pants.

I rest my head against the rock. Now that I know it's here, I can feel the evil emanating from this place. I can't believe Maggie wanted to let it inside her. Was she really in that much pain? Did she really feel so alone and so lost? Or was it the opposite—that she didn't feel enough? That she wanted to feel more?

"Maggie," I whisper.

When I look up, there's a ledge two feet above me, rock jutting out in an overhang. I swear it wasn't there a moment ago. I launch myself up and onto the ledge, gasping with relief to not have to hold up the weight of my own body anymore. The rock opens—a dark, gaping mouth.

"Carolina," I call. "Come here." I kneel at the edge, my body trembling, as I wait for Carolina to make her slow, arduous way to me. Once she's next to me, I grip her hand. "This is it," I say. "He must be in there."

"Do you have a flashlight?"

I pull my phone out and navigate to the flashlight button. My hand trembles so badly I can't hold the phone steady. Carolina takes it from me gently. "Are you ready?" she asks.

I nod. This is what I came here for. This is what I suffered for. To see Kincaid's bones with my own eyes.

Carolina points the flashlight into the opening. A skeleton lies in the darkness, its head propped on a rock. There is no skin, no hair, only white and gleaming bone. A tattered brown jacket with a moldy shearling lining, the patch torn from the breast. Blue jeans. One shoe missing. It's Kincaid.

"How do we know it's real?" I ask. "How do we know it's not another of the canyon's tricks?"

Carolina leans forward and touches the shoe. She pulls the knot in the laces free. "Feels pretty real to me," she says.

"He's really dead," I whisper. This is the first time I've ever believed that might be true. Fully believed it, as a fact my soul knows.

"He's really dead," Carolina agrees. "We won Killer Quest." She lets out a broken, uneven laugh.

"Well, does it help?" I ask.

"Does what help?"

"Are you sure now that you aren't like him?"

Carolina stares at me, her face pale in the glow of the flashlight. "I already knew I wasn't."

"When did you figure it out? After—after Noah?"

She nods. "After I killed him and I remembered everything that happened with Michael. But it wasn't only that. It was how it felt to kill him, how painful and awful it was. And I only did it to protect you, and even knowing that, I still felt so guilty and horrible. And I knew I never wanted to do it again." She hangs her head. "But now that Maggie's dead—"

"That wasn't your fault. You couldn't have done anything to stop it," I protest. "She tried to kill us. The whole thing is my fault, and not just because I pushed her. I'm the one who went along so eagerly with all her plans. I'm the one who let her talk me into everything. I was so desperate not to be weak that I almost let myself become a monster. I'm the guilty one here."

"But it wasn't only Maggie you were up against," Carolina says. "It was this place, this evil fucking place. And him," she adds, nodding at Kincaid's skeleton.

"I guess so," I say. But I'm honestly not sure how much blame I can put on Maggie, on the canyon. "Being good is a lot less straightforward than I thought."

"Yes, and maybe being evil is too," Carolina says. She meets my eyes. "Will you feel safe now, out in the world, knowing that he's really dead?"

I take the phone from her and train the light on Kincaid's face. His eye sockets stare back at me, empty. He's just matter now, devoid of personality, intent, or danger. So is Noah, and so is Maggie.

"After we killed Noah," I say, "I felt so free, like I'd never be afraid again. But the real villain was walking right beside me. They can hide in plain sight. They can even hide inside us."

"So is that a no?"

I shake my head. "I think it's just that there is no such thing as safety. Not really, not completely. So if safety doesn't actually exist . . . I may as well stop looking for it and live my life."

Carolina laughs. "I think Maggie would approve of your new philosophy."

My gut twists. I wish it hadn't ended this way. Despite the horrible things she did, I wish I could bring her back. I wish I could have saved her.

"So do we just leave Kincaid here, or do we claim our prize money?" Carolina asks.

"Oh, no, we're not letting this canyon keep him. His victims' families deserve to know he's dead. Everyone deserves to know." I turn on my camera app and snap a picture of the body.

"Do you have any cell signal?" Carolina asks. "My phone's completely dead."

I look at my screen. "No, none. We'll have to walk back and tell them where to come find him."

I take one last look at Kincaid, the man who broke my life. He's dead, and I'm not. And maybe there are more Kincaids out in the world. Maybe they are even here in this canyon, or walking the streets of my neighborhood, or coaching my softball team. But I'm done living my life in their shadow.

We climb down the wall of the canyon and find our way back to the path. We are bruised and bleeding, filthy and exhausted. There is such a long way back to camp and so many questions to answer once we get there. A part of me wants to lie down in the dead leaves and let the canyon cover me over.

But Carolina takes my hand, and we trudge doggedly up, up, up, through the drifting, reaching fog and back into the light.

# *HUMAN BEASTIES* PODCAST, EPISODE 400
## PARTIAL TRANSCRIPT

**KEVIN:** Lucy, welcome to the show. I'm so glad that we're finally getting the chance to sit down and talk with you.

**LUCY:** I can't really say the same, Kevin, but a promise is a promise.

**KEVIN:** [laughs uncomfortably] Right.

**SANDRA:** I know this will be difficult for you to talk about, Lucy, so thank you so much for coming on to tell your side of the story. There have been so many rumors and theories, so many different perceptions about what happened to you in Cloudkiss Canyon—both on the day you were abducted by Joseph Kincaid as a fifteen-year-old, as well as during the murky events of our Killer Quest contest in November, during which two people went missing.

**KEVIN:** Maggie Rey, a nineteen-year-old student at Duke University, and Noah Sapp, a twenty-year-old student at

UT Chattanooga, both disappeared during the course of the contest and have never been found. Maggie was on your team, Lucy.

**LUCY:** Yes, she was. I considered her a friend.

**KEVIN:** And you had several unfortunate run-ins with Noah during the contest.

**LUCY:** Yes, that's true. And I'm not the only one. I think you'll remember that when Kiersten Powell woke up from her coma, she said that it might have been Noah who caused her to fall down the stairs. She wasn't sure, but she thought it was him. And a search of his personal laptop raised a lot of red flags, didn't it?

**SANDRA:** Police believe that Maggie's and Noah's disappearances are linked. Noah was seen talking to Maggie shortly before he disappeared. Do you think it's possible that one of them killed the other?

**LUCY:** Anything is possible, Sandra. That's sort of the point of true crime, isn't it? That anyone is capable of just about anything?

**KEVIN:** You've been surprisingly unwilling to commit to an opinion about what may have happened to them, both in your statements to the police and the press. Why is that? Don't you think that Noah killed Maggie?

**LUCY:** I'm not a podcast host, Kevin. I don't deal in speculation.

**SANDRA:** [clears her throat] Let's talk about the other big mystery of the contest, then. Joseph Kincaid. You claim to have found his body.

**LUCY:** I did find his body. I saw it with my own eyes, as did Carolina Cassels.

**KEVIN:** Your *girlfriend*, Carolina Cassels. Not exactly an unbiased source.

**SANDRA:** But you have a picture to prove it, logged on your phone at the time you said you found him, with the coordinates of the place you said you found him.

**LUCY:** Yes. Everyone has seen that photo.

**SANDRA:** And yet rangers and police were unable to locate the body. They went exactly to those coordinates. There was no body. There was not even a ledge and cavern in the rock where you said it would be. Just a blank wall. All you could offer us was an aviator patch that you said led you to the body.

**KEVIN:** How did you fake the photo, Lucy?

**LUCY:** How did you fake your graduate degrees, Kevin?

**SANDRA:** [snorts]

**KEVIN:** I'm so glad to see that you're as pleasant as ever, Lucy. Wouldn't want you to lose that winning personality of yours.

**LUCY:** [sighs] I didn't fake the photo. I wouldn't even begin to know how to do it. And I can't explain why the body wasn't where we found it. Maybe we got the coordinates wrong. But I joined the Killer Quest contest to find his body, to give myself the peace of mind of knowing he was truly dead, and I did that. I'm satisfied. I don't care whether anyone else believes me.

**SANDRA:** I'm glad to hear that our contest gave you peace of mind, Lucy. I can't imagine living with the idea that your abductor might still be out there, might still be a threat to you. Tell me, what was it like to return to the place where your life nearly ended, where, if police had arrived later, if a ranger hadn't recognized Kincaid's car, if you hadn't turned at just the right moment before Kincaid drugged you, you might have ended up like his other victims? What was it like to return to Cloudkiss Canyon?

**LUCY:** Honestly, it was hellish. I saw Kincaid everywhere I looked, I didn't trust the other contestants, and I was afraid every single second.

**KEVIN:** You had a really negative opinion of our podcast when you arrived. Did you feel any differently after meeting our fans?

**LUCY:** Have you met your fans, Kevin?

**SANDRA:** I think what Kevin is asking is did you discover anything redeeming about true crime and the communities that spring up around it?

**LUCY:** [pauses] Why do you need my approval so badly?

**KEVIN:** Are you aware that we donated the twenty-thousand-dollar contest prize to Cloudkiss Canyon, to support the national forest's preservation and education work there? I would think that would make you happy as someone who plans to go into that kind of work yourself. I understand you're majoring in environmental science at UNC Chapel Hill.

**LUCY:** There is no work I think is more important right now than conservation and environmental stewardship, but I'd burn Cloudkiss Canyon to the ground before I'd give it a single cent.

**SANDRA:** Wow, Lucy, you feel that strongly? Do you believe the legends of the place?

**LUCY:** There's a reason locals don't camp there. I'll never ignore local lore again, I'll tell you that.

**SANDRA:** [laughs weakly]

**KEVIN:** Do you think Joseph Kincaid would have killed those five people and abducted you if it weren't for the paranormal influence of Cloudkiss Canyon?

**LUCY:** That's just another way of asking the thing podcasts like yours are always asking. What makes a serial killer? How does someone become one? Could I become one too? Serial killers fascinate us because they contain all the parts of humanity we're too afraid to look at—the parts of ourselves we're too afraid to look at.

**SANDRA:** That's a profound thought, Lucy, especially coming from you.

**KEVIN:** [laughs] She's absolutely dead wrong, but it's an interesting thought nonetheless.

**LUCY:** We'll agree to disagree, Kevin. As usual.

**SANDRA:** So what's next for you, Lucy? You're a smart, articulate, resilient young woman. You could write a book about your experiences. I'm sure it would be a best seller. You'd probably have every movie studio in Hollywood knocking on your door for the film rights.

**LUCY:** [laughs] I can't imagine anything worse.

**KEVIN:** So you're ready to leave this part of your life behind forever? You're ready to move on?

**LUCY:** I already have.

**SANDRA:** Lucy, it was so generous of you to come and talk with us about such a painful time in your life. I'd like to ask you one more question before I let you go back to your studies.

**LUCY:** All right.

**SANDRA:** What would you say to our listeners who feel afraid, who worry about something terrible—like what happened to you—happening to them?

**LUCY:** I'd tell them to stop listening to your podcast.

**SANDRA AND KEVIN:** [sigh]

**LUCY:** Honestly, I don't have any brilliant advice to give. I'm just a person who went through something, got messed up by it, and somehow managed to live through it. That's not unique, even if the particulars of my story are. Joseph Kincaid tried to kill me, but I survived him. Human beings are remarkably good at surviving. It's living that we seem to struggle with. But, if you'll excuse me, I'm going to go and give it a try.

# ACKNOWLEDGMENTS

To all the brilliant, beautiful people who helped make this book happen: I am endlessly grateful for you.

Thank you to my agent, Lauren Spieller, for going over (and over and over and over) the initial synopsis with me and guiding me away from the most terrible of my ideas. Thank you to my editors, Alice Jerman and Clare Vaughn, for believing in this project and helping me get it into the best possible shape. Thanks also to my fantastic teams at HarperTeen and Triada US Literary Agency for treating me and my books with so much care.

John, thank you for traveling to foggy places with me and for listening to me complain about this book every single day. Logan, thanks for being my walking buddy and sounding board. Cayla and Alder, thank you for reading the early, rubbish pages and giving me good, honest, and affirming feedback. Thanks so much to all my writing pals, whose commiseration and companionship help keep me writing. You deserve all the good things.

Finally, thank you to my readers. Your support for my books means the world to me.